# THE CLA

# A THRONE
# BETRAYED

# THE CLAN WARS
# A THRONE BETRAYED

Julie Kagawa
& J.T. Nicholas

First published by Aconyte Books in 2025
ISBN 978 1 83908 290 0
Ebook ISBN 978 1 83908 289 4

Copyright © 2025 Asmodee North America, Inc.
Legend of the Five Rings and the Legend of the Five Rings logo are trademarks or registered trademarks of Asmodee North America. The Aconyte name and logo are registered or unregistered trademarks of Asmodee North America. The Asmodee name and logo are ™ and © 2019-2025 Asmodee Group SAS. All rights reserved.

This novel is entirely a work of fiction. Names, characters, places, and incidents are the products of the author's imagination or are used fictitiously. Any resemblance to actual events, locales, organizations or persons, living or dead, is entirely coincidental.

Sales of this book without a front cover may be unauthorized. If this book is coverless, it may have been reported to the publisher as "unsold and destroyed" and neither the author nor the publisher may have received payment for it.

Cover art by Mauro Dal Bo.
Rokugan maps by Francesca Baerald.
Internal illustrations by Axel Hutt.

Printed in the United States of America and elsewhere.
9 8 7 6 5 4 3 2 1

**ACONYTE BOOKS**
*An imprint of Asmodee North America*
Mercury House, North Gate,
Nottingham NG7 7FN, UK
*aconytebooks.com*

*To all those who have
journeyed with us through
the Emerald Empire
over the years.*

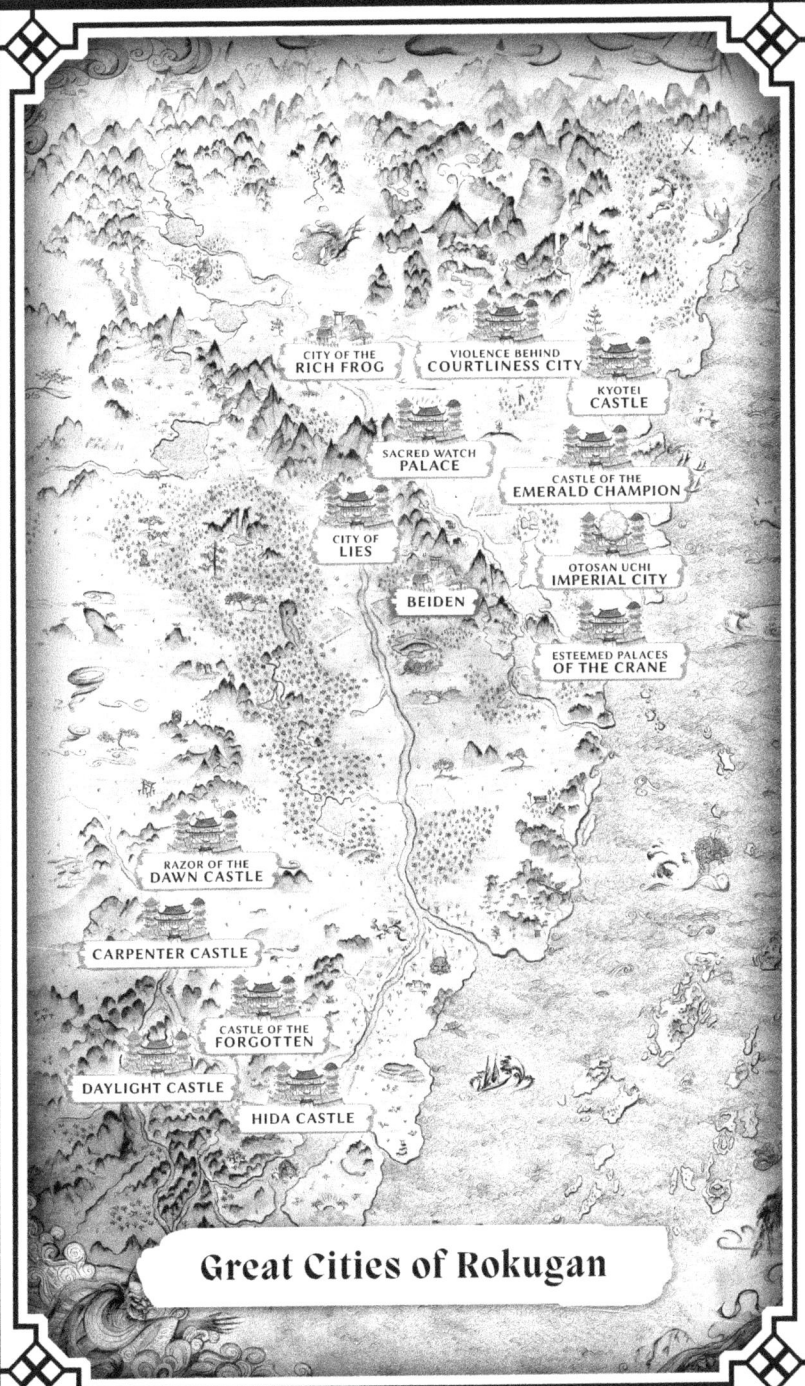

# List of Characters

### THE COMPANY OF TOTURI THE RŌNIN
Toturi the Rōnin (formerly Akodo Toturi)
Daidoji Daisuke, a samurai
Toku, a peasant
Yohei, a peasant

### THE CRAB CLAN
Hida Kisada, daimyō of the Crab Clan
Hida Yakamo, a samurai
Hida O-Ushi, a samurai
Hida Sukune, a samurai
Kuni Yori, advisor to Hida Kisada
Hiruma Bunzō, a samurai
Hiruma Momoe, a samurai
Kaiu Yoshikuni, a scout

### THE CRANE CLAN
Kakita Yoshi, the Imperial Regent
Kakita Toshimoko, Master of the Kakita Dueling Academy
Doji Hotaru, Crane Clan Champion
Doji no Tsume Takashi, a commander

### THE DRAGON CLAN
Mirumoto Hitomi, a samurai & duelist

## THE IMPERIAL FAMILY
Emperor Hantei 38th (deceased)
Hantei Hochiahime, the dowager Empress
Hantei Sotorii, a prince
Hantei Daisetsu, a prince

## THE LION CLAN
Matsu Tsuko, leader of the Lion Clan
Matsu Agetoki, a general
Akodo Sachio, a commander

## THE PHOENIX CLAN
Chukan Hanako, a courtier

## THE SCORPION CLAN
Bayushi Kachiko, Mother of Scorpions
Bayushi Shoju (a traitor, now deceased)
Ayame, a spy

## THE UNICORN CLAN
Utaku Kamoko, a Battle Maiden
Ide Yoritsugu, a courtier

# THE CLAN WARS
# A THRONE BETRAYED

# 1
# Toturi

"Are you one of the bad men?"

The rōnin looked down at the boy, who stared back with an expression equal parts wonder, excitement, and fear. The child had emerged from the bean fields at the edge of the village, his tousled black hair waving above the green fronds like a banner. He was seven or eight years old and fell in step with the warrior, taking two strides for each one the rōnin made, their footfalls raising puffs of dust from the packed-earth path that served as the village's main street. The boy wore simple peasant garb: short, loose-fitting trousers and a sleeveless tunic, both woven from undyed hemp. His arms and legs thrust out of the garments like the spindly limbs of a scarecrow that had lost its stuffing, and the boy himself looked nearly as underfed.

It took courage for a peasant boy to approach anyone carrying the daishō – the paired katana and wakizashi that only the samurai were permitted to wear – even one as tattered and travel-stained as the rōnin. For a moment, as he pondered the warring emotions flicking across the boy's face, he felt an ache deep in his chest. His failure, his shame, meant that he would never wed, never have children of his own. Never get to instill such courage in another.

He crushed the thought beneath the discipline that had been ingrained into him in the monastery of the Dragon Clan, forcing his mind away from the past, from a future that would never be.

"Are you? One of the bad men, I mean?" the boy asked again, interrupting his contemplation.

"What bad men are those, boy?" His voice sounded rough to his own ears, gravelly from disuse. They had passed the first line of houses now, and the rōnin took a moment to truly see the village. The buildings all had their sliding shutters closed, transforming the modest homes into nondescript wooden shacks. The shutters kept the people safe from the ravages of storms; perhaps they hoped they would also keep them safe from the ravages of men.

The rōnin knew better.

Few people moved in the streets, and those that did kept their heads downcast and walked with a furtive haste that spoke more of fear than industry. They did not meet his eyes, gave no sign that could be taken as courtesy… or challenge. In fact, one might be convinced they paid him no mind at all, if it were not for the wide bubble through which he moved, and the occasional worried glances at the boy walking beside him.

"My mother says the bad men are bandits!" the boy exclaimed, his eyes guileless and bright with the excitement of it all. "Bandits come to make the village pay trib… tribu…"

"Tribute."

The boy nodded. "What's tribute?"

"A failure by those tasked with protecting you," the rōnin muttered. He felt his hands tightening into fists. These lands had been under his protection once. All the Empire had been under his protection. It was the duty of the samurai to protect the peasants, just as it was the peasants' duty to work the land, coaxing forth the crops needed to ensure everyone's survival. That balance, that harmony, handed down from the Celestial Order of Heaven itself, was fundamental to the structure and well-being of the Empire. To allow one of the villages under your protection to be tormented by armed thugs was shameful. And in the lands of the Lion? He clenched his jaw. Were he Clan Champion, he would have more than harsh words for whichever samurai claimed this village as their own.

But he was not Clan Champion.

Not anymore.

The rōnin drew a calming breath. Held it for a moment. Exhaled. He forced his hands to relax. His own failures had led him here; could he so easily hold another's failures against them? He glanced down at the boy, still watching him with a blend of fear and fascination. The rōnin could see the hardship of the village clearly in the child's lean limbs and sunken eyes.

"Please, my lord samurai. Please. He means no harm!"

The rōnin looked up to see a woman wearing the same homespun tunic and trousers as the boy, rushing from the shelter of one of the nearby houses. She threw herself on her knees before him, bowing until her head rested in the dirt, arms outstretched before her. The boy blinked in confusion, glancing back and forth between the rōnin and what must be his mother. Seeing her obvious terror, the fear that had been dancing across the boy's face solidified. Tears welled in his eyes, and he shied away, moving behind the kneeling woman and outside the rōnin's grasp.

The rōnin sighed.

"I am not here to hurt you," he said to the woman. "Or your boy. He was merely keeping me company as I walked through your village."

The woman said nothing, holding her bow, but he could see

the quiver in her shoulders. Fear, or relief? "Where is your lord or lady?" he asked. "Where are the patrols meant to keep the roads open and the villages free from bandits?"

"Gone, my lord," she said. She did well to control her voice, but the rōnin could still hear the barest hint of bitterness beneath it. "Marshaling to fight the Crane."

The rōnin allowed a small frown of disgust to break through the emotionless mask he wore. The effects of the Emperor's death at the hands of the traitor, Bayushi Shoju, still echoed throughout the Empire, amplified by the fact that the Bayushi family had been seen as one of the most loyal families in the Empire. Hantei 38th's reign had not been the time of peace and prosperity for all Rokugan that the samurai may have wished, but with his death and the disappearance of Princes Sotorii and Daisetsu, the clans' territorial disputes and endless infighting reignited. And, it seemed, had already spread to the villages.

*And you are to blame,* the rōnin thought. *It is your failure that caused this. And it will be villages like this one that ultimately suffer for it.*

What was it that the *Teachings of Shinsei* said?

*The coward sees what is right and does nothing.*

The rōnin felt another weight settle across his shoulders. "Where?" he asked with a sigh.

"My lord?" she asked.

"Where are the brigands?"

The woman said nothing, keeping her face pressed into the dirt, but he saw a new tension in the set of her back. What would happen to this woman, he wondered, if he found himself facing more enemies than he could handle? What vengeance would they exact if they felt the townspeople had held out on them, and instead put their resources into hiring rōnin? More than one village had been razed by bandits, even during years when the whispers of war had not spread across the land. Perhaps it would be better for everyone if he left things alone. To let the strong prey upon the weak, as they always had.

To ignore the fear that rolled off the woman in waves. To ignore the resigned looks of the villagers. To ignore the underfed and malnourished boy.

To see what was right and do nothing.

His jaw tightened. Turning to the boy, who had edged far beyond his reach, he tried to put a soothing note into the gravel of his voice. "Where are the bad men, boy?" he asked, ignoring the way the child flinched away from him, his earlier curiosity completely swallowed by fear.

The boy pointed a shaking finger, indicating a side road that branched off from the main village path. The rōnin nodded his thanks and stepped around the still kneeling woman. She made no sound as he passed, no movement except for the slight trembling in her back and shoulders. As he strode away, he heard a cry, and glanced back to see the boy fling himself into his mother's arms. They clung tightly to one another, weeping, as the rōnin continued his path into the village.

His stomach felt sour. If that was how the people viewed the samurai, were they so much better than the brigands?

The path took him past small workshops and businesses. Like the homes, they, too, had their shutters in place, walling themselves off from the rest of the town. All save the sake house. The rōnin had seen dozens like it; a square, squat building of wood with a clay-tiled roof that overhung the broad windows, casting them in shadow but protecting them from the torrential rains that sometimes fell. From within came the sounds of raucous laughter and shouting, the clatter of cups against tables, and the calls for more drink.

The rōnin stepped up the single stone stair and onto the encircling, veranda-like engawa before pushing open the door and ducking inside. The ceiling nearly brushed his head as he took a moment for his eyes to adjust. A half-dozen low tables were scattered around a central fire pit, the sullen glow of its embers barely visible against the infiltrating sunlight. Wisping tendrils of smoke danced as they drifted toward the hole cut in the roof above the coals.

The four tables closest to the fire spilled over with rough-looking men – too many rough-looking men. The tunics and pants of their samue were a nondescript brown, stained and dirtied from long wear. They could have been farmers, taking their ease after a long day working the fields, except for the short, broad-bladed swords that rested by their sides, and the carefully expressionless features of the serving girl kneeling to place another tray of sake cups on one of the tables. The tension in the set of her shoulders, the stiffness in her back as she knelt, and the mocking laughter and crude remarks from the men at the table told the rōnin nearly everything.

The expression of the older man standing toward the back of the shop, a sliding panel partially open to reveal a kitchen beyond, told him the rest of the story. The woman – his daughter, judging by the resemblance and age difference – was better at controlling her expressions than the man. His face danced between an impassive mask and an angry, helpless scowl in a series of contortions that would have made a Kabuki actor proud. In the dim interior, the rōnin could barely see the large bruise that covered half the man's face, but it bore mute evidence as to the treatment of the town at the hands of the brigands.

The fifth table, closest to the door, sat empty. The final table was set closer to one of the windows and occupied by another man. This was no bandit or villager; the man wore a light gray haori over dark gray hakama. He wore no clan or family crests, but the daishō tucked into his obi named him samurai as surely as his flowing hair, dyed a brilliant white, named him a Crane.

He was young, scarcely passed his gempuku, and slight of build. A stone teapot sat on the table before him, and he sipped from a matching cup. As his eyes met the rōnin's he offered a small bow, little more than a bare inclination of the head, before returning his watchful gaze to the revelers. The young man was a Crane, and therefore born to the machinations of court, adept at concealing his emotions. Even so, the rōnin could see the faintest tightening around his eyes, the stiffness to the mocking set of his lips, and the slight furrow of his brow that told the rōnin he might not be entirely alone in what was about to happen.

One of the men at the nearest table of ruffians noticed him. "In or out," he grunted, a harsh note of command in his voice. The rōnin watched as the man's eyes flicked over him, pausing for only a moment on the swords before dismissing them with a grunt. "Rōnin." He spoke the word like a curse.

The man was big, nearly as big as a Crab Clan berserker, with broad shoulders and a thick, barrel-like chest. His arms were the size of the rōnin's legs, and he had the broken and scarred face of someone who was no stranger to battle. He also had nearly a dozen of his friends by his side.

Twelve men against one. In the stories, the greatest of the samurai could cut down whole armies while barely breaking a sweat. But the rōnin knew the truth of battle, the harsh realities of war. The stories were simply that: stories. In the real world, one man did not fight twelve and live to see the next dawn.

The wise thing to do would be to leave.

Though it shamed him to admit, the rōnin knew the town's situation was by no means unique. It was the samurai's duty to protect such places, but the samurai could not be everywhere, and the strong had preyed upon the weak since the Founders first fell from Heaven. Even Hantei's reign had not been free of such happenings; with its fall, the rōnin feared that this tableau would be playing out across the Empire as old rivalries reignited and the scabs over wounded pride tore free. The clans, both great and minor, would pull their forces back, leaving the villages and the people who lived there defenseless. This village had likely survived dozens of tributes paid to bandits and rough treatment at their hands throughout its history. No matter what he did here today, it would survive dozens more.

All he had to do was walk away. Walk away and leave a frightened mother, a starving boy, a battered father, and a beleaguered girl in the hands of those who would do them harm. Walk away, like he had from his duty. Walk away, like he had from the Empire.

The rōnin was tired of walking away. The looks of utter hopelessness in the faces – not just in this room, but in every town he had passed through – haunted him, a constant reminder of his own failures. He could not undo those failures. He could not erase his shame. And he could not single-handedly right the Empire from its current course.

But he could try to help these people.

"I will go outside," he said, speaking loud enough to fill every corner of the room. "And you will follow. You will take your men, and you will leave this village. You will not return. Or" – he offered a flat, uncompromising smile that had served him well in Court, and spoke the words that would seal all their fates – "you will die."

# 2
# Hotaru

Doji Hotaru felt the shiver of ancient enchantments as she passed through the gates of the inner wall. Otosan Uchi spread around her, the city flowing out from the Imperial Palace perched upon Seppun Hill as surely as water flowed down from the mountains. The tingling, she knew, came from the spirits bound to the inner wall, infusing the barrier with a strength far greater than simple stone. Those walls had never been breached, never fallen to any siege engine, invocation, or dark ritual.

For all the good that did.

The vaunted walls of the Imperial City had done nothing to stop the murder of the Emperor. They had not turned aside the traitor's blade. They had not closed around Prince Sotorii or his brother to keep them safe. No. For Hotaru, the walls were a stark reminder that here, in the Imperial City, the dangers one must fear the most came not from without, but from within.

She emerged from the long tunnel that passed through the wall and into the sunshine once more. The outer city was a hub of trade and commerce, a place as much for the peasants as the samurai, full of a bustle and industry that was almost vulgar. The outer city thumped like the frenetic beat of the war drums that accompanied the samurai to the field of battle. By contrast, the inner city was calmer, more refined. The plucked strings of a biwa resonating in a council chamber, the soft melody of a koto fading into the background of a moon viewing party. Peaceful. Elegant. Sophisticated.

Hotaru nearly snorted. For all the poise and courtesy, she suspected that far more blood was spilled within the inner city than without.

"Now that is a sour expression for such a lovely face."

A smile broke free as Hotaru turned to the sound of the voice. Her hand reached unconsciously up to push the stark white strands of hair from her face, which had slipped loose during her travels. The man before her had drilled her incessantly about the need to keep her vision clear. Her uncle and teacher, Kakita Toshimoko, stood there, leaning casually against the sacred enchanted wall as if it was his school back in Tsuma. Actually, that wasn't fair. He would have treated the walls of his school with more respect than he did the walls of Otosan Uchi. Despite the fine cut and weave of his kimono – a drab and washed-out gray that may have begun life as the vibrant cyan of the Crane but now could only be called blue if one were being generous – he still managed to look slightly rumpled and unkempt. His silvery-white hair, a color bestowed as much from age and care as the dyes that Hotaru used, was pulled back in a warrior's tail that only accentuated his retreating hairline. He had a broad smile on his own face and a hint of laughter in his eyes, showing far more emotion than was appropriate in such a public place. He did not look fearsome or serious, despite the blades at his side. Any who did not know Kakita Toshimoko would barely give him a second glance.

And yet.

Even Hotaru, who had trained with her uncle from the moment she could properly hold a bokken, could not look at him without feeling the edge of danger. A katana housed in a battered and chipped sheath was no less deadly than one wrapped in silk. And Kakita Toshimoko, master of the Kakita Dueling Academy and one of the highest-ranking nobles among the Kakita family, was the finest swordsman in the Empire, its sharpest blade. There were a few skilled samurai who, perhaps, came close to matching his prowess, but all those who had chosen to put the matter to the test had left some of their blood behind for their efforts.

"Uncle!" she exclaimed, a note of genuine affection underlying her voice. "It is good to see you. Though I assume it is not mere chance that brings you here."

"Bah," he grunted, and unceremoniously pushed himself off the wall. He stood tall and was blade-thin, but Hotaru stood as tall, easily able to look him in the eye. "Nothing happens by chance in this city. There are more spies, informants, and gossips here than grains of rice in all the Empire." His lips pursed as if he wanted to spit, but not even Toshimoko would go quite that far in breaking the bonds of courtesy. "The palace knew you were arriving an hour before you passed the gates of the outer city," he went on. "By now, every courtier in Otosan Uchi knows where you've stabled your horse."

He turned a disapproving eye to the naginata she held loosely in her right hand. "Though you didn't leave your weapon with it, eh?" He said *weapon* in a voice that implied the exact opposite. "Still carrying around that overgrown walking stick? It saddens my heart to think of all the years I wasted teaching you the sword."

Hotaru whirled the naginata in a quick spin, the curved blade at the end of the lacquered wooden shaft flashing in the sun. "Training at the Kakita Academy was the happiest time of my life," she offered as Toshimoko raised a brow, unimpressed. "And I value the skill you drummed into my head beyond measure."

She didn't point out that, despite bringing the naginata with her into the city, she still wore the daishō at her side. Toshimoko could see that as plainly as any, just as he knew that most of the techniques he'd taught her applied just as well to the naginata, but the man couldn't resist poking at his favorite student. Another smile danced across her lips as she said, "Besides, as the Crane Clan Champion, it's only fitting that I be the best at *something*, and Fortunes know, as long as you live, it won't be the sword."

Toshimoko laughed. "True enough, student." There were few people who could address her so casually, but her uncle and former teacher – still her teacher in many ways – was certainly counted among them. He raised a billowing sleeve to the city. "Now, to business. We must get you to the palace so you can see the regent and learn of all the horrors facing the Crane. And the Empire, of course."

Hotaru kept her face impassive at Toshimoko's words, stifling the frown that pulled at her lips. His tone may have been casual, bordering on flippant, but Hotaru knew he could be every bit as precise with his words as he was with his blade. Putting the Empire second, behind the Crane Clan, was no mistake, and the implications underscored why Hotaru had felt compelled to come to the capital in the first place.

Like Toshimoko, the Imperial Regent, Kakita Yoshi, was one of Hotaru's uncles. The wily courtier had served the Crane well in his position as both ambassador to the Imperial Court, and Imperial Chancellor. When the Emperor had fallen to foul treachery, the stewardship of Rokugan had passed to Yoshi. At least, until the princes could be found and the line of Hantei restored to its proper place. But Yoshi, for all his time in the capital, was a Crane through and through. Hotaru had rejoiced, as any Crane should, with her clan's sudden rise to power. But as Clan Champion, she could not allow herself to be unaware of the dangers, even when they came from within.

Even before the murder of Hantei 38th, there had been whispers among the other clans that the Crane had risen too high, that they exerted too much control over the policies of the Empire. The empress was a Crane before she was blessed with marriage to the Light of Heaven. The Imperial Chancellor was a Crane. Many of the most influential courtiers and members of the diplomatic corps were Cranes, as were a disproportionate number of the lesser court functionaries. Of the key positions within the court, only those of Emerald Champion and Imperial Advisor had been filled by individuals with no ties to the Crane. The role of Imperial Advisor – once held by the traitorous Scorpion – now stood empty and was unlikely to be filled. Akodo Toturi had held the position of Emerald Champion, but he had abandoned it, and his duty, after the Emperor's death.

The Scorpion Clan, the Crane's only real rivals when it came to matters political, was in shambles, disgraced by the actions of the traitor. No Scorpion would dare show their face at court, though in the quiet places of her heart, Hotaru wished that at least one would. The Lion still reeled from Toturi's abdication of power. The Crab cared only for the Wall. The Unicorn were practically outsiders, despite having been returned to the Empire for centuries. The Dragon spent too much time staring down at their navels and the Phoenix too much time staring up to the Heavens. There were few obstacles to the political ascendency of her clan.

But Hotaru knew that the other clans, particularly the Lion, would not sit idle while the Crane rose to dizzying heights of power. And since the Lion were known not for their political expertise, but rather the strength and fervor of their armies, if the balance of power was not corrected, the situation along the Crane-Lion border would only worsen.

"When will the regent see fit to call for a new tournament to name the Empire's next Emerald Champion?" she asked Toshimoko. Traditionally, the Emerald Champion acted as the protector not only of the Emperor, but of all Rokugan. In practice, that meant both leading the Imperial Legions and serving as a mediator in martial disputes between the clans. A neutral third party with the backing of Imperial might would go a long way to easing the tensions.

"There will be no tournament," Toshimoko said, making Hotaru's brows shoot up. With a wry twist of his lips, her uncle opened his kimono slightly, revealing the emerald badge of office hanging from a thin silver chain around his neck. They had begun walking down the broad avenue that led straight up Seppun Hill to the palace proper, but seeing the amulet made Hotaru stop in her tracks.

"You?" She tore her gaze from the badge to blink up at him in confusion. "How? Even traveling, word of the tournament would have reached me."

"By Imperial decree," Toshimoko said. That wry smile still adorned his face, but Hotaru could see the worry that simmered in his eyes. "My brother, in his wisdom, decided that there was little point in holding a tournament when he could simply appoint me to the position." He shrugged as they began walking, and the lazy swagger returned to his stride. "Not that there would have been any doubt as to my victory in such a tournament." There was no bravado in Toshimoko's words. And why should there be? So far as Hotaru knew, he had never lost a duel.

"I don't particularly want the position," he continued. "It's more politics than I care for. And it keeps me away from my students longer than I'd like. But if it is the will of the Imperial Regent and for the good of the clan…" He shrugged.

"I wonder how good it will be for either," Hotaru replied, her mind spinning in worried circles. The traditions of the Empire were iron bound. Breaking them in such a blatant fashion would not be taken lightly – or well – by the other clans. To say nothing of the gathering of so much power in the hands of her own clan. "I'm sure you've heard the whispers. The other clans grow uneasy with the power of the Crane. The Lion stalk closer to our borders, and there is talk that they have Toshi Ranbo in their sights."

Toshimoko snorted as they continued the long climb to the palace gates. "The Lion ambassador took it poorly when my brother appointed me Emerald Champion," he said wryly. "But he's not the one we must worry about. Matsu Tsuko arrived in the city five days ago, along with a retinue at least fifty strong. Not enough to challenge the guards in the Imperial Palace, but more than enough to get up to some mischief."

Hotaru felt a chill slide up her back. Matsu Tsuko had no love for her; it was Hotaru's arrow that had claimed the life of Tsuko's betrothed, Akodo Arasou, at the gates of Toshi Ranbo. She felt no guilt over the matter; the battle had been fought well within the bounds of both law and tradition, and every samurai who stood to battle knew the risks. She felt confident that Arasou's spirit bore her no ill will. His widow, on the other hand, was a different matter. Would Tsuko let the personal enmity between the two drive their clans to full-scale war? And potentially tear apart the Empire in the process?

"Can she be reasoned with?"

"A Lion?" Toshimoko asked incredulously. "You might as well try to convince Lady Sun to rise in the west as reason with a Lion." He snorted. "You'd have a better chance of success."

That was perhaps unfair to the Lion, Hotaru thought, as they continued their way through the outer city. As a clan, the Lion were known to be unyielding and inflexible, but they were also brave, loyal, and fearless in battle. And they cared more about their personal reputation than any other clan in the Empire. Surely, Matsu Tsuko could be reasoned with, if Hotaru chose her words very carefully.

They had reached the palace walls, and Toshimoko waved at the guards standing at crisp attention at the gate as they passed. No one challenged them. Whether that was because of Toshimoko's newfound position as commander of the Imperial armies, or if they recognized Hotaru as Champion of the Crane – or both – she could not be sure. Still, in the wake of the Emperor's murder, she would have expected a little more scrutiny.

Once inside the walls, Toshimoko grabbed the first functionary he saw, a young courtier who barely looked old enough to pass her gempuku. From her dress, the girl was a Dragon, slight of build, wearing a silk kimono in Dragon green and gold.

"Lord Kakita," the girl said with a proper bow. "How may I help you?"

"Take the Crane Champion's pointy stick to her quarters in the palace, if you would," he said, waving one hand at Hotaru's naginata. "We must present ourselves to the regent, and I'm sure the guards would be a bit upset if Lady Hotaru brings it with her."

Hotaru shook her head in amusement as she passed the naginata to the courtier, who held it like the stick her uncle claimed it to be. "As you wish, Lady Kakita," the girl said with another bow. She turned and glided off in the direction of the Crane living quarters that stood near the east gardens.

Hotaru and Toshimoko walked through the palace grounds and Hotaru, who lived in the Doji Palace surrounded by the finest works of art that the finest artisans in the Empire could produce, still found herself marveling at the beauty around her. The gardens were tended daily by an army of highly skilled workers, and each leaf, flower, and blade of grass was maintained just so. Drought never touched this place, nor did the ravages of storm or flood leave any scars upon it. The statues and other works of art that lined the winding paths were all from the greatest artists to walk the Empire. Many depicted the heroes of old, while others honored nature or the Fortunes, but they were all sculpted with the tools of a master.

The people she passed, whether peasant or samurai, seemed to reflect that beauty, as if the backdrop of the palace grounds lifted them to heights of elegance those who lived outside could never obtain. It was an illusion, she knew. A silk and makeup disguise over the harsh realities of palace life. But it was an illusion that she allowed herself a moment to enjoy. Even her uncle, rumpled and unkempt, somehow managed to look like the graceful blade he truly was within the backdrop of the Imperial grounds.

And then Hotaru saw her.

She perched demurely on the edge of a fountain, one hand trailing in the waters, ripples of light dancing across her skin. Her hair spilled down her shoulders like a dark river, framing a face whose beauty pained Hotaru to look upon. The lacy butterfly mask reflected the light of Lady Sun in a way that made it seem almost alive, somehow only adding to her beauty rather than concealing it. Her kimono, woven of the finest silks and thin enough to border on the scandalous, flowed across her body like a caress, highlighting both the strength and softness that Hotaru knew lingered there. The kimono and mask were both the deep crimson of the Scorpion Clan, making the woman stand out like a splash of blood against the alabaster stone of the fountain.

*Kachiko.* Hotaru felt her breath catch as she gazed at the Scorpion, her heartbeat suddenly loud in her ears. She had no doubt that Kachiko had staged it, had planned every little detail from the crook of her knee that emphasized the curve of her hip to the twist of the shoulder that pushed her breasts against the silk of her kimono. Everything the woman did was planned; Bayushi Kachiko, Mother of Scorpions, widow to the traitor and murderer Bayushi Shoju, played politics in her sleep and never let even a moment's advantage pass her by. Hotaru could not fault her for it; it was simply who Kachiko was.

But she still wore the mask that Hotaru herself had gifted her so many years ago.

Hotaru swallowed hard. Kachiko shouldn't be here. The Scorpion were pariahs, their entire clan bearing the shame for the murder of the Emperor. It was only by the grace of the Fortunes that the clan had not been disbanded, their ambassadors and diplomats – or spies and assassins depending on whose tale you believed – retreating to within their own borders. The clan's power was broken, at least for a time. It was dangerous for any Scorpion to be outside of the lands they controlled, and no place more dangerous than here. Hotaru's heart quickened at the thought of Kachiko placing herself into that danger.

Why had she come?

It didn't matter. All that mattered was that she was here, now.

Then Kachiko's dark eyes lifted, meeting Hotaru's gaze, and the glimmering emotion within easily snuffed out everything else. Thoughts of the regent, the Lion, the dangers to the Crane, vanished. Without thinking, Hotaru turned and strode to meet the woman whose delicate fingers were irrevocably tangled in the strings of her own heart.

# 3
# Yakamo

"They're coming again!"

Hida Yakamo tightened his grip on his iron-studded tetsubō and tried to ignore the stench that threatened to raise the bile in his throat. All around him, the Great Carpenter Wall seemed bathed in blood and carpeted in the bodies of the dead Shadowlands creatures and his fellow Crab warriors alike. This close to the foul domain of Fu Leng, the curse that loomed over all the Emerald Empire sank its blackened claws into everything, even the recently deceased. Their flesh festered and rotted far faster than it should, and though Yakamo had learned to ignore it, sometimes the foul miasma seemed to have a life of its own, forcing its way into his nose and lungs and filling him with a nausea ill-suited to a warrior.

Yakamo shook his head, as if to violently fling the thoughts – and the stink – from his mind. He shrugged his massive shoulders and shifted his feet, the heavy plates of his armor – once the deep blue of the Crab Clan but so covered in blood and ichor it might as well have been black – grating against one another. He did not have the time to dwell on such matters, for the enemy was nearly upon them. The last wave had broken no more than ten minutes ago and he had sunk down, placing his back against the parapet to catch a few moments of rest. The water bearers, Crab youths not yet old enough to hold a weapon and stand a watch – had not made it to his position, and his throat felt dry and thick. Still, despite his thirst, he pushed himself to his feet and turned to face the onrushing darkness.

The Great Carpenter Wall rose more than a hundred feet into the air, topped with the banners and pennants of his clan. Despite the rigors of battle, the banners still flew, the Crab emblem that was the namesake of his people dancing in the fetid winds. Perched atop the Wall, Yakamo had a clear view of the wastelands that stretched out to the south. Broken earth and blasted rock spread as far as his eye could see. The land was barren; no tree or bush pushed its way through the crags, no hint of grass poked through the rubble, no bird or bug flitted through the air. The tableau was empty. Dead.

Except for the army crouched beyond the wall.

The forces of the Shadowlands milled about just outside of the range of the great siege weapons that dotted the Wall's watch towers. From the lofty height of the Wall itself, he could not make out much of the enemy. But he didn't need to. All Yakamo had to do was look at the bodies of the monsters that had twice now made it over the parapets and onto the battlements.

Goblins were the least of them. The spindly, green-skinned creatures stood no bigger than a child and were no match for a warrior. Not in a stand-up fight. But the Jigoku-damned things bred faster than rats or rabbits, because there seemed to be thousands of them in every assault and an infinite reserve just waiting to break their needle-like teeth against the Wall. They fought more like wild animals than disciplined warriors, but a pack of rabid dogs could take down a man, if there were enough of them.

Worse things marched at the goblins' side. Ogres towered over their goblin allies, dwarfing even Yakamo who was used to being taller and broader than any of his kin. Their thick hide was nearly as hard to pierce as boiled leather and one blow from their broad blades or axes could tear through the Crab's steel and lamellar armor like paper. And still that wasn't the worst of it. Yakamo could slaughter goblins by the dozen, and no ogre would drive him to fear. Even the lesser oni, demons summoned or escaped from the pits of the Realm of Torment itself, did not fill him with the creeping horror that could overcome any who fought the nightmare beasts of the Shadowlands.

For Yakamo, that feeling only came when battling the dead.

They were out there, too. All too often wearing rotting kimonos and broken armor bearing the colors and the crest of the Crab. Warriors who had gone into the Shadowlands and never returned, their bodies reanimated and pressed into the service of Fu Leng. Yakamo could think of no worse fate, and in his bleakest moments, he would wake from dreams where the dead coming for him wore the familiar faces of the samurai under his own command.

If I die here, he thought, at least I die clean.

The roiling mass of the enemy was moving now, surging forward again, as relentless as the tide rolling up the shore. He heard the thump of the siege engines, and watched the hail of rocks sailing overhead. Most fell short, but some crashed among the enemy. Where they did, they exploded, the invocations the shindōshi had inscribed onto them reacting to the foulness of the Shadowlands Taint, detonating with the fury of Fire and Earth. The holes that opened in the enemy lines closed almost at once, the forces of Fu Leng absorbing the losses with unflinching fanaticism.

"Ha! Look at them fall!" The voice was deep, like rumbling

stones rolling down a mountainside, but at the same time full of laughter. A smile came unbidden to Yakamo's lips as he stared at the onrushing horde. He turned to see the grinning face of Hiruma Bunzō, whose eyes glittered with cheerful indomitability. "We will fling them back into the holes they crawled out of," the man crowed. "They will cower in the darkness and rue the day they dared to cross the Crab!"

For all the deep rumbling of his voice, Bunzō was slight of build, almost scrawny, even in his armor. He moved with the exaggerated swagger of a man twice his size, like a Kabuki actor claiming the stage. The dark blue lacquer of his armor was stained and chipped with battle, but a smile hung on the man's face. The men and women under Yakamo's command laughed as the wiry soldier strutted by, and with the laughter came the sense of a weight lifting. The enemy still surged forward – soon they would be within easy bowshot and the archers could begin their bloody work. Not long after that, the goblins would gain the battlements, and the world would regress to exertion and pain and death. But in that moment, they all laughed.

It was a welcome reprieve, and one that reminded him of his duty.

"Get the battlements clear," Yakamo ordered. "Return the bodies of the Shadowlands filth to their fellows and start seeing to our own dead."

His forces turned grimly to the task. No one wanted to touch a corpse; doing so was considered unclean and usually reserved for peasants. But the Crab had long since come to terms with the fact that, on the Wall, polite and proper had to give way to pragmatic and necessary. Unpleasant though the task might be, it was difficult to fight atop a blanket of corpses. His soldiers muttered, but they started grabbing goblin bodies and hurling them over the parapets. Yakamo grabbed a pair of dead goblins by the scruff of the neck, his massive muscles bulging as he lifted them easily from the stones. With a casual toss, he threw them over the edge, sending the creatures back to the Shadowlands where they belonged.

"That's a lot of goblins coming," Bunzō muttered as Yakamo wiped his hand on the wall and turned his attention to the body of an ogre. The enormous monster lay sprawled on the battlements, its grayish skin covered in dozens of wounds from sword and arrow, one limp claw clutching a rusty axe. Gritting his teeth, Yakamo grabbed the ogre's tree stump arm and levered his weight beneath it, striving to heave the body up the wall.

Bunzō set his lean shoulder into the mountain of flesh as well, lending his strength as Yakamo struggled to push the eight-foot body of the beast through one of the embrasures. "Do you think they'll make the walls again?" Bunzō grunted as they both shoved to rid themselves of their disgusting burden.

Yakamo's answer was interrupted by the sound of hundreds of bows firing at once. Yakamo had no archers under his command; they were concentrated in the bastions that stood every thousand feet along the length of the Wall. But with the advantage of height the bastions offered, the yumi-armed ashigaru and samurai could range along the front of the Wall between their towers. Only a narrow corridor a hundred and fifty feet wide was relatively safe from their arrows, and it was in that gap where Yakamo's troops held the Wall.

Yakamo still could not decide if it was a sign of respect, or a punishment. His father, Hida Kisada, the Great Bear himself, had ordered him here, at the very heart of the current assault on the Wall. It was the position most likely to be tested, and the one most likely to fall.

It was the place where a young commander might prove himself to his lord. Or where an heir who didn't quite live up to his father's expectation might find himself conveniently removed.

*Is that why I'm here, Father? To finally rid you of your disappointment?*

"They will make the Wall," Yakamo grunted, crushing thoughts of his father beneath the weight of the ogre and the task before him. He and Bunzō heaved the ogre through the embrasure and together watched it tumble down the sloped face of the stones. Even as he said it, the first of the enemy reached the base and began scrambling up, climbing more like spiders or insects than anything human.

"Good," Bunzō replied, kicking a severed goblin head off the backside of the battlements. His voice rose in volume, carrying to all those nearby. "It's boring to sit up here and watch the archers and engineers have all the fun, and my blade hasn't claimed nearly enough goblin heads. What a wonderful day to be a Crab!"

Yakamo could only chuckle. The Laughing Crab, as Bunzō was known by his fellows, was irrepressible. And it was a blessing from the Fortunes that he was. The pragmatic Crab Clan, Yakamo among them, fell all too easily into a stoic shell, shutting out the horrors of their everyday life. But that often meant shutting out the little moments of joy that could be found, even here. Bunzō's antics reminded them all that the grim reality of their sworn duty as samurai and Crab didn't have to turn them into numb, emotionless killers. All along the length of the Wall, Yakamo saw the samurai and ashigaru in his charge casting glances at Bunzō and heard the laughter that rose in their wake.

A smile tugged at one corner of his mouth. Trust Bunzō to rouse the fighting spirit of the troops; now it was his turn to wake them up entirely.

"You heard him!" Yakamo shouted, raising his voice to be heard by his entire command. "Lady Sun shines upon us, and the Fortunes cheer us to victory. Let us meet our guests and show them what it means to have a good day on the Wall."

Newfound laughter and roars met his words as the Crab warriors tossed the last of the goblin corpses over the Wall. They plummeted down the fortification and, in some cases, smashed into the faces of their fellows, the lead elements of which were now less than fifty feet below the parapets, still climbing with the alien grace and speed of arachnids. They would gain the heights in a few moments, and once more, the battle would be joined.

"So many of them. They just keep coming."

Yakamo looked over at Bunzō, shocked not at the words, but at the tone. The laughter was gone from his voice as he peered over the Wall, and he spoke in a near whisper that only Yakamo, standing right beside him, could hear. Despite the bravado from only a moment before, Bunzō now seemed deflated, folded in on himself as the goblins scrabbling up the wall drew ever closer.

Yakamo narrowed his eyes. How much of Bunzō's laughing persona was an act, put on to bolster his own courage and those of his companions? He couldn't be sure, but he knew that all of them wore masks, as surely as any Scorpion. And they all needed support when those masks began to slip.

"We have been here a hundred times, my friend," he said quietly, "and we will be here a hundred times more before we're done. Besides," he added as Bunzō glanced up at him, "if we let this filth overrun us, my father would have Kuni Yori pull us both from our graves just so he could tell me what a disappointment I was."

Bunzō gave something that was half snort, half shudder at the mention of the shindōshi's name. "Don't invoke that one lest you summon him," the Laughing Crab warned, in a voice that was only half mocking. "I'd rather face all the demons of the Shadowlands than Kuni Yori. Or your father." He leaned and spat over the Wall, a breach of courtesy so shocking anywhere else in the Empire that it would almost certainly lead to a duel. Then he snorted again. "Not that it matters now. Our guests are arriving."

Yakamo glanced over the parapet and saw that the goblins were mere feet away, shrieking furiously as they climbed. "Then let's give them the welcome they deserve," he growled. The first leathery green fingers grasped the embrasure in front of him and he smashed his tetsubō down, feeling bones crush between the iron-studded wood of his club and the unforgiving stone of the wall. The goblin fell away with a shriek, but there was another to replace it.

There was always another to replace them. As Bunzō said, they just kept coming.

"Steady!" Yakamo roared, bashing the second goblin off the Wall and back to the Shadowlands. "Push them back! They gain nothing but death here today."

All along the length of the Wall, battle was joined. Bowstrings still thrummed from the bastions, and the regular thud of the catapults and ballistae launching their deadly missiles into the massed troops below still sounded, but for Yakamo, the world shrank down to the hundred or so feet of the Wall that was his responsibility. The goblins scaled the Wall, and the Crab met them, smashing them from the ramparts and sending them tumbling into the waiting darkness. But for each goblin that fell, two more seemed to take their place.

Yakamo grunted as the jagged point of a goblin spear shattered against the steel plates of his armor, the inferior weapon splintering into a dozen fragments. He turned and swept his tetsubō in a broad arc, connecting with the creature and feeling its ribcage shatter even as it was flung off the Wall, plummeting to the ground far below. His muscles strained as he stopped the momentum of the massive club and snapped it back in the opposite direction, faster than would have been possible for a weaker man. The iron studs rang as they shattered a goblin's hastily raised shield and sent that one, too, disappearing over the Wall. Another spear slipped along his armor before catching behind his kote and digging a shallow furrow in his flesh. He roared and smashed his club straight down, crushing the goblin as easily as swatting a bug.

And still more goblins came. They poured over the walls now, those behind shoving those ahead bodily into the waiting line of Crab, uncaring as their comrades fell to the blades, hammers, polearms, and clubs. Should they gain a firm foothold on the walkway, reinforcements would swarm like ants until the Crab – at least those under his command – would be consumed.

"Push them back!" Yakamo bellowed. "Push them from the Wall!" He drove forward like a man possessed, weapon raised high. His muscles burned with fatigue and breath came in panting gasps. He ignored the pain as he drew a ragged breath. "Hida!" he shouted as his tetsubō smashed through the hastily raised sword of a goblin less than half his size. "For the Crab!" He bodily kicked another goblin, ignoring the biting teeth and hooked claws that scratched the lacquer of his armor. "For the Empire!"

He fought without grace, without precision, a desperate brutality that left his enemies broken and dying before him. He could not help but revel in the fury and violence of it all. It was the way of the Crab. Let the Crane have their duelists, the Dragon their sword masters, and the Lion their grand strategists. Let the other clans train in their pristine schools where the mats were freshly swept and mistakes were corrected with soft words and guiding hands. Let them fight their clean wars where cultured warriors exchanged pleasantries and played at politics when they should be spilling each other's blood.

The Crab couldn't afford any of those luxuries. If they faltered, even for a moment, the Shadowlands would overwhelm them. And the soft, fat lands beyond the Wall would fall as surely as wheat to the scythe.

The pressure eased and Yakamo realized he had pushed all the way to the parapets, driving the goblins before him. His samurai and ashigaru had followed suit and pushed the invaders back over the Wall. A quick glance showed him that the same scene had played out at every point between the two bastions, and it looked like the goblins were in full retreat, scrabbling down the wall more quickly than they came up it.

"Run, you cowards!" Bunzō cried, waving his blood-spattered ono in the air as he shouted at the goblins' retreating backs. "Go back to the foul pit that spewed you forth!"

He was answered by a trumpeting sound that was half-shriek, half-roar. It came not from the ground below, but from the skies overhead. Yakamo cursed as he tore his gaze from the retreating goblins and scanned the slate gray sky.

It was all too easy to dismiss the creatures of the Shadowlands as mindless, animalistic monsters. And some of them were exactly that. But not all. There were beings in the lands of Fu Leng with enough cunning to put a Scorpion to shame. And there were others, creatures like the oni or Fu Leng's dark necromancers, who had a deep understanding of tactics and strategy.

Deep enough to use a ground assault by the goblins to draw the Crab's watchful eyes away from the real threat.

"There!" an armored warrior shouted, stabbing a finger toward the washed-out clouds. But it was already too late. Another trumpeting scream sounded, directly above, and creatures unlike anything Yakamo had seen swooped from the sky toward the Wall.

Yakamo's skin crawled. These monsters had long, emaciated bodies with the bones beneath their leathery skin clearly visible and thick, lizard-like tails. Two legs, birdlike, stretched out behind them as they flew. Yakamo could see with crystal focus the massive, curved talons at the end of those feet. Their arms, if arms they were, were thick and powerful, far longer than would be normal for a human, and ending in hands that looked disturbingly like those of a man. A membrane stretched from the creature's wrists to a point halfway down the powerful tail, creating something more akin to a sail than a wing. The creatures had long necks, two-thirds the length of their bodies, and arrow-like heads that reminded him of the herons he had seen in the Imperial City. Except, these creatures didn't have beaks, just long, fleshy proboscises that he had little doubt were full of razor-sharp teeth.

Yakamo did not know how birds flew, but nothing of these creatures resembled the liquid grace of a bird in flight. They beat at the air like they were trying to bludgeon it into submission, and their angry cries echoed with as much pain as hate.

But still they flew. Directly for the Wall, and Yakamo's forces that waited there. Arrows flew at them, the archers quickly responding to the sudden threat from above, but the few that struck the creatures did nothing to slow them down. They soared over the Wall, silhouetted black against the mottled clouds. Yakamo felt the chill of their shadows as they glided over him. It mirrored the chill that shot up his spine at the sight of the beasts. He fought back the fingers of fear – there was no place for it on the Wall – as his eyes tracked the beasts.

At some unseen signal, the creatures reared up, flaring out their wings and, as one, dropped from the sky. Their taloned feet crashed into the broad walk atop the Wall, striking with enough force to crack the stones. Yakamo stumbled, clutching his tetsubō, as the creatures turned on them with an ear-splitting wail. The beasts were huge, each towering nearly twice the size of a man and half again as broad, even with their wings folded. They moved on all fours, upper limbs reaching out as their powerful legs and tail drove them forward in something that was half slither, half crawl. A dozen of the demons had dropped onto his section of the Wall. Behind him, Yakamo heard the triumphant howls of the Shadowlands army as they prepared to charge once more.

Scarcely a second had passed since the monsters crashed into their midst, and his samurai were already reacting. The first to reach one brought his ōdachi slicing down, the long, slightly curved blade moving with the speed and force that only desperation could bring. Yakamo watched in horror as the razor-edge of the weapon met the leather flesh of the monstrosity… and bounced. That blow could sever the head from a man, but all it left behind on the beast was a thin, shallow cut leaking black ichor.

Almost casually, the monster reached out, curved talons closing around the torso of the samurai. Its proboscis opened, peeling back in four separate, tentacle-like appendages, each lined with barbed protrusions that were somewhere between teeth and the suckers of an octopus. The mouth where those four appendages met was circular and lined with more teeth. The same cry – half rage, half agony – thundered forth as the massive muscles in the creature's legs flexed, and the samurai, armor and all, was crushed.

A moment's stillness settled over the Wall. It couldn't have been more than a heartbeat, but to Yakamo, it felt like an eternity. In that frozen moment, as he watched the nightmare slaughter one of his own with casual ease, Yakamo saw death. Worse, he saw the complete and utter failure of his duty.

But that duty remained, no matter how hopeless.

*If I die here, at least I die clean. I swear it.*

He raised his tetsubō above his head, drew a deep breath, and shouted, "Charge!"

# 4
# Toturi

An absolute silence had fallen over the sake house as the patrons of the establishment stared at him in stark astonishment. Not that the rōnin could blame them; he was outnumbered ten to one, and he doubted that bandits who would stoop to crushing a peasant village beneath their heel would have any compulsion to fight fair. What he had just proposed was tantamount to suicide, and it seemed to have stunned the raucous crew into a moment of shocked stillness.

Then the big man who appeared to be their leader began to laugh. It was a coarse, guttural laugh full of cruelty. "I don't know where you're from, rōnin, or what polite court you think this is," he sneered. "But out here, your pathetic Akodo Code isn't going to help you." As he spoke, he pushed himself to his feet, having to tilt his head to the side to avoid bumping the ceiling. The men at the other tables stood as well, picking their sheathed blades up from where they rested on the ground.

The rōnin said nothing. Instead, he stepped outside and

gestured to the man, waving for him to follow. He moved from the engawa and back down the stairs, coming to a stop in the middle of the dusty track. He turned to face the door to the sake house and waited.

It was not a long wait.

The large man was the first out the door, squeezing his bulk through the small opening. But he was not alone. Every patron of the house followed him. The brigands arrayed themselves behind their leader, forming a rough wedge, and they held their broad, short-bladed swords in their hands. The Crane had come out as well, and he, too, stepped from the engawa, though he did not position himself with the brigands. Nor did he position himself with the rōnin. He stood apart, a light smile playing on his lips and his left hand resting easily on his katana's scabbard.

The rōnin was aware of eyes watching from the buildings around them, the villagers peering from the safety of their homes while the rōnin prepared to die for them. Why was he doing this? Why risk his life for people who would not defend themselves?

Because it was his duty. Because it was right.

They stood there for a long moment, the only sounds the soughing of the breeze and the small shifting movements of the men arrayed against him. The rōnin could feel the heat of the sun upon his back, the balmy warmth a soothing lie of comfort. He felt the building tension, the almost physical weight of the animosity rolling off the brigands. He let their anger, their hatred, wash over him like a wave crashing against a rock, and when it passed, it took with it his own anger, his fear, and even, for the moment at least, his litany of shame and regrets. When that wave receded, it left him standing in near-perfect calm, eyes locked on the bandit leader, waiting for the imperceptible motion that would signify the start of the battle.

He was moving before he was consciously aware that the

moment had come. One instant, the brigands were standing before him, hefting their weapons and waiting for their overlarge leader to give the order to kill him. The next, they were surging forward. But the rōnin moved with them, his katana sweeping from its scabbard with liquid grace, slicing upward in a crescent moon.

The cut caught the first man to reach him, opening him from hip to chest and spilling his life into the dirt. The rōnin barely felt the resistance as the razor-edge of his sword parted cloth and flesh, and he continued the swing into the upper guard before flowing back down into a blinding strike. Another brigand joined his fellow on the now-muddied earth, but the precious seconds it took to fell the two foes did not come without a price.

The others were upon him, and the rōnin knew that the bandit leader had spoken true. The greatest samurai of Rokugan were near legendary in their abilities, and while the rōnin might not count himself among their ranks, his training and skill far outstripped those of his opponents. Had he met these men on the dueling field, he could fight them one by one and kill them at his leisure, and all it would cost him would be a few droplets of sweat. But when it came to the chaos of battle, when concepts of fairness were crushed beneath the booted heel of pragmatism, one man could not win against ten.

But that was no reason to make it easy for them.

He shifted his stance from the rushing flow of water to the ever-shifting currents of air as the enemies' swords came for him. He danced with the bandits, weaving an impenetrable wall of steel, his feet moving with the quick, balanced steps of the swordsman, always angling to keep his attackers in front of him, to try to funnel them to his blade one at a time. He moved with the unpredictability of the spring breeze and the quickness of the summer storm. He managed to keep the enemy steel from his own flesh, but each time an opening to strike back presented itself, he had to twist away, intercepting a different strike from another opponent.

The rōnin knew it was not a battle he could win. Sweat streamed down his face, and he could hear his own breath growing panting and ragged. Fatigue burned in his muscles and the slight quiver in his legs told him that time was running out.

It was strange to think that, after walking in the highest palaces of the Empire, serving at the side of Hantei 38th himself, and leading armies that numbered in the tens of thousands, he would die in the alleys of a village, the name of which he did not know.

A blade finally slipped past his guard, the edge slicing across his chest. The heavy hempen cloth of his kimono parted under the slashing blade, slowing the steel. Pain flashed through the rōnin, but the wound was shallow. He reacted with lightning speed, letting out a roar as he shifted from his graceful dance into a direct and ruthless assault upon his enemy. His blade was no longer a shield against the attacks of his enemies, but instead a questing flame, savage and relentless. Two quick parries cleared the way as he lunged into a piercing strike, the tip of his katana sinking home. It cost him two more minor wounds, but a third foe was now down.

Leaving only nine more to go.

The bandits howled their rage and flew at him. The rōnin spun, a defiant and tight-lipped smile creasing his face as he began to silently compose his death poem.

And the Crane entered the fray.

The young samurai stepped with the delicate grace that seemed the birthright of his clan and yet moved with deceptive speed. He glided into battle, his katana appearing in his hands as if summoned by the elemental spirits, darting out with the speed and precision of a calligrapher's brush. The rōnin recognized the techniques as the Crane's blade wove a net of steel. Though there were subtle differences from the way he had learned them, it was a dance as deadly as the rōnin's own, and it took the brigands by complete surprise.

Two more corpses decorated the village road, and then the Crane was by his side. He said nothing, merely offering a faint smile that was as precise and intentional as his swordplay. It lent his face a smug cast, though perhaps that was more the rōnin's own preconceptions than reality.

The Crane's entry into the battle had also bought the rōnin some much needed rest, for with close to half their number dead or dying, the remaining bandits appeared to be having second thoughts about their mortality. Raising his head, the rōnin stared them down.

"You can still leave," he said, fighting to keep the tiredness from his own voice. "Stop this foolishness, leave this village, and never return. Whatever tribute you thought to gain will be lost, but you will still have your lives."

"Kill them!" the leader shouted, his voice loud enough to shake the shutters of the buildings around them. "The rōnin is wounded, the Crane is a boy. Kill them!"

Still, the bandits hesitated, looking at one another and at their late companions lying in pools of their own blood.

"Perhaps if you led from the front?" the Crane suggested, that faint smile still shadowing his face. His voice was a crystalline, high tenor and the words carried the biting edge of sarcasm. "It is necessary at times to set a proper example, after all." As he spoke, he flicked his katana to the side, clearing some of the blood from it in an arcing wave of crimson. "I wouldn't want it to get on my clothes," he said, his tone more conversational and the words spoken to no one in particular.

The bandits exchanged more uncertain glances and for the barest moment, the rōnin thought they might break. But with a roar of his own, the leader charged directly at him, swinging his nata-like sword in a broad chopping motion.

The Crane's words proved prophetic, for his men rushed after him, snarling out their own fury. The Crane peeled off, intercepting three of them and leaving the rōnin to deal with the leader and a trio of his followers. As they charged, the rōnin yanked his wakizashi from its scabbard and hurled it toward one of the trio heading his way in a technique he hadn't practiced in years. He did not have the instant to spare to see if it was effective, for even as the hilt left his fingertips, the bandit leader crashed into him.

The rōnin's katana intercepted the brigand's blade and though he angled his own steel to shed as much of the force as possible, he still felt the impact through his shoulders and shivering down his spine. Their blades screeched against each other as both fought for the superior position. The rōnin was aware of the other two bandits angling around, looking for an opportunity to drive their swords into his back.

But from a nearby alley, another shadow darted. It was a peasant boy, no more than sixteen years of age, clutching a masakari – a single-bladed, hatchet-like peasant axe – in his hand. He swung the weapon without skill, but with more than enough ferocity, and his surprising charge bowled one of the bandits over, sending the pair sprawling to the ground. The rōnin could not spare much thought for the boy's action, save to offer a mental word of thanks to the Fortunes that at least one villager had found their courage.

The other bandit continued to close in on the rōnin's flank while the brigand leader tried to overpower him. There was no time for subtle swordplay. In one swift movement, the rōnin brought his knee high, sinking on his other leg as his foot shot out and up, slipping past the bandit leader's guard to connect his heel with the man's chin. With their blades locked and the weight of the brigand bearing down upon him, the rōnin was too off balance to generate much power, but it was enough to send the surprised brigand stumbling back. As he did, the rōnin whirled, darting two quick steps forward and plunging his blade through the chest of the bandit who had been circling him.

He saw that the peasant and the bandit he'd tackled still struggled on the ground. There was blood there, and plenty of it, but he couldn't tell whose. With that much blood, it would be over soon, one way or the other. He spun back in time to parry the leader's sword once more, then a second and third blow. They separated for a moment, both panting for air. The rōnin spared a quick glance at the Crane, but the man had already dropped one of his foes and seemed to be having little trouble handling the two that remained.

That just left the leader for the rōnin to worry about. The brigand snarled and lunged forward, sword questing for the rōnin's blood.

The man attacked with an angry flurry of strikes driven by the weight of his considerable size. The rōnin could not pick out any discernible techniques – unsurprising, since those were only taught in the formal schools of the samurai – but size, strength, and speed had a certain technique all their own. And the man was not completely unskilled; the rōnin supposed that in the world of bandits and thugs, the one most able to kill his fellows was the one most likely to lead.

But the rōnin was not one of his fellows, and now that he didn't have to worry about being outnumbered ten to one, his own abilities were more than up to the task. He met the fury and strength of the attack with speed and grace, shedding the brigand's heavy blows or dodging them entirely, watching the frustration build on his opponent's face. Their blades clashed again and again, the furious ringing of steel blending into one long, continuous cacophony.

The rōnin saw his opening and began the sequence of strikes

known as whirling tempest. His blade moved like a leaf caught in a dust devil. With each swing he subtly changed the angle of attack, slowly building up the speed of his strikes until he was raining down a torrent of blows that the brigand had little hope of stopping. The frustration on the man's face shifted to concentration and then to panic as the rōnin's gliding blade showed no sign of slowing. With a final twisting cut, the rōnin slipped past the brigand's guard and felt the slightest resistance as his katana bit home.

Two hollow thumps sounded as the brigand and his head fell separately into the dirt.

He whirled to move to the aid of the peasant and the Crane, but it was unnecessary. The white-haired samurai already had his blade sheathed and was looking down at the muddied and corpse-littered road, no expression at all playing across his handsome features. The peasant boy had regained his feet and was staring down in horror at both the bloodied axe that he held and at the body of the brigand he had killed.

The rōnin snapped his blade out to the side to clear it of blood and slid it back into its scabbard. He was aware of the eyes upon him as he did so. A glance toward the sake house showed that the proprietor and his daughter had moved out onto the engawa, staring at the aftermath of the battle with wide eyes. He thought he saw the girl mouth a name – Toku? She started to move toward them – toward the peasant boy, the rōnin realized – but her father stopped her with one hand on her shoulder.

They were not the only ones watching. The fight had not taken long, a minute, two at the most. But it had been loud, and it had drawn the attention of everyone in the village. The rattling sound of shutters sliding open echoed all around them, and the rōnin, the Crane, and the peasant boy found themselves standing in a ring of wide-eyed onlookers.

It was the Crane who broke the silence. "Well," he offered, "that *was* surprising, wasn't it?" His gaze slid to the bodies in the road, and that faint smile fluttered over his lips. "I didn't really expect to be fighting today. Thank the Fortunes that I left my silk kimonos back home." His tone was conversational, as if he were discussing the weather, not the casual slaughter of a dozen brigands. "The servants are adept at cleaning them, of course, but no matter how good a job they do, I can never seem to forget that the blood was there. I find it rather… distasteful." His gaze shifted to the rōnin, and one silver brow arched. "Wouldn't you agree?"

The rōnin appraised him in silence for a moment. The boy – no, no matter how young he seemed, he had clearly completed his gempuku, and that made him an adult in the eyes of the Empire – stood among the dirt and blood, an artless smile on his face. Despite his surroundings, despite the dead that lay at his feet, he seemed as poised and refined as if he stood in the great Doji palace. The rōnin had no idea how he was going to answer the Crane; the chances of being recognized as the rush of battle fled were too high. And yet, the Crane deserved some answers. He had, after all, saved the rōnin's life.

He looked instead at the peasant boy, who was still staring in horror at what he had done. It allowed the rōnin to turn his face away from the Crane, without stretching the bounds of courtesy too far. "It was a brave thing you did, boy," the rōnin said. "You have my thanks."

"I killed him." The words were barely a whisper, but the rōnin's ears caught them. He had seen the reaction before. No matter how hardened a warrior thought they might be, there came two moments, in close succession, that would determine the course of that warrior's life. The first was the moment when the first battle was joined; some broke at that instant, unable to ignore the stomach-churning fear and get past the blood and fury. And then, if they were lucky enough to survive their first battle, there came the moment immediately after, where the newly blooded warrior had to come to terms with what they had done.

"You did what you had to do. To save your village. And to save my life. And for that, I am grateful." The rōnin offered the barest bow.

He was spared the need to say anything further as the sake house proprietor's daughter shook free from her father's restraining hand and rushed to the boy, throwing her arms around him. She whispered something to him, something the rōnin could not hear, but the hatchet slipped from the boy's fingers and he raised his bloodstained arms to return the girl's embrace.

"Ah, young love," the Crane said sardonically.

The girl's father also came forward and bowed deeply, sinking to his knees, uncaring of the blood and bodies that he knelt beside. A moment later, another villager joined him, then a third, and then, like water flowing past a breaking dam, more villagers emerged. They bowed to the rōnin, heads pressed to the ground, indifferent to the corpses of the bandits that shared the space with them. "Thank you, my lord," the sake house owner said. "You have saved our village. All that we have is yours."

The words were courteous and proper, but not without their own undercurrent of fear, and the rōnin had to keep the bitter twist from his lips. He could not fault the villagers; they had no idea who he was. From their perspective, they may have just traded a bad situation for a worse one.

"No thanks are necessary," he said, pitching his voice like he once had on the fields of battle, to carry easily to the most distant of those gathered. "It is the place of the samurai to protect villages like these. You owe us nothing. It was our duty to serve." He returned the bow, though his was little more than the slightest dip of the waist. "Please," he added, as the villagers remained prostrate before him. "Return to your own duties. And see to the dead."

At his words, the rōnin felt the attitude of the village shift. The sense of dread that had hung over the place like a foul miasma lifted. As the villagers rose to their feet, he could see the genuine gratitude on their faces. But it was more than that; it was more than the muttered words of thanks they directed at him and the Crane. It was a father's gentle touch on his daughter's shoulder as he led her away from the peasant boy. It was the smiles of a pair of farmers as they strolled toward the fields. It was the squeals and shouts of the children that seemed to suddenly fill the streets, pouring out from the unshuttered homes, and bringing life and vibrancy to the village.

In their simple joy, the rōnin found a moment's respite. The weight of his failures eased. The burden of his guilt lessened. These were people who the rest of Rokugan had forgotten. Was there a truer duty for any who claimed the title of samurai than to see to the needs of the people? They *were* the Empire, after all, as much as those who led armies or played the games of the court.

"That was certainly interesting," the Crane said. He moved to one of the bandits' corpses, a faint curl of distaste pursing his lips. It was, the rōnin could see, the bandit who had been impaled upon his hurled wakizashi. The blade was buried halfway to the hilt in the man's chest. In one swift motion, the Crane reached down, grasped the blade, and pulled it free. He snapped it to the side, clearing the blood, then stepped back to the rōnin, presenting it to him hilt-first over his forearm.

The rōnin nodded his thanks as he took the blade and slipped it back into its scabbard. "Without your help," he said, "I would have died here today. You have my gratitude." He bowed low, lower than he had to any but the Emperor himself for many, many years. He did not ask the Crane's name, nor give his own. Courtesy might force his hand, but if the rōnin could avoid walking that path, he would.

The Crane returned the bow. "When I decided to walk the

warrior's pilgrimage after my gempuku, I did not expect to find myself crossing blades with bandits so soon. But it was a pleasure and an honor to fight by your side." He looked at the peasant boy, who had finally taken his eyes away from the corpses and was watching as the sake house owner and his daughter moved back inside. "And you, peasant," he called. "What is your name?"

The boy blinked for a moment and shook his head. He was, the rōnin saw, a good-looking boy, broad of shoulder with well-muscled arms, no doubt from swinging the hatchet with which he had felled the bandit. "Toku, my lord," he said, and took a step to prostrate himself before the pair.

The rōnin caught him before he could. "You do not need to bow so. Not after coming to my aid."

"Yes, well, I suppose that's true for me as well," the Crane added, though the rōnin heard the hint of distaste in his voice. The demands of courtesy ran paramount to the Crane Clan, and even minor breaches went against the grain. And peasants prostrated themselves before samurai; that was how it had always been, how it was supposed to be.

The rōnin ignored the subtle barb. To the Crane, he said, "You are a credit to your teacher and your school." It was true. The Crane was scarcely older than the peasant boy, probably no more than seventeen winters, a decade the rōnin's junior, but he had fought with the poise and grace of a hardened veteran. "I owe you a debt," he went on. "If it is in my power, it will be paid." The words were a polite formality; after all, in what circumstance would a Crane call upon the debt of a rōnin?

"And you as well, Toku," the rōnin added, glancing at the peasant. "If there is something I can do to assist you, you need only say the word."

"Take me with you."

The boy blurted the words and seemed almost surprised to

hear them drop from his mouth. But then a grim determination settled over him. The rōnin could see it in the set of his shoulders, in the tightening of his jaw. "I wish to learn," he went on. "To fight. Like you did here today. I don't ever want to be at the mercy of these..." He waved a hand at the bodies of the bandits, still being dragged away by the other villagers. "I want to be able to help my family," the boy finished. "Please, my lord samurai, allow me to accompany you and teach me." He did drop to his knees this time, pressing his forehead to the blood-spattered dirt.

A quiet chuckle echoed beside him. "It seems you have quite the way about you," the Crane said, a wide smile playing across his handsome features. "And I must say, our young friend here has the right of it." He paused for just a moment, as if weighing his words, then continued. "For repayment of my efforts here today, I would ask that you allow me to travel by your side, as well."

The rōnin blinked in astonishment. First a peasant boy, and now a Crane?

The boy he could understand easily enough; without training, the peasants were at the mercy of every bandit and brigand that stumbled upon their villages. He could recognize the desire to stand against that; there was merit in Toku's request, and given what the boy had done for him, he would be hard-pressed to refuse it.

The Crane was another story. He might be following the old tradition of wandering the Empire for a year as rōnin, gaining a deeper understanding of the land and the people before assuming his formal duties, but the rōnin's own pilgrimage was of a very different sort from that of the Crane. He had walked away from his life, from his family name, from more power than the Crane could possibly understand. He had not done so out of some vague desire to wander or learn, but as a penance for his failures.

He still did not know exactly how the debt those failures incurred could be paid, but he suspected that he had found a tiny piece of it in helping this village. It had left the beginnings of… not an idea… but the *idea* of an idea. Though the rōnin knew his pilgrimage would not be the stately tour of the countryside with a focus on sake and geisha houses that the Crane might expect.

And yet, the Crane truly had saved his life, even more so than the boy, and he had acknowledged that debt. His responsibility was clear. "Are you certain, Lord Crane?" he asked. "You truly owe me nothing. I will not hold it against you should you wish to leave."

"I have never been more certain," the Crane replied immediately. A mischievous light danced in his eyes as he glanced briefly at the peasant. "I'll even help you train the boy. A Crane teaching a peasant the ways of the samurai; what a scandalous tale that will be." He did not prostrate himself before the rōnin, but he did offer another bow.

The rōnin sighed. It seemed his path was clear. For better or worse, he had picked up two traveling companions. He just hoped that, by following him, their paths would not fall to misfortune. "You are welcome to join me," he told the Crane. "And you, boy… Toku? I will teach you what I can. But I must warn you, I travel rough and I have no plans to visit any major cities."

Toku said nothing, but the rōnin saw the tension leave the boy's back.

The Crane smiled. "The Fortunes have set my feet on a strange path indeed," he mused, more to himself than anyone nearby. "I am Daidoji Daisuke," he went on, giving his family name followed by his given name as he bowed deep to the rōnin. His smile took on a slightly mischievous cant as he rose. "And I cannot wait to see where you lead us… Akodo Toturi."

# 5
# Hotaru

"Dōji Hotaru."

The words, spoken in low, dulcet tones that hovered just above a throaty whisper sent a shiver down Hotaru's spine. As she approached, Bayushi Kachiko rose from her languid perch on the fountain's edge with the liquid grace of a dancer. The Scorpion bowed, perhaps a touch lower than courtesy would have dictated, her kimono shifting to reveal the pale rondure of her breasts. As she straightened, a slight smile pulled at the corner of her lips.

"Lady Kachiko," Hotaru returned, only her years of training among the Crane allowing her to keep her voice calm and even. Her heart was suddenly pounding, and it felt as if a dozen butterflies fluttered within. She knew that the tableau, from location to wardrobe, was carefully chosen by the Scorpion for maximum impact; Kachiko had always made use of every weapon in her arsenal to achieve her aims, whatever they might be. But knowing that the scene had been constructed specifically for her did not slow the beat of the butterflies' wings. "I did not expect to find you here."

She longed to take the woman into her arms, to feel those full lips pressed against her own. But she could not; Bayushi Kachiko was the widow of the most notorious traitor the Empire had seen in generations and the Scorpion were the chief political rivals of the Crane besides. No matter her feelings toward Kachiko, Hotaru could not weaken the position of her clan. Not here, in the Imperial City, with the clans on the brink of outright war.

Not where the eyes of the court could see.

"Oh?" Kachiko asked as she straightened from her bow. Her eyes met Hotaru's. Was that longing she saw there, or was that only what Hotaru wanted to see? "And where else would I be?"

"I would have thought the palace grounds might prove… less welcoming to the Scorpion these days." Hotaru tried to keep the worry from her voice, but felt Toshimoko, who had approached behind her, stiffen. Whether it was from her failed attempt at casualness, or just the sight of the Scorpion before them, she didn't know.

"Perhaps," Kachiko allowed with a small smile. "But despite my late husband's actions, I still have many friends here at the palace. They keep me safe enough." Her eyes flickered, very briefly, to the man at Hotaru's shoulder. "And I will not allow the Scorpion to be shuffled off into the darkness. If the regent wishes us to disappear, it will take more than cold treatment and the casual arrogance of the Crane."

"That can be arranged." Toshimoko's voice was cold. He took one half step forward, one hand resting casually, not on the hilt of his katana, but tucked into his obi, close enough to make the threat clear.

"Uncle!" Hotaru exclaimed, feeling her face redden.

"I will not listen to insults against the Crane or the regency,"

Toshimoko went on, ignoring Hotaru to stab a glare of ice at the Scorpion. "Not from anyone, but certainly not from the widow of the man who murdered our Emperor." His voice took on an almost contemptuous edge. "No matter what games the two of you may play at."

Hotaru almost flinched at that, but she managed to maintain her mask of calm. Dalliances were common enough among the clans; marriages were almost always arranged matters in the Empire, built on a foundation of politics rather than love or mutual attraction. Such pairings could grow to become something deeper, more personal, but just as often they were alliances founded on duty. There was no shame in seeking love elsewhere… unless that elsewhere was in the arms of an enemy. The Crane and Scorpion had been at odds since the Founders fell from heaven, and no one in either clan would look kindly on seeking comfort in the company of the other.

Were it anyone else, facing down both the Emerald Champion and possibly the best duelist in all Rokugan, they would have paled, apologized, begged forgiveness. Kachiko, however, simply let a tiny, amused smile cross her lips. "How brave you are, Emerald Champion, to make such threats against an unarmed woman. I can see why the regent appointed you." The inflection she put on the word "appointed" was subtle yet carried more than enough venom to justify the name Mother of Scorpions.

Hotaru could feel the anger boiling within Toshimoko, and knew Kachiko well enough to recognize the woman was baiting him. "Enough," Hotaru snapped, taking a step forward before things went too far. "Both of you."

"I will not–" Toshimoko began, but Hotaru cut him off with a sharp gesture.

"Go," she ordered. "You may be the Emerald Champion, but I am still your Clan Champion. Go." She softened her voice.

"Please, Uncle. Leave us for a moment, and then I will follow you to the regent."

Toshimoko gave her a flat stare before he offered a stiff, formal bow, turned on his heel and moved away. No more than ten paces, but he at least took his hand from the hilt of his blade. Hotaru stifled a wince. She knew that her uncle would have words with her later and it would not be a pleasant conversation.

More than a little exasperated, she turned back to Kachiko, who was watching the scene play out with that subtle amusement Hotaru found both infuriating and irresistible. "That was unfairly done, Kachiko," she accused, causing the Scorpion to arch a delicate brow at her. "I don't know why you provoked him on purpose, but Toshimoko is not just my uncle and my teacher; he is a friend on both the personal and political level. I cannot afford, nor do I *want* to alienate him."

"I'll send him a formal note of apology later." Kachiko's voice was anything but apologetic. She took a step forward, close enough to teeter on the very edge of scandalous, but not past it. Hotaru's heart leaped in her chest, and she had to stop herself from reaching out to the woman in front of her. "Now, hush," Kachiko ordered, her voice low. "We don't have much time. You shouldn't be seen with me for very long, no matter how much I'd wish otherwise."

Hotaru felt a rush of emotions at Kachiko's words: a minor surge of annoyance at being hushed followed by a flush of warmth at the thought that Kachiko wanted to not only spend time with her, but to be *seen* spending that time with her. Still, no matter the surge of emotion, she couldn't ignore the situation. Kachiko was here for a reason. Nothing she did was ever by chance.

"Do you ever stop playing politics, Kachiko?"

"*Playing* politics?" Kachiko replied, a hint of both amusement and affection breaking through her mask. It caused a glow of warmth to bloom in Hotaru's stomach, but the Scorpion shook her head. "No," she replied, still sounding subtly amused. "If I did, I probably would have died with Shoju." Hotaru did wince at that, but Kachiko didn't give her time to speak. "Matsu Tsuko is here."

"I know." Hotaru nodded. "Toshimoko told me she arrived with a large contingent of samurai."

"Her samurai don't matter," Kachiko said, waving a dismissive arm. "They're adornments here in the palace, nothing more." Hotaru nodded again. Not even the Lion would attempt violence within the palace walls, not so soon after the death of the Emperor. "But there is another who arrived with them," Kachiko said, and her voice was a warning now. "A woman named Chukan Hanako."

"Chukan?" Hotaru frowned. Like every Crane, she had been drilled relentlessly not only on her own clan's families, but on those of every clan and household, great and minor, that could claim the title of samurai within the Empire. It took her a moment to place the name; the Chukan were a minor client family of the Phoenix. They weren't even one of the main families, but rather a distant branch of the Asako line, too far removed to bear the name. "What is a Phoenix doing with the Lion?" she wondered.

"I do not know… yet," Kachiko admitted. Though her face hid it well, Hotaru could see the edge of frustration in the tightening of her red-painted lips. Bayushi Kachiko prided herself on knowing everything about everyone. The fact that she hadn't discovered all there was to know about this Chukan was testament to the Phoenix. Testament to what, Hotaru wasn't exactly sure, but Kachiko seemed highly annoyed about it. "They've been here less than a week, and already this Hanako seems to have access to secrets and whispers that should be beyond her." She drummed her fingers against her arm, her eyes narrowed in thought. "She is building a network, Hotaru," Kachiko went on. "A network of spies and informants to rival my own, and she is doing it faster than I have seen it done before." She gave a little sigh and pursed her lips. "I would be impressed, were it not for the things my own informants are telling me."

"And what is that?" Hotaru asked. "And why did you have to insult Toshimoko and drive him away? If you think this Phoenix a threat, shouldn't the Emerald Champion know about it?"

"Because I do not know if he is a tool of the regent, the Crane, or the Empire," Kachiko replied. "And until I am certain, until I know where his loyalty would fall if the players at court turned on each other, I cannot afford to trust him."

The words sent a little chill down Hotaru's spine. It was a reminder that, despite her beauty and seeming softness, despite the feelings that Hotaru held for her, the Scorpion saw most people as stones to be placed on a Go board. Go was a game of tactics, where one sought to surround the opponent's stones with their own, trapping them and winning the game. In the far more dangerous game of court, Kachiko was a master, and she used people as surely as any Go tactician used the game pieces to their advantage, placing and removing them at will.

Hotaru wondered if she was something more to the Scorpion than a favorite Go stone.

She banished the thought from her head. "Can one not be loyal to all three?" she asked. Her hand itched to rise and stroke Kachiko's cheek, to show her that there was a time to drop the masks and put away the politics. But she did not; there was a time for such things, but that time was not now.

The effortless control that Kachiko maintained over her own expression slipped, if only for an instant. The look she cast at Hotaru was a heady mix of disbelief and fondness, of humor and caring. "My dear Hotaru," Kachiko whispered. "Do not ever lose that innocence. I think it is the thing I love most about you."

Then, as swiftly as it had vanished, before Hotaru could fully comprehend the words that had just been spoken, the mask fell back in place. Kachiko didn't answer her question, her tone becoming businesslike once more.

"This Hanako has the ear of the Lion," she said. "Perhaps Matsu Tsuko is not fully under her spell. But the Lion give the words of this minor noble far too much weight. You know as well as I that a whisper in the right ear can lead to war, or worse than war, and this Hanako is whispering for all she's worth. Guard yourself, Hotaru." Kachiko gazed at her again, a hint of that earlier warmth glimmering in her eyes. "I fear she might seek the total destruction of the Crane, and if you fell to her warmongering, I don't know what I would do."

Hotaru swallowed the thickness in her throat. The urge to embrace Kachiko was becoming overwhelming. It was an effort to keep her voice light, her tone glib, to offset the churning emotions within. "I'm sure you would think of something, Bayushi Kachiko."

Kachiko smiled. "I'm sure I would. Still…" She took a step back, her eyes never leaving Hotaru's. "Be careful. The court feels like a tinderbox these days, and one small spark can turn it into an inferno. Farewell, Hotaru. Fortunes willing, we will see each other soon."

With that, Kachiko turned and glided from the garden, and Hotaru could do nothing but watch as she walked away, disappearing among the topiary.

"His Imperial Regent, Kakita Yoshi."

Hotaru kept her face calm and composed as the herald called out the words, banging his staff of office against the floor with three sharp reports. Despite Toshimoko's insistence that she speak to the regent at once, Kakita Yoshi had kept them both waiting here in the throne room for the better part of an hour. While the delay and implied discourtesy grated at her, it did give her time to contemplate the Emerald Throne.

It was here that Akodo Toturi had found Bayushi Shoju standing over the body of the slain emperor, ancient sword of the Hantei line grasped in his bloodstained hands. It was here the two had fought, on the sacred dais of the throne.

She could see the marks on the throne itself, where their blades had scratched the polish of the stone. The pillars that rose to either side of the throne bore ancient inscriptions, as old as Rokugan itself. To the right of the throne, the characters read: All is right in the world; to the left: Revere Heaven, love people. Those words struck Hotaru as a bitter irony, standing here in the place where the Emperor was murdered. All was certainly not right in the world, not with the Emperor dead, the Empire on the brink of war, and the very line of Hantei threatened.

What would become of the Empire if the Hantei's sons could not be found? If, Heaven forbid, they were already dead? She suspected at least one member of her clan had their own plans should that unfortunate scenario come to pass.

In a sudden flurry of motion and movement, Kakita Yoshi strode into the throne room, surrounded by a group of Imperial functionaries. He was issuing orders as he walked, and his followers bowed deeply and peeled away as each was given their instructions. Hotaru had to smile; whatever else her uncle might be, he understood how the games of court were played. She had no doubt he had carefully crafted this entire scenario to showcase his own power and set the tone for their conversation. First by making her – his own Clan Champion – wait upon his arrival and then by entering in the midst of what she could only presume to be official Imperial business, showing her that he was forced to make important decisions regarding the fate of the Empire, showcasing his own importance.

It was a well-executed bit of courtly theater, but one that was wasted on her. She watched impassively as the functionaries were dismissed to their tasks until her uncle stood before Hotaru and Toshimoko alone.

He was a tall, handsome man, his ivory hair pulled back into a neat bun, but with artful locks falling to frame his face. His kimono was of the finest silks, dyed the vibrant blue of the Crane – appropriate given that, despite the title of Regent, he was still a member of Hotaru's clan. She also noted the subtle pattern of white flowers worked into the design. Not just any flowers, but tiny chrysanthemums, so finely stitched that each of their petals measured a single thread wide. Unease flickered within her. There was no prohibition against using the flower that was, in many ways, synonymous with the throne, but in this place, at this time, it made a definitive statement.

Kakita Yoshi was the current power on the throne of the Empire, and he was not afraid to make others aware of that fact.

"Dearest niece," he said, offering the slightest of bows to her. "Brother," he added with a bare nod to Toshimoko.

It was another brilliant gambit, worthy of the finest courtiers the Crane could produce. By addressing Hotaru as family, Yoshi had sidestepped the question of precedence and had bypassed the need to acknowledge the fact that Hotaru was Clan Champion, and his technical superior. Of course, it also allowed Hotaru to ignore the fact that Yoshi was now Imperial Regent… and her technical superior. It was, she reflected, an odd scenario; when it came to matters of the Empire as a whole, Yoshi had authority over her, yet, at the same time, he was a Crane and under her command. Given how he had made her wait here in the throne room – and how could anyone not see the Imperial power here? –

she suspected Yoshi was most concerned with not being forced to recognize her authority over him.

"Yoshi," Toshimoko said simply, taking the regent's words at face value and dropping all titles. Or perhaps he would have addressed his brother so, no matter what. He had not with Hotaru's father. But then, Doji Satsume had not been the best of men.

"My Lord Regent," Hotaru said. She offered no bow. "Your new duties seem to suit you."

Yoshi offered a tight smile. "I serve the Empire, and the Crane. Which is why I requested your presence when I heard you were arriving in the Imperial City." He put no particular emphasis on the word *requested*, but Hotaru felt the irony in it, nonetheless.

"The Crane are honored to serve the Empire," Hotaru replied, the phrase coming automatically to her lips. "Whatever is required of us." *Including you, Uncle,* she added silently. *You, despite everything, are still a Crane.*

"Then I must warn you, for the good of the Empire, that the Lion are once more threatening the stability of the land," Yoshi said. "I think my regency sits uneasy for them, and they seek to undermine it by pressuring the Crane. We cannot allow them to do so. The Empire must be seen as strong, by those within and without. For the good of all."

*For the good of all?* Hotaru managed not to narrow her gaze. *Or to ensure that you remain firmly in power?*

"Perhaps they fear an empire delivered into the hands of their rivals," she said calmly. Years of training in the Doji Palace allowed her to keep her voice light and conversational, despite the subject at hand. There was no accusation in her tone, no matter what she might have felt within her heart of hearts. "Now that there is a Crane regent and given the… irregularities of appointing a Crane Emerald Champion, how could they not?"

"I had little choice in that," Yoshi replied, his well-trained baritone revealing no emotion. "With Akodo Toturi abandoning the position, the Empire needed a strong military mind and a firm guiding hand. I am many things, Hotaru, but a military strategist is not one of them. The Empire could not afford to look weak, and we lacked the time to provide the usual spectacle. And there are none in all the Empire who would deny Toshimoko's skill. My advisors all concurred with the decision."

And how many of those advisors, Hotaru wondered, were themselves drawn from the ranks of the Crane?

"Still, Uncle," she replied, "you must be able to see it as the Lion see it. Of their past two Clan Champions, one died by my hand at the siege of Toshi Ranbo and the other abdicated his position the moment a Crane regency was announced. The Lion Emerald Champion has been replaced with a Crane Emerald Champion, but with no Emerald Championship to guide that decision. And you still have not officially acknowledged Matsu Tsuko as the true head of the Lion. Whether we have done it on purpose or not, we have backed them into a corner."

"A she-lion backed into a corner is a dangerous thing," Toshimoko muttered, one hand scratching idly at his pate. "A dangerous thing indeed."

Yoshi waved it off. "Until such time as an emperor sits on the Emerald Throne, *no* new Clan Champion can be formally recognized," he stated. "That is the Emperor's duty, and there is nothing in our laws or traditions that suggest a regent can do it in the place of the Voice of Heaven." He snorted in a most un-Crane-like fashion. "And all the Lions in the world cannot stand against the might of the Empire.

"But she will raise arms against *you*, Hotaru." He glanced at the throne as he spoke. While he stood closest to it, he had made no move to climb the dais. It would be blasphemy of the highest order to ascend that throne, but Hotaru thought she could see a faint hint of longing in his eyes. For all his talk of the authority of the regent, it was clear to Hotaru that he wished for more. It caused a chill to crawl up her spine.

To his credit, though, Yoshi turned away from the throne. "She will draw you into conflict," he went on, "to prove the weakness of the regency to the rest of the Empire. Not just at Toshi Ranbo, where they have long claimed that they hold rightful sovereignty, but all along the borders of our northern holdings as well."

Once more, Hotaru could not help but notice that Yoshi said "our" when referring to actions being taken against the Crane. He seemed like a moth drawn between twin flames, one representing the glory of the clan and the second the power of the throne. She knew that if he drifted far enough in either direction, he would burn. But there was little she could do about it, and that had her clenching her teeth in frustration. Yoshi's mistakes might be his own, but they could drag the Crane – the entire Empire – into conflict on a scale that hadn't been seen for centuries.

She was also all too aware of the aggressions of the Lion. The border raiding along the northern lands of the Crane was a constant, low-grade headache for her. But the Lion had, for the most part, kept that conflict within the traditional bounds, unlike the warbands that they sent to harass Toshi Ranbo. If Yoshi was suggesting something more, something closer to full-scale war, Hotaru had to admit that the Crane were ill-prepared for it. The crop that year had not been good; both famine and sickness threatened to sink their teeth into her people. If it came to open war with the Lion, the strain on the peasantry would be severe. Starvation and plague were certain to follow.

Which was part of the reason she had come to the capital in the first place. The price the Crane would pay for stopping the Lion on the field of battle would be far too great. A different solution had to be found.

"I will meet with Matsu Tsuko," Hotaru said. "It is my hope that we can find a diplomatic and peaceful solution. War would not be good for either of our clans, and certainly not for the Empire. I believe she can see reason, to understand that finding Sotorii and Daisetsu and restoring the line of Hantei to the throne is the paramount duty for all of us."

She paused, aware of their surroundings and that the man who had, until scant months ago, been subject to her orders, could now issue edicts backed by the will of Heaven. Still, it must be said. "But she must not feel pressure, Uncle. Not from you or your advisors. If she thinks that the Crane are trying to blunt her ambitions, or are attempting to position themselves above the Lion, she will dig in her heels and not budge for anything."

"And what about her personal vengeance against you, Hotaru?" Toshimoko asked. "It was your arrow that claimed Akodo Arasou's life at Toshi Ranbo. I doubt she has forgiven you for the death of her betrothed."

Hotaru opened her mouth to respond but was cut short as a harried-looking courtier rushed into the throne room. They offered a hasty bow, even as they said in a breathless huff, "The Lion are coming, my Lord Regent."

The Crane scarcely had time to look down at the servant before the door to the throne room banged open once more.

"No." The armor-clad woman strode into the throne room with the arrogance that only the Lion could muster. Under one arm she carried her helm, its broad lion-like plumage fluttering with the wind of her stride. She wore the daishō at her side and was flanked by more of her armored kinsmen. Behind them trailed a line of kimono-clad courtiers. "The Lion are here."

# 6
# Yakamo

The hulking bird-like monstrosity screamed again as Yakamo closed on it. He was aware of his soldiers turning on the other creatures, breaking off into groups of ten or so to try to overwhelm the monsters and bring them down. He was aware of the arrows arcing in from the bastions, finding purchase where they could in the flesh of the enemy.

And he was aware, in that distant part of his mind that knew the broader tactics of battle, that the army below the Wall was surging forward once more, taking advantage of the distraction to try to create a breach. Yakamo ground his teeth in frustration but knew that there was nothing he could do about it, not until the walkway was clear once more.

So, he lowered his head and charged, swinging his tetsubō with every ounce of strength he could muster even as he ducked under the lashing arm of the beast before him. He felt the shiver of impact as the iron-shod club slammed into the Shadowlands spawn, landing a foot behind the creature's front shoulder where the ribcage should be. The flesh of the creature felt oddly rubbery beneath the strike, but he heard the crack of bone and felt something shifting beneath the weight of the club.

The howl of the creature this time was more pain than rage. The proboscis peeled back and the flesh tendrils that surrounded its sucker-like mouth reached for him as the thing's head darted forward, quick as a striking viper. He dove low, rolling on his shoulder and letting his momentum carry him back to his feet as the monster's head passed over him.

Hot, oily spittle – or was it venom? – dripped from the gaping maw, burning and itching where it found his flesh. The creature's talons dug gouges into the stone as it whirled its massive body, seeming unhampered by the ribs Yakamo was sure he had broken. It lunged again, and this time it was all Yakamo could do to ward away the grasping tendrils with short, quick movements of his club.

Then Bunzō was there, screaming his own battle cry as his ono bit into the leathery hide of the creature. Black ichor spurted forth, spraying both men. More warriors from his command arrived, thrusting with their yari, smashing down with massive hammers, and slashing with their swords. The thing before them responded to the sudden onslaught by bellowing out another cry of pain and rage as it went into a frenzy, whirling in tight circles and lashing out with tooth, claw, and tail.

A samurai screamed as the four tentacle-like appendages around the monster's mouth closed around her arm, tearing and ripping the limb free in a gout of blood. Another was caught by the swinging tail and flung hard enough into the battlements that the impact sounded like a stone from a siege engine crashing into the Wall. A third was pinned beneath one of the taloned feet, a strangled cry escaping as the claws dug into him.

But the others kept striking, despite their losses, and Yakamo saw his own opportunity. He brought his tetsubō up in a short, vicious arc, hammering it hard into the snakelike neck of the monster, just beneath the thing's chin. The creature's head snapped back with the impact, and Bunzō took advantage of that fact to swing his axe like he was chopping down a tree. The blade bit deep, parting the leathery flesh and more ichor flew, but the creature was not done.

It pushed off its powerful legs, drawing a horrific coughing sigh from the samurai it still had pinned beneath its talons, and leaped into the air. Its membrane-like wings beat furiously, the force of the winds hurling bits of dust and debris, causing Yakamo to blink his eyes rapidly against the barrage. Through his blurring vision, he swung the tetsubō again; he could not allow this creature to get away, only to torment the Crab at some other position along the Wall. He put all of his considerable strength into that swing and felt a satisfying crunch as the very end of the club smashed not into the creature's head or ribs, but rather into its shoulder, crushing bone and wreaking havoc on the joint. The limb stopped its furious pumping and the creature fell back to the stone of the walkway, howling in agony.

The spears and axes of his samurai were waiting for it. The monster gave a last furious shriek as the weapons rose and fell, and finally died.

Yakamo drew one gauntleted fist across his eyes, wiping the sweat from them and ignoring the streak of oily ichor his battle-stained armor left behind. His breath came in short, ragged gasps as he took a moment to survey the top of the Wall. Up and down the line, he could see his warriors putting an end to the last of the flying monstrosities. But by the Fortunes, the ancestors, and the Founders, it had cost them. He felt a pang deep within that was equal parts loss and rage. It had cost them dearly. He had started the day with a hundred soldiers, hardened veterans of the Wall one and all, under his command. Fewer than fifty were still on their feet, all of them gasping and panting. A dozen of the flying Shadowlands spawn lay alongside his own dead and injured.

And still the battle was not done.

"To the parapets," he shouted, or tried to. It came out more as a gasping croak, loud enough to carry a dozen feet, no more. Those around him took up the call as they shuffled once more to the defensive bulwark that separated them from the Shadowlands. He was aware of Bunzō at his side, leaning heavily against his axe and panting for breath.

Before the assault from the flying creatures, every embrasure on Yakamo's section of the Wall had held an ashigaru or samurai prepared to push back the Shadowlands hordes. Now, every other embrasure stood empty, with his command spread thin to cover their assigned frontage as best they could. He could hear the servants and healers moving behind him, trying to sort the living from the dead and tending to the wounded. Some of those wounded would return to their duties, ignoring their splints and bandages and standing once more to battle. Others would never again hold a sword or spear, their bodies permanently damaged from their injuries. And many, many more would succumb to their wounds, the foul infections of the Shadowlands plaguing them with fever that would ultimately claim their lives.

Beneath him, he could already see the bald, pockmarked heads of goblins scurrying up the Wall, now more than two-thirds of the way to the parapets. More flowed from the gathered army, rushing toward them like a black river of death. They had been killing the creatures all day, but to his eye, the forces arrayed before him seemed undiminished. Yakamo felt the cold hand of despair gripping his heart. Bunzō had the right of it. They never stopped coming. There was no reprieve, no rest to be had.

Anger flickered. There was not a single ashigaru or samurai

with him who was not of the Crab. The other Great Clans played at politics and war, and he and his people suffered and died in endless battle.

*Why?* Because it was his duty, his clan's duty, he knew that as well as anyone. He was reminded of it every single day. But was duty alone enough of a reason? And why was it the sole duty of the Crab? Where were the samurai from the other clans, willing to risk their lives for the good of the Empire? Where were the Imperial Legions, whose might could turn the tide against these relentless attacks?

Too embroiled in their own meaningless squabbling to see that death awaited the entire Empire if the Crab were overrun. Too content to let the Crab be the ones to bleed and die while they flounced about in their peaceful gardens and shining palaces.

As Yakamo stared into the red, hate-filled eyes of death, he silently cursed them for their indifference.

The battle raged throughout the day, and somehow, Yakamo and his soldiers fought on. Twice, his father had sent reinforcements to bolster Yakamo's position. Once, a Kuni shindōshi, not Yori, thank the ancestors, had called upon the elemental spirits of Water to ease the suffering of his wounded, returning several to their places on the Wall. Now, Lady Sun had sunk below the horizon and Lord Moon's luminescence bathed the battlefield in pale light.

"Why do they still stand at muster?" Bunzō grunted, looking at the rough formations of creatures in the distance. Yakamo had no farseer, only his naked eye with which to survey the enemy, so he couldn't tell what exactly was standing there. Goblins, ogres, demons, the dead. What did it matter? He was so exhausted that he couldn't bring himself to care.

"You don't think they'll attack at night, do you?"

"Why not?" Yakamo grunted. "The Jigoku-damned things see better in the dark than we do."

"Well," Bunzō replied, "it wouldn't be very courteous of them. I heard from a visiting Asahina that courtesy was the most important dictate of the Akodo Code. Of course, the Asahina was here to paint a landscape of the Shadowlands for a viewing back in Phoenix lands, so make of that what you will." He snorted and rubbed his face, seemingly oblivious to the smear of blood and dirt his hands left in their wake. "Maybe if we explain that to them, they'll just…" Bunzō flicked his hands in a sort of shooing gesture.

Yakamo barked a short burst of laughter. He raised his own hands before his face, examining them in the pale light of Lord Moon. Like Bunzō's, they were dark with blood and ichor. The water bearers couldn't carry enough of the precious liquid to waste it on something as mundane as washing, and to a person, his soldiers were caked with dirt, sweat, blood, and far, far worse things.

He had no doubt that their appearance would have sent their delicate cousins in the north retiring to their chambers to recover from the horror of it all. He silently wished for the ability to do the same; by all the Fortunes, he was tired. More than tired. He and all his soldiers had pushed well past tired into a level of exhaustion that was hard to distinguish from the walking dead that, he knew, would eventually scramble their way up the Wall as well.

They should have been relieved of their position hours ago, but the forces of the Shadowlands were pressuring all up and down the length of the Wall, and Yakamo had received the same orders as everyone else: hold. They had eaten a hasty meal, despite being covered in the filth of battle, and drank their fill as the water bearers rushed along the length of the Great Carpenter Wall. But they had not been given the order to stand down.

"If they do visit us this night," he said in response to Bunzō,

"I'll be sure to let them know how rude they are being." His jaws creaked in a massive yawn and he reached his hands high overhead, stretching until he heard the muscles in his back creaking in protest.

Bunzō tried to respond, but he was cut short by a yawn of his own, which spread up and down Yakamo's command. There were a few chuckles at that, and Yakamo smiled. If they could still laugh, then hope was not lost. And as long as the Crab had hope, the foul creatures of Fu Leng couldn't break them.

A cold wind blew across the battlefield, howling out of nowhere and carrying the carrion stench of the Shadowlands to his nose. It tore at his hair and mustache and kicked up a fine mist of grit that clawed at his throat. Then, as suddenly as the wind had risen, it stopped. A silence followed in its wake, as if the world itself held its breath in anticipation. There was something about that silence that was unnerving; it wasn't the stillness of a calm evening where the insects still chirped and the grasses rustled, but rather the total stillness of death.

Something was wrong. Yakamo could sense it, and drew in a breath to start shouting orders to his men.

But no sound came forth. His eyes widened and he turned to Bunzō, who was staring back at him with the same wide-eyed alarm on his face. Bunzō's mouth moved, but Yakamo heard nothing. He tore his gaze from Bunzō and looked up and down the Wall, seeing all the ashigaru and samurai gathered there looking in his direction, confusion and fear on their faces. They had turned away from their positions on the Wall and were shouting at each other; at least, their mouths were wide in a caricature of speech. Others had dropped to their knees, arms reaching for the Heavens as if in prayer.

None of them were paying attention to the enemy.

Yakamo turned his attention back to the parapets and to the Shadowlands forces. They still stood there, in tight regiments, waiting. He saw something, a swirl of shadow, a flicker of light and one of the enemy formations seemed to shrink, collapsing in on itself the same way the formations closed ranks when the Crab archers or siege engines tore lines in their ranks. But no engine or arrow could reach so far. Where had the enemy gone?

He had his answer a moment later.

The carrion wind rose once more, though he still heard nothing. But when it died down, the smell returned tenfold, pouring off the dozens of corpses that now lay upon the battlements.

One instant the broad top of the Wall was clear of enemies. In the next, Yakamo's waking nightmare materialized. The bodies of the dead stood before him, given a horrific facsimile of life through the dark magics of necromancers and blood sorcerers. All of those he could see were human, clad in the rotting remnants of their former lives. Samurai in broken bits of armor, peasants wearing tattered wisps that had once been farmers' garb, even a few who looked to be clad in the white funeral robes that preceded their cremation. All were in various states of decay, ranging from those who looked like they had fallen scant hours ago to those who were scarcely more than skeletons, their bones yellowed with age.

He was grateful for the mystical silence that had befallen the Wall, for the sudden appearance of the dead pulled a reflexive, fearful cry from him. He felt his hands go slick with sweat as the undead lurched forward, moving with a jolting, unnatural gait. They fell upon his soldiers, and though they had little more than rusty, broken weapons, the chaos caused by the incantation of silence, coupled with finding the enemy abruptly in their midst, took its toll. His soldiers fought back, but it was a wild, instinctive thing lacking discipline or unity. They dealt wounds, but the dead ignored wounds that would stop the living. One by one, his soldiers were pulled down.

Pulled down beneath the hands of the dead.

Dead that were once Crab. Dead that might have stood on this very spot on the Wall, defending the Empire against the Shadowlands.

Yakamo felt a surge of fear unlike anything he had ever known. He grabbed Bunzō as the man tried to surge forward into the fray. Bunzō looked at him, and Yakamo could only shake his head, pointing back toward the bastion some forty yards away. They had to fall back. They were too battered, too tired. At least that's what he told himself.

Bunzō looked confused, but Yakamo was his commander and samurai obeyed their orders. Together, they started to get the attention of warriors on both sides of the clump of rotting zombies, gesturing for them to fall back. It was all Yakamo could do not to drop everything and run, such was the fear that gripped him. His heart raced harder than it had in the thick of the battle against the flying creatures and his breath came in short, ragged gasps. Beneath the fear, he felt the shame, closing around his heart like a fist. He was abandoning his position, falling back without orders to do so.

He had failed.

His soldiers were dying, and he could do nothing but retreat. He knew he should order a glorious charge; if they hit these creatures hard enough, fast enough, perhaps his samurai could overwhelm them, drive them from the Wall. If not, their deaths could buy others the time to get into position and brush the filth from the Wall. But he couldn't give the order.

Yes, they were silenced by the incantation. Yes, his forces were split in half by the sudden appearance of the undead. Yes, many had fallen in the initial surprise attack. But even if all those things were untrue, Yakamo was still not sure he could have given the order. Fear had him firmly in its grasp, and he couldn't shake its grip.

They were being driven back, giving ground before the zombies, keeping them at bay but doing little real damage. The breach grew wider, and the portion of Yakamo's mind that could still think clearly despite the fear, wondered if the goblins and ogres were already rushing forward to take advantage of his failure. But even that thought could not reverse the tide, and step by step, he and the tattered remnants of his command retreated. Yakamo sent up silent prayers to the Fortunes, to his ancestors, to the Founders themselves that he would reach the safety of the bastion before the cold hands of the dead closed around him.

Without warning, sound returned, a cacophony of noise slamming his ears. One moment, all was silence. The next, he heard the screams, the chattering and groaning of the undead, the twang of bowstrings and the heavier thumps of the siege engines. And over it all, he heard the sound of a horn, the deep note calling for the charge. He recognized the specific call being played. His eyes swept the Wall, looking past the dead to see the ancestral banner of the Crab Clan. It took two soldiers to hold the ancient standard aloft, but they held it high as reinforcements rushed into the enemy ranks.

That banner filled him with a different kind of dread.

His father had come.

# 7
# Toturi

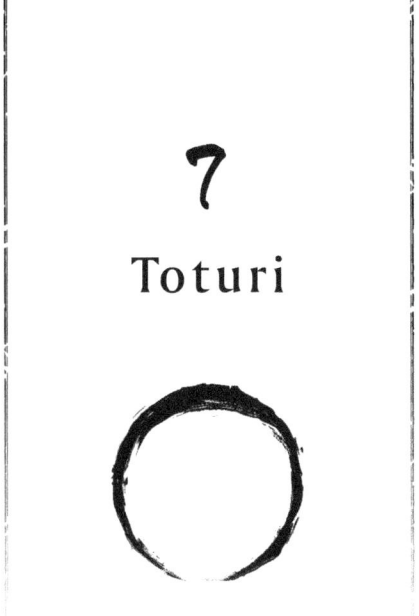

The body of the Emperor, Hantei 38th, lay on the floor in a spreading pool of blood.

Over the crumpled form of the wizened man who had been not just his emperor, but also his confidant and friend, stood Bayushi Shoju. The Scorpion was a picture of poise and grace, his red and black kimono perfectly arranged and not a single hair of his topknot out of place. His mask was polished wood, lacquered crimson. It covered the entirety of his face save only his mouth, revealing the slight, condescending twist to the man's lips. The mask was carved in a pattern of swoops and whorls that drew the eye to all the wrong places, somehow making the man more sinister than the oni menpō many samurai wore into battle. In his hands he held the ancestral sword of the Hantei line, its edge darkened with the blood of its rightful master.

Toturi was not one for jumping to conclusions. He was the Emerald Champion; he understood that, sometimes, things were not always as they appeared. If this scene had occurred anywhere else, if it had not been a Scorpion standing there, if it had been anyone but the Emperor of Rokugan lying in a pool of his own blood, perhaps rational thought would have prevailed. Shoju was smarter than this. Shoju had no reason to kill the Emperor; the Scorpion Clan Champion, while a force to be reckoned with both in the court and out, seemed content with his position and never held aspirations for the throne. Or so Toturi had always thought.

And yet, the blood of the Hantei was fresh, both on the floor and the blade Bayushi Shoju still held. And the Scorpion was the only one in the room.

"Traitor!" Toturi bellowed. His own blade leaped into his hands as if of its own volition. His shout echoed through the cavernous throne room, filling the room with the accusation. Traitor… traitor… traitor…

For just a moment, Shoju paused. A mere heartbeat, as the last echoes of the accusation died away overhead. Then, he turned, a slow smile spreading over his masked face.

"Am I?" Shoju replied, his low, silky voice, a voice that Toturi had heard countless times in council, seeming to profane the scene with its casual indifference.

Toturi's jaw clenched. Anger was building, as shock gave way to a disbelieving rage. Shoju's question, mocking and defiant, solidified the man's guilt and drove all hesitation from Toturi's mind. "Why?" he demanded. "Why would you murder the Emperor? Have you gone mad? He was your friend!" He moved forward as he spoke, each footfall bringing him closer to the traitor.

That little smile which was all of the man's face Toturi could see twisted into something sour, but otherwise unreadable. Then, with three quick strides, Bayushi Shoju climbed the stairs of the dais and dropped unceremoniously into the seat of the Emerald Throne. "What I do, dear Toturi, I do for the good of the Empire."

He casually drew the edge of the Hantei sword along the carved throne, first along one side of the blade, then the next, clearing the blood – the Emperor's blood – from the steel and smearing it on the throne itself.

The sheer effrontery of the act seemed to paralyze Toturi. His mouth dropped open, but several heartbeats passed before he could find words. His mind spun. He had no love for the Scorpion, nor for their daimyō, but this? It made no sense. The Scorpion couldn't truly believe that he could claim the throne through such a murderous act.

But the story before him was clear: the Emperor was dead, and Shoju sat on the throne.

"You shame yourself, your clan, and your ancestors," Toturi grated as he continued to step forward, making his way down the length of the long throne room. "You are a murderer and usurper. Fortunes find mercy on you if you have harmed the princes, for no one else will." He stopped at the foot of the dais and looked up at the man draped so insolently on the most sacred symbol in all the Empire, as if daring Toturi to speak the words he knew he must. He drew a deep breath and spoke, his voice taking on the studied formality of his office. "Bayushi Shoju, I accuse you of the murder of the Emperor. Do you have anything to say in your defense?"

"I have already said it, Toturi. What I do, I do for the good of the Empire."

Toturi barely heard the words. What *could* the man say in his defense, with the blood of the Hantei staining the sword he held? "Then, as is the duty of my office as Emerald Champion and based upon your words and the evidence of my own eyes, I judge you guilty. The sentence is death."

The Scorpion uncoiled from the throne, standing to his full height and gazing down with a faint smirk on his face. The Hantei ancestral sword, which he had been holding in a light, languid grip, rose before him as he stepped into the high guard. "If it is my life you wish, Akodo Toturi, it is yours. All you have to do is claim it."

Something in Shoju's tone made Toturi pause. The smugness and arrogance of the Scorpion was still there – when was it not? – but there was something deeper as well. It wasn't regret, nor shame for his heinous act, a fact which inched Toturi's anger up further. Something else… a fatalism, perhaps?

"If you had even a shred of integrity, Scorpion, you would surrender and face the judgement of the people."

Shoju snorted. "Your talk of integrity means nothing to me, Lion. Here, I will make it easier for you." With that, he strode back down the dais, giving up the advantage of the higher ground. "Your choice is simple: acknowledge me as your Emperor, or we will see which of us is truly the better swordsman. It is something I've wondered about."

Toturi had, as well. It was inevitable given how often he, in his role as Emerald Champion, had clashed with Shoju when it came to matters of council. There had been more than once when he had dreamed of settling their differences over steel. Toturi may not have numbered among the very greatest blades in the Empire, not when it came to the purity of his forms and techniques. But he had always found a way to exploit the weaknesses of his enemy and win.

Bayushi Shoju, on the other hand, *was* considered among the best Rokugan had to offer, and the blade in his hands was one of the finest weapons ever forged. In truth, Toturi did not know if this was a fight he could win. But as he stared at the body of the murdered Emperor, he knew there was no other choice. "Then let us both satisfy our curiosity."

He had barely finished the words before rushing forward like raging fire, his blade flashing. He struck out, slashing toward the Scorpion's eyes, hoping to momentarily blind him. When the Scorpion's sword – no, when the *Emperor's* sword – turned his blow aside, he flowed with the motion, driving the hilt of his katana at Shoju's temple. But the Scorpion was like smoke, and he slipped the blow with easy grace. The furious exchange continued for several seconds, each cut and thrust from Toturi questing for a vital area; each time, his blade was met with steel or empty space as Shoju danced around him, as elusive as the air itself.

They separated, both their breaths coming a little harder than before. "Your style lacks refinement," Shoju said, voice still calm. "Not unexpected, I suppose, coming from a Lion."

"And yours relies too heavily on deception," Toturi countered. "Exactly what I would expect from a lying, disloyal Scorpion."

"Loyalty?" Shoju mused, a thoughtfulness in his voice that, to Toturi's ear, sounded entirely genuine. "Loyalty is a tricky thing. You are so certain of my treachery, and yet, I stand before you with no doubt that my time on the Celestial Wheel is done. Should death claim me today, I go to the Realm of the Blessed Ancestors." That little, mocking smile flashed once more. "You, on the other hand, who have sworn to keep the Emperor safe above all else, seem to have failed in your first duty." The Scorpion cast a deliberate glance at the body of the Emperor, still lying unceremoniously in a cooling pool of blood. "What do you think the next rotation of the Wheel will bring for you?"

The hot flare of rage that surged in Toturi was tempered only by the shame that came with Shoju's words. The Scorpion spoke truth. Hantei 38th was dead, and the entire Empire would suffer as a result. Because of him. He felt his resolve falter as the Scorpion's words bit deeper than any blade.

But he was Akodo Toturi, daimyō of his clan and Emerald Champion of Rokugan. He could not undo what had been done; he would gladly trade his life for that of the Emperor, but the Fortunes had already spoken. His failure was complete, but his duty was not. He could no longer protect the Emperor, but he could see that his killer faced justice. The consequences of his failure could wait until that task was completed.

"Perhaps you're right, Scorpion," he acknowledged, tightening his fingers around the hilt of his blade. "My failure in this life may well haunt me in the next. But if you think that your time in this realm is done, then I will be happy to be the one to send you off!"

He charged forward again, this time foregoing precision in favor of raw power. He was heavier, stronger than the Scorpion daimyō, and he let out a low roar as he swung his katana like it was a hammer or tetsubō, putting all of the power he could generate from his hips, back, and shoulders into each swing. His blade crashed against Shoju's hastily raised defenses, steel grating against steel as the Scorpion tried to shed the blows.

Step by step, Shoju was driven back, until his heels hit the dais and he was forced once more to climb toward the throne. Toturi followed, unrelenting in the power and fury of his strikes, until the two of them fought before the Emerald Throne itself. He was aware of the blasphemy he was committing by being upon this platform, but Toturi knew that it meant little enough when compared with the death of the Emperor.

He put it from his mind as they both stepped back, as if by unspoken accord. Now their breathing came in sharp, ragged gasps as the demands of their duel drew on their last reserves. The Scorpion truly was a master swordsman, and Toturi's blade had not managed to draw even a single drop of blood. Nor had the Scorpion landed any blows of his own, though there was a nagging part of Toturi's mind that could not help but notice that, so far, Shoju had made no effort to actually kill him. It was as if the Scorpion was goading him, driving him to put more and more effort into the attack, but was doing nothing but defending in return.

Why? Was it some Scorpion trick to create a false sense of security before he struck? He tightened his hands on his katana and tried to get his breathing under control. If it was a trick, Toturi knew that he wouldn't see it coming. He may have been a great tactician and strategist, but when it came to deception, the Scorpion could not be beaten. The only way to circumvent the machinations of someone like Bayushi Shoju was to refuse to play the game.

"It is time to end this," Shoju said abruptly. "I believe our exchange has drawn attention."

Toturi could hear it as well, the rush of booted feet making their way down the halls of the palace. The Imperial Guard was never far from the Emperor, even here, in the seat of his power. Their fight had lasted only moments, but the sound of battle in this place would bring a swift response. Toturi could wait. He could fight defensively, biding his time, and let the guards arrive. Perhaps, with their help, he could even subdue Shoju, capture him and then give the man the true traitor's death that he deserved.

But a glance at the Emperor's body drove the thought from Toturi's mind. His mentor lay dead, and Toturi could not bear the thought of waiting for someone else to avenge him. He gave Shoju a brief salute with his blade, and was surprised when the Scorpion returned it. "Let us be done with it, then."

As before, he charged, bringing his blade down in heavy strikes, relying on strength and speed to overwhelm his opponent. This time, as Shoju shed his blows, Toturi's own blade slid down his guard and struck the Emerald Throne, gouging and tearing at the lacquered wood. He saw that mocking smile flash again and felt another surge of anger. It was one more blasphemy, one more shame, for him to bear. He ground his teeth but drove forward.

His focus shrank to the man before him, and the rest of the world faded from existence. He knew Shoju, who still had not attacked him directly, must be preparing whatever ploy he had in store, waiting for the opportunity to deliver a single, killing blow. He had to be, for the Scorpion's time was running out. Once the guard arrived, if Toturi still drew breath, then no matter the fate that ultimately befell Toturi, Shoju's murderous coup would be finished.

If Toturi wanted to end this, he had to strike before Shoju's moment came. But he could think of only one tactic that would break through Shoju's immaculate defense, and it was one that would almost certainly cost him his life. The Emperor lay dead, and it was his failure. Shoju may have wielded the blade, but the duty had been his. If Toturi died while avenging the Emperor's murder, he would be absolved of that shame.

A sense of peace washed over him as he made the decision.

In the midst of the unrelenting assault upon the Scorpion, Toturi shifted his balance. His blade dipped as he prepared to lunge forward. There was a moment, no more than half a heartbeat, where his blade was positioned low enough that he could not bring it quickly back to guard. With his weight shifting forward and his blade low, there was an instant where Toturi knew he was open to a counter. In that moment, with his guard compromised by the sudden shift in tactics, Shoju could strike. But Toturi did not care; if avenging the Emperor meant sacrificing his own life, then so be it.

He saw the realization in Shoju's eyes, saw the ancestral blade of the Hantei shift into the position that would mean his death. He could do nothing to stop it, but neither could Shoju do anything to turn aside his own blade.

And in that fraction of a second, the Scorpion did something completely unexpected. That same strange, sour smile twisted his lips… and his blade turned aside. Toturi felt it catch in his kimono, the razor-sharp steel slicing through the tightly woven silk as easily as sliding into water, but the edge did not touch his flesh. His own blade slammed home, the point slipping beneath Shoju's breastbone and angling upward into his heart.

There was a clatter as the ancestral sword of the Hantei fell from Bayushi Shoju's weakening grasp and tumbled to the dais. The Scorpion slumped, his hands falling to his sides as he sank to his knees, sliding down the length of Toturi's sword as he did. His lips opened, and it seemed to Toturi that he tried to form words, but all that came out was a hoarse cough and spray of blood. His head slumped, and he was still.

A shudder passed through Toturi as the weight of what had just happened fell upon him. Emotions battled within him: shame at his failure to protect the Emperor, rage at the man still impaled upon his blade, and a growing sense of unease. With the stroke of Shoju's blade and the stroke of his own, he knew the Empire had just changed forever.

Where would this day lead?

The door to the throne room burst open, and the Imperial Guard rushed in. But when they saw the tableau laid out before them – the body of the Emperor dead at the foot of the dais, the Emerald Champion standing atop it, his sword buried in the chest of the daimyō of the Scorpion – they could do nothing but stop in their tracks.

Toturi felt the shame of his failure burning deep as the eyes of the guard fell upon him. But he turned, raising his voice to carry across the chamber. "Emperor Hantei 38th is dead, slain by the traitor Bayushi Shoju," he announced, his own voice sounding flat in his ears. "Go to the princes. Find Sotorii and Daisetsu. See to their safety. Send runners to all the Imperial Advisors and staff and all of the senior ambassadors. They must be summoned at once." He paused, looking down at the body of his friend. "And find someone to see to the remains of the Voice of Heaven. The Empire mourns."

The guards just stared at him, their faces showing shock and uncertainty and doubt, and his shame burned even deeper. "Go!" he demanded, striding down the steps of the dais and snapping his sword out to clear the blood before slamming it home into its scabbard. "Ancestors curse you, go!"

They went, leaving Akodo Toturi, Lion Clan Champion, Emerald Champion, and avenger of a murdered Emperor alone with his failures.

"My lord."

For a brief moment, Toturi was in two places at once. As his eyes blinked open, he could see the low flame of their campfire, the makeshift shelters they had built just off the main road. But over it hovered the ghosts of memory: the Emerald Throne, and the body of his friend. He blinked rapidly, telling himself that the burning he felt behind his eyes as the dream faded was from the smoke.

"I told you not to call me that, Toku," he grunted, looking up at the boy.

"Yes, Lord Toturi," the boy said with a bow. "As you say."

Toturi grunted. The boy had refused to call him anything other than "my lord" or "Lord Toturi" since they had departed the village. "Why did you wake me?" he muttered.

"A horseman approaches."

Toturi blinked and glanced at the horizon, which had only just started to lighten as Lady Sun and Lord Moon continued their perpetual chase across the sky. This horseman was either up very early or riding very late. Horses were not common in the

Empire, though this close to the lands of the Unicorn, they were not unheard of, either. If they ignored it, the rider would likely pass their camp with nothing more than a slight bow as they went about their business. But they might have news of the Empire, which Toturi was highly interested in. On his quest to find the missing princes, even a small amount of information could be crucial.

"Wake Daisuke," he said to Toku. "We'll go and meet with this rider."

# 8
# Hotaru

Matsu Tsuko strode into the throne room with her head thrown back and a haughty expression on her face. Her kimono, a subdued brown with bright yellow threading depicting the walls of Last Breath Castle, was cut in a utilitarian, almost aggressive fashion. Hotaru felt the familiar itch in her palms, the one she always got when she wanted the comforting weight of her naginata in her hands. This was the woman who was behind the current Lion aggression. It didn't matter if she had not been formally recognized by the regent as the rightful Clan Champion; the Lion did as Matsu Tsuko bid, and that was all there was to it. And right now, those same Lion were harrying the Crane borders and threatening to reignite a war that she thought had been put to rest.

Not for the first time, Hotaru wondered if she had done her clan a disservice when she took that fateful shot at Toshi Ranbo. How different would the Empire be today if Akodo Arasou had lived? He had persecuted the war between the Lion and Crane with calculated precision, but Hotaru had never sensed in him that there was anything personal in it. It had been almost a matter of tradition between the clans. That was not the case with Matsu Tsuko.

Her husband's death had filled her with a hatred for the Crane that, at the time, had seemed of little relevance to Hotaru. After all, with Arasou's death, it had not been Tsuko, but rather Arasou's brother, Akodo Toturi, who was named Clan Champion. Despite his monastic upbringing, Toturi had proven an able and capable leader, and with his responsibilities as Emerald Champion, Toturi had slowly moved his clan away from the violent conflict over Toshi Ranbo.

But that had all changed with the death of Hantei 38th. And Matsu Tsuko had become far more dangerous. If it was just a personal vendetta against Hotaru alone, she wouldn't have worried as much, but the Lion seemed to want more than just her blood.

She wanted to see the Crane destroyed, young and old, root and branch, samurai and peasant alike.

"Matsu Tsuko," Yoshi said, interrupting her thoughts as the Lion contingent came to a stop before them. "You were not summoned to this council." Though the words were spoken in the calm and polished tones of a master courtier, making it almost more of a question than a statement, Hotaru had to suppress a wince. No matter how pleasant the tone, the words themselves were a clear reprimand.

"Do I need a summons to bring my grievances before the throne?" Tsuko barked back, her light tenor filling the room. "I thought it was the right of every champion to voice their concerns at court."

Yoshi gave an exasperated and exaggerated sigh. "Lady Tsuko, you know that the regency does not have the authority to formally recognize new Clan Champions. That is the purview of the emperor and the emperor alone."

"On the contrary, Lord Regent." It was not Matsu Tsuko

that spoke, but another young woman, who looked barely out of her teens. She moved effortlessly through the crowd of Lion functionaries to stand beside Matsu Tsuko. She was clearly not a Lion herself, clad as she was in the twisting orange and red flame motif of the Phoenix. This, then, must be Chukan Hanako, the woman Kachiko had warned her of.

She was exquisitely beautiful, her features fine and delicate, her skin flawless and flushed with the vibrancy of youth. Her silk kimono, like Kachiko's, was cut to emphasize her figure, though the two could not have been more different otherwise. Kachiko was fully aware of her beauty, and carried herself with a sensuality that set everyone's passions, Hotaru's included, aflame. This woman was the promise of becoming, a caterpillar just emerging into a butterfly, with an air of naivety that seemed to call out for a guiding hand. There was something innocent there, but also something eminently… corruptible.

Hotaru felt a ripple of temptation through her insides, a spider of need crawling under her skin. Alarmed, she closed her eyes, blocking the woman from her sight, and the sensation faded.

Hotaru shuddered. What, by all the Fortunes and ancestors, was *that* about? She'd never felt that way before and it left her feeling… unclean.

The young woman's voice continued, unaware of Hotaru's momentary lapse. "There are at least three instances of regents confirming Clan Champions in the past, Lord Kakita," she was saying, her voice light and crisp. "These instances have been documented, of course. I have brought the relevant scrolls from the archives for you to review."

A servant moved forward, bowing low, offering up a wooden box stained dark and chased with silver filigree. Another servant, this one wearing the Imperial livery, seemed to materialize out of thin air to take possession of the box of scrolls. Yoshi, Hotaru noted, hadn't even glanced at the box. His eyes, like those of most of the people in the room, seemed to be locked on Hanako. The young woman, now that her task had been completed, bowed and faded back into the Lion.

Yoshi blinked as the Phoenix disappeared. "Yes, well." He cleared his throat. "We will, of course, review whatever supporting documents you may have, Lady Tsuko," he said, turning his gaze back to the Lion. "But it will take time. We are, as I am sure you are aware, quite busy with other matters."

Tsuko snorted. "Busy with more Crane conspiracies, you mean," she said. "Do not think to deceive me. When the Crane Imperial Regent, the Crane Clan Champion, and the Crane Emerald Champion meet and whisper behind closed doors, those of us with grievances against the Crane take notice. We will not sit idly by while you plot to use the forces of the Empire against those who are not Crane." Her hand twitched, as if she, too, longed to feel the weight of her weapon in it.

"You forget yourself, Matsu Tsuko," Yoshi replied, a slight quaver of anger breaking through the edges of his control. "I do not serve the Crane in my current capacity. I serve the Empire. You would do well to remember that."

"Or you will bring the weight of that Empire down upon us?" Tsuko snapped, voice rising. "How convenient that would be for your clan, *my Lord Regent*." She practically sneered the title.

Toshimoko stepped forward. He did not place himself between Matsu Tsuko and the regent, but he did put himself within easy sword's reach of the Lion. Every person in the Lion contingent stiffened, and more than one hand strayed to a weapon. Such was her uncle's reputation.

Hotaru drew in a furtive breath, her heart thumping a little faster than before. Should steel be drawn here, for the second time in six months, she was certain that the Empire would fall into a war unlike any it had seen before. That would serve no one.

She stepped forward as well, placing one hand on her uncle's arm. She could feel the tension in Toshimoko's muscles; the man was like iron cord stretched tight and thrumming with potential violence. None of it showed on his face, which now held his customary, almost arrogant, smirk. He didn't have to speak; his presence was threat enough. Hotaru hoped she could provide a counterbalance.

She offered a bow to Tsuko, which was not returned. "Lady Tsuko," she said, ignoring the slight. "I understand your concerns. For my part, I assure you, I have no intention of trying to bring my uncles – either of them – into the disagreement between our clans. It is a matter that should be settled between us and us alone. I hope that you and I can speak on it while we are both here in the Imperial City, for nothing would make me happier than to find a solution to our problem that does not end with yet more deaths among both our people."

Matsu Tsuko said nothing, only stared at her in icy silence, so she turned instead to her uncles. "Lord Regent," she said with another bow. "Emerald Champion. With your permission, I will take my leave of you."

Yoshi nodded regally, and Toshimoko twitched one eye in what might have been a wink. Matsu Tsuko continued to glare at her, while the rest of the Lion studiously ignored her. Hotaru offered one final bow and spun on her heel. As she strode from the chamber, she kept her back straight and her shoulders relaxed, not giving any outward sign of the frustration – and worry – that swirled within her at Tsuko's intransigence.

"I told you that girl was trouble," Kachiko purred.

It was later – much later. Hotaru had left the throne room, intent on meeting with the Crane ambassadors at court. Partly to get their input on their Lion counterparts – and Hanako – and partly to see just how much of their direction they were still taking from Yoshi. He had been the senior Crane courtier before being elevated to regent, and Hotaru needed to make sure her other courtiers understood that they no longer reported to him. She needed to put clear lines between the regency and her clan, and not only because of the Lion's accusations.

But her intentions had gone out the window when she found Kachiko waiting in an alcove outside the throne room. It had been the better part of two years since they had a chance to be alone together. They had exchanged correspondences over that time, and Hotaru had sensed that they had both been drifting, letting their duties drive a wedge between them.

It would have been for the best, Hotaru told herself. Even before Bayushi Shoju's betrayal, any relationship between them was destined to end in sorrow. The Crane and the Scorpion were intense political rivals, enemies in both love and war. Now, with Shoju's atrocity still fresh in the mind of every citizen of the Empire, the Scorpion were pariahs, unwelcome in any court, serving as reminders of how swiftly one could fall when playing the games of politics.

But when she had seen Kachiko in the garden, and then when she found the woman waiting for her, the divide between them had vanished.

It had taken some time to properly reintroduce themselves to one another.

"She didn't say much," Hotaru countered, one hand idly running her fingers through Kachiko's silken hair as they reclined on the futon. "She provided some scrolls she claims support the notion that the regent can, in fact, recognize a newly named Clan Champion."

Even now, alone in Hotaru's chambers, Kachiko still wore the lacy butterfly mask. It moved with her skin, creasing slightly as she crinkled her nose at the idea. "She is doing far more than that, Hotaru." As she spoke, she shifted against Hotaru, the warmth of her body as she moved sending tingles up and down Hotaru's spine.

"I cannot give you hard proof – not yet – but you know how many eyes and ears I have in this place. Matsu Tsuko hates you, and that is a fact. But she holds you, not your clan, responsible for Arasou's death. It is this Hanako who is whispering poison into her ear and filling her head with the notions of obliterating the Crane, by whatever means necessary." Kachiko frowned and drummed elegant fingers on Hotaru's knee. "I do not know what game she is playing at, or what the Phoenix have to do with this at all. But do not let her innocent façade fool you. She might be one of the most dangerous people to have ever trod the halls of the Imperial Palace."

Hotaru felt a chill. Kachiko herself was a master of the court, and wielded politics like the sharpest blade. If she said someone was dangerous, you would do well to believe her. Which raised a different question in her mind.

"Kachiko," she said softly, almost afraid to speak the words aloud. "Why are you still here?" Before the woman could answer, she rushed on. "I am glad, truly, to see you once more. But the Imperial Court has always been a dangerous place, and by both your words and my own eyes, it has grown more so since the Emperor's death. Given what happened" – she didn't mention Shoju by name – "wouldn't you be safer back in Silk and Shadow Palace?"

She felt Kachiko stiffen, just slightly. "I would," she admitted, though it sounded painful for her. "But what would you have me do, Hotaru? Tuck my tail between my legs and run? Abandon everything the Scorpion have worked for? Allow the other clans to drive us into the darkness to be forgotten?" She paused for a moment, her tone becoming sad but with an edge of steel beneath. "I might not wear the daishō, but that does not mean I am defenseless."

Her voice was calm, but Hotaru was reminded of the fact that while Kachiko might consider Hanako to be one of the most dangerous people to walk the halls of power, the woman sharing her futon had held that distinction for years. Not so very long ago, a whisper from Kachiko could end a life as surely as a strike from Hotaru's blade.

It probably still could.

"I know, Kachiko," she said, going back to stroking the Scorpion's hair. "And you are not a coward; forgive me if I implied otherwise. But you know the dangers of this place far better than most. Better than I do," she added. "And if I can see the danger, surely you can as well? What is there to gain by remaining, save the chance that some assassin's blade comes for you? Unless you have your own plans, as well?"

There was a long moment of silence, and Hotaru wondered if she had gone too far. Their dalliances had been just that; moments of pleasure stolen from their responsibilities and duties. In the quiet moments when she could be completely honest with herself, Hotaru could admit that it was not Kachiko's beauty alone that had first drawn her to the woman. Some part of their attraction stemmed from the forbidden nature of it. Theirs had not been the first such dalliance between a Scorpion and a Crane, but there were certain unspoken rules that were normally observed.

First among them was the simple fact that they should never interfere with the internal politics of the other's clan. To do so would cast doubt on the nature of the relationship, particularly where the Scorpion were involved. As a clan, they were known to do what they perceived as their duty, no matter the personal cost, even if that cost meant dabbling in intimate relationships with their rivals. Hotaru's words were not exactly a violation of that unwritten rule, but they teetered on the very edge of crossing the line.

She narrowed her eyes. Realm of Torment take the line. Their dalliance may have started with mutual attraction seasoned with the lure of the forbidden, but Hotaru had come to care deeply for the woman in her arms. And she knew – she hoped – Kachiko felt the same way, whatever their clans might think.

Still, being between a Scorpion and their duty was not a comfortable place to be.

The Scorpion pulled away from her and rose, moving with a grace to put the finest Kakita dancer to shame. The light of Lord Moon filtered in through the screens, and for a moment, Kachiko was a vision, the pale light caressing her bare flesh like a lover. Then she slipped into her kimono, wrapping the obi loosely around her waist, and turned back to Hotaru.

"I appreciate your concern, Hotaru," she said, allowing a slight smile to dance on her lips. "Truly, I do. And you are correct. The palace is far more dangerous than it has ever been before." She turned, gliding across the floor to the window. Hotaru's personal quarters, as the Champion of the Crane Clan, were a large suite of rooms set high in the palace and overlooking one of the many imperial gardens. The view of the palace grounds was breathtaking; pools of still water framed by carefully cultivated cherry blossom trees and sighing forests of bamboo.

It could not compare to the sight of Kachiko framed in the window, the breeze stirring her hair and billowing kimono, the light of the moon setting her skin aglow.

Hotaru rose from the futon and went to stand behind the Scorpion, slipping her arms around her waist. Kachiko leaned back slightly, pressing against her, and for a moment, both were content to stand like that, mingled in each other's warmth.

"I can't leave," Kachiko finally said, her voice a determined whisper. "I understand the anger against my people. The Scorpion have always been the Empire's villains; we *chose* to be the Empire's villains. And yet, I do not know why my husband" – to Hotaru's surprise, she spoke the word without rancor – "did as he did. Perhaps it was madness and ambition as the courtiers say. Perhaps he worked toward some greater duty that he saw fit to keep from me. Or perhaps it's something else entirely. But it doesn't matter." She sighed and settled deeper against Hotaru. "Whatever his reasons, I doubt I will ever learn them."

Hotaru said nothing, sensing that Kachiko was not yet done. She just held her, letting the Scorpion gather her thoughts. Kachiko was silent for several moments, her light fingers trailing circles on Hotaru's skin, sending shivers all the way up her arm.

"There is something stirring in the halls of the palace," Kachiko said at last, her words barely audible. "Something dark. Our courtly games have always had an edge, but with Hantei's death, something changed. The entire Empire is gripped in rage and fear. And that rage could easily settle upon – or be directed at – the Scorpion. My people fear that the other clans will demand retribution, despite the fact that none of us – none of us, Hotaru – had any idea what Shoju was planning."

The fingers tracing Hotaru's arm clenched into a fist. "The Scorpion have returned to our ancestral lands, but we are not hiding," she murmured. "We are not cowering in shame. We are preparing. We make ready for the reprisal we fear is coming. And if it does come, Hotaru, it will be for the very existence of the Scorpion."

Hotaru felt a chill. The end of the Scorpion. That was what Kachiko feared. It had been a miracle that their entire clan had not been disbanded for the blasphemous crime of their champion.

Even now, the Scorpion clan was not out of danger. Even now, reprisal might come. The chill Hotaru felt spread to her whole body. Should anything like that come to pass… it would be the Crane that issued the order.

Kachiko sighed and then straightened, standing on her own rather than leaning against the Crane. She did not, Hotaru noted, pull away from her encircling arms. "I cannot fight in that kind of war," she said quietly. "But I can work here, in the palace, to try and stop it from coming to pass. Which is why I haunt the halls of the Crane, watching, listening. I will use whatever I can find to aid the Scorpion."

Hotaru tried to ignore the sick feeling in her stomach. She tried to keep the accusation from her voice, accusation borne of dismay and hurt, accusation that was not befitting someone of her station, but it slipped out anyway. "Is that why you came to me tonight, Kachiko?" she whispered.

"Hotaru." Kachiko's elegant shoulders slumped. One hand came to rest on Hotaru's arm, fingers curled gently around her wrist. "If that was true, if my only purpose was to use the Crane Clan Champion as leverage for my own devices, do you think I would have told you any of this?"

Hotaru's throat closed. She knew she shouldn't believe Kachiko. She knew she should be cautious when dealing with the Scorpion, any Scorpion. They used words as weapons, twisting them so the truth was unrecognizable. They told you what you wanted to hear, weaving a garrote of lies and trickery, and when your guard was down and your back turned, that's when they tightened the noose. The unspoken mantra, whispered in every courtier school across the Crane lands, echoed loudly in her thoughts: *never trust a Scorpion.*

But it was too late. And perhaps she was being foolish, putting her faith in one of the most infamous Scorpions in the Empire, second only to the traitorous Bayushi Shoju himself. But if Kachiko said that Hotaru was *somehow* not entangled in the Scorpion's machinations to preserve her clan, Hotaru believed her. And the fact that Kachiko was willing to share those plans with her spoke of a trust that filled Hotaru with a warmth more comforting than the fire laid in the hearth.

"So, now you know why I am here." Kachiko was silent for a long moment, letting the words hang in the air. For just a moment, she seemed strangely vulnerable. "Would you do any different, Hotaru?"

Hotaru thought of the Lion pressing the borders of the Crane, of Matsu Tsuko's rage over the death of Akodo Arasou. Of the fear that her uncles, now both in positions of considerable power outside of the clan, would, knowingly or not, usurp her authority and attempt to rule the Crane in her stead. And of the untold thousands of peasants who would suffer and die if war came to her people. She was here for much the same purpose as Kachiko – to prevent more fighting, more death. To serve as a shield between her people and the ravages of war.

"No," Hotaru said at last. "No, Kachiko. I could do no different." She tightened her arms, pulling the Scorpion against her once more. "I would risk my life as surely as you are risking yours… but I do not like to think of you in danger."

The Scorpion turned her head as she leaned back further, her lips tantalizingly close to Hotaru's own. "Then let us not think of it," Kachiko murmured. "Our duties will still be there in the morning. We can steal one night for us." Her lips met Hotaru's and the world shrank down to just the two of them.

Kachiko was right. Their troubles would still be there in the morning.

# 9
# Yakamo

Yakamo stared into the polished steel mirror and didn't recognize the face that gazed back at him.

He had never been accused of being handsome, not with his broad features, heavy brow, and close-set eyes. In fact, he cultivated his long mustache, carefully trimmed and falling down on either side of his chin, to draw attention from the rest of his face. But now, that face looked haggard and far too old for his years. Deep bags had settled under his eyes and one cheek was marred by a blotchy purple bruise. He had more injuries, a dozen minor cuts and scrapes that he hadn't bothered seeking the healing blessings of the shindōshi for. Better that they saved their powers for those who truly needed them. The wounds left him tired and irritable, and he wanted nothing more than to rest in his chambers until his next duty rotation.

But that was not to be.

Two days since his father's forces had come to his aid and driven the dead from the Great Carpenter Wall. Two days since the forces of the Shadowlands had stopped their attack and abruptly pulled their forces back, as if waiting. Two days, and only now had his father deigned to summon him.

To Yakamo, it felt like a stinging rebuke. Why had his father not included him in his planning? Why had he been sent to his chambers like a wayward child and left to his own devices for days? Had his failure truly been so great?

The Great Bear's forces had crashed down upon the dead like an avalanche, bursting through Yakamo's own lines to sweep the monstrosities from the Wall. Hida Kisada himself had been there, leading from the front, shouting orders and wielding his own tetsubō with a speed and grace that belied its massive weight. Yakamo had modeled every aspect of his own fighting style on his father and had tried to do much the same with his personality and command style. And yet, he still fell short.

Where his forces had been driven back, Kisada's reserve, admittedly fresh compared to Yakamo's troops, had made short work of the undead horrors. His father had spared him and his warriors barely a glance, telling Yakamo only that they were relieved of their duty atop the Wall until further notice and to get what food, rest, and medical attention they needed.

And that was the last he had heard from Hida Kisada until the servant arrived, bidding him to come to his father's war room.

Yakamo took one last glance at his face in the mirror and straightened his kimono. It was a simple affair by the standards of the northern clans, made not of silk, but a light breathable wool more suited to the mountains. It bore no ornaments and the pattern woven into it was a simple motif of crabs with their claws upraised for battle, subtle shades of gray against the darker blues of the cloth. He would have much preferred to wear his armor, but it was still under the ministrations of the Crab clan smiths, repairing the damage it had suffered in his last foray on the Wall.

He grabbed his daishō from the stand and tucked the blades into his obi as he turned for the door.

Bunzō was waiting for him when he stepped into the hall. The Laughing Crab was also without his armor, making the wiry man seem even smaller than usual. He still wore a smile, only slightly marred by the long cut that ran from his left temple, narrowly missing his eye, and terminating in the precise center of his chin. Yakamo couldn't remember when Bunzō had acquired that wound, which probably meant it had come from the undead. "Did you have that looked at by the healers?" he asked, gesturing at the cut.

"A pleasure to see you, too, Lord Yakamo," Bunzō replied with a grin. "I did, indeed. And I'm happy to report that I also washed behind my ears and changed my undergarments."

Yakamo grunted. "Why are you here?"

Bunzō shrugged. "To escort you to Lord Hida, of course. We fought a great battle atop the Wall. It is only right that you have a retinue with you."

Yakamo couldn't tell from Bunzō's tone whether the man was serious or not. They had not won a great battle; the reserves had to relieve them. But no one, not even his father, could deny how hard they fought. Yakamo felt the sting of his failure down to his bones, but he would not subject Bunzō and the other survivors of the battle to that. It was *his* failure, not theirs.

"Lead on, then," he said. "Let us go see what my father has for us."

The war room of the daimyō of the Crab Clan was built into the largest bastion – really more of a fortified palace unto itself – atop this section of the Wall. Like most of Crab architecture, the focus was on function over beauty, and that function was obvious in the thick walls, narrow windows, and twisting hallways. Any enemy who breached this fortress would find themselves in a bloody battle with surprises and ambushes at every turn.

Yakamo barely noticed. He had played in these halls as a youth, and they were as familiar to him as his own quarters. His mind was focused on the chamber ahead, where his father waited. The guards outside wore full armor and leaned on long nodachi. They were gruff men, veterans of the Wall and older than Yakamo by three decades. They had earned their place among their daimyō's honor guard through years of dedicated service, but he knew that they would gladly abandon their largely ceremonial role and go back to fighting atop the Wall if the need arose.

Briefly, Yakamo couldn't help but wonder if that was all that was before him. Would his entire life be nothing more than an endless series of watches, fighting an endless string of battles, until, at some point, he made a mistake and died at the hands of some Shadowlands beast? Since before he could walk, he'd been taught that to die gloriously for the good of clan and Empire was his duty and greatest privilege. But was there truly no better way to keep the Empire safe than to shunt that duty to a single, slowly dwindling clan? A clan that, by the very Empire they protected, was scorned as uncouth barbarians?

The guards pulled the door to the chamber open and Yakamo strode in, Bunzō at his side. The large room was dominated by a broad table stretching ten feet in length and half again as wide. Upon it, in painstaking detail, was built a model of the Wall and its surroundings. It did not detail the full two hundred and fifty plus miles of the Great Carpenter Wall; even with the massive size of the table, it would have been tactically useless. Instead, the center of the table was dominated by the fortress they stood in now, with the Wall stretching away to either side.

Yakamo knew that each length of the Wall spreading from the fortress to the table's end represented about fifteen miles, half the distance in either direction to the next fortress. Each fortress commanded about thirty miles of the Wall's length, with a dozen total fortresses being spread along the border with the Shadowlands. Between those fortresses, every hundred yards, were the bastions that held the massive siege engines and served as lighter fortifications if the Crab ever needed to fall back and regroup.

The model was covered in painted stones representing the Crab warriors scattered along its length. Yakamo knew that those tiny bits of rock depicted thousands of his fellow clansmen, and that the decisions made in this room would determine how many of them lived and how many died.

Standing over the table, peering down at it with his brows drawn together, stood Hida Kisada. The Great Bear, daimyō of the Crab Clan… and Yakamo's father.

He towered over everyone else in the room, save only Yakamo, and was broad enough to make two of most men. His strength and ferocity on the battlefield were legendary, as was his acumen as a general. While Yakamo took after him with his own size, his father's features were more traditionally handsome, in a rugged, chiseled sort of way. He wore his great armor, the heavy overlapping plates of steel that could take a blow from an oni's club and remain intact, with easy familiarity. He barely glanced up when Yakamo first entered the room, and in that lack of acknowledgement, Yakamo sensed disappointment.

He was not alone in the room. Three others were present. Yakamo's younger sister, Hida O-Ushi, stood at his side. Where Yakamo was tall and broad like their father, O-Ushi took after their mother, long and lean, with fine features. She was considered a great beauty by many, and not just among the Crab Clan. But her lean frame hid surprising strength, and she served as ably on the Wall as any Crab, wielding her warhammer to brutal effect. Instead of the great armor that many Crab warriors wore, she wore a lighter suit of lamellar that allowed her to be more mobile on the field of battle.

Beside his sister stood Yakamo's younger brother, Hida Sukune. Sukune had neither the height of Yakamo nor the breadth of Kisada. He was a capable enough warrior, though by far the least skilled of Hida Kisada's children. What he lacked in physical strength, he made up for with a sharp and twisting mind that lent itself well to strategy. Despite his physical shortcomings – at least in the eyes of their father – his tactical expertise had earned him a place in the Great Bear's councils of war. He wore the signature armor of his own design, forged by the finest artisans among the Crab. The steel plates had been carefully worked to mimic the appearance of an actual crab. The jutting points and odd angles struck Yakamo as useless, perhaps even counterproductive, but he could not deny the effect. Despite his physical shortcomings, when Sukune donned that armor and put on his helmet, he became a living banner of the Crab.

Yakamo reluctantly turned his gaze to the final person in the room, and a shiver coursed down his spine.

Kuni Yori, his father's chief councilor and advisor on all things related to the Shadowlands, was a shindōshi, one of the shindōshi that called upon the elemental spirits through the use of prayers and invocations, willing them to lend their power to the beseecher's cause. The Crab boasted many such shindōshi, and they were essential to the defense of the Wall. Without them and their ability to call upon the spirits of Water and Earth, many warriors would succumb to their wounds or, even worse, be taken by the infection of the Shadowlands Taint. Without their invocations to the Fire spirits, the siege engines that could tear great rends in the enemy forces would be reduced to throwing sticks and stones. The clouding Air invocations that confused the enemy with shrouding fogs or slowed their progress with torrential winds would vanish. Yakamo knew their value well and had nothing but respect for those who took up the calling. They were the spiritual shepherds of the Empire as surely as the Little Teacher was.

Despite all that, Kuni Yori still set his teeth on edge.

The man was tall and gaunt, with a slight hunch to his shoulders that twisted his form and stole inches from his height. His features were thin and sharp, the bones seeming to press against the reedy skin of his face like they were trying to break free from their fleshy prison. He wore the white and red makeup of the Kuni Purifiers, making his face seem even more skull-like. Yakamo knew that Kuni Yori was his father's age, perhaps a little older, but between his twisted back, his pallid features, and his skeletal frame, the man looked to be at least twenty years older.

To Yakamo's eye, he looked like a walking corpse. Perhaps that was why he felt such unease in Yori's presence.

Yakamo stepped forward and sank into a deep bow, waiting for his father to notice him. Bunzō bowed at his side, deeper than Yakamo, bending nearly double. They held that pose for long moments as the silence in the room stretched, and a flush of embarrassment crept up his face as he felt the eyes upon him.

"Yakamo," his father said at last, finally looking up from the stones scattered across the table. He didn't bother to acknowledge Bunzō. "Now that you have deigned to arrive, we can begin."

Yakamo's flush deepened at the minor reprimand. "As you say, Lord Hida," he replied formally, rising from his bow. Kisada scarcely seemed to notice, turning his eyes back to the model of the Wall.

"Sukune, what is the latest news?"

Yakamo's younger brother straightened, clearing his throat

slightly. "The Shadowlands army has withdrawn," he said, gesturing to the table that was, Yakamo noted, bare of the paper slips denoting enemy forces. "They abandoned their positions two days ago, shortly after your forces cleared the undead from between bastions twenty-three and twenty-four. Runners have been sent up and down the length of the Wall, but so far, we have no reports suggesting that they have moved to attack other positions." He offered a slight shrug, the plates of his armor creaking. "We are still awaiting word from the farthest positions."

"Perhaps we struck a deeper blow than we realized," O-Ushi offered. "This latest was not a normal attack. We have never seen those flying Shadowlands creatures before, nor the strange incantations that allowed them to move their undead soldiers to the top of the Wall."

Yakamo shuddered at the memory of the dead materializing in their midst, but O-Ushi continued without pause. "Perhaps their entire strategy hinged on winning that battle," she finished, "and whatever fell powers they needed to achieve it were expended at their failure."

It was as good an explanation as any Yakamo could have offered, and a reminder that while he was, technically, his father's heir as the Crab followed the old tradition of passing the authority of the daimyō down through the male line, there was nothing to stop Kisada from changing that tradition, as many other clans had long ago. His sister, or his brother for that matter, could just as easily be named successor. Yakamo had little desire for the position, but he wasn't sure he could bear the shame of being deemed so unworthy.

"Bah," Kisada grunted, shaking his head. "The bastards had plenty of their filthy kind left to pressure the Wall." He peered at the table, thumb idly stroking his chin. "This is something more than a simple withdrawal. There's something else happening." The Great Bear glared down at the empty space beyond the representation of the Wall as if it had personally insulted him. He stabbed a finger at the dark rock and sand meant to represent the barren landscape of the Shadowlands. "They're out there, somewhere."

"I agree, Lord Hida," Kuni Yori said. He spoke softly, his words scarcely above a whisper. "The spirits are uneasy, and they hint of more darkness to come."

"There is always more darkness," Kisada said flatly. "The Shadowlands spew forth nothing else."

The Kuni offered a slight bow. "As you say, Lord Hida. But I submit that this is something… different." He paused, tilting his head to one side as if considering. The movement was almost insect-like, and it sent another little shiver down Yakamo's spine.

"This latest siege has been ongoing for weeks. The Shadowlands did not suffer a major defeat; we did not break their army or drive them away. On the contrary, they have gained the Wall multiple times, and have only been pushed back by the strength and fortitude of our warriors." To Yakamo's surprise, the shindōshi offered him a slight bow as well. "So, what has changed?" he went on. "Why pull back now at this moment? Are we to believe this is merely the will of the Fortunes smiling upon us?" He shrugged, and Yakamo would have sworn that he heard the bones of the man's shoulders grinding in their sockets as he did.

"That is the key question," Sukune said. "I don't like the idea of leaving anything to chance, but we do not have enough information to know what is going on."

"Then send the Hiruma scouts," O-Ushi said. "It is their purpose, after all. Let them go into the Shadowlands and find where this vanishing army has gone. If our enemies are hatching some scheme, then they must still be close."

"That is quite dangerous, sister," Sukune countered. "If the Shadowlands army has not truly withdrawn, our own scouts could walk right into them. And even if they have, the creatures of Fu

Leng are sure to have scouts of their own. There is no guarantee that anyone we send will make it back."

O-Ushi's lips twisted slightly in distaste, but she said, "It will tell us more than we know now."

Despite the callous nature of the words, Yakamo knew that his sister was right. The lords of the Shadowlands could be fickle, and no one among the Crab claimed to understand what they were after, at least not beyond the destruction of the Empire and the death of everyone within. But he had never seen an army massed outside the Wall withdraw so completely. He had seen them ground down to remnants, until they no longer had enough bodies – warm or cold – to throw into the teeth of the Crab. He had seen them break and flee, as the cowardly nature of the goblins and lesser creatures overtook the fear of their masters. But he had never seen them simply… quit the field.

In its own way, it was more worrisome than having the enemy camped at their gates. They were all familiar with that scenario, comfortable with the ideas of battle and siege. But the situation also presented an opportunity. His father had to rescue him atop the Wall when the dead gained the ramparts. Perhaps he could atone for that failure.

"I will go," he said. "I will lead a small contingent of scouts beyond the Wall and uncover what the filth are planning." He looked at Bunzō, the lithe man not only a Hiruma by birth, but also a graduate of their scouting school. "I will take Hiruma Bunzō and a half-dozen other scouts, no more. We will move swiftly and silently, and I swear by the Fortunes and our revered ancestors that we will return."

# 10
## Toturi

Toturi and Daisuke followed Toku through the camp, moving out to meet the rider. Even with the remnants of the dream – a dream that seemed like it was from another life entirely – rattling in his mind, Toturi still couldn't help but shake his head in disbelief at the "camp" in question. When he had entered that nameless village and fought the bandits, he had been alone, a rōnin seeking redemption. He had wanted little more than to find the missing princes and restore the line of Hantei. When he walked out of it, that very same day, Toku and Daidoji Daisuke had been at his side. After long months of searching for the princes in solitude, he had accepted, even reluctantly welcomed, the companionship. But he had not expected where it would lead.

Had he known, he might have denied them both and slipped away like a whisper in a storm.

Now, ten days later, nearly two dozen men and women moved around the camp, doing the morning chores as the sun climbed over the eastern horizon. Most didn't have so much as a cloth to stretch between two branches for shelter. They had brought very little in the way of personal gear or provisions with them, but every one of them carried a weapon of some sort. Most of those were repurposed farm implements, timber axes, and makeshift spears, but Toturi knew that their crudity made them no less effective. They bowed low and muttered, "Lord Toturi," as he passed, despite him having told them repeatedly not to.

"Why can none of you understand that I am no longer anyone's lord or general?" he grunted after the third such greeting.

"They respect you, Lord Toturi," Toku said. "All the Empire knows that you are a man of fairness and virtue."

Toturi grunted again. He was many things, but he had lost his right to call himself virtuous when he failed in his duty to the Emperor.

"You might not want to be anyone's lord, my Lord Toturi, but you're still an old wolf in need of a pack. Besides," Daisuke added in his light, somewhat mocking tenor, "they need you. Or at least they need hope. Since the Emperor's death, their lives have become harsher. You offer them a chance at something different."

He glanced at the Crane. Daidoji Daisuke did not look like someone dragged early from his bed; nor did he look like he had been on a cross-country journey on foot for the better part of two weeks, living out of his pack and nothing else. His kimono might have been an unadorned gray wool, but it was clean and unrumpled. His flowing white hair was pulled back into a perfect topknot, not a single strand out of place, and he walked with the casual grace of a dancer, as if the muddy track that passed for a road was the grand hall of a palace.

Toturi sighed, shaking his head as another man bowed to him with a low "Lord Toturi."

"I haven't promised them anything," he muttered. "And I'm not looking for any sort of pack."

"Yet here we are," Daisuke replied.

"Lord Daisuke is right, my lord," Toku said. "I have spoken with all of those who have come. They all say the same thing. Something is broken in the Empire. It began with the Emperor's death, yes, but that is not all. It has pushed out from Otosan Uchi into their villages and homes. They want to help fix it, but they don't know how. In following you, they believe they will find the way to help."

Toku, unlike the Crane, showed every mile they had walked in the travel-stained tunic and pants of his samue and his dirty, disheveled face. Toturi made a mental note to talk to Toku about that. He had been spending the evenings teaching the boy to wield the axe he carried, and he found him to be a quick student with a mind almost as agile as his feet. But if he was to be representing Toturi – whether Toturi wished him to or not – he should make some effort to keep himself presentable.

Toturi sighed again and returned his attention to the peasants who had stoked last night's fires and were now setting pots of rice porridge to boil over the flames. They had arrived in ones and twos as Toturi and his companions walked across the countryside. How word of his actions had spread, he had no idea. Peasants rarely traveled far from their own fields, and he and the others had left the village before anyone could carry word ahead of them. And yet, it was as if the Air spirits themselves had whispered the tale on the winds, because every time they passed through – or even near! – a village, a handful of hopeful peasants would rush out to join them.

As Toku had said, their stories were always the same. The Empire as they knew it was failing. The murder of Hantei 38th and the rising tensions between the clans meant that the attentions of the samurai were drawn away, leaving the villagers to the mercies of bandits or unscrupulous rōnin. Imperial magistrates carrying the Imperial Seal and the word of law with them no longer traveled the roads, and criminals went uncaught and unpunished. The men and women that rallied to him like a living banner were those who were tired of waiting for the nobles they served to notice the needs of their people.

Toturi could understand their plight. But he had no idea why, by all the ancestors and Fortunes, they had settled on *him* to address their grievances.

He was no longer champion, daimyō, or general and he wanted no part of it. He had tried to turn the peasants away, to tell them that they would not find what they sought with him. But no matter what he said to his would-be followers, they simply bowed and agreed. And followed him anyway. He had tried leading Daisuke and Toku away from the roads, avoiding the villages entirely. And still they found him. In the end, Toku's quiet, hopeful eyes and Daisuke's gentle needling had forced him to relent. Both the peasant and the courtier apparently saw something he didn't in the gathering villagers, some portent or sign of a way forward.

If only they could share it with him.

"I hope this rider was worth getting out of bed for," Daisuke muttered as they passed the last of the tents and made their way out to the road. Toturi, unable to leave behind some aspects of his military training, had ordered a watch stationed, and a single peasant bowed to them as they approached. "It is still too early for any but farmers to be up and alert."

"She must have traveled throughout the night, Lord Daidoji," Toku replied, an audible note of excitement in his voice. "And she asked to speak to Lord Toturi by name," he added. "It must be a matter of importance."

"She, you say?" Daisuke asked, preening a bit. "Well, that *does* sound interesting. Tell me, Toku, is she pretty?"

The peasant boy blinked. He opened his mouth as if to speak, closed it, then opened it again. Toturi could almost feel the emotions surging as Toku tried to answer the Crane's impertinent question. There was, of course, no good answer; to say no would be offensive to the rider, who had to be of a much higher station than the boy to afford a horse; to say yes would make it appear as if Toku, a peasant boy, were lusting after his betters. To say nothing would be rude to all present. It was the kind of game that Cranes and Scorpions like to play at court, but Toturi had no patience for it. The boy didn't know the rules, anyway.

"Enough," he said. "You can see for yourself."

The Crane flashed Toku a lightning quick grin and a wink that passed so fast, Toturi wasn't even sure he saw it. Was Daisuke playing typical Crane games, or just teasing the boy? He started to ponder the question but stopped when he saw the horse.

He had expected a Rokugani pony, one of the small, sturdy horses used for both riding and the field. What he saw instead was a sleek Utaku steed, the mounts used almost exclusively by the Utaku Battle Maidens of the Unicorn Clan. The horse was lean and lithe, larger than a Rokugani pony but smaller than some of the warhorses fielded by the Lion. Its coat was pure white, and its tack included not just saddle and bridle, but lamellar barding lacquered the deep purple of the Unicorn Clan. A broad-tipped spear hung alongside the saddle, within easy reach of its rider. Even standing almost statue-still, the creature was a living embodiment of grace and speed, agile in a way no other horse in the Empire could compete with.

A woman stood beside the creature, one hand lightly holding the reins. She, too, wore armor in the purple of the Unicorn, her helm tucked beneath one arm. She was in her early twenties with the slim, athletic build of someone who spent most of their life on horseback. She was pretty, if not beautiful, but there was something in her features that seemed almost untouchable, a certainty of purpose in the intensity of her eyes and the set of her shoulders.

"Lord Toturi," the woman said as he approached, offering a bow deeper than was required to a rōnin but less than would have been polite had he still been Emerald Champion. Even the bow seemed infused with a crisp energy.

"You have me at a disadvantage, Lady Unicorn," he said, addressing her by her clan and returning her bow. He matched it as precisely as he could, offering the woman exactly the same courtesy that she had offered him. "I am afraid I do not know how to address you."

"Forgive me, my lord. It has been a long night and a long ride." The woman shifted the helm beneath her arm and nodded. "I am Utaku Kamoko."

"A Battle Maiden," Daisuke almost purred. "Fascinating. I have great interest in the schools of the Unicorn. Perhaps we could speak on the matter later… at some length." He smiled, his handsome features catching the first rays of the rising sun and seeming to take on a glow of their own.

The insinuation in the Crane's voice seemed lost on the woman. "If time permits, Lord Crane," she said briskly. "But I fear it will not. Time grows short for us all, I think." She focused her attention on Toturi. "I have news you must hear, my lord."

The words sent a chill down Toturi's spine, and he had no idea why. But something in the way the Unicorn spoke them seemed… significant.

"Come, then," he replied. "Such news should not be heard on the side of the road. Let us find a place that is more private."

They returned to camp, the peasants gawking at the Battle Maiden and her horse. For the first time in months, Toturi felt a little surge of shame at the humbleness of his surroundings. He could provide the Unicorn little more than hot tea, a bowl of porridge, and a log pulled by the fire to serve as a seat. While he oversaw those preparations, Kamoko had quickly and efficiently stripped the barding and tack from her mount and brushed the horse down. She had no shortage of hands willing to help; Utaku steeds were a rare sight in the Empire, but the Unicorn insisted on taking care of her mount herself. Toturi was grateful the Battle Maiden allowed him the few minutes necessary to provide at least some sort of welcome, even if it was hidden in settling her horse.

Now they were settled around the fire, Kamoko still clad in her armor but seeming at ease perched on the stump that served as a camp stool. Lady Sun had revealed herself in full, and the bright light of the morning washed across the camp. Toturi could see that he had not misjudged the Unicorn Battle Maiden's beauty, but he had, in the dim light of dawn, missed the worry and exhaustion that shadowed her face. Daidoji Daisuke perched on another log and Toku knelt in the grass, tending to the fire.

"Please forgive the meager nature of our camp, Kamoko," Toturi began, offering a seated bow. "We did not expect to be attended by those of a noble nature."

"Lord Toturi means that *he* did not expect it," Daisuke teased. "I, on the other hand, have no doubt that peasant and samurai would flock to his banner. If he would only do us the courtesy of raising one."

Toturi ignored the Crane while Toku passed around bowls of hot porridge. He tried not to dwell on the fact that the boy's hands were visibly dirty. Kamoko didn't seem to notice or care as she took her bowl with a small nod of thanks. "The Battle Maidens travel light, my lord," she replied. "I see nothing untoward in your camp, or your followers."

It was a polite fiction, and they all knew it, but so long as everyone agreed to accept it, it was indistinguishable from the truth. "You spoke of a matter of some urgency, Kamoko," he said, "and you have been more than patient as we have tried to put our best foot forward. Please" – he nodded at the bowl in her hand – "eat, but as you can, tell us why you have sought us out. And please, there is no need for titles. I am no longer Lord Toturi. Now, I am only Toturi, the rōnin."

Kamoko bent to her food, and some of her exhaustion seemed to fade with each bite. Around mouthfuls, she told her tale. "Like you, my lord," she said, ignoring his admonition against the title, "I set out on a pilgrimage to find the princes. I do not think the Empire can heal until the line of Hantei is restored to the throne."

Toturi nodded at that, some part of him rejoicing that his search for the princes, and the reasons to find them, was shared by another like-minded warrior. "But in these recent months, something has changed," Kamoko went on. "The Lion – and forgive me, my lord, for I know they are your clan and kinsmen – are moving aggressively, and not just against the Crane."

"There is little new in that," Toturi sighed. His clan held glory in battle as one of their highest tenets, sometimes to their detriment. If the Lion had no battle before them, they would, at times, go out of their way to create one. As Clan Champion, Toturi had been working to guide them away from that practice, though it had not been easy. There were few things more difficult to change than entrenched tradition, and challenging those traditions, no matter his official position, had been met with tacit resistance.

Kamoko shook her head, sending her dark locks swaying. "It is different this time, Lord Toturi," she said. "The Lion are known for their drive to battle, but it is not fortresses or border stations or even garrisoned towns that have drawn their eye. Their efforts seem focused on small Crane villages, places that have no ashigaru, no samurai, not even a militia that can be mustered."

She sighed and set aside her not-yet-empty bowl. "I have seen the aftermath of these raids firsthand," the Battle Maiden said quietly, her lips twisting with distaste. "They commandeer the food stores and then raze the village. They set fire to the fields, and any villager that objects too harshly is slain. The survivors are turned out with nothing, and driven from their lands." She raised her eyes, grief and horror shining like tears in her gaze. "I passed some of those survivors on this very road, my lord, or rather, I passed their corpses. Dead from sickness and starvation as they tried to make their way to a sympathetic town willing to take them in." She shook her head. "The Lion did them no mercy by sparing their lives."

"This is happening to the Crane?" Daisuke demanded. And Toturi heard a note in the man's voice that he hadn't heard before, a burning anger that undercut his normally mocking tone.

"Yours and others," the Unicorn replied. "Bands of Lion move up and down the river between the City of the Rich Frog and Toshi Ranbo. They have hidden their mon and lacquered their armor black like rōnin or bandits, but there is no mistaking them. They have raided Crane villages the most, but also those of the Unicorn and even the Dragon."

"Why?" Toku asked, and blinked as the three other gazes turned to him. Clearly, he hadn't expected to be heard. "Forgive me, lord samurai," he added with a hasty bow. "But I don't understand. Why would samurai need to burn villages and drive out the people? We are not warriors. Why attack those who cannot defend themselves?"

"It makes the regent look weak," Toturi said, voice flat. He didn't want to believe it, even of Matsu Tsuko. His late brother's widow was impetuous, hot-tempered even, but she was never cruel. She saw the Crane – and Doji Hotaru – as her personal enemy, but he would not have thought her capable of unleashing this type of chaos on innocent villages. Apparently, he was wrong.

"The Lion-Crane war is still fresh in everyone's mind," Toturi continued. "And to Matsu Tsuko, to most of the Lion, the Crane have risen too far, too fast in the wake of Hantei's death. By showing that Kakita Yoshi cannot keep the peace in Rokugan, she wears away at the foundation of his authority. Those villages are simply a statement for her, a necessary price to pay for checking the power of the Crane."

Toku looked sickened by the thought, and, looking at the boy's face, Toturi couldn't help but feel a wave of guilt wash over him. Guilt, because the thought of making war on the people of a rival clan as a way of exercising political power… was all too common for him to feel remorse. War was a tool in the kit of any daimyō, and the peasants were the ones often caught in the crossfire. He found the idea unpleasant, distasteful even, but it did not sicken him.

And that realization sat like a cold lump of grease in his gut.

"Well, that's certainly terrible," Daisuke said, idly brushing at an imaginary speck of dirt fouling his kimono. His voice had regained the lilting, mocking tone that Toturi was beginning to believe was an affectation, but the Crane's eyes still held a smoldering anger. Still, he smiled a courtier's perfect smile at the Unicorn. "And I do very much appreciate your passion in defense of the Crane, Kamoko. But why did it drive you to ride through the night seeking out our reluctant leader? Surely, this is news that could have waited long enough for you to travel in the daylight."

Kamoko leaned forward, her eyes taking on an intensity of their own. "Because, Daisuke, I know where they're going to strike next." She glanced at the camp, at the score of poorly armed peasants and the makeshift shelters before her eyes returned to Toturi.

"The Village of the Golden Blades lies not three days from here. Forces from Matsu Agetoki's" – she said the name through gritted teeth – "army march to burn it. A small detachment only, led by one of his lieutenants. I heard from a passing farmer that you were on the march, and that you were raising an army, to fight for the good of all Rokugan." She swept another glance over the camp. "I admit, this isn't exactly what I was expecting."

"I am not raising an army," Toturi replied, trying to keep the note of weariness from his voice. He glared at Daisuke and Toku. "And I'm not sure why or how such a rumor is spreading." It seemed like Daisuke, Toku, and now even Kamoko, were bound and determined to force him from his chosen path. "I seek to find the princes and restore the line of Hantei, nothing more."

"A noble goal," Kamoko acknowledged. "And one I support as well." He heard the emotion in her voice, the passion, but also anger as she continued. "But what empire will we restore the princes to? One that knows peace, or one that has dissolved into an unending series of clan wars? If the Lion reignite hostilities with the Crane, it will not be long before other clans seek to resolve their grievances through battle, and war will spread across all the lands. Finding Sotorii and Daisetsu will do little good if there is no empire left for them to preserve."

Toturi considered her words. Kamoko wanted to fight for what she perceived as the greater good: peace and stability for the Empire. It was a noble goal, but when Toturi looked at Toku, he saw nothing of noble desires. In the boy's face he saw only horror as he learned of the realities of Rokugani politics, of the suffering that could be inflicted, almost casually, on those who had no real stake in the conflict.

Just as the boy's village had been under the heel of bandits, the Crane village would suffer simply for being an easy target. The Village of the Golden Blades would be destroyed; the generals would admire the military tactics employed and the courtiers would measure the shift of power. But what about the people? It was the duty of Doji Hotaru and her local daimyō to protect their towns. But what about the duty of one person to another?

Kamoko was right about the political situation, but much to his surprise, Toturi found that the politics didn't move him. It was the look on Toku's face: a slow realization of what war and politics really meant for people like him, that did. It may have been the Crane's duty to protect their villages from the ravages of war, but that did not mean that it wasn't his responsibility. He wasn't sure what he and his not-quite two dozen followers could do. All he knew was that he had to try.

"Toku," he said. "Tell the others that it is time to break camp. I want to leave within the hour. We march for the Village of the Golden Blades."

# 11
# Hotaru

Matsu Tsuko scowled across the table, making no effort to maintain the carefully controlled mask of polite society. Hotaru, in her turn, wore a small smile, the barest curving of the lips, just enough to be noticed by a careful observer. It was a polite smile, though it was neither kind nor welcoming, and Hotaru did not let it touch her eyes.

She couldn't afford for the woman across from her to see it as a sign of weakness.

This meeting had not come about by accident. It had taken Hotaru the better part of a week to arrange it, and even that would not have been possible without leaning on some of the ambassadors from the other clans. The Lion were not inclined to speak directly with her Crane diplomats. There had been no formal declaration of war – yet – but whenever her people tried to engage the Lion in conversation, some pressing matter always seemed to materialize. Only by using the Unicorn and Dragon ambassadors as go-betweens had Hotaru's own diplomats been able to gain any traction at all. Still, their efforts had borne fruit, and now Hotaru found herself face to face with the woman who, more than anyone else in the Empire, wanted her dead.

They were in one of the palace gardens, surrounded by the beauty of the late spring growth. Tatami mats had been spread over the manicured grasses and a low table placed atop them. Hotaru knelt upon a silk cushion, while Matsu Tsuko sat in seiza directly upon the mats. A pot of tea steamed between them, with a porcelain cup set before each. A servant, borrowed from a minor Seppun samurai, had filled their cups and knelt attentively by, though neither Hotaru nor Matsu Tsuko had touched the steaming brew.

They were not alone in the gardens. Each had a dozen retainers arrayed in a pair of neat ranks behind them. That had been the agreed upon number, and while no provision had been made as to the makeup of the retainers, Hotaru noted that almost all of those arrayed behind the Lion wore the daishō of a warrior. At least none of them wore armor; such a thing was too much a breach of courtesy, even for the Lion.

There was, however, one in their ranks that was not a warrior, nor even a Lion. Chukan Hanako stood in the center of the front rank of the Lion's line, directly behind Matsu Tsuko, her demure and innocent face downcast as she waited, still and silent as any of the statues that decorated the gardens.

For her part, Hotaru had called mostly upon her ambassadors and diplomats, though at least two of those diplomats had trained with her at the Kakita school and were deadly duelists in their own right. Four guards from the Daidoji Iron Warrior School flanked the courtiers. Hotaru had faith in her people, and in her own abilities at the negotiating table, but if something were to go terribly wrong, it would be Matsu Tsuko and eleven warriors against Hotaru, four warriors, and a pair of duelists.

It would be best if nothing went terribly wrong.

"You have my thanks for agreeing to this meeting, Lady Tsuko," Hotaru said, breaking the silence that had stretched between them as they both sat at the table, allowing a moment for their retainers to get situated.

"It is a formality," Tsuko replied. "Nothing more."

Hotaru tilted her head in perceived confusion. "I do not understand. I had hoped we could discuss the troubles between our clans and come to some resolution other than war. There has been enough death on both sides, wouldn't you agree?"

"I would not," the woman across from her replied. It was said so casually, Hotaru had to keep her shock from spilling over her face. The Lion leaned forward, placing her hands on the table and leaning close to Hotaru. "But if you wish to discuss terms to keep the Lion from grinding your clan into dust, then so be it. Withdraw your forces from Toshi Ranbo. Return the city and its surrounding demesnes to the Lion. Return to your lands in the south. Do that, Crane, and we will stop the bloodshed. That, and nothing less."

Matsu Tsuko used her words like clubs, offering three separate insults in as many sentences. She wished for more Crane to die. She believed her clan could grind the Crane to dust, as if it would be such a simple task. And she continued to push the lie that Toshi Ranbo was rightfully the domain of the Lion, despite the Crane's indisputable claim to the city. Hotaru could feel her warriors stiffening behind her as the barely veiled insults landed, though her ambassadors managed to control their reactions. It took all of her years of careful training for Hotaru to maintain the precise smile.

Those words had been no accident, but rather, careful calculation. To offer them here, in this place, when the purpose of the meeting was to sue for peace, was justification enough for Hotaru to challenge Matsu Tsuko to a duel on the spot. Such duels had to be signed off on by the office of the Emperor, but with Yoshi as Regent and Toshimoko as Emerald Champion, that was a mere formality. She could challenge the woman and resolve their personal enmity on the fields of honor.

Which, she realized, was exactly what Matsu Tsuko wanted. The Lion was trying to maneuver Hotaru into a position where the current prevalence of the Crane in the Imperial Court might be viewed as favoritism, continuing to undermine the Regent's rule and drive a further wedge between the clans. And casting the Lion as the ones standing up for righteousness and tradition.

It was the twisting plan of a Scorpion, and not what she would have expected of Matsu Tsuko. Her eyes flickered for an instant to Chukan Hanako, who still stood with eyes downcast. Was there a slight smile on the Phoenix's face? Kachiko had warned her that the woman was far more dangerous than she appeared, and Hotaru was beginning to suspect that the Scorpion might have even underestimated the danger. Did she truly have enough influence over the Lion to convince Tsuko to set such a trap?

Still, if Hotaru's own death or Tsuko's would have any impact on the looming conflict, she may have taken the bait. The Lion Champion was a fierce warrior, but Hotaru was not a green samurai who had barely drawn steel. It would not be an easy fight, but it was a fight that she was confident she could win.

*And then you will have slain the past* two *Champions of the Lion Clan*. Hotaru furtively grit her teeth in frustration. She could think of nothing more likely to guarantee war to the bitter end between their clans. Her own death would have much the same result, with her clan swearing their own vengeance upon the clan of her killer. It truly was a trap worthy of Kachiko herself.

Her eyes flashed once more to Hanako. The Phoenix were pacifists, more interested in studying the secrets of the elemental spirits than they were in worldly pursuits. Who, then, was this woman, scarcely out of girlhood, who had a warrior like Matsu Tsuko dancing to her tune?

"An interesting proposition, Lady Tsuko," Hotaru said at last, after allowing the silence to stretch on perhaps a bit too long. "It has the advantage of simplicity, at least." She widened her smile briefly. "Unfortunately, I do not think the withdrawal of the Crane from *our* northern holdings will be possible."

Tsuko's eyes darkened, and Hotaru's heart sank. These negotiations would go nowhere. She knew that now, given Tsuko's opening gambit. But she had to try. She could not give Tsuko what she wanted, but perhaps the woman would meet her halfway. Her people needed peace, and she was willing to give up much to ensure that they found it. "We may, however, be able to come to some kind of agreement with regard to Toshi Ranbo. We will not renounce our claim to the stronghold or its lands, but I acknowledge that it has changed hands many times over the course of history. Perhaps we could come to some accommodation; a shared stewardship reminiscent of that in the City of the Rich Frog."

This time it was her own courtiers at her back that stirred. She hadn't discussed this possibility with them because she had known exactly what their response would be. The City of the Rich Frog sat at a juncture where the territories of three major clans met, and was considered one of the most vital river ports in all the Empire. Because of its location, and its economic significance, its dominion was not given to any one clan, but rather divided between the Lion, Unicorn, and Dragon, and administered by an Imperial governor.

Toshi Ranbo had no such economic significance, but just as she might leverage the current position of the Crane at the Imperial Court to sanction a duel between her and Matsu Tsuko, Hotaru could leverage that same influence to come to some sort of compromise regarding the city.

Giving up all control of Toshi Ranbo was unthinkable. The city had been at the heart of conflict between the Crane and Lion for far too long. It would not – quite – be admitting the superiority of the

Lion, but it would come close enough that Hotaru's status as Clan Champion would be called into question. Even the shared stewardship she was offering could cause her significant political fallout if Matsu Tsuko accepted her offer. In fact, it may well result in her being ousted from her position and sent back to the family lands in shame.

But it would also mean that thousands of Crane, peasants and samurai alike, would live untroubled by the touch of war. It was not only a sacrifice she was willing to make; she could not see how anyone, given the option, could make any other choice.

The scowl had left Matsu Tsuko's face, and her expression had become unreadable. Hotaru made careful note of that fact. She had thought the Lion firebrand incapable of donning the emotionless mask that all samurai were expected to wear, but now it seemed that her scowls and outbursts were as much a part of the woman's strategies as any tactics she applied on the fields of war. One thing was clear: the Lion had no more expected her offer than her own kinsmen had. For one long, hopeful moment, Hotaru thought that Tsuko might accept her offer and that her people, both their peoples, might know peace once more.

And then Chukan Hanako lifted her downward gaze.

Her eyes met Hotaru's and the Crane felt a shiver race down her spine. The innocence and naivety that she had first witnessed in the young Phoenix woman was nowhere to be seen in those eyes. They were cold, empty pools, like the void of a moonless sky. Her face was unreadable, but those eyes caused a thin sheet of sweat to break out beneath Hotaru's kimono.

Then they blinked, and returned to that doe-eyed innocence. "Lady Tsuko," Chukan Hanako said. Her voice was light, demure, and yet somehow insistent. When she spoke, all eyes shifted to her, and a faint blush suffused her alabaster skin, as if she were embarrassed by the attention.

But Hotaru would not – could not – forget the threat that she had seen boiling just beneath the surface of the woman, nor the shiver of fear it had sent through her. No one had made her feel that way before; she had felt fear on the fields of war and again in the dueling arena. In both places, she had risked everything, never certain if she would return whole – or at all. And that had unsettled her far less than that momentary glance from Chukan Hanako.

"Such an offer, while magnanimous," the woman was saying, "is best considered carefully and not accepted – or rejected – in haste." She offered a low bow, bending nearly double as she spoke, the silk of her flame-and-flower themed kimono flowing over the curves of her body like water. The motion was liquid grace and Hotaru could sense that more than one eye was now looking hungrily upon the young woman. She wanted to shake her head, to physically force the conflicting thoughts and emotions from it. What power did this Hanako have that she could manipulate those around her so easily, that she could shift from exuding innocence to fear to that terrible corruptibility?

"Yes," Matsu Tsuko said. She spoke slowly, the single word almost slurred. "Yes, you are correct, Hanako." The Lion stood and went so far as to offer Hotaru the slightest of bows. Her face was still unreadable as she said, "You have given me something to consider, Lady Hotaru. I was not expecting your offer. We will speak again." With that, the Lion turned on her heel and strode from the garden, her soldiers falling in line behind her.

Chukan Hanako waited for the soldiers to file out, falling in at the end of the line. As she glided from the garden she threw a glance over her shoulder, and Hotaru met her eyes once more.

They glittered like obsidian, and the smile that passed across the woman's face chilled her to her bones.

Hotaru sighed as the servants began the process of removing her formal robes. Her day had started with preparations for the meeting with Matsu Tsuko, and, despite the unnerving intervention of Chukan Hanako, those negotiations had gone better than she had anticipated. She at least had some hope that she might yet come to peaceful terms with the Lion, as unlikely as that seemed. But she was not at court often and there had been many more obligations to attend, including meeting with the Dowager Empress, wife of the late Hantei.

The empress had been a Doji before marrying into the Imperial family, and the obligations of family and clan ran deep. Hotaru had tried to keep that conversation light, telling of the gossip of the Crane courts and the intricate alliances and betrayals that made sure there was never a dull day in the Esteemed Palaces of the Crane.

The empress had been a companionable hostess, but Hotaru could tell that the woman not only still grieved over the loss of her husband, but worried for her sons, of whom no word had come since the fateful night of Shoju's betrayal. Hotaru knew that samurai from all the clans had taken to wandering the Empire in search of the missing princes. At times, she wished she could join them; how wonderful would it be to leave behind the burdens of Clan Champion in exchange for the clear purpose of finding the princes? But her first duty was to her people.

The servants finished removing her formal kimono. She waved them away, dismissing them as she stepped into her closet and donned the simple jinbei – the short trousers and tunic in a light breathable cotton – that she preferred to wear in the evenings. As the servants slid the door shut, she walked once more to the window overlooking the gardens. Lady Sun had retreated behind the western horizon more than an hour ago, and the palace servants had lit the lanterns that dotted the garden paths. She could see people, some alone, some in pairs, some in small groups, walking those paths. She knew that some did so in meditation, others in pursuit of romance, and others played at the never-ending game of imperial politics. The picturesque vignette outside her window held countless tales, and more than one were plans to bring down her or her clan.

Hotaru sighed as she gazed down at them. She was tired, and the weight of her station pressed down on her. Was she wasting her time attempting to bring Matsu Tsuko and the Lion to the peace table? She was a warrior at heart; her uncle Toshimoko had trained her to be one of the deadliest blades in the Empire. Her father, for all his faults, had instilled in her the skills of not just a warrior, but a leader, a general. It would be so much easier to find Matsu Tsuko, challenge her to a duel, and once the Lion woman was dead, to rally her forces to war. The Lion's armies outnumbered her own, but warfare was not the simple equation that most Lion thought it was. The Empire would not – could not – allow a state of war to exist for long, and she had little doubt that, when that time came, her own courtiers could secure an armistice that favored the Crane.

It would be so much easier. But it would also come with so much bloodshed. So many deaths.

Hotaru was tired of it.

It seemed there was no problem facing the Empire that didn't eventually result in bloodshed. Most often, it was blood shed by those not even directly responsible. The butcher's bill settled most heavily on the peasants and ashigaru, paying the price for the games that the samurai played. It had been the way of the clans, the way of the Empire, since the Founding, but Hotaru could not make herself believe that that made it right.

So, she strove for a peace that she didn't believe she could obtain, and she worried that her own people would see her as all the weaker for it. Her mind worried at the thought, recounting the meeting with Tsuko yet again, as she stared into the gardens below.

"Hotaru! Down!"

The voice came from behind, and Hotaru reacted without thinking, dropping to the ground. As she did so, she felt a flash of fire along her cheek and heard the *thunk* of an arrow slamming into the wall of her room.

Shock flared, even as her body had moved on instinct. The reaction had been drilled into her by her father and Toshimoko, both of whom understood that assassinations, no matter how frowned upon as a political tool, remained a real threat to anyone in power. But here, in the Imperial Palace? The idea was unthinkable… or had been, until the Emperor himself had been murdered within these very walls. Hotaru hit the ground and rolled, taking cover in case more arrows came at her. It was only then that she realized she recognized the voice that had shouted the command.

Kachiko?

"Get up! They're coming. Make yourself ready."

Kachiko slid into her bedchamber like a shadow. The woman still wore her clinging silk kimono and butterfly mask. Her makeup was applied with skill and precision, accentuating her features and adding a calculated allure. She still moved with the grace of a dancer.

But she held a blade in each hand, short, slightly curved daggers that were neither kitchen knife nor tanto, but something else. The blades did not glimmer in the moonlight, as if their metal had been darkened with soot. She glided into the room, moving along the wall and sliding the door shut behind her.

"Who?" Hotaru asked, the initial shock fading. She had questions, so many questions, but that was the chief among them. She didn't wait for an answer as she moved to the corner of the room where her naginata rested next to her sword stand. Given the confines of the room, she ignored the spear in favor of her katana, grabbing the sheathed weapon from its place on the stand.

"Assassins," Kachiko said shortly. She had prowled around the room and, at some point, had snatched up a blanket. With a few deft motions, she managed to drape it over the window, dropping the room into deeper darkness, but making it so that whatever archer lurked outside would have to fire blind into the room.

It also prevented any witnesses from seeing what might occur, and for a fleeting moment, Hotaru couldn't help but wonder at the timeliness of Kachiko's arrival. But if the woman wanted her dead, all she would have had to do was… nothing. The arrow could easily have claimed Hotaru's life.

"How many?" Hotaru asked, moving away from the wall as no more arrows came through the now-shrouded window. Her door had been unguarded. To station soldiers outside of her chamber would have been a grave insult to the Emperor – or the regent – implying that her safety could not be assured by their rule alone. She had a small contingent of warriors, but their chambers were some distance away. Far enough that they were unlikely to hear the din of battle… or the screams of the dying.

"I don't know." Kachiko didn't look at her as she spoke, her gaze focused on the door to the room. "But they will be here soon. I learned of the attempt only a few moments ago, and the one who warned me is dead. It might be that the archer is the only one we must face, but I don't think so. Others will be coming to finish the task."

There was an intensity to the woman that Hotaru had never seen before. She had always been focused, always graceful. When it came to matters of court, she had also always been deadly. But this was a different Kachiko, another face to the woman Hotaru thought she knew. Kachiko held her twin blades with obvious competence and surveyed the room with a tactician's eye. Was this, then, the woman's true face? Not just the spymaster, but a capable agent in her own right?

Hotaru had received training in the blade, in warfare, and in diplomacy. As a favored daughter of the clan, much had been expected of her, but much given to her as well. What training had Kachiko received, she wondered? Rumors of the Scorpion dabbling in forbidden arts had long persisted, but Hotaru had not given them much thought. Now, as she watched Kachiko, standing there alert but relaxed, she could not help but wonder.

She did not have much time to dwell on it, for as soon as it crossed her mind, Hotaru heard the soft footfalls outside her door. She stood calmly, sheathed blade held in her left hand, her right resting across her stomach, fingers a few bare inches from the hilt of the katana. Kachiko moved to her side, then drifted a half step behind her, giving Hotaru room to wield her longer blade.

The door burst open, and masked assassins poured into the room.

They wore dark clothing with close-fitting hoods and veils wrapped around their faces, leaving only their eyes visible. Even the little exposed flesh around their eye sockets had been darkened, and their weapons, like Kachiko's, did not glint or reflect the faint light that filtered in from the lantern-lit halls. They carried a variety of weapons: straight-edged swords longer than a wakizashi but shorter than a katana, club-like tonfa, curving kama, and more. Hotaru had no idea how many there were, but they flowed into her room like a river.

She took in their appearance in an instant, but she was already moving as her mind registered the details. She took two steps forward, planting herself not directly in the doorway, but far enough from it that she could use her katana to full effect. She saw the slight widening of the invader's eyes as he burst through the door to find her, sheathed sword still held at her side, waiting for his arrival. Those eyes narrowed and he extended his blade, lunging forward, the chisel-like point aimed straight at her heart.

It never got close to her.

With the speed and grace that was the hallmark of the Kakita duelists, she drew her katana, striking in an upward arc with the same motion. Years of relentless practice allowed her to time the strike perfectly, and the edge of her sword found purchase in her opponent's flesh, catching him just above the clavicle and slicing upward across his neck. His sword fell from suddenly limp fingers, and his hands moved to the gaping wound that opened, trying to stem the flow of blood as he crumpled to the ground.

But the others were already charging into the room behind him.

Hotaru breathed slowly, eyes watching the assailants as they began to spread out before her, wary now that they faced a fully armed and ready opponent. She was aware of Kachiko, still standing slightly behind her, keeping out of the way of Hotaru's longer blades, but with her own knives at the ready. Hotaru offered a silent prayer to the Fortunes that the Scorpion truly was able to defend herself, because she doubted that she would be able to defeat her would-be assassins if she had to worry about keeping Kachiko safe.

As if in answer to the thought, something whirred past the edges of her vision and she heard a meaty *thunk*. One of the attackers made a choking, gasping sound and fell back, hands reaching for the hilt that had blossomed, flower-like, in the hollow of his throat. She spared a quick glance at Kachiko in time to see the woman draw another knife from somewhere on her person, her face as expressionless as stone. Then the black-clad assassins surged forward.

Her mind registered their numbers even as her body moved with responses so ingrained that they had become reflex. Nine attackers had made it into the room. The archer, presumably still out there somewhere, made ten. She had killed the first to step into her chamber, and Kachiko had killed another with her thrown blade. Seven assailants surged toward them. Her chambers were large, but not large enough for nine people to engage in a pitched battle. But that was a problem for her attackers, not for Hotaru.

She moved with speed and grace, always in perfect balance, giving small amounts of ground as she worked to keep her attackers before her. Kachiko's presence on her left let Hotaru put most of her focus on those to her right, within the easiest reach of her blade. The confines of the room only allowed three of them to attack at once, and Hotaru used their numbers against them, letting them crowd each other.

As they pushed forward, she swept her sheath up to intercept a heavy swing from a tonfa while pivoting away from the thrust of a straight-bladed sword. The third attacker wielded a pair of kama, the farming scythes turned weapons blurring down at her as he swept them forward. She twisted back, narrowly avoiding the tip of one of the arcing sickle-like blades as her katana thrust upward. The man fell, and as he did, Hotaru saw Kachiko dart in, eyes dispassionate as she knifed the tonfa wielder in the back even as the man spun toward Hotaru. He, too, fell. In the split second before the other attackers could push forward, Hotaru struck again, three quick cuts that battered through the swordsman's guard and ended with another body on her bedchamber floor.

Perhaps ten seconds had passed since the would-be assassins had invaded her room and five now lay dead, their blood soaking into the tatami.

The four remaining cast nervous glances at the pair of women and at the bodies of their fallen companions. They did not run; she hadn't expected them to. She did not know who had sent them, but however cowardly their methods were, they would not leave the task undone, even if it meant their lives were forfeited. Hotaru found a smile coming to her face. She tossed her blade's sheath to the futon and took up her katana in a two-handed grip, shifting her feet once more as she pointed the tip of the sword at the heart of the nearest assassin. "Come, then," she said. "Let us finish this before we're interrupted by the palace guards. I would hate to bother them with so trivial a concern."

It was a calculated insult, dismissing the attack as a minor inconvenience, underscored by the bodies that now served almost as a bulwark against the other attackers. Had all four moved in concert, supporting one another, she and Kachiko might have found themselves overwhelmed. She was confident in her skill, and Kachiko had proven herself deadly as well, but battle could be swayed by numbers as readily as by skill.

And these opponents were not *unskilled*, so much as they had been unprepared for the swiftness and lethality of the response. Now, knowing what they were facing, had they proceeded with care and caution, they could have made a fight of it.

Instead, one of them allowed himself to be incensed by her words and charged forward, a step ahead of his fellows. They charged after, following their misguided leader and sealing their fates. As the first man leaped over the bodies of his fellows, Hotaru's blade flicked out. She swept his own sword aside with contemptuous ease, and a twist of her wrists sent it darting back again, taking the man's throat. Kachiko had left her side at the charge and cut off one of the attackers whose stature suggested she was a woman, though Hotaru could not be sure. The assassin wielded a chain weighted at both ends with metal balls.

Hotaru had only a moment before the next attacker was upon her, but in that moment, she saw Kachiko slip to the side as one of the weights flew past her face, crashing into the wall. Before the assassin could recover, Kachiko's leg flashed across her body like a crescent moon. Her foot crashed into the collarbone of the assailant who let out a muffled cry as her chain clattered to the floor. Kachiko's knives made short work of the enemy after that.

The last two assassins closed in, and Hotaru could see acceptance in their eyes. They knew they were about to die, and by the set of their shoulders and the determination in their stride as they stalked forward, they would do whatever they could to take her with them into the halls of the dead.

She raised her blade in salute, acknowledging that only one side would leave this conflict alive. One of the pair carried a broad, heavy looking sword that flared at the top, more suited for chopping through thick brush than battle, though she suspected it would part flesh with equal ease. The other carried a short, spear-like weapon, no more than two feet in length and tipped with a steel head. They moved toward her slowly, setting their feet carefully on the now uneven floor. Hotaru gave ground before them, stepping with equal care, drawing them deeper into the room. They would charge in a heartbeat, and she would be ready.

That heartbeat never came. Kachiko stepped behind the pair, driving her knives into the back of their necks with a cold savagery Hotaru had never seen of her. They dropped like marionettes with their strings cut, landing face first on the floor. The hilts of Kachiko's black knives still protruded from the base of their skulls.

Hotaru breathed deep as silence fell as abruptly as a stone. It was over; the assassins were dead, and they still breathed. She could feel her arms shaking as the adrenaline of battle faded, and gazed down at the dead men before her. "That was not a very fair strike, Kachiko."

The Scorpion tilted her head to one side. "Fair?" She sounded vaguely amused. "They tried to kill you with an arrow through your bedchamber window. And when that failed, they sent nine more assassins to your door. They do not deserve a fair fight." She looked down at the bodies, including the two that now had her knives lodged firmly in their spines, and her nose crinkled with disgust. "Could you retrieve those for me?"

Hotaru couldn't help it. She laughed. Perhaps it was the giddiness of surviving the attack, or the last remnants of adrenaline coursing through her system, but whatever the reason, the picture of Kachiko standing there, kimono splattered with the blood of the assassins, not wanting to make contact with the bodies of the men she had just killed, filled her with a sense of the ridiculous. That, and a strange pride, not in her own skill, but in that of the Scorpion.

"Well, I'm glad one of us finds this amusing." Kachiko raised a brow at Hotaru's laughter. Then she sighed. "The bodies will have to be dealt with. Give me a few moments and I'll have this… seen to. Unless you wish to bring it to the attention of the regent?"

The fight had been short, two or three minutes at most. But it had not been quiet. Neither she nor Kachiko had called for help, but the clash of steel on steel and the cries of the dying had been loud enough that they should have attracted attention, from the palace servants if no one else. The fact that they hadn't hinted at a broader conspiracy. She could not believe her uncle Yoshi involved in it; for all the man's foibles, he wanted two things: personal power and the ascendency of the Crane. The man had no love for her, niece or no, but killing her now, in this way, would serve little purpose. He could place the blame on the Lion, but a war between the Crane and Lion would make the regent appear weak and out of control of the Empire.

That might be enough reason for the *Lion* to attempt such an assassination, and that thought made Hotaru's blood run cold. Not because of the attempt on her life, but to think that a clan like the Lion – the paragons of duty in many ways – could fall so far.

Had Hantei's death been such a poison to the Empire that the clan of Akodo, the Founder of the Code, could have come to this? Did Matsu Tsuko's hatred and lust for vengeance run so deep that she would betray the most sacred tenets of her people? Hotaru didn't think so. Matsu Tsuko had seemed honestly interested in her offer of a shared administration of Toshi Ranbo. Or had that interest been feigned to drop her guard as preface for this attack?

"This was not the work of the Lion," Kachiko said, as if reading her mind. She had produced a linen cloth from somewhere and was carefully cleaning the blood from her fingers. Her eyes, now dark and mysterious pools, looked at the bodies, but Hotaru could see that Kachiko wasn't really seeing them. Her mind had already turned to the task of unraveling the intrigue before them, in all its tangled threads and layers. Hotaru offered silent thanks to her ancestors that the Scorpion was on her side.

"Had the Lion sent assassins, it would have been armored warriors," Kachiko went on, sounding thoughtful. "These are not samurai, but nor are they peasants. They are skilled, but not at infiltration. Their attack was sloppy; they got in each other's way when they should have been working in unison. It is obvious that they have not done this type of thing before."

Listening to Kachiko, Hotaru felt an odd tug of both admiration and unease. The way she spoke of the assassination attempt, with disdain and familiar expertise, was another reminder that Kachiko herself belonged to the shadows. The world of assassins and shadowy infiltrators was one she knew all too well.

"I suspect these were rōnin," Kachiko finished with a dismissive gesture. "Hired by someone with coin and a promise of redemption. For all the good it did them." She shrugged and glanced at Hotaru. "Whoever they were, you must decide how you want to handle it. I can have the bodies removed and your chambers cleaned so that no one will know what happened. The palace will hear that you were working a vigorous training session this evening, sparring multiple opponents to hone your skills." Her lips twisted in a faint smile. "Some will know the truth, of course, but in these halls, a truth unspoken is no different from rumor."

Hotaru thought about it. She did not have Kachiko's talent for deciphering the endless webs of the court, but she was no novice either. If the assassination attempt was revealed, she could see how it would play out. The Lion would bear the brunt of the suspicion, and any chance that Matsu Tsuko would accept a deal would perish. The second, and in some ways more troubling, path would be that the blame fell upon *Kachiko*. It did not matter that the Scorpion had almost certainly saved her life; it didn't matter that Kachiko was here, that her blades had claimed several lives of the would-be murderers. At the moment, the Scorpion were the court's pariahs, and even if they weren't, when the assassin's arrow or poisoner's cup found their mark, the fingers always pointed at the Scorpion.

She almost felt a sense of admiration for whomever had set this up. If they had been successful and Hotaru had died, war between the Lion and Crane would have been inevitable. If they failed, and Hotaru did anything other than keep silent, that same outcome was the most likely. It was a trap worthy of the Scorpion, and if she didn't know in the deepest recesses of her heart that Kachiko was uninvolved, she might've come to the same conclusion. Instead, as she looked at the blood-splattered woman, Hotaru felt a rising wave of emotion that brought moisture to her eyes. It had not been her guards, nor her uncles who had watched over her this night. It had been a woman that, by the traditions of her clan, she was supposed to distrust, if not despise. What she felt for Kachiko in that moment could not have been any further from those expectations.

"Summon your people."

# 12
# Yakamo

The bleakness of the Shadowlands stretched out before Yakamo and his party.

The land was blasted and barren, dry and cracked as if from drought, with rock formations breaking through the earth like broken bones jutting from a wound. The sky above was slate gray and featureless, as if a woolen blanket stretched from horizon to horizon. Lady Sun touched this land, but only from afar, and her glowing face never seemed to break through the gray to allow her warmth to bless the earth. The winds that blew shifted from chilling to blistering from one moment to the next, and both carried the charnel scent of death with them.

Yakamo hated this place.

They were scarcely a week's journey beyond the Great Carpenter Wall, and it already felt as if he were in another world, another realm of existence, perhaps walking through the hellscape of the Realm of Torment itself. It had taken two days to gather the scouts, sufficient provisions, and a small cache of jade before they set out. He felt the comforting weight of the blessed stones tucked into his obi, secure beneath his armor. The sacred stone helped to ward off the curse of this land. Already, nearly half of the jade they had brought had blackened and crumbled to dust, succumbing to the all-pervasive taint. Soon they would be faced with a decision: accept that there was nothing to find and turn back while they had enough jade to ward off the taint of the Shadowlands, or press on and hope that, once the last of the jade crumbled to dust, they had the spiritual fortitude to resist the dark temptations.

Ahead, Hiruma Momoe raised one arm, and their group came to a halt, squatting down to lessen their profile against the featureless sky. The woman was nearly twice Yakamo's own age, wed and with grown children of her own, but she was also one of the best scouts the Hiruma School had ever produced. She ranged a good fifty yards ahead of the party, moving swiftly and silently, their first line of defense against the countless dangers of the Shadowlands.

She seemed frozen in the distance, the grays and blues of her armor blending into the bleak terrain with surprising efficacy, to the point where Yakamo had to focus hard to keep his eyes from sliding off her. Her arm waved back and forth, twice, before going still again, indicating that the others were to make their way – carefully – to her.

"I'm so glad you volunteered me to go on this mission of yours, Yakamo," Bunzō whispered as they began low crawling across the intervening distance. "Where else could I find such blessings from Lady Sun and such truly incomparable views."

Given that Yakamo was at the front of their formation, with Bunzō crawling right behind him, he had no doubt the view in question was not a particularly pleasant one. "I thought they called you the Laughing Crab, Bunzō. Not the whining one," he grunted as he moved on elbows and knees across the harsh landscape. He winced each time his armor ground against the exposed rock, emitting a sound like a low, tortured scream.

The Shadowlands seemed to welcome the wail.

"I always have laughter in my heart," Bunzō replied loftily. "Even when I get dragged along on dangerous missions that I never asked to be a part of. Especially when one of the people on said mission – and I'm not mentioning any names, you understand – is a giant lout of a Hida who can't put his feet down without it sounding like a drum being banged before battle."

Yakamo snorted, trying to keep the sound quiet, or at least quieter than the scraping of his armor against the rocks. "I thought you were a Hiruma, Bunzō; a graduate of the esteemed scout school," he countered. "Every Hiruma scout I've met insists the Shadowlands are their own personal demesne, and that the horrors of this place are as nothing to them." Such were the boasts of the Hiruma School, but being here, Yakamo understood how hollow those words really were. Traveling through these blasted lands wore not just upon the body, but upon the spirit as well. He understood why the scouts made the boasts; the stoic Crab had a long tradition of making little of hardships. But no one who had been beyond the Wall could deny the impact of it. "What do the Hiruma claim, again?" Yakamo went on. "You were born for this."

"No one was born for this," Bunzō muttered, as they continued their long, arduous crawl. The other pair of scouts that rounded out their party, both also graduates of the Hiruma School, moved in silence behind them, and Yakamo could not understand how they managed to keep their own armor from scraping against the rocks. "But *some* of us could benefit from lessons in crossing enemy terrain."

The banter continued for another minute or two, until they were close enough to Momoe's position that even their whispered conversation might put the group at risk. They crept the last dozen yards in silence. Hiruma Momoe was lying prone at, what from Yakamo's perspective, was the barest rise in the land. However, the topography of the Shadowlands was deceptive; the bleak and wasted plain rose and fell more than one would guess at a casual glance. He made his way to the older scout's side and stared in horror at what he saw laid out before him.

Beyond Momoe's position, the broken earth of the Shadowlands sloped away. It wasn't a drastic slope, but a long gradual slide stretching hundreds of yards. By the time the plain flattened again, the difference in elevation had to be close to fifty feet, creating a broad basin.

It was a basin large enough to conceal an army. Which spread to either side like a pool of ink at the bottom of a bowl.

"Ancestors protect us," Yakamo whispered as he gazed down into the hollow. The Shadowlands force that had withdrawn from the Wall had numbered in the tens of thousands. This massive force was easily ten times that.

The camp stretched beyond his line of sight to the east and the west, a surging sea of Shadowlands horrors. He couldn't tell if it encompassed the army that had broken its teeth against the Wall, but that didn't matter. There was only one reason for such a force to be gathered so close to the border: an attack on the Great Carpenter Wall on a scale that had not been seen in a dozen generations. A stab of fear shot through him at the thought and a cold sweat burst from his pores. How could the Crab stand against such a force?

He glanced to either side, to see Bunzō, Momoe, and the other two Hiruma studying the army with trained eyes, their faces pale and grim. The seasoned scouts would no doubt come up with more accurate estimations of the enemy numbers than he would; that was their job, after all. Still, he turned his attention back to the seething mass, scanning for anything that would be of tactical significance to their defense. Fortunes knew the Wall would need all the information it could get.

The bulk of the forces he could make out were the omnipresent goblins, but there were worse things among them. He saw full troops of the boar-like creatures sometimes used as cavalry mounts by the Lost, those samurai who had fallen to the dark temptations of the Shadowlands and abandoned the Empire to serve the forces of Fu Leng. As far as he knew, the creatures didn't have a name; most among the Crab simply called them hellbeasts. Mingled among the goblins were packs of slimy-skinned marsh trolls and dozens upon dozens of ogres, towering above their lesser kin. He shuddered as he saw the undead, standing motionless in their ranks. They were too far away to see anything beyond the unnatural stillness of their formations, but their numbers made Yakamo's blood run cold.

But even the reanimated dead were not the worst of it. Even at this distance, Yakamo could see the oni. No two of the Jigoku-damned demons were the same, and they varied in size from scarcely larger than a man to towering over the tallest ogre. Some were monsters woven of nightmare, like the centipede creature that curled in a tight ball, its blood-red carapace seeming almost to glow. Based on the massive size of the ball, Yakamo suspected that when the monster unfurled to its full length, it would be over forty feet long.

Oni had no place in the mortal realm. Most of the time they had to be called forth from the Realm of Torment and bound to the will of a blood sorcerer. But once summoned, powerful oni lords could, in turn, call forth more demons from the pits. There had to be at least one, and more likely several, oni lords mixed in with the army spread before them.

Yakamo's stomach twisted, fear and anger like sour bile in his gut. There was enough strength gathered in that basin to tear a rend in the Wall and flood the lands beyond with Shadowlands spawn. Even if they made it back to report on the horde, what could his father do?

The Crab might – *might* – be able to stop this army, but doing so would require stripping every other tower and bastion on the

Wall, leaving the Empire defenseless against whatever might slip through the cracks. He could see an empire overrun with the Shadowlands filth, pouring from the breaches, skittering into Rokugan like so many cockroaches when the lanterns were lit. Those that slipped through would be small in number, much smaller than the force gathered in the basin, but with the forces of the Crab fully engaged against this army, who would stand against them?

The lands of the Crab would be laid bare. The peasants that farmed the fields and the merchants that turned the wheels of commerce were the ones that kept the warriors fed, providing the resources enough to maintain the Wall and their own equipment. If monsters from the Shadowlands attacked their villages and killed the people, the Crab would be finished. And if the Crab fell, the Wall fell. The Empire would soon follow.

There was no solution, no answer that might save them all. Staring into that basin filled with creatures from his deepest nightmares, Yakamo felt something within him… shift. He had been certain all his life of the superiority of the Crab. They were the strongest in the Empire; they were the defenders and protectors of their lesser cousins, who were too cowardly or too concerned with the meaningless intrigues of court to understand the true duty of a warrior. They were the ones who put the well-being of the Empire above their own personal desires. They were mocked for it, called brutes and barbarians by those who failed to see that it was those brutes and barbarians who kept the demons from kicking down their doors. This mockery, too, they bore with grace.

But in that basin, Yakamo saw the end of the Crab. And he doubted any of the other clans would rally to their cause, too blind to realize that it was the Crab, not the court, not the Emperor, not the diplomacy of the Crane or the machinations of the Scorpion or the armies of the Lion, but the Crab, standing resolute, that kept the Empire together.

Yakamo gazed into that basin and felt despair unlike any he had known before.

"Yakamo." It was Bunzō, his voice low and urgent. Yakamo realized that Bunzō had been saying his name for several moments. When he looked into the Laughing Crab's eyes, he saw the same realization, the same fear, reflected in them.

"We must go," he said. "We have the counts and disposition. We must make for the Wall with all haste."

"Yes," Yakamo agreed, his mind still fuzzy. "Yes." He shook his head, trying to break free of the despair that threatened to paralyze him. They had to move. His father had to know what was coming. For what little good it might do them. They set action to the words, crawling back from the basin's lip.

They moved a score of feet before Hiruma Momoe pushed herself to her feet. She did not stand to her full height but moved to something closer to a low crouch. "We focus on speed, now," she said to the others, who nodded in understanding. Even Yakamo, who towered over the woman and was the son of her daimyō, deferred to her in this. The woman had more successful forays into these lands than any other, and if she said that speed was what would see them safe, Yakamo was not about to argue.

They set out in an awkward shamble for another hundred yards, keeping their bodies as close to the ground as they could while still keeping their feet under them. Then, when Momoe judged the distance between them and the army at their backs sufficient, she rose to her full height, barely coming to Yakamo's shoulder, and they all lengthened their stride.

They traveled in a loping jog that covered distance but conserved energy. The scouts wore the lighter ashigaru armor where Yakamo had opted for the lacquered armor that, while lighter than the plate he wore atop the Wall, still afforded him better protection than the ashigaru kit. That protection came at the price of weight and decreased mobility, and Yakamo soon found himself sweating and panting as he strived to match the scouts' pace. Bunzō threw a glance over his shoulder, looking worriedly at him.

"Go!" he ordered between panting gasps of breath. He wanted to tell the man that they had to get the information to the Wall and that they had too many miles to go to worry about the possibility of Yakamo lagging behind. To leave him and carry word to his father if they must. But he didn't have the breath, so he just waved an arm, ducked his head, and focused on not catching his booted feet on the uneven terrain. He just had to keep placing one foot in front of the other and trust the scouts to lead him home.

It had taken them nearly a week to discover this army, but that had been moving slowly, carefully, with their focus on not being discovered. If they could maintain this pace, stopping only for brief rests during the darkest hours of the night when they would not have enough light to travel, they could cut that time more than in half.

Assuming Yakamo could keep up.

As the minutes stretched to hours and he felt the sweat pouring from him, he considered tossing his tetsubō aside. He considered ordering a brief stop so he could strip off his heavy lamellar armor. He considered calling for the fastest among them to run on ahead, cutting down the time it would take for the message to arrive even further. But each thought came with the knowledge that this place hated them.

Fu Leng and the forces of the Realm of Torment had been the enemies of Rokugan since the Founding, and only the Day of Thunder and the sacrifices of the Seven Thunders had kept the Emerald Empire out from beneath Fu Leng's heel. Fu Leng's shadow stretched all the way to the Wall – and some said, even deeper into the Empire itself. Yakamo knew that no matter how much distance they put between themselves and the army at their backs, there was no safety until they were on the other side of the Wall. He feared he would need his weapons and armor, and that they would all need the strength of their numbers, if they were to carry news of the army back to Hida Kisada.

No. They needed to stay together, to stand together. They had reached the basin where the army hid without incident. They could make it back. He felt a surge of confidence that seemed to ease the pain of his labored breathing. They *must* make it back. The Great Bear would know what to do; his father had always kept the borders of the Empire intact. This time would be no different. But they had to reach the Wall.

He ducked his head and ran on.

They almost made it.

For three days, they ran, loping across the wasteland in a mile-devouring stride. They ate and drank as they moved, stopping only for a few brief hours each night to steal what rest they could. Each morning, when Yakamo woke, he felt as if he had been beaten all over his body with bundles of reeds, and he dreaded the thought of strapping on his armor and continuing the torturous run. His feet were blistered and bloody, and his flesh had been worn raw in a dozen places where his kimono shifted under the weight of his armor with each jolting step. Despite their lighter armor and better conditioning for long distance travel, the Hiruma scouts were not in much better shape. But in the distance, they could see the Wall itself taking shape against the horizon, and Yakamo knew that another day would see them there.

That was when the oni struck.

They had no warning. One moment, Hiruma Hidetaka, a wiry,

taciturn man who had borne the hardships of their journey in stoic silence, was leading their ragged line, his steps unflagging despite the fatigue burning in all of their muscles. The next, there was a thunderous crack, like a rock shelf splitting from a cliff wall, and a monster surged forth from the black stone.

Yakamo had only an instant to take the creature in; it was large, towering nearly a dozen feet into the air, but its proportions were strange, almost comical. Its round head seemed several times too large for the body that dragged along behind it. He got only the vaguest impression of that body, something long and lizard-like, but with too many legs and a short, club-like tail. The hide of the creature was mottled black and gray and blended seamlessly with the surroundings.

But it was the head of the oni that drew his attention. It was a sphere almost eight feet in diameter, covered in leathery hide stretched so taut that it looked less like a skull and more like a distended, over-inflated bladder about to burst. Set close together toward the top of the head were three pairs of frog-like eyes stacked one on top of the other. At first, Yakamo thought the creature had no mouth, but then it's head split, hinging open in a vertical line that passed right between its rows of eyes and opening into a maw that split the creature's head in half. He only had a moment to glimpse the rows of needle-like teeth stacked in multiple rows and jutting from everywhere within the gaping mouth. Then the jaws snapped shut again.

Taking Hiruma Hidetaka with them.

Momoe reacted first. Her bow appeared in her hand and two arrows were in the air before Yakamo could even tear his tetsubō – which he had strapped across his back for their flight across the Shadowlands – from its lashings. One of the arrows, tipped with broadheads honed to a razor's edge, opened a shallow cut in the oni's flesh, leaving a trail of black ichor. The second sank into the flesh just below one of the sets of eyes, but Yakamo could still see the glint of the arrowhead. It had penetrated perhaps an inch, no deeper, and when the oni reared back its head and opened its mouth to unleash an earth-shaking roar, the arrow was flung free.

Still, Momoe had bought Yakamo, Bunzō, and the other scout, Kaiu Yoshikuni, time to act. Bunzō had his axe at hand and Yoshikuni held his katana before him in a two-handed grip. Yakamo answered the oni's roar with one of his own as he charged forward, aware of another arrow flashing past his head. The oni reared onto its hind legs, and rather than biting as Yakamo expected, it slammed its head down, striking as fast as an uncoiling serpent. The move took Yakamo by surprise and he had to throw himself bodily to the side as the massive head smashed into the earth with enough force to crack rock and crush bone.

Yoshikuni and Bunzō, flanking him on his charge, had managed to avoid the attack more easily, each darting to their respective sides as Yakamo dove out of the way. Yoshikuni's blade slashed in, drawing another line of oozing ichor even as Bunzō swung his axe with the furious rhythm of a crazed lumberjack. The heavy weight of the axe head bit deeper into the oni's flesh and it reared back again, its maw opening in another cry of pain. Another pair of arrows flashed by, sinking into the softer flesh of the creature's mouth.

Yakamo felt a little surge of hope as he rolled back to his feet. The oni was on the defensive; if they could keep up the pressure, they still had a chance. He closed the distance, swinging his tetsubō with all the strength his considerable frame could generate, putting his hips and back fully into the swing. The iron-studded club crashed into the oni's side, and Yakamo thought he heard the crack of breaking bone.

But if the demon was injured, it didn't show in the lightning speed of its counterattack. As its forelegs came back to the ground it whipped its head and tail in opposite directions. The bulbous head flashed toward Yoshikuni, who raised his sword in defense. The blade – made of the finest metal that the master smiths of the Crab could forge – might as well have been a bundle of sticks for all the good it did the man. The oni's head crashed through the scout's guard, snapping the steel, and slamming into the samurai with enough force to hurl him bodily through the air. He landed in a heap a dozen feet away, the shattered remnants of his katana bouncing from his fist.

Bunzō reacted faster than Yoshikuni, spinning and driving his axe directly at the club-like tail that swept toward him. Unlike its body, the knob at the end of the creature's tail was not covered in the leathery hide but looked instead like exposed bone. The sound of axe and tail slamming together was like a thunderclap and once more the oni's vertical mouth opened wide in a roar of pain. But while Bunzō's axe struck true, shattering the bony end of the appendage, he could not stop the raw force of the oni. The axe was torn from his hands and the tail, splintered bone and all, crashed into Bunzō. He, too, went flying through the air.

Hiruma Momoe continued to pepper the oni with arrows as Yakamo swung his tetsubō with renewed vigor as he found himself alone before the monster.

He felt another bone crunch beneath the force of his club. The oni's head whipped back in his direction, gaping maw snapping toward him. The thing was so fast that he had no choice but to dive again, jumping out of the way as the teeth snapped closed inches from him. The oni's massive head still slammed into him, sending him bouncing along the stony ground. His armor absorbed most of the force, and his years of training allowed him to roll with the impact. He staggered back to his feet. He had managed, barely, to maintain his grip on the tetsubō and he raised it before him as the creature's eyes whipped back and forth between him and the still forms of Yoshikuni and Bunzō.

Another arrow sank home into its flesh; the razor-edged broadheads might as well have been fly bites for all the good they were doing. Several arrows poked from the oni's leathery hide, the points buried in the flesh, but most of the shafts stuck out like the quills of a porcupine. A quick glance in Momoe's direction showed him that the seasoned scout had come to the same conclusion; she had dropped her bow and pulled her own sword and was stalking forward.

It was easy to forget, when faced with such strange and bestial creatures, that the oni were not just mindless animals. Some were exactly that, but others had intelligence equal to any samurai in the Empire, and others still had an intellect that matched the greatest tacticians Rokugan had ever produced. All of them, from the most animalistic to the most brilliant, were possessed of a feral cunning that told them exactly how best to hurt their foes. Yakamo was reminded of that fact as the lashing head of the oni settled not on him, but on the form of Yoshikuni. The creature charged, its low, powerful legs cracking the stones beneath its feet.

It was too quick, too unexpected, and Yakamo was too far away. Momoe was not. She charged the oni, her katana arcing down in a powerful two-handed grip. The edge struck hard, opening the largest wound any of them had managed to inflict, showering her with a spray of black ichor. But the oni only screamed and continued its charge. Its heavy, clawed feet trampled over the body of Yoshikuni, who gave a garbled cry and was still.

But Yakamo had not watched idly while another of his scouts was killed by the foul denizen of the Shadowlands.

Now, he stood side by side with Momoe as the oni turned back to face them, the blood of the fallen Yoshikuni fresh on its claws. His mind raced as he tried to come up with some plan, any plan, that would save them. The oni was wounded; he knew he had broken its bones, and what passed for blood poured from several wounds. But those wounds hadn't slowed the creature at all. Three of his scouts were down, two dead for certain. Yakamo had no idea if Bunzō still drew breath, and worry for his friend gnawed at the back of his mind.

"What do we do?" Momoe gasped, her sword wavering before her. The woman was a veteran of the Wall and the Shadowlands both, and Yakamo found no fault in her fear. His own hands shook as he stared at the multiple eyes of the oni as it stalked closer. The thing almost seemed to be playing with them now, confident that the pair of humans would pose little threat.

Yakamo had no answers. "We fight," he said at last. "And if we die, we pray to our ancestors that this foul land lets our spirits return to the Wheel."

"No." Hiruma Momoe straightened, a deep resolve settling onto her weathered features. "Someone must make it back," she said, raising her katana with determination. "The Wall must be warned. Lord Yakamo, it has been an honor."

Momoe leaped forward, charging with the same bullishness of the oni, her blade held above her head, point forward. Her sudden surge took Yakamo by surprise, but he was not the only one. The oni, too, seemed startled, at least enough that its advance stopped and it recoiled slightly. Then its mouth split open, stretching wide enough to swallow a full-grown man, and it unleashed another bone-chilling roar.

Momoe never slowed. She charged into the literal teeth of the creature, katana thrusting forward with not only her weight, but all her momentum concentrated behind the point. Yakamo realized her plan, then, her sacrifice, even as the blade struck home. They had struggled to penetrate the oni's hide, but the arrows that Momoe had fired into its open maw had sunk deep, showing that, with many things, the inside was squishier than the outside. Her blade bit home even as the jaws of the oni snapped shut. Hiruma Momoe, veteran of dozens of forays into the Shadowlands, died in that single crushing embrace.

But she did not die alone.

The oni's mouth opened again, and Momoe's mutilated form fell forth, dropping lifeless to the hardpan. But with it came a stream of black ichor, vomited forth from the oni as it stumbled. It managed one step, a second, and then collapsed atop the body of the samurai that had sent its soul – if it had such – back to the pits of the Realm of Torment.

For a moment, Yakamo could only stare. The fight had lasted… how long? A minute? Two? He was no stranger to death – no one who served on the Wall was – but in that moment, he felt an almost overwhelming wave of despair wash over him. What was the point? No matter how hard they fought, no matter how many battles they won, the Shadowlands always seemed to have another horror to throw at them.

Then, as the shock and adrenaline slowly drained, he remembered Bunzō. The warrior had been smashed aside by the oni's tail, but Yakamo hadn't seen what had happened to him after that. The tetsubō dropped from his nerveless fingers as he spun, searching for the body of his friend.

He caught sight of Hiruma Bunzō, perhaps fifteen feet from where he had been thrown. He reclined, almost casually, against a small boulder that jutted from the blasted landscape. For a moment, Yakamo felt a surge of relief, for Bunzō was clearly alive. Then he saw the trail of wet, glistening blood that led to the boulder, the unnatural angle of the man's legs, and the little flame of hope twisted into writhing dismay.

He hurried to Bunzō's side and knelt beside him, trying to gauge the nature of the injuries. A sick feeling rose inside him. Both of Bunzō's legs were twisted and broken. Yakamo could see the glistening white of bone within the wounds. He swallowed the bile that threatened to crawl up his throat and did his best to smile at his friend.

Bunzō coughed, the noise sounding wet and painful. "Stop

gaping at me like that, Yakamo," he rasped. "You look like you're about to burst into tears and shame us both."

"It's not as bad as it looks," Yakamo lied. "Setting and binding the wounds will hurt. But you will live." He started to cast about for something the man could bite down on while he tried to push the bones back into the right position.

"No," Bunzō replied, voice thick with pain. "No matter what you do, I will not be able to walk. And if you are forced to carry or drag me, the enemy will catch you. Momoe was right; someone must make it back to the Wall. And I'm not fit to walk there myself." He chuckled, but halfway through it turned into a cough, and Yakamo saw flecks of red in the spittle that stained Bunzō's lips. There was more broken than just the man's legs.

"Your ancestors curse you, Bunzō," Yakamo growled. "I won't leave you here." That wave of despair that he thought had receded came crashing back, carrying with it the thousand little defeats that every Crab carried in their soul.

Bunzō's hand shot out and latched on to the front of Yakamo's breastplate. The weak pull the man exerted was not enough to move Yakamo, but he leaned forward anyway, bringing his own face close to his wounded friend. "You will," Bunzō said, his voice hard and eyes fierce. "By all our ancestors, by the Fortunes and the Founders, you *will* leave me, Yakamo. If you do not, Hidetaka, Yoshikuni, and Momoe all died for nothing. If you do not, *you* will not reach the Wall in time for it to matter. We will *both* die, and the Wall with us. If the Crab fall, the Empire falls. My life means nothing next to that."

Yakamo felt hot tears burning behind his eyes and he blinked rapidly to keep them from spilling forth. How many of his fellows had done as Bunzō was now doing? As Momoe had done? How many had died? How many had sacrificed themselves fighting a war that only the Crab seemed to care about? The damnable thing of it was, Bunzō was right. Yakamo knew it. He had known it even before Bunzō spoke the words. The oni's presence was proof that the Shadowlands army had scouts and other forces stationed between the basin and the Wall. Even without Bunzō, there was no guarantee that Yakamo could make it back. If he tried to take Bunzō with him, he would certainly fail.

"Bunzō…" he began, but the Laughing Crab, now with another weak smile pulling at his lips, cut him off.

"Go, Yakamo. For the good of the Crab; for the good of the Empire. You must. Go."

Yakamo gazed down at his friend. His duty was clear: the life of one Crab could not be weighed against the well being of the Empire. He knew it. Bunzō knew it.

Why? By the ancestors, why?

Somewhere, deep within him, Yakamo felt the twisting strands of hatred taking root. Fortunes take Fu Leng and his cursed lands. And Fortunes take the mewling masses of the Empire, too concerned with their meaningless games to fight against the true evils of the world. As things stood, they deserved each other. The Shadowlands could have them, for all he cared.

He reached down and took Bunzō in a rough embrace, drawing a pained cough from the man. But Bunzō's arms closed around him, despite the shiver of pain that coursed through the samurai's broken body as he gripped his friend hard. Yakamo felt Bunzō's ragged breathing, the struggle to draw air, the labored rise and fall of his chest. But the Laughing Crab's grip did not relent. They stayed that way for a long moment, before Bunzō released Yakamo and pulled away.

"Go," he said weakly. "If the Fortunes are kind, we will see each other in the next life."

Yakamo went.

# 13
## Toturi

The Village of the Golden Blades spread out before them. Fields of winter wheat enfolded the buildings, the burnished stalks of grain swaying in time to the late spring breeze. A track of hard packed earth with worn cart ruts wound into town from the outlying farms, no doubt joining with one of the few trade roads that crossed the Empire. From the crest of one of the rolling hills that spread out before him, Toturi could see that the fields were mostly empty. He knew that the wheat would not be harvested until the last days of spring, at which time the village would come alive with activity. The fields would fill with men, women, and children gathering the bushels, plowing the fields, and making ready for the planting of the summer wheat that would take place almost as soon as the winter grains had been pulled from the earth.

He imagined it for a moment, the pastoral scene playing out in his mind's eye. A stark contrast to reality.

There was no one in the fields. There was also no one in the city streets. Even more so than in that nameless village where he had picked up Toku and Daisuke, this village looked empty, deserted. From his vantage point, it was as if the villagers had simply moved on, abandoning their homes and their fields, though the scattered billows of smoke, rising through several rooftops, gave away the lie. The people were still here. Toturi did not blame them for hiding in their homes.

An army had come to the Village of the Golden Blades.

In their three-day journey to the village, more than a dozen peasants and nearly half as many rōnin had joined Toturi's band, swelling their numbers close to fifty strong. They were no threat to a true army, but it was a not-insignificant fighting force. More than once, he had heard his followers jokingly refer to themselves as Toturi's Army, and he knew that the harder he tried to step on the moniker, the faster it would spread.

Most had brought little beyond their bodies and makeshift weapons, and their already thin supplies were now stretched to the breaking point. They needed to help the Village of the Golden Blades, but even more, Toturi needed the help of the village. They would have to buy supplies, or he would find himself at the head of a starving and ragtag group, too weakened by hunger to fight or do anything useful. He was aware that the threat of starvation might convince some to leave, and if enough of them left, he could go about his own business. But his sense of duty would not let the people under his command starve.

Even if he didn't *want* them to be under his command.

He had started organizing the group on the march, putting the more trustworthy of the rōnin in charge of groups of peasant levies, instructing them to try and instill some measure of training into them. It was an impossible task; counting Daisuke and Kamoko, Toturi had perhaps a dozen trained samurai. He had three times that in untrained peasants, most of whom had never swung a blade or shot a bow at a living target not intended for the cook pot. If Kamoko was correct, they would find themselves facing roughly the same number of Lion. Assuming they could convince the people of Golden Blades to defend their homes, they would actually end up having the numerical advantage, but Toturi knew better than to think that would give them an advantage. The Lion would be a trained fighting force composed of skilled warriors, with weapons and armor far superior to that of his own force. Numbers always had some effect, but if Toturi and his followers were to have any chance at victory, it was not numbers alone that would win the day. It was taking advantage of every tactical edge that could be found in the defense of the village.

And they had little time to do it.

"How long before the Lion arrive?" he asked Kamoko, who stood at his side. She had left her horse back with the main body of the force as she, Toturi, Daisuke, and Toku crested the hill to survey their destination.

"Four days. Perhaps less," the Unicorn replied. Her eyes, too, were locked on the village, and Toturi could see the same calculation there. The Battle Maidens were known for their skill at warfare – not just combat, but strategy, tactics, planning and execution. If he could put a dozen trained riders under her command, they would be able to make short work of the Lion infantry. But he didn't have a dozen trained riders. Or a dozen horses for them to ride.

"Then we had best be about it," Toturi said, and straightened. "We four will go into the village," he announced. "The rest of the… troops… will remain outside. No need to scare them any more than they already are. Toku, let them know what is happening."

The boy instantly jumped to his feet. "Yes, my lord," he said, and sprinted back down the hill toward the soldiers.

Kamoko surveyed the village for a moment more before she turned back to the camp as well. "I'll need my horse," she said. "It will take but a moment."

Toturi only nodded. They would make more of a spectacle as they entered the town with the Unicorn astride her mount, but there was no avoiding it. It would take far more persuasive power than he had to convince a Battle Maiden to go on foot into a potentially dangerous situation.

As Toturi watched the Unicorn stride back toward the camp, Daisuke stepped up beside him. "You *do* know why she's here, don't you, Lord Toturi?" he asked.

The seeming non-sequitur took Toturi by surprise. He glanced at the Crane, frowning slightly. "Kamoko?"

"Of course," Daisuke replied, watching as the woman disappeared into the hills. "Her name is not unknown within the courts. Nor is that of her mother, Utaku Kumiko. You have heard of her, yes?" The Crane paused expectantly, raising his brows, but Toturi only shook his head. The name meant nothing to him.

"I don't have time to play courtly games, Daisuke. If you have something to say, out with it."

The Crane gave a faint smile. Toturi had the feeling the other found his weariness for courtly games amusing, but all he said was, "You are, of course, aware of the animosity the Lion bear the Unicorn?"

Toturi grunted. He wasn't keen on a Crane telling him how his clan felt about any other, but he could not deny it; there were those among his clan who viewed the Unicorn as outsiders, ever since their return from the lands of the foreigners, though that had been more than three centuries ago. The loudest among them advocated for exactly the kind of war that it seemed Matsu Agetoki was pursuing against the Crane. That type of intolerance existed in all the clans, each judging the others against their own standards and finding them wanting. It was yet another excuse to justify the unrelenting conflict. "Your point?" he asked the Crane warrior.

"My point is this, Lord Toturi. While your late brother was busy prosecuting the Lion-Crane war, Matsu Agetoki was leading a campaign against the Unicorn. Unlike the conflict with my clan," he added, "there was no real grounds for it. The lands he raided were not disputed territory; the villages he burned had offered no insult to the Lion."

Matsu Agetoki. Toturi knew the man. The Lion general had a reputation as a cold and calculating tactician, willing to use whatever tools at his disposal to achieve victory. He was a blind adherent of the Akodo Code, putting the wisdom of the Lion Founder above all else. That single-mindedness made him a dangerous opponent and, to his own superiors, the ideal weapon to point at an enemy. With Agetoki, all one had to do was identify the objective and order the man to achieve it.

If Agetoki had been invading Unicorn lands, Toturi could see where this was going.

"The Unicorn did not take the raids into their lands lightly," Daisuke continued. The mocking lilt was gone from his voice, and his eyes were shadowed. "They sent their own troops to answer against the Lion aggression, and the Battle Maidens were at the forefront. There are many tales sung in Crane lands about the bravery of those women against the Lion; songs of their victories gave hope to my own people at Toshi Ranbo and the countless other skirmishes the Lion brought to us."

The way Daisuke spoke caught Toturi's ear. There was something in his tone that suggested he was speaking firsthand. The Crane, for all his love of stories and storytelling, had spoken little of his own past. He was a boy, scarcely two years past his gempuku ceremony, and too young to have fought at Toshi Ranbo or any of the other major battles in the Lion-Crane war. But those battles had not been fought in a vacuum; they had taken place in villages, towns, and strongholds, and there were always children and other non-combatants present. It was an undeniable fact of warfare that many of those innocents lost their lives, killed in the confusion… or worse. He wanted to ask Daisuke about his experiences during the Lion-Crane war, but the Crane was continuing.

"One of the songs that was sung most frequently was that of Utaku Kumiko. To hear the song tell of it, she swept down from the Unicorn lands at the head of an army of Battle Maidens. Under her leadership, they cut through the Lion like scythes through the wheat, taking vengeance upon those who would invade their lands. She was so successful, in fact, that Matsu Agetoki determined the Battle Maidens – and Utaku Kumiko in particular – could not be allowed to live. He called in his forces, pulling together the raiding parties that had spread out across Unicorn lands, until a great army had gathered under his control.

"Then, so the story goes, he sent word out through the villages and towns, letting the Unicorn peasants know that any who harbored the Battle Maidens would be put to the sword, their villages burned, and their fields salted so nothing would grow again. But any village who told the Lion of the Battle Maidens' arrival, and managed to keep them there long enough for the Lion to arrive, would be spared. Not just in this conflict, but in all conflicts between the Unicorn and the Lion, from that day, until the end of days.

"It didn't take long for word to reach Matsu Agetoki of Utaku Kumiko's location," Daisuke continued, a wry smile twisting his lips. "His army marched, and they encircled the village where she and her Battle Maidens rested. True to his word, Matsu Agetoki spared the town, allowing the Battle Maidens to take to their horses and fight the Lion outside the boundaries of the village."

Toturi found himself spellbound, not just by the tale, but by Daisuke's telling of it. It wasn't the words he was using, but his tone and cadence, drawing Toturi deeper into the story. He was a

Lion, had been the Clan Champion, and he knew he should be on the side of his clan. He also knew the outcome of the story already. But he still found himself hoping that Daisuke's story would take a surprising turn and that the Battle Maidens would triumph.

"The Unicorn were outnumbered ten to one. The Lion could have finished them with archers and taken not a single casualty, but, to their credit, they did not. They encircled the Unicorn in the fields next to that village and they awaited the Unicorn's charge." Daisuke sighed and looked pensively down at the Village of the Golden Blades.

"If it were just a song, the brave Unicorn would have broken through the lines and escaped, living to harass the Lion and protect their people another day. But that wasn't what happened. The Unicorn were slaughtered, to a woman. An entire contingent of Battle Maidens, butchered by Agetoki and his soldiers. According to the song, it was Matsu Agetoki himself who slew Utaku Kumiko, but not before the Unicorn had single-handedly felled a half-dozen of his personal guard." Daisuke looked back at Toturi, a sad smile on his face. "And that is how the story ends, with those who set out to protect their people lying dead on the field, leaving the spoils to the victor. It's a very Rokugani tale, don't you think?"

Toturi said nothing. Daisuke was correct; it *was* a very Rokugani story, with the reward for courageously upholding duty being a heroic death – and with little further mention of the plight of the peasants that had triggered the heroic response. "What happened to the village?" he asked at last.

"When Kamoko learned of her mother's death, she swore vengeance on all those involved," Daisuke said. "She gathered a band of Battle Maidens and returned to the village where her mother died. True to his word, Agetoki had left them in peace. Kamoko did not." Daisuke, ever the talented storyteller, left it hanging there, leaving him wanting for the details.

"Did she kill them?" he asked at last, when it was clear that the Crane wasn't going to volunteer any additional information. She would have been within her rights; no clan could allow the villages and towns that swore their loyalty to the samurai to betray them without reprisal. It would set a precedent that could tear apart the very fabric of the Celestial Order of Heaven.

"She did not," Daisuke said. "But she did drive them from their homes, burn their village to the ground, and salt the earth so nothing would grow there again, just as the Lion threatened to do to them." He shrugged. "A poetic sort of justice I suppose. Of course, now Matsu Agetoki is doing the same to the Crane. From the stories I've heard, Kamoko also swore to take her vengeance upon the Lion by claiming the head of Agetoki." He smiled a bright, disarming – and entirely false – smile. "But I'm sure Utaku Kamoko finding us with Matsu Agetoki nearby was mere coincidence."

Toturi felt the first fingers of doubt. Assuming the Crane was telling the truth – and that these "stories" he had heard were accurate – he was glad the Unicorn did not have the blood of her own clan upon her hands, even if they were peasants. Nor could he take issue with anything she had done. She had every right to seek out the one who had slain her mother. But it did call into question the woman's motivation. Was Kamoko only using him to confront Matsu Agetoki and claim her vengeance? Or did the dead Crane villagers, driven from their homes the same way she had driven the Unicorn villagers from theirs, weigh upon her conscience, too?

Vengeance or redemption? It seemed a question that too many of the samurai of the Empire found themselves facing.

Since the death of Hantei, the line between them seemed vanishingly thin.

The village headman met them in the center of town.

He was a wizened man, bent by years and with skin browned and weathered by long hours in the fields. He wore a simple woolen kimono, bereft of any pattern but in a faded Crane blue. He groaned slightly as he prostrated himself in the town square before them, knobbly knees sinking into the dirt. He was alone; none of the other villagers had come out to meet them, but Toturi could feel eyes peering at him from behind the closed shutters.

"My lord samurai," the headman said, his forehead pressed to the ground. "You honor our humble village with your presence." He said nothing else, waiting in silence to see if the Fortunes had brought him his death.

Toturi looked to Daisuke; it was a Crane village, after all. But the Crane only gave him a slight bow in return, indicating that Toturi should take the lead. Toturi sighed. "Stand up, man," he said, reaching down to offer the elder a hand. The man took it, somewhat hesitantly, and Toturi pulled him to his feet. "What is your name?" he asked.

"I am called Yohei, my lord samurai." The old man bowed again, folding himself nearly in two. "Forgive me, lord samurai, but I do not recognize your clan. Unless you are all part of the Unicorn?" Toturi was dressed in his usual featureless black kimono and Daisuke wore similar garb, though in a light gray that could almost be mistaken for a muddy blue. Only Kamoko wore clan colors, though in her case, they were scarcely needed as she sat atop her horse.

"No, Yohei. We are not of the Unicorn, though Battle Maiden Kamoko is. I am called Toturi; there is no need for a title. You see the Unicorn, Kamoko. These other two are Daisuke, once of the Crane, and Toku." He nodded at each in turn. "We are rōnin." He could sense Kamoko tensing at that; the Unicorn was clearly not a rōnin. There was no disgrace – necessarily – in walking the land as one of the wave men. Many, like Daisuke, undertook such a journey not long after their gempuku to experience more of the Empire… and perhaps to sow a few last wild oats before the full weight of their duties fell upon them.

But the path of the rōnin was also the last refuge of the disgraced samurai, those born of noble birth but deemed unworthy of service and forced to make their own way in the world.

"I fear there is not much the Village of the Golden Blades can offer you, my lord," the headman said, politely ignoring Toturi's instructions. "And it is not a good time to be here. Lion raiding bands have been seen in the area, and it is likely they will be coming here. I fear it is not safe for you, or anyone, in the village."

"What are you doing about the Lion?" Daisuke asked. There was no reproach in his voice. He asked the question as casually as he would have asked for a cup of tea, but Toturi was not fooled. Despite the man's tone, he could see intense interest behind his eyes.

The headman shrugged. "What would you have us do, Lord Crane?" Despite the unrelieved gray of Daisuke's kimono, his white hair marked him as a Crane as clearly as the daishō marked him as a samurai. "We are farmers. We have no weapons with which to fight, nor knowledge in how to use them. The warriors of the Crane are far from here, staying close to Toshi Ranbo where the samurai suspect the main attack will take place. If the Lion come, we will flee."

"If you flee, you will die."

It was Kamoko who had spoken. She had used the conversation to slip from her mount's saddle and was now standing beside the horse with a quiet intensity on her face. "I have already seen it," she went on, and Toturi could hear the pain in her voice. "The bodies of women and children driven from their homes. The burned wreckage that was once villages just like yours." She waved at the houses around them. "And I have seen the fields, set aflame so that when the harvest comes, the Crane will have nothing. No rice for the storehouses nor grain for the mills. If you abandon your village, the Lion will destroy everything. And when there is no summer harvest and the snows of winter set in, your clan, peasant and samurai alike, will starve."

Yohei smiled at her, a sad, tired smile that deepened the lines of his craggy face. "I know, Lady Unicorn," the man admitted quietly. "We all know." He straightened to his full height for the first time since they had found him there, in the center of the seemingly abandoned town. Toturi was surprised to note that the old man stood nearly as tall as he.

"But what you are not saying, is that if we stay and resist the Lion, we will still die. They will put all those who raise a weapon against them to the sword and the rest will still be driven from their homes. The houses will be razed and the fields burned. Our lords and masters will not get their tithe, and obi will be tightened across the lands of the Crane. But my people will still die, killed before they ever set foot on the roads. If we flee, some of us may survive. If our choice is between some of us living, and all of us dying, we choose life."

Those last words hit Toturi like a physical blow. We choose life. How often did the samurai of the Empire choose life? He had seen men and women waste their lives for pride, for glory, even for the status of their clan within the Empire. But he had seen others die, not for some nebulous gain, but to protect others. Daisuke and Toku both had done that, risking their lives to help him and the village. The disaffected rōnin and desperate peasants who followed him now had made the same choice. They had chosen to fight, but was that a choice for life or death? Could one choose life by putting their own at risk?

For the first time since Kamoko had joined them, Toturi's doubts about his present path eased. Helping these villagers was as much a part of helping the Empire as finding the princes. It was choosing life.

"If you fight," Toturi said, "you will not fight alone. I told you my name is Toturi, and it is. Akodo Toturi, formerly Emerald Champion and Lion Clan Champion." The headman's eyes widened as Toturi named himself, recognizing the titles, if not the man. "I forsook my position in failing to protect the Emperor. But, through the grace of the Fortunes and Ancestors, I find myself at the head of a fighting force. We will defend your village, headman. Whether you stay and fight with us or flee before the coming Lion, we will do our best to protect you and yours."

The headman was silent for a long moment. Then he asked, simply, "Why?"

The confusion on his face was another blow to Toturi. The man could not fathom help coming from someone who had nothing to gain from offering it. Had the Empire always been this way, or, in the months since Hantei's death, had it shifted so rapidly? "Because your people should not fear being slaughtered simply because of the names of your rulers," he answered. "Because the Crane should not face a choice between war and starvation. And most of all, Yohei, because it is the right thing to do." He offered the man a small, tight smile. "We will send for our warriors. Should we tell them that you will be evacuating the village, or will you be standing with us?"

The old man did not answer for a long moment, his eyes boring into Toturi. Toturi realized that it might well be the first time the elderly headman had ever looked one of his station in the eye. The Lion met his gaze and somewhere within the headman's eyes, a glimmer of hope began to shine.

"We will stand."

# 14
# Yakamo

Yakamo ran.

He was beyond exhaustion, beyond pain. There was only the broken hardpan of the Shadowlands and the growing height of the Wall, inching upward before him with every staggering step. Some distant part of his mind knew that he had pushed himself too hard, that the shaking of his fatigued muscles told him that he was not far from collapse. That same part of his mind knew that the coppery taste of his own ragged breath was a bad sign, a very bad sign. As was the blurriness of his vision and the stabbing pain in his side each time his right foot hit the ground. But he didn't care.

Yakamo ran and he did not know if he was running toward the Wall, or running away from an image he could never escape.

In his mind's eye, he saw Bunzō, the Laughing Crab, broken and bleeding. Broken and bleeding, but still very much alive.

He had left him. He had left his friend in the Shadowlands to die. Or worse than die, surrounded by the corruption of Fu Leng.

All so that he, Yakamo, could report back to his father of the doom that was certain to befall them all. All so that the Crab could make a stand against an evil that the rest of the Empire scarcely seemed to notice.

It made him want to howl in frustration, but he didn't have the breath to spare.

And then the gates of the Great Carpenter Wall were before him, rising a dozen feet, the iron-bound oak weathered and battered with the scars of a thousand sieges. Yakamo stared blankly at the gates, unsure of how he had reached them. He had no idea how long it had been since he and the scouts encountered the oni; it might have been only hours, or it might have been days. It was like a fever dream; he had only flashes of trudging endlessly across the broken wasteland interspersed with images of his dying friend.

His eyes moved up, taking in the vastness of the Wall, until they fell upon the Crab ancestral banner, barely visible above one of the bastions. That banner had been the standard of Hida, the Founder of his clan, who had battled Fu Leng and the Shadowlands and whose son would become one of the Seven Thunders. It signified the triumph and glory of the Crab Clan and their dedication to the protection and preservation of the Empire.

Now it belonged to his father. Whom he had once again failed.

He realized he was just staring at the Wall, looking blankly at the barrier before him. He raised a hand as if to knock on the massive gates, but barely had the energy to place it against the wood. Then he found himself leaning against the massive doors, head low, suddenly aware of every single bruise and broken bone that plagued him. His breath came in short, ragged gasps and his vision swam. He felt a sense of falling as the darkness claimed him.

"He will recover."

The words came from somewhere far away, and the voice that spoke them, thin and dry, like dead leaves crumpling underfoot, sent an involuntary shiver down his spine. He steeled himself against the pain that was sure to follow the spasm, but no pain came.

"Wake him."

That voice, he recognized. Hida Kisada. The Great Bear. His father. Was there concern in the voice? Yes. Yakamo could hear it. But was it for him, or the mission he had undertaken?

"It could be dangerous."

His father didn't even hesitate.

"Do it."

Yakamo was slipping back into the velvet of unconsciousness when that dry, rustling voice began to chant. He didn't recognize the words; they weren't in Rokugani, at least, not in any dialect that he understood. But it was clearly an invocation, calling forth the elemental spirits. He had felt the healing touch of the Water spirits many times before, but this was something different. It was as if his blood momentarily turned to fire, filling him with a searing pain unlike anything he had felt before. His eyes shot open, and he felt a scream try to tear its way forth from somewhere deep inside, but his muscles were locked, convulsing, and the best he could manage was a garbled groan. The pain passed as quickly as it came, leaving him stark-eyed and gasping.

He found himself staring up into the painted face of Kuni Yori. The purifier looked down at him, his painted features an unreadable mask. "He is awake, Lord Kisada."

The Kuni stepped back, and Yakamo found himself looking up into the grim eyes of his father. He spared no word of kindness for Yakamo, no expression of concern over the wounds his son had suffered, or the fact that he alone had returned from the foray into the Shadowlands. Instead, he offered only a single word.

"Report."

Yakamo did. As concisely as he could, he told his father everything he had seen or could remember. The location of the enemy horde; the vast numbers that made up its ranks; the Shadowlands creatures that had all united under one banner. The deaths of Bunzō, Momoe, and the others at the hands of the oni. That was how he reported it: the death of Bunzō. Every time he thought of his friend lying there, his mind seemed to skip and stutter, but his father's probing eyes would brook no delay. He told of Momoe's sacrifice to slay the oni and his own journey back to the Wall, at least as far as he could remember it.

"They are coming, Father," he said as he had the last of the tale out. "In numbers greater than I have ever seen. How can we stand against that?"

His father was silent for a long moment. Then, instead of answering Yakamo, he turned to Kuni Yori. "Can he travel?"

"The spirits have answered my call," the shindōshi replied. "By sunrise, he will be back on his feet. He can travel."

"Good." His father stared down at him again and Yakamo felt the need to stand. He tried to rise, but his muscles, despite whatever healing Kuni Yori had provided, would not budge. His father put one massive hand on his chest, pressing him firmly back onto the futon. "I think you are not yet done with desperate journeys, Yakamo," he said ominously. "You leave in the morning for Otosan Uchi."

Otosan Uchi. The capital? His confusion must've shown on his face, for his father continued. "Tell the regent of what you have seen," he ordered. "Tell every worthless courtier and clan ambassador you can find. Let them all know of the doom that comes for us. Convince the regent to release the Imperial Legions, Yakamo. Convince the clans to send their warriors to aid us. We must have their support if we are to survive."

"Why me?" Yakamo managed to croak. It was not an argument; he would do as his father commanded, always. But he was a warrior, not a courtier, and the only way he knew to convince people of anything was on the field of battle.

"Because you are the one who ventured into the Shadowlands," Hida Kisada replied. "You are the one who saw the army that comes for us. You are the one who returned. A firsthand account will carry more weight. And because you are my son and heir. I cannot go, not with what awaits us, so you must go in my stead."

Yakamo wanted to argue, wanted to convince his father to send Sukune or O-Ushi to the capital. But for the first time in years, it felt like Kisada truly needed him. Not another body to defend the Wall; not even a commander to lead troops in battle, but *him*. He could prove his worth to his father, not just as a warrior, but as the next Crab Clan Champion. He could not bow, not from his back on the futon, but he closed his eyes and ducked his head. "As you will it, my lord."

They left with the dawn.

Yakamo rode at the head of a dozen warriors, all that his father could spare given the Shadowlands army that would soon befall them. It was nearly five hundred miles from the Wall to the Imperial City, a journey that would normally take over two weeks, even for a small group moving swiftly. Yakamo intended to cut that time to ten days. In addition to the horses that the men rode, they each led two tough Rokugani mountain ponies. Those ponies carried their supplies for the journey, and the finery that was required in the Imperial Palace. Yakamo had also ordered their armor stored away onto the pack beasts. Not wearing armor as they traveled was a risk; the lands on the Imperial side of the Wall were not free from Shadowlands creatures. The Wall, for all the effort the Crab put into it, was not truly impermeable; single creatures and small groups could and did slip through. They could encounter such creatures in the lands of the Crab. And outside those lands, there always seemed to be problems with bandits and rōnin.

But their horses would travel faster without the added weight of armor, and speed was of the essence. They would ride for one hour, pushing the horses to a canter, and then dismount and run alongside the beasts for an hour. They would repeat that pattern, day in, day out, rising with the dawn, riding and running until Lady Sun vanished and the light of Lord Moon was not enough to see the path before them. It was grueling, nearly as grueling as his desperate flight back to the Wall, but Yakamo could almost feel the hours slipping away like sands falling through an hourglass.

Armies moved slower than individuals or small groups; significantly slower. It would take a fortnight for the army of Shadowlands creatures to reach the Wall. They would not immediately attack; it would take some more time for them to array their forces properly, make their camps, and prepare for their assault. But even with all of that, Yakamo knew that, in the best of circumstances, the battle would be joined long before he could bring help from the capital.

*If* he could bring help from the capital.

But his father would be able to hold, at least for a time, against the armies of Fu Leng. He just needed to convince the regent or the clans to send aid. And he needed to be quick. Every hour they wasted on travel, every hour they spent in polite courtesies, would be paid for in the lives of Crab warriors.

So, they traveled light, and they traveled hard. And for every grueling mile they crossed, whether Yakamo was in the saddle or panting alongside his horse, he had two images fixed in his head. One was Bunzō, bloody against the black rock of the Shadowlands, urging him to go, to run. To leave him. The other was his father, looking down at him and telling him he was needed. Those two images were twin lashes that drove him like nothing in his life had before.

The miles and days blurred as the small troop made its way through the Beiden Pass and deeper into the Empire. Once they were through the pass, even the relentless pace and the thoughts of his father and Bunzō could not keep Yakamo from seeing the softness of these lands. The villages they passed were unwalled, unguarded, open for attack at any time. They passed by no patrols, and the only time they encountered warriors from the other clans was at formal border crossings. He could have taken his men off the main roads and traveled cross country, and the samurai whose lands through which they passed would have been none the wiser. In the lands of the Crab, these soft villages would be burned to the ground, their people slain, their warriors overrun.

It was another reminder of the sacrifices the Crab made to keep the other clans safe, and what little they received in return for their efforts. The thought twisted and festered inside him.

Momoe had died for these people as much as for the Crab. He had abandoned Bunzō to a fate that may well be worse than death, for these people to keep the oni from their doors. And did any of them care? Were any of them even aware of the sacrifices the Crab made every single day? And now he had to come before them, a beggar in their house, trying to remind them of what should be a sacred duty. To beg and plead for their help, when instead he, and every Crab, should be revered as heroes.

But they were not seen as such. He had learned that lesson the last time he had ventured from the lands of the Crab and into the broader Empire. That had been for his gempuku ceremony nearly a decade ago. He had been among those fortunate enough to be invited to participate in the Topaz Championship in the town of Tsuma, home of the Kakita Dueling Academy. The other competitors, regardless of their clans, all seemed far more refined and cultured than he. He remembered the barbs from the other young samurai competing in the tournament. He had endured the jibes and thinly veiled insults as best he could, focusing on the competitions where his size and great strength were giving a respectable showing. He had known going in that he stood no real chance of claiming the title of Topaz Champion, not when the Kakita set the rules of the tournament.

The culminating event – and the one that carried the greatest weight with the judges – was the iaijutsu duel, focused on the art of quickly drawing and attacking with the katana. One cut, one kill, or so the mantra went.

It was the sort of foolishness that would get you killed on the Wall. Let the Kakita duelists try keeping their blades sheathed until the last instant when ten thousand monsters were bearing down upon them. By the Ancestors, let them choose a katana at all when an ogre larger than a horse was standing before them. Their tactics worked well enough on the dueling fields, and maybe even on the fields of inter-clan warfare. But against the true enemy?

After an ignominious defeat on those dueling fields, Yakamo had indulged in a bit too much shōchū and shared his thoughts – loudly – at the sake house. Word had spread, and though he wasn't quite sure how things had escalated so quickly, he found himself leaning on his tetsubō and staring across the field at the Dragon who had placed second in the tournament. One Mirumoto Satsu.

The Dragon had challenged him, demanding that he put his claims to a true test. Looking back, Yakamo realized that Satsu, for all his skill in the blade and years of training, was untested in the ways of battle. Yakamo, on the other hand, had already stood watches upon the Wall and fought against goblins and even an ogre. There was a difference between those who had trained to fight and those who actually fought, and on that day, Yakamo demonstrated it.

He hadn't intended to kill the Dragon.

Satsu fought like many of his kin, katana in one hand and wakizashi in the other, allowing him to parry and attack in a single motion. Just as the Kakita were known for their speed and precision, the Mirumoto were known to be masters of the double blades, using a wakizashi to turn aside enemy strikes and create openings where none were before. It was a tactic that worked well against another swordsman, or even against the thrusting point of a yari.

Against the crushing weight of Yakamo's iron club, driven by the full force of his massive frame and fueled by the rage of a thousand tiny indignations, the perfectly canted blade of Mirumoto Satsu, angled just so to slide Yakamo's weapon aside and leave him open for the counter thrust, did precisely nothing. He remembered the clang of iron striking steel as his tetsubō smashed into, and then through, the Dragon's raised guard. He remembered the ease with which the club crushed Satsu's skull, dropping the man bonelessly to the ground. He remembered standing stupidly over the corpse, staring down at the man he had just killed.

And he remembered the shriek of the little girl that came flying out of the crowd, holding a wakizashi in both hands like it was an odachi as she reared it back over her head. He had reacted without thought, kicking out at the girl, his sandal striking her in the chest and flinging her back. She had landed in a heap, wheezing as she fought for breath, the blade – taken from where it had landed near her brother's body, he had realized – flying from her grasp. The other Dragon had closed in, then, forming ranks around the girl and carrying her, screaming and crying, from the field of battle.

That had been the end of the matter. Mirumoto Satsu had challenged him, and though the fight should not have been to the death, only a single blow was struck. It was agreed by all that such things happened, and that law and tradition were satisfied. It was a tragedy, yes, but a blameless one.

But Yakamo had never been able to forget the cries of the girl. He had heard something broken in those cries. He hadn't understood it, not then. But now? As he thought of Hiruma Bunzō, of the army coming for his clan, of the seeming inevitability of it all, he understood. The girl's cry had been the cry of someone who found themselves faced with an impossible situation and knew, deep in their soul, that there was absolutely nothing they could do about it.

"The walls of Otosan Uchi, Yakamo."

The words pulled him from his past and back into the moment. Why had the memories of that duel come to the forefront of his mind? Perhaps because that had been the last time he had left the lands of the Crab. Or perhaps it was because of his newfound understanding. He pushed the matter from his mind; he had an impossible task before him, and he had to focus.

His clan was counting on him. His father was counting on him.

He would not fail.

# 15

# Hotaru

The throne room still filled Hotaru with a sense of unease. The shadow of the Emperor's assassination hung over the chamber, and the Emerald Throne itself seemed to loom over the hall, its emptiness a stark reminder to the dangers the Empire still faced. Her formal kimono seemed unusually hot and heavy today, and her hair, piled atop her head in elaborate patterns and held in place with countless pins, was giving her a headache.

Her general irritability had another source, and she knew it. Nearly a week had passed since assassins had tried to claim her life. Kachiko, true to her word, had made it as if the attack had never happened. She had no idea how the Scorpion had managed it, but within minutes of the death of the last assassin, a cadre of servants had moved in. Hotaru, who prided herself on paying attention to such things, did not recognize a single one of the servants, despite them all being clad in Imperial livery. The bodies had been quietly removed, the soiled floor cleaned, and any cushion, curtain, or coverlet that had so much as a single drop of blood upon it had been replaced.

In less than half a glass, all evidence of the attack upon her was simply… gone. She had no idea what had been done with the bodies, nor did she particularly care. She supposed that some poor soul would find them floating in the river.

In the intervening days, life at court had returned to the routine. Her time was spent visiting the ambassadors and courtiers of the other clans, engaging in seemingly meaningless talk and activities, while trying to subtly guide them into pressuring the Lion for peace. She saw little of Matsu Tsuko, though the Lion Champion was still at court and had not yet accepted nor rejected Hotaru's proposal. She *had* seen more of Chukan Hanako. In fact, she seemed hardly able to avoid the woman, who somehow always managed to be nearby. Never intruding. Never obviously watching her. But every time Hotaru looked over her shoulder, Chukan Hanako was there. There was nothing threatening in her presence, but each time Hotaru's eyes found her, a chill passed over her. She couldn't explain the feeling, but something about the Phoenix made her blood run cold.

Kachiko's warnings about the young woman had been more than justified and Hotaru wondered, not for the first time, if the Phoenix was somehow behind the attack on her. It was so out of character for the pacifistic clan that each time she thought it, her mind automatically dismissed it. And yet, at least according to Kachiko, when Hanako wasn't watching her, she was whispering in Matsu Tsuko's ear. Despite the reputation of the Phoenix, Hotaru did not think Chukan Hanako was pushing the cause of peace.

But until she had an answer from Matsu Tsuko, she could not leave the capital. As long as there was a chance – however slim – that the Lion would see reason and that the enmity of their clans could be put to rest, she had to stay the course.

And it was that, not her discomfort at formal clothing or the burgeoning headache from the pins pulling at her scalp, that was causing her irritation. Her people were dying. She received reports every day of groups of Lion raiding her borders and burning her fields. But more, many more, would die if she gave the Lion what they wanted. If she engaged in wholesale war against them, the destruction, which for the moment was contained to a few villages, would spread across all their lands.

And she suspected it would pull the rest of the Empire, already teetering on instability, into war along with it.

Today's court was unlikely to improve the situation.

Kakita Yoshi had summoned the ambassadors and ranking samurai in attendance to the throne room. There was, he had said, an important matter to be put before the court.

The Crab had come to Otosan Uchi.

Hotaru had arrived in the chamber early enough to watch the others file in. Matsu Tsuko was the only other Clan Champion in attendance. She, too, wore formal attire, including a massive leonine headdress that framed her face and somehow highlighted the stern set to her features. She was accompanied – as always – by Chukan Hanako, the young woman wearing a simple, understated kimono in Phoenix orange and red. Next to the elaborately plumed Lion, she looked almost like a simple peasant, exuding that same air of innocence that was starting to set Hotaru's teeth on edge. The ambassadors of the other clans filed in, along with their various attendants, until even the large throne room seemed crowded.

A silence fell over the hall as the next person entered, a silence followed almost immediately by the hum of whispered words behind hastily raised fans. Hotaru turned her eyes to see a vision in red and black. Kachiko had joined them.

Hotaru wasn't surprised; the regent had called for the

representatives of all the clans to gather for this meeting, and Kachiko was the only Scorpion remaining in the palace. Though, thinking of the horde of servants that had seemingly materialized out of thin air at Kachiko's call, perhaps it was better to say that she was the only Scorpion *openly* remaining in the palace. Hotaru suspected that the stir at her arrival was largely theater; the courtiers would have been just as scandalized had she disobeyed the regent's summons and not shown up. Regardless, there was not a single ambassador, courtier, or warrior in the hall that could deny that Kachiko knew how to take control of a room.

As she entered, every eye was upon her, and it was clear the Scorpion knew it. She, too, was clad in her formal best, but where Hotaru's cerulean kimono consisted of layers of the finest silks trimmed in silver and gold thread and wound about her until it felt nearly as heavy as her armor, Kachiko's garb was gossamer in comparison. The quality was evident in the sheen of the silks and the artisanry with which it shifted and slid over her body with each measured step, revealing brief glimpses of bare flesh. There was nothing about the garment that failed to meet the expected standards of the occasion… and yet, it seemed to flaunt those standards, adding a sensuality that had no place at such a gathering.

Kachiko came to a stop not far from Hotaru's own place in the hall, a bubble of space opening around her. To be fair, that bubble would have opened even before the Scorpion had been cast into the role of pariah. Now, Hotaru could not be sure if that space was because Kachiko was, at least for the moment, a social outcast, or because her presence was a stark reminder to the court that while the Scorpion might currently be on the downswing of political power, they were still dangerous.

Hotaru longed to go to her, to stand by her side. To show Kachiko that she was not completely alone in this court. But that was personal solidarity. Hotaru might stand with Kachiko, but the Crane did not stand with the Scorpion. In matters political, she did not expect Kachiko to be on her side, and she knew the same was true when it came to the Scorpion's expectations of her.

She wished it didn't have to be that way; life would be much easier if the Crane and the Scorpion could put aside their enmity. But with the Scorpion disgraced over the shame of Shoju and the Crane on the brink of open warfare with the Lion, neither side made attractive allies. Besides, this day's court had not been called to discuss the problems of the Lion, the Crane, or the Scorpion.

It was the Crab that brought them here today.

The clan responsible for the security of the Empire's southern border against the Shadowlands had an envoy at court, of course, though it was the smallest delegation from any of the clans. But this was different. It was not an envoy that was coming, but the son of the Great Bear himself. And if her sources were correct, young Yakamo was coming with a plea for aid, a request not seen in the Empire in living memory.

The throne room fell into silence as the doors at the side of the chamber opened and Kakita Yoshi strode in. Her other uncle, Kakita Toshimoko walked beside him, looking irritated in what appeared to be a new kimono, with none of the faded colors or wrinkles that his standard attire bore. A wave of bows followed in their wake as the pair stopped at the foot of the dais leading up to the Emerald Throne. Toshimoko took several steps to the side, leaving Yoshi alone before the edifice that signified the absolute power of the emperor. The Crane, wearing a kimono of Imperial white but with a barely visible pattern of cranes in fine blue thread, looked out seriously over them, conveying an air of somberness. His face was drawn in obvious concern, and the set of his shoulders suggested that he bore the weight of the Empire upon them.

Hotaru had to give credit where it was due. Her uncle certainly knew how to project just the right image to the gathered samurai; he was the very picture of the concerned regent, burdened by his duties, but determined to meet them head on.

"Thank you all for coming this morning," Yoshi said, his voice full of the same grave concern that lined his face. "There is a matter of some seriousness before the court, one that could have consequences for all the Empire. There have been some concerns voiced over the impartiality of my regency," Yoshi continued, a droll note entering his well-trained voice. As if on cue, a chuckle passed through some members of the crowd, including, Hotaru noted, her own Crane ambassadors. She felt a prickle of annoyance even as she kept her face still. She had already spoken to those representatives here in the capital and informed them – in no uncertain terms – that they were not to throw their support behind Yoshi simply because he was a Crane and their former superior. But old habits die hard, apparently. Several of those present were casting less-than-subtle looks at the Lion, whose efforts to undermine the regency had become the subject of many whispered conversations in the gardens and teahouses of the palace grounds.

"In order to alleviate those concerns," Yoshi went on, "I thought it best to greet this emissary and hear what he has to say in court, rather than behind closed doors." With that, the regent nodded and the doors at the far end of the throne room were opened once more.

The sound of hard soles striking the tiles of the throne room echoed throughout the chamber as the Crab marched in. Unlike the rest of the people present, they did not wear their finest kimonos. It was a statement, Hotaru knew. No matter how uncouth they might appear by the standards of the Empire, the Crab did possess courtly finery, and knew how to wear it. But they had chosen to make their first appearance at the regent's court garbed not as courtiers and nobles, but as warriors. To a man, they wore armor, and not just any armor, but the layered plates of the great armor that was worn only by the Crab, and then, almost always upon the Wall itself. The armor rendered them almost inhuman in appearance, taller and broader than any citizen of the Empire and carved of hard lines and sharp angles. The tortured oni-inspired masks of their menpō only added to the illusion. All of them also wore their daishō, though, Hotaru noted, despite the armor, none had been quite so brazen to come into this hall bearing the massive weapons typically brought against the Shadowlands.

It was a small group, as such things went, a dozen soldiers arrayed behind their leader, who Hotaru assumed to be Hida Yakamo. It was impossible to tell, at least until the group came to a stop perhaps fifteen feet from the regent and, as one, bowed. It was an impressive feat that filled the room with the tortured squeals of metal grinding against metal as the plates of their armor shifted against one another. When they straightened, the form in front, who stood a full head taller than his already impressive clan members, unstrapped his menpō and removed his helmet, tucking it beneath one arm.

Hotaru had met Hida Kisada, the Great Bear, many years ago. Hida Yakamo could have been a younger version of the Crab clan daimyō, so closely did he resemble his father. The young man was not handsome, not in the way of the Crane or Scorpion, but there was a ruggedness about his features and a hardness in his eyes that was not unattractive. It suggested a depth of experience, even at Yakamo's relatively young age, that many of her own clan could not match.

"I thank you for your welcome, Lord Regent," the young man said, his voice a low rumble that, again, reminded Hotaru of his father. "And for giving us this opportunity to speak with the gathered representatives of the clans."

Hotaru caught the edge of uncertainty in his voice. This was clearly a man more accustomed to the battlefield than the courts, despite the fact that he was a Clan Champion's son. Such was to be expected of the Crab, but as she let her gaze slip to the professional courtiers, ambassadors, and politicians filling the room, she could easily read the disdain in their eyes. No matter how formidable Yakamo and his samurai might be in the thick of battle, here, in this place, they were easy prey.

"We bring word from the Wall," Yakamo continued. His voice rose, taking on the tone a commander would use to be heard by his troops over the din of combat. It was entirely unnecessary; the acoustics of the chamber were excellent, and more than one courtier frowned at the display. "The forces of Fu Leng have gathered in great numbers," Yakamo went on. "They march on the Wall!"

He paused, as if waiting for the crowd to react to his proclamation, but the gathered courtiers and ambassadors remained silent. The lack of response seemed to fluster the Crab. "I have seen them myself," he insisted, "spread across the Shadowlands like a plague. Tens of thousands, perhaps hundreds of thousands. Creatures of nightmare, and they are coming!"

Still the crowd said nothing, though Hotaru could feel a tension in the room, and even rising in her own breast. The Shadowlands seemed very far away, but every child had grown up on stories of the horrors that awaited there, eager to carry off children who didn't listen to their elders. The Crab stood as a wall – even more so than the Great Carpenter Wall – against the Shadowlands, but Hotaru seldom gave it – or them – much thought. She had too many other matters on her plate to worry about threats on the far borders of the Empire.

"Which is it?" a voice demanded, breaking the tense silence. The words were light and mocking and came from the ranks of the Lion contingent. "That's a large disparity, after all. I know our Crab cousins are vaunted and courageous warriors above all else, but surely, we can expect them to know the difference between ten and one hundred?" The jest broke the tension and several chuckles spread through the gathering as the faces around her relaxed. Most of the faces. Hotaru could see the fury building beneath the carefully blank expression on Yakamo's face.

"It is not a laughing matter," he cried. "If this army sweeps down upon the Wall, the Crab will be overrun. And if we are, what will stop the hordes of the Shadowlands from sweeping into *your* lands, from destroying *your* crops and stealing *your* children for their cookpots? Mock us, if you must," he growled, "but surely even you weak northerners have the sense to understand that if the Crab fall, you are all next."

The laughter had cut off instantly at "weak northerners" and to Hotaru's keen eye, the offense was clear on more than one expressionless face. Insulting your rivals at court was a time-honored tradition among the clans of Rokugan, but one that had rules of its own. The Lion were far from masters at the craft, but whichever of Matsu Tsuko's lackeys had made the jest about the Crab, they had first complimented them and then merely implied that the Crab as a people were too stupid to be able to count. The insult, however crude, was indirect. Unlike Yakamo's response.

Before the mood in the room could turn uglier, Yoshi stepped in. "What is it you would have of us, Yakamo?" he asked. "What is it you request of the Empire?"

"To honor your oaths," the Crab growled. His face had darkened and Hotaru saw the young man visibly try to regain control of his emotions. "The first duty of any samurai is to protect the Empire. The largest threat the Empire has ever faced grows on her southern border. Order the Imperial Legions to march south, Lord Regent," Yakamo declared. "Give us the aid we need to keep the Empire safe."

"I see," Yoshi said. He folded his hands into his billowy sleeves in a picture of worried contemplation. "We will consider your request, Lord Yakamo, and the reports that I am sure you will deliver to us on this matter. For now, however," the regent added, "it is perhaps best if we all retire to the gardens and discuss things in a more informal setting." He clapped his hands once, and the doors of the throne room were thrown open. The various courtiers, ambassadors, and functionaries began to file out, leaving Yakamo and his armored Crab standing like rocks in the midst of a flowing river as they watched the others leave.

"A child playing at the games of court. It will not end well for him."

Hotaru turned, a smile coming unbidden to her face as Kachiko approached. Her presence drew more than one disapproving glance from Hotaru's own cadre of ambassadors, diplomats, and courtiers, but they would dare not speak out against their champion. Besides, most of them had already begun to flow with the crowd, moving to the gardens where the court would turn the news from the Crab into rumor and scheming as each worked to find advantage – for themselves or for their clan – in the tidings. Such was the way of things in the Imperial City.

"Perhaps, Kachiko," Hotaru replied. "But even a child can carry a warning. And Yakamo is not much younger than us, after all." She hadn't really thought of it until she had said it, but it was true. The Crab daimyō's son was in his early twenties, only a few years shy of Hotaru and Kachiko. Why, then, did he seem so young? The man had doubtless faced as many battles as she – more even, if half of what she heard of the Wall was true. Was it just his naivety in court? Or was it something else?

"Did you notice who made light of the Crab's warning?" Kachiko asked, cutting into her thoughts as the throne room continued to empty.

Hotaru sighed. "Yes. The Lion. It always seems to come back to them, doesn't it?"

"They are the ones who would be most impacted if the regent called forth the Imperial Legions. Many of their most promising young officers also boast commissions in the legion and would be forced to muster if called. A legacy of Akodo Toturi's time as Emerald Champion. But their departure would leave the remaining Lion forces severely lacking in leadership." A small, satisfied smile tugged at her full lips. "In fact, such a thing would make it very difficult, very difficult indeed, for the Lion to wage war upon the Crane."

Hotaru sighed. Kachiko was right, of course. If she could convince her uncle that it would be in the best interests of all to muster the legions, it would cool the Lion's ability to wage war upon her clan. And if she used her relationship with the regent and his allegiance to the Crane to thwart the Lion, she would be validating every fear that Matsu Tsuko and her clan had about the situation. It made her head ache. The constant politicking, the attempt on her life, even the subterfuges around her relationship with Kachiko, all were beginning to wear on Hotaru. "Do you ever wish it could be different, Kachiko?" she asked softly, aware that there were still too many ears that might overhear their conversation. "That we could live our lives on our own terms without the weight of clans, empires, and duty always pressing down upon us?"

The Scorpion was silent for a long moment. Long enough for the remaining nobles to depart the room, leaving them alone before the Emerald Throne. Kachiko gazed at the edifice, her eyes locked on the scars slashed across the ancient stone. Scars,

Hotaru knew, from Bayushi Shoju's blade when he fought Akodo Totori after murdering the Emperor. "I wish for many things, Hotaru," she said at last. "I wish for the strength and prosperity of my clan. I wish for the well-being of my people. And I wish my son could have grown up under the watchful eyes of his father instead of fleeing this palace in disgrace."

Her gaze slid from the throne and back to Hotaru, and Hotaru saw the liquid black pools of her eyes had turned to obsidian. "But whatever I might wish, Hotaru," the Mother of Scorpions said in a voice that matched her eyes, "I live in the world. And if it is not the world that I wish it to be, then I will bend it to my will until it is at least a world where those I love need not live in fear."

With that, the Scorpion turned and strode from the room, leaving Hotaru alone with her thoughts. Could there ever be a world where *Yakamo*'s loved ones did not live in fear? She did not think the young samurai would travel to the capital only to lie or to exaggerate the threat the Crab faced. Would it be better for the Empire to put aside politics and march in force to the Wall?

Probably, she acknowledged, if only to herself. And if a Hantei still sat upon the throne, perhaps that is exactly what would be done. But with the Empire balanced on a razor's edge, with the fates of many of the clans uncertain, and with the growing threat of widespread war, Hotaru knew that it would not be.

The Crab would stand alone.

# 16
# Toturi

"We've gathered everything that might be used as a weapon."

Toturi nodded, noting the exhaustion in Toku's voice as the boy rubbed his still dirty hands through his freshly cropped hair. "And every member of our band who knows how to fight has been training the villagers in how to use them." He shook his head. "Do you think it will be enough, my lord?"

Toturi did not answer, not at first. Instead, he looked down at the map spread on the table before him. It was simultaneously beautiful and crude; Daisuke had sketched it, and the Crane's hand with a pen was firm and flowing, leading to a creation of bold lines interspersed with surprising flourishes. But while the Crane may have been an artist with both the sword and the brush, he was not a cartographer. The map showed the location of the main buildings in town: the mill, the inn where they were now gathered, and the storehouses that held the rice and grain of the village. Near those structures, the Crane had sketched in the closest houses, paying some attention to the scale of things, but the farther one went from the center of town, the less detailed the map was. On the outskirts of the village, vague outlines of buildings simply blended into waving fields of wheat.

Given that Daisuke had pulled the map together in less than a day, Toturi could not complain. It was enough to give him a sense of the Village of the Golden Blades, and that sense was enough.

"Have the scouts reported anything?" he asked instead.

The "scouts" consisted of Kamoko and a handful of villagers who had kept their families fed by hunting off the land. A somewhat disturbing practice to the samurai, but one that Toturi did not begrudge. They might be killing and touching dead flesh, but it gave them the same skills that a good scout needed: sharp eyes, a familiarity with the terrain, and the ability to move quickly and quietly through the bush.

"Nothing yet, Lord Toturi," the peasant boy replied. "Lady Unicorn says they've encountered a few from outlying farms that carry word of the Lion, but they did not actually see any of the soldiers. And they haven't ventured out beyond a day's journey to see for themselves. My lord, why…?"

He paused, stopping himself from asking a question that might seem impertinent. Peasants did not question samurai, even disgraced samurai. Toturi had been encouraging the boy to speak his mind; Toku was surprisingly intelligent and had a quick mind for matters of war and strategy, but he was fighting a lifetime of habit and expectation. But if the boy was to serve him, that confidence – and a willingness to question his superiors – was vital.

"Out with it, boy," Toturi said, eyes still locked on the village map.

"Why haven't you ordered the scouts to venture farther, my lord? If they knew exactly where the Lion were, wouldn't that give us a better advantage?"

Toturi smiled at the question and nodded; it was the sort of thing any samurai past his gempuku, even those not attending military schools, would already know the answer to. He did not hold the lack of knowledge against the peasant boy – after all, Toku had not had the opportunity to learn such things. But he smiled because the boy spoke with a confidence that he had not possessed even a month before. He was learning.

"It would be good to know as early as possible, Toku," he began, "but only within our limitations." He held out one hand, fingers curled into a fist. "We have a limited number of scouts, yes?" Toku nodded, his eyes on the fist hovering a foot from his face. "My fingers are those scouts, Toku, and my hand the Village of the Golden Blades. If those scouts stay close, my fingers touch, yes?" He turned his hand, first one way then the next, showing the boy that there were no gaps. "But what happens if those scouts move farther out?" As he asked, he opened his hand, spreading his fingers wide.

The boy was nodding even before Toturi completed his demonstration. "You open gaps, Lord Toturi," he said. "Gaps that the enemy might slip through."

"Yes, Toku," he said, and the boy straightened at the praise. "It means we will have – at most – a day's warning, and likely less, unless it is Kamoko that finds the enemy first. But when weighing military matters, you must look at not only the reward – knowing the enemy location at the earliest possible moment – but also the risk. In this case, that risk is the Lion taking us completely unaware. That risk far outweighs the potential reward."

The boy nodded thoughtfully. Toturi could see that he was not merely agreeing, but actually contemplating the problem. "I understand, my lord," he said with a formality he hadn't possessed earlier. "Thank you for the instruction." He bowed – a much more precise and confident bow than he had offered before, and Toturi smiled grimly. It seemed that he was not the only one taking time to teach the boy; both the bow and the proper words had Daisuke written all over it.

Toku sat down then, his curiosity satisfied, and Toturi went back to studying the map.

There weren't many defensible buildings in the Village of the Golden Blades; the structures of the town were made of wood, with roofs consisting of either wooden shingles or thatch weighed down with lattices and stones. In short, every building in town was eminently flammable. If they fought the Lion within the confines of the village, the Lion did not even need to draw their blades. They could use a few torches to do their work for them. It was far from respectable, but Toturi was a veteran of enough battles to understand that the Akodo Code was sometimes ignored in favor of pragmatism, and Matsu Agetoki had a reputation for doing what was necessary to achieve his goals.

"What do you see, Toku?" he asked, pointing at the map.

"My lord?" the boy replied, uncertainty creeping back into his voice.

"The map, boy. The town. What does it tell you? What weaknesses do you see?"

The boy's eyes turned to the ink and parchment, then to the inn where they currently stood. Toturi could see the boy's mind working as he turned the problem over in his head. "The buildings," Toku said slowly. "They're all made of wood, and the roofs are all thatch."

"And what does that mean?"

"That they will burn," the boy replied, and a slight shudder coursed through him. "It means that if we try to defend them from inside, they could set fire to the thatch and drive us out… or trap us in."

"Correct," Toturi agreed. He was impressed. Most, even among the samurai, would see the buildings as the obvious point of defense, favoring fortifications over meeting a superior foe on the field of battle. But Toku had been raised a farmer, and could imagine the worst possible outcome when it came to attacks on the village.

"What then, do you think we should do?" Toturi went on. "If you were to fight this battle, how would you deploy your forces?"

"Deploy my forces?" the boy asked, stumbling over the unfamiliar words. Toturi realized that he had, perhaps, gone too far outside the boy's experience. Still, if Toku was to follow him, then it was his responsibility to teach the lad, and there was no better time than the present.

"How many people fight under our banner?" he asked instead. "Including the villagers that have joined us?"

"Perhaps a hundred and fifty."

"And how many of those are trained warriors, Toku?"

"You, Kamoko, and Daisuke," the boy replied. "And maybe twenty rōnin."

"Correct. Those are your forces. Understand?" Toturi asked. The boy nodded; slowly, but he nodded. "Then, knowing what we know about the Lion, where would you put them? In order to defend the attack we know is coming?"

The boy chewed his lip in thought. "Not in the buildings," he mused. He stared hard at the map, dark eyes tracing the buildings and streets. "If we can't be in the buildings, maybe we can be between them?" He pointed to certain points on the map, where houses had been built close enough together to create long alleyways. It was difficult to tell the exact width of the alleys from the sketch – there was no truly consistent scale despite Daisuke's efforts – but Toturi had already examined them. They were wide enough for three men to fight side by side, perhaps four if they were armed with spears or other thrusting weapons. "If we could draw the Lion into these alleys, they would have to fight us one on one."

"Perhaps," Toturi agreed. "And that would not be the worst plan, if we could be certain that they *had* a numerical advantage. But what little information we've been able to gather suggests that we could just as easily be facing fifty men or five times that number."

The villagers had confirmed that the Lion were operating in the area, but there had been conflicting reports as to exactly how many Lion were out there. The uncertainty of numbers was no surprise to Toturi, who had helped write some of the doctrine that Matsu Agetoki was presumably operating under. Of course, he had intended it as a tool to be used if war was declared among the clans, not to terrorize villages, but he recognized it all the same.

If they were following the doctrine, then Agetoki would be in command of five hundred soldiers. Those would be broken into five contingents, each a hundred strong, and spread out across a broad area. But each of those contingents could be broken down further, into groups of fifty, twenty-five, or even fewer, each with a capable kashira to carry out orders. It allowed for a high degree of flexibility to pursue a variety of differing objectives. It also meant that the village could be facing anywhere from a few dozen to a few hundred enemies. That uncertainty made a coherent defense of the Village of the Golden Blades difficult.

But not impossible.

"We cannot be sure of the enemy numbers, Toku," he said. "If Matsu Agetoki or one of his commanders get word that I am present, they will surely send the full weight of their forces down upon us. Without reliable fortifications, what do you think we should do if faced with five hundred samurai?"

"Run," the boy said, without a moment's hesitation. It was the right answer, and one that many of his own station would have been unwilling to provide.

"Yes." He smiled faintly. "There is little we can do against those numbers. Though we could call it a retreat or strategic withdrawal to save face. However…" He tapped the map with a finger. "If we find ourselves facing *fifty* men – fifty well-armed, well-trained Lion samurai – what could happen if we drew them into those alleyways?"

Toku spoke slowly, as if weighing each word before it slipped from his lips. "Then, the Lion samurai could trap us there," he muttered. "If we have superior numbers, but worse trained soldiers in tight confines…" He trailed off, brow furrowing as he followed the twists of the tactical problem.

Toturi nodded. "In that situation, much of the village could be slaughtered," he said. "In a classic defense, it is the defenders who are outnumbered, and so they retreat to fortifications. But we lack true fortifications. If we use the village as such, the Lion do not have to defeat us, only set most of the buildings alight and retreat. If the village is burned down, it defeats the purpose of our defense."

"Then why don't we retreat?" Toku cut in, a note of frustration entering his voice. "We could evacuate the village and move them to another settlement. And we could protect them on the road until we get there."

It was a fair question, and one that he had hoped Toku would raise. It would do well for the boy to understand the harsher calculus of war. He looked at Toku, taking in his stained clothing and dirty hands. When they had met only a few weeks ago, he had been thin, but what little spare weight the boy might have been carrying had been worn from his bones with the long walking and light rations. Now, he looked almost skeletal. "What did you have for breakfast this morning?"

The boy shrugged. "There was no breakfast this morning."

Toturi nodded. "And lunch."

"Rice porridge," the boy replied.

"And what do you think we shall have for dinner, Toku?"

"More rice porridge," the boy acknowledged, though there was no disgust in his voice as he said it. For him, meager meals of thin, watered-down porridge were routine.

Toturi nodded. "Armies have two options, Toku. They can carry what supplies they need to march and fight, or they can forage in the territories through which they march. But foraging is not what you might think; it is not digging up wild tubers and hunting game. When we talk of foraging on the march, what we really mean is taking from the land of our enemies. We steal their crops and animals, their carts and wagons, and sometimes their people." He shook his head. "It is necessary at times, but it has never sat well with me. I will not do it here, in the lands of people who have asked us for protection.

"Which means that we must find another way to feed ourselves. If we evacuate the Village of the Golden Blades, we will carry what we can and burn the rest so that it does not fall into the hands of Matsu Agetoki. But most of those provisions will go to the villagers, so they can have some hope of reestablishing themselves. And 'Toturi's Army,'" he said the words with a rolled eye, "will find ourselves right back where we are now: short on food and with few prospects of how to get more, short of turning to banditry ourselves."

Toku nodded, staring at the map. "But if we win," he countered, "then the villagers here still have homes and everything they've stored. They can give us more food."

"And shelter us for a time, so we can strengthen ourselves. And, in their gratitude, I have no doubt they would allow us to take a cart or pack animal when we depart." It sounded cold and calculated to his ear; more of the villagers would ultimately survive if Toturi and his band helped them flee.

The headman had spoken of choosing life, but what Toturi offered was not the solution that would save the greatest number of his people, at least not in the short term. Of course, everything the villagers had would be lost, and he had little doubt that some of them would still succumb to starvation and cold and sickness if they became refugees. Which was better: to immediately save the greatest number of lives by fleeing, or to save the village and everything its people had worked for their whole lives? And did the fact that he and his own followers would benefit affect that choice? More questions that added to the ever-growing weight upon his conscience.

Life had been much simpler when the only morality he need concern himself with was the will of the Emperor.

Toku continued to stare at the map, brows drawn together. "So, what do we do, Lord Toturi?" he asked. "We cannot fight in the buildings, or the Lion will burn us out. We cannot fight between them, because the Lion are better fighters. And we can't run, because then we'll all starve. What would you have us do?"

He looked up, and Toturi saw the deep concern in the young man's eyes. But there was something else, too. Something that both scared him and stirred a sense of deep duty to life. He saw trust, and he saw hope.

The door to the inn banged open.

Utaku Kamoko strode in, still clad in her lacquered purple armor. Her plumed helm was tucked under one arm, and Toturi could see the sheen of sweat that covered her face. As the door swung shut, he caught a glimpse of her mount, nostrils flaring as if it had been ridden hard. "They are coming," the Unicorn said by way of greeting. "And they are close."

Toturi pushed himself up from the table, straightening his shoulders and drawing a deep breath. The time for lessons was over. "Come, Toku," he said, a grim resolve settling over him. "And I will show you how we will deal with these Lion."

# 17
# Yakamo

Yakamo wanted to scream.

He wanted to take his tetsubō and smash every wall in this Fortunes-forsaken palace. He wanted to take every smarmy-faced courtier he had seen, hurl them from the top of the Wall, and make their fellows watch as they were ripped apart by the horrors they seemed to think scarcely more than figments of the Crab's imagination.

But he did none of those things.

Instead, he offered a polite smile to the man who sat across from him, a representative of the Unicorn clan who wore a kimono cut in a foreign style and dyed a shade of purple that, Yakamo was certain, had not come from any dye in the Emerald Empire. The man seated in the small teahouse was not even the official Unicorn ambassador to the court, but rather a functionary several steps removed, with no authority to send aid to the Wall. Yakamo had requested to meet with Ide Tadaji. Yakamo had *expected* to meet with Tadaji. When this man, Ide Yoritsugu had appeared instead, it had taken all his years of discipline and training not to throttle the man.

As Yoritsugu spoke, that discipline was rapidly fraying.

"You must understand, Yakamo, that the Unicorn are not disposed to fight behind fortifications. Our cavalry would be of little use to you, on the borders of the Shadowlands. You would do better to seek out the Lion or the Dragon. Their warriors would be better situated to assist you in the defense of the Wall." Yoritsugu sipped delicately from his teacup, a pregnant pause into which Yakamo did not leap. The fop was probably trying to tell him something by the angle at which he was holding the cup or some other such drivel, but Yakamo had neither the interest in nor the time to indulge the trivialities of the court. When he said nothing, Yoritsugu said, "Or perhaps you would be better waiting for the regent to decide if the Imperial Legions can be spared at this time."

"Spared?" Yakamo snapped, his own teacup trembling as he felt his fingers tighten to the point of shattering the porcelain. He drew a breath and set the cup back on the table. "Spared from what, Yoritsugu? They do nothing but sit in their barracks, paying lip service to the idea of protecting an empire they have already failed. The man they were most sworn to protect lies dead. And all of us will join him if the regent does nothing."

Yakamo cursed himself as he caught the hint of a smile that flashed across the Unicorn's face. He hated these northern games. They goaded you into speaking the truth, and then turned that truth into whispers and rumors to use against you. Where were the vaunted warriors of the Empire? Where were the samurai who would fight to protect the land and its people? So far, he had encountered nothing but dithering politicians, and he was acutely aware of time slipping through his fingers. He had no idea how long the forces of the Shadowlands would muster in the basin, but even if they had lingered there a week, by his reckoning they would now be closing upon the Wall. Soon, battle would be joined, and the Crab would begin to die.

And in the week he had been here, in the capital, he had accomplished nothing. The regent had put up a wall of his own, this one made of minor court functionaries and administrators that always seemed to waylay him just when he thought he was making progress. He had turned his efforts to the ambassadors of the clans with as little success.

The Lion, for all their staunch lip service to the Akodo Code, were more concerned with tormenting the Crane. The Phoenix were as pacifistic as ever, and filled his ears with mystic nonsense about a "greater darkness" rising. As if any darkness could be greater than Fu Leng's army tearing down the Wall. The Dragon would not even speak to him since he had killed a scion of the Mirumoto family all those years ago. And now, the Unicorn ambassador seemed more interested in besting him at the petty games of court so that he could increase his own standing. That left only the Crane and the Scorpion.

Doji Hotaru, at least, had agreed to meet with him in person, that very evening. He had little hope of convincing the Crane clan daimyō to release any forces to the Wall – not when her clan was heartbeats away from war with the Lion. But the regent was her uncle, so perhaps he could at least persuade her to help with the release of the legions. As for the Scorpion… well, the Crab were desperate, it was true, but Yakamo was not certain he was that desperate. If all else failed, he might have no choice but to approach Bayushi Kachiko. But if all he could muster to the Wall were Scorpions, maybe dying beside his clanmates and leaving the rest of the Empire to its fate was the better choice.

But he still had to finish his dealings with Ide Yoritsugu. Not that anything would come of it, but he had to try. For the sake of his people and his own sense of duty, no matter how futile it was. He ignored his own outburst and keyed in on the last meaningful thing that the Unicorn had said. "There is a place for cavalry soldiers at the Wall, Yoritsugu. While they may not be useful on the battlements, mounted samurai would be most useful in patrolling the Crab lands behind the Wall, hunting down the bands of Shadowlands creatures that inevitably find a way past our defenses and into the Empire. Even a small number of Unicorn detachments could free up significant Hiruma forces currently dedicated to that task."

The Unicorn made a small, noncommittal sound. "As you say, Yakamo," he said. "I will, of course, take your words into consideration and present them to Ide Tadaji. He will determine if it is necessary to send them on to Shinjo Altansarnai." The smile he offered did not touch his eyes. "I'm sure it will take no more than a month or two to have an answer for you."

Yakamo ground his teeth in frustration as he executed a small, seated bow. "My thanks, Ide Yoritsugu," he said, fighting to keep the anger from his voice. "I am sure the ghosts of my people will be excited to hear what decision the Unicorn Clan Champion arrives at." He stood abruptly, bumping the low table as he did and sending tea sloshing from the cups. He did not apologize or look back. He had no doubt tarnished the reputation of the Crab as discourteous louts even further, but Yakamo could not bring himself to care.

Could none of these people see the danger they were in? Did none of them care about the lives of his clan? Lives that they willingly put at risk to protect the rest of the Empire? As he stormed back to his quarters to change his clothes yet again, in preparation for yet another meeting that would result in no help for the Wall, he wondered why his father had sent him. Of all the people that could have been chosen for this task, surely he was the least suitable. His firsthand accounts of what he saw in the Shadowlands were politely ignored. His calls for aid were met with courtesy and vague promises, but no actual action. And his ability to hold his temper in the face of indifference was rapidly fading.

He was beginning to wonder if even the most skilled member of the Yasuki School could have made any progress. Perhaps *that* was why his father had sent him here. Perhaps it wasn't to convince the other clans of the need to support the Crab. Perhaps it was to prove to him that such a task was impossible. That the Empire, at least as it stood, was too concerned with its own politics to understand the real threat.

The thought filled him with a swell of pride; if his father wanted him to experience these things, it must be because he valued him not just as a warrior, but as a son and heir. But there was a discontent that swelled right along with it. If he could not convince anyone to send aid, he would return to the Wall a failure and his people would suffer for it.

He ground his teeth in frustration as he tried to still his mind. There was still the Crane to speak with. He had not failed yet.

The imperial gardens glowed with the light of Lord Moon cloaking the open spaces with a pale luminescence. The lanterns burned on their lowest settings, providing just enough light to move without tripping over one's feet. Almost two dozen samurai had gathered in the gardens to gaze upon Lord Moon and bask in his glory. Or some such foolishness.

Yakamo had no quarrel with Lord Moon, but the night was not something to be revered upon the Wall. There was no rest to be had when Lady Sun was chased from the sky and when Lord Moon turned his full face upon the world. It only meant that attacks were just as likely to come at night as with the dawn. That these people looked upon the night as an alluring time of celebration, and that the ghostly light of Lord Moon filled them with wonder instead of fear, was just more evidence of how soft the northerners truly were.

Still, even Yakamo could not deny a faint stirring at the beauty around him. Those who had gathered were courtiers for the most part, and they came to the moon viewing party in elaborate costumes that were probably specially made for the event. The patterns and imagery on their kimono had been embroidered and highlighted with a silken thread that, when the light of Lord Moon brushed it, seemed to glow with an inner light of its own. The effect of that glow muted the clan colors and put emphasis on the intricate details and artistry of their garb. If he unfocused his eyes, it looked like the hundreds of fish, flowers, dragons, and other designs had come to life, dancing in the moonlight to the rhythm of their wearers' movements.

There were two exceptions: Yakamo himself, whose deep Crab-blue kimono, while the best he owned, contained none of the strange luminescent threads, and Bayushi Kachiko. Why the woman was even still at court was a mystery to him, but he could not deny that she was a striking presence. Her kimono was more a silken slip that clung and shifted with every sinuous move she made. That alone was not surprising; Yakamo was aware of the Scorpion's reputation. But the entire garment appeared to have been woven of the same luminescent silk that embellished the kimonos of the other courtiers, with only thin lines of crimson piping to show her clan colors. It made the woman glow like a divine spirit, as if one of the Fortunes themselves walked among them.

"Stunning, isn't she?"

Yakamo realized that, despite his best efforts, Kachiko had captured his attention to the point that he had failed to notice his own surroundings. He silently berated himself and plastered a polite smile to his face as he turned his attention to the speaker.

Doji Hotaru stood at his side, her own gaze on the Scorpion gliding through the gardens, never stopping to speak with anyone, but drawing every gaze as she wandered the edges. Yakamo offered a hasty bow to the Crane Clan Champion. He had been taught that the Crane spent far too much time on politics and art and not nearly enough preparing for the inevitable wars, but even the Crab respected the abilities of the Kakita smiths and the tenacity of the Iron Warriors. There would be worse allies to stand with on the Wall. "Lady Doji," he said. "Thank you for agreeing to this meeting. Though, I will say I am surprised at your choice of venue."

Hotaru, like the others present, wore a kimono embroidered in glowing threads, outlining graceful cranes winging over peaceful waters. Her white hair, piled intricately atop her head with a series of needle-like pins, glowed almost as brightly as the cranes. For a moment, Yakamo felt as if he had been transplanted to another reality. He knew, on some level, that the entirety of the Empire could not match the excesses of the Imperial City, but the thought of others living like this while his people fought and bled and died was frustrating.

"I have spent my days in the capital much the same as you, Yakamo," Hotaru offered with a smile that struck him as more sincere than those plastered on the faces around him. "Trying to garner help for my people against unwarranted attacks. I grow weary of tea houses and council chambers. I hope you do not consider it discourteous to meet here, under the light of Lord Moon."

"Lady Hotaru, I would meet with you at any place or time if I thought it would bring a chance to aid my people. And through them, the Empire."

Hotaru nodded. "A noble sentiment, Yakamo. Word of the trouble facing the Wall has spread throughout the court; all have heard of your brave journey into the Shadowlands and the discovery of the army massing on our southern border."

She put no emphasis around the word "brave", but it still stung, bringing that image of Bunzō, broken on the rocks, to the forefront of his mind. "I did my duty," he said, doing his best to keep the edge from his voice. "Nothing more. I wish more people of the Empire could say the same."

"You are young," Hotaru said. She raised a hand even as she spoke, forestalling his words. "I know. You are not so much younger than I. But you *are* young, nonetheless. And you have lived your life with a singularity of purpose. That gives you a clarity many could never understand."

She smiled again, and Yakamo felt the tension in his shoulders ease a little. "It is a clarity of purpose that I truly wish I had," she went on. "Your duty has been singular: fight the Shadowlands. It is a virtuous calling, a noble one. You have a clear enemy to stand against. It must be strange for you to come to the heart of the Empire and watch us play these games. But these games stem from duty as well."

"I understand, Lady Hotaru," he replied. "But these games pale in comparison to the army that comes for us. There will be no empire if the Shadowlands is not stopped."

Hotaru nodded. "Perhaps, Yakamo. But what happens if I send my soldiers to the Wall and the Lion do not? They will destroy my clan. My people will die, and it won't matter if a single Shadowlands creature has crossed the Wall." She sighed, and in it, Yakamo heard a note of frustration, perhaps even defeat. "And, ancestors help me, from the Lion's perspective, what empire is there to preserve if it has been taken over by their ancestral enemies, with Crane in every position of power? I have no doubt that Matsu Tsuko sees that prospect as every bit as dangerous as a Shadowlands invasion. It is my duty to protect my people, Yakamo, as it is the Lion's duty to protect theirs. You should be able to rely on us for help and, were it another time, I have no doubt you would receive it. But the Empire today is not the same as it was before."

Yakamo felt the growing frustration, not just his, but Hotaru's as well. In that moment, he knew that he had failed. Hotaru was quiet for a long moment, as the courtiers in their glimmering kimono drifted across the garden. "I will think on your words, Yakamo," she said at last. "I cannot sacrifice my people to the Lion. But we are working toward peace; perhaps it will come." She did not sound as if she believed it. "I will say this, and on my word as Clan Champion: if I can get sureties from the Lion that the invasions into Crane lands will cease, then I will send the Iron Warriors to the Wall. If I don't get those sureties… well, perhaps some soldiers can still be found. It is all I can promise you now."

Yakamo bowed deeply, nearly bending double. It was not what the Crab needed, and it might not have any impact at all, but it was more than he had expected. "I can ask for no more," he said as he straightened. "Thank you, my lady."

Then he frowned. Across the gardens, Bayushi Kachiko was making a beeline for him and Hotaru. The seductive sway of her gait was gone, replaced with a purposeful stride that should have been impossible in the kimono she was wearing. But she managed it anyway, and Yakamo felt himself tensing again as the traitor's wife approached.

"This is a private meeting," he declared as she reached them. "We have no need of the Scorpion in this discussion." He stood to his full height, towering over the woman, casting her in his giant shadow.

"Shush," she said. "If you listen very carefully, I might just save your life."

Yakamo was so shocked at being shushed by this… creature… that he could only blink in confusion. He felt the heat climbing up his face, but then Hotaru stepped forward. There was an odd expression on her face, almost as if she was holding back amusement.

"That was rude, Kachiko," she said, and the easy familiarity with how she addressed the Scorpion shocked him even further. "But, Yakamo, in my experience, if Kachiko comes bearing warning, it is best to listen."

Before he could answer, Kachiko smiled. "Do not worry, Crab. I will keep it short and use small words. Mirumoto Hitomi is coming to kill you."

# 18
## Hotaru

Kachiko's words, delivered in a cool, matter-of-fact tone sent a shiver down Hotaru's spine. Yakamo appeared just as stunned, and his mouth dropped open slightly as if to speak, but no words came forth. "What do you mean, Kachiko?" Hotaru asked.

"I mean exactly what I said," the Scorpion replied, maintaining that same aloof tone. "*Lady* Hotaru," she added, placing particular emphasis on the title, reminding Hotaru that they were in public and, whatever else might be happening, it would be best to keep up appearances. "The court is abuzz with the fact that Mirumoto Hitomi arrived in Otosan Uchi this very night and she is headed here." Kachiko smiled and turned her eyes back to Yakamo. "It seems word of your arrival at the capital has spread far and wide. I hope you are ready for her."

Hotaru looked from Yakamo to Kachiko. She still had no idea what was going on. "Why would Hitomi want to kill Yakamo?" she asked at last.

"Because I slew her brother," Yakamo replied, voice distant.

"Legally, from what I have been told," Kachiko added. "In a fair and just duel. And for which Hitomi has been training all her years since. If you are to leave, I would do so, quickly. She is not far away now."

Several emotions flitted across Yakamo's face before he could restore the impassive mask of the Crab. Hotaru saw anger in the set of his jaw and frustration boiling in his eyes. Beneath that frustration, though, she saw an empty well of hopelessness covered with a thin patina of shame.

She did not see fear.

"I will not turn my tail and run," he said at last. "That may be acceptable behavior for a Scorpion, but I could not call myself a Crab if I did."

"Good!" a new voice, high and true like a silver trumpet, sounded. "Then you can stand and die!"

A woman followed the words across the garden, and Hotaru had to admit, she cut an impressive figure. Unlike the others, she was not dressed for the moon viewing party. Instead, she wore her lacquered armor, the green-hued segments shining like emeralds under the light of Lord Moon. She wore no helmet, and her head was clean-shaven, her bald pate seeming to glow in the pale moon light. It lent her a strange cast, making her look less a beautiful young woman and more an angry spirit that had animated a suit of armor.

The Dragon's appearance, and her warlike mantle, had already sent a storm of whispers hissing across the garden. A crowd was gathering, with Yakamo and Hitomi standing in the center.

Mirumoto Hitomi raised a gauntleted hand, pointing at Yakamo. "For the murder of my brother," she said, her voice taking on a formal tone, "and for the insults you cast on me and my family, I challenge you, Hida Yakamo."

She bowed deeply to the man and eyed him expectantly. Hotaru realized that Kachiko had already slipped away, merging into the crowd and disappearing as easily as a shadow in the night. This was neither the time nor the place for such a challenge to be issued; in fact, for it to truly meet the legal standards, it would require sanction by the Emperor. Not the regent… the Emperor. But with no emperor upon the throne, Hotaru knew there was little anyone could do to stop it.

"I have no wish to fight you, Hitomi," Yakamo replied, though Hotaru thought she could still hear the anger simmering under the edges of his words. "And I regret your brother's death. Though I know it changes nothing, I did not wish to kill him."

"But you did," Hitomi replied, her words coming out low and forceful. "And for that you will pay. Unless you are a coward, Crab. I have heard much of your clan, but cowardice is not often a word associated with them."

Hotaru saw Yakamo's eyes narrow and his jaw muscles clench. When he spoke, it was through gritted teeth, but the words were not what Hotaru expected. "If you wish to see the bravery of the Crab, Hitomi," he said, "come to the Wall, and bring your warriors with you. A great horde gathers in the wastes, and if we do not all stand against it, it will sweep over our borders and into the rest of the Empire." He returned her formal bow and said, "I beg you. Gather the Dragon and march, not for vengeance, but for the good of us all."

More whispers flitted through the gathered courtiers and Hotaru had little doubt that this was the most excitement they had had since word of the Emperor's death swept through the palace. For her part, she felt a surprising admiration for Yakamo; even in the face of the challenge and a direct insult, he was still trying to advance his mission and gather allies for the Wall. She knew it would be to little effect; but then, Yakamo probably knew it as well. He was rough around the edges, but an asset to his clan nonetheless. She offered up a silent prayer to the ancestors that this night not end in bloodshed.

Mirumoto Hitomi laughed. It was a bitter, mocking sound, and one that sent another ripple of shock through the gathered crowd. It was unseemly behavior in a samurai, particularly at such a delicate moment, but Hotaru could see the gleam of madness shining in Hitomi's eyes. "No Dragon will *ever* march to the defense of you or your family, Hida Yakamo. Not so long as I draw breath." Her lips twisted in a vicious grin. "But I will swear to you in front of all these present: if you slay me here and now, then the Dragon are yours. On my word, with my dying breath, I will order all the forces I command to the Wall. But you will have to fight me for them."

"Clever." The word was whispered in her ear, and Hotaru turned to find Kachiko once again by her side, a frown upon her face. "Or perhaps she is mad. But Yakamo will not refuse, now."

Hotaru could see the truth of Kachiko's words in the building anger on Yakamo's face. Here was a target for all the frustrations he had faced since coming to court; here was a way he could "negotiate" on the Wall's behalf. All he had to do was kill one insulting samurai. "I accept your terms, Mirumoto Hitomi," Yakamo growled. "You have your duel."

"Then die!" Hitomi snarled, and her blade seemed to materialize in her hand. Hotaru recognized the technique as a modification to those taught at the Kakita school and wondered where the Dragon had picked it up. The Mirumoto were some of the most renowned sword fighters in all the Empire, but they didn't favor the iaijutsu style of the Crane duelists. The blade seemed to gather in the light of Lord Moon, looking like a shining bar of silver as it flashed toward Yakamo. There was no way the Crab would be able to draw his sword in time to block the cut.

But while he may not have been a duelist, Yakamo was a veteran of more actual battles than most samurai north of the Wall could comprehend. He made no effort to draw his own katana. Nor did he try to give ground before the swing; Hotaru knew that such a tactic would just delay the inevitable, allowing Hitomi to follow up her initial strike with an unrelenting onslaught that would, eventually, drive the larger Crab into the ground.

Instead, Yakamo did the unexpected, raising his knee and stabbing his foot out like a thrusting spear. The front kick was a brutish move, and one that had little place in a formal duel, but Hotaru understood what many of the courtiers around her did not. This was no duel. This fight was tantamount to sanctioned murder, whichever way it went. That thought gnawed at her mind, even as Yakamo's kick struck home.

The unexpected strike caught the swordswoman as much by surprise as it did the crowd of onlookers, and the outrushing *oof* of air from Hitomi's body as she was flung backward was drowned in the broader gasps of the spectators. But the Dragon was also no novice to battle. The power of Yakamo's kick hurled her back bodily, but she kept her grip on the blade and her balance, despite stumbling back several yards. She was moving forward again, a blur across the grass. But the strike had bought Yakamo enough time to clear his own sword, and this time, as the Dragon's blade flashed out, it was met by the cold steel of Yakamo's katana. The sword might not have been a weapon favored among the Crab, but it was clear to Hotaru that they did not shirk their training in it.

Yakamo handled the sword with skill and ease, moving the blade in precise counters, the steel in his hand an impervious wall that shed the Dragon's strikes. His own attacks, she noted with clinical detachment, lacked the crispness that would be found in the Kakita school, relying instead on the massive size and strength that only a Crab could put into each arm-numbing swing. For her part, Hitomi danced among the blows, meeting the force of Yakamo's fury with a carefully angled blade that slipped each strike with scant fractions of an inch to spare. Her counters *were* crisp, the swift stings of a thousand darting wasps, but none of them reached the Crab.

The fury of their clash subsided for a moment as both stepped back, each leveling an assessing gaze at the other while they panted for breath. Neither spoke; they were both committed now, long past the point where a peaceful solution could be found. In that brief instance, Hotaru wondered if she was witnessing an allegory for her own quest to find peace with the Lion. But if that were so, was she Hitomi – unrelenting to the point that her other duties were forgotten entirely – or Yakamo – so stymied by his failures that any chance, no matter how dangerous, was worth taking?

She had only a frozen moment to think upon it, and then Yakamo unleashed a howl of rage as he surged forward. His katana blurred, and it, too, took on the aspect of a silver bar of light under the face of Lord Moon. He struck not with speed and precision, but with an earth shattering strength that Hotaru could practically feel as Hitomi flicked her own sword in response. Each crushing strike was met with steel, but where those blades touched, sparks flew from the impact. Gone were the perfect parries as the Dragon fought desperately to keep her blade between herself and the enraged Crab. Hotaru could see each strike taking a physical toll on the woman, driving her back, forcing her guard lower and lower.

And she saw the trap into which Yakamo was blindly rushing.

She could do nothing but watch as, step by step, Hitomi was driven back, pushed almost to the edge of the crowd that had come to view Lord Moon and instead found a far more entertaining spectacle. Then, as Yakamo roared again, he swung his blade in a broad arc, catching Hitomi's katana just above the guard. The blades rang like bells as they recoiled. Hitomi's arm was flung wide, and Yakamo took advantage of the perceived opening. His left hand lashed out, closing around the wrist of Hitomi's sword arm, lifting the woman to her toes as he pulled upward. He drew back his own blade, prepared to thrust it through the seemingly defenseless woman.

It was then that Hitomi sprung her trap. The Dragon were known for many things – their monasteries and temples, their desire to look inward to find peace, the mystical nature of their tattooed monks – but not the least among them was the twin-blade style of the Mirumoto school. Hitomi had engaged Yakamo with only her katana. Were this a proper iaijutsu duel, that would be only right. But this wasn't a formal duel, and Hotaru suspected that the Dragon had no intention of limiting her own fighting style.

So, it came as no surprise to Hotaru when Hitomi's left hand blurred, the blade of her wakizashi slicing upward in a single, graceful cut that would make any Kakita proud.

The razor edge of the wakizashi caught Yakamo just below the elbow, parting skin, muscle, and bone with equal ease. Hitomi dropped back to the ground as Yakamo gave a howl, his sword slipping from the nerveless fingers of his sole remaining hand. The Crab staggered back, clutching the bleeding stump to his chest as he desperately tried to stem the flow of blood with his right hand.

Hitomi unleashed a cry of her own, a defiant scream of victory and anger and a dozen other emotions, as she stepped forward and brought her blade down at Yakamo's head.

It clanged, bell-like, off another sword.

Her own, she realized. She hadn't consciously made the decision to enter the fray, but she had. Stepping in between the triumphant Dragon and her defeated quarry, who was, even now, fighting to maintain consciousness.

"What are you doing, Crane?" Hitomi demanded, her piping soprano raw and breathless with emotion. "Stand aside, or by Mirumoto's spirit, I will cut you down. I *will* have my revenge."

"You have had it, Hitomi," Hotaru replied, refusing to step back.

"The duel is done. By every law of Rokugan, it has ended. Your opponent lies defeated and unable to fight. It is over."

"I don't care!" the Dragon spat. She pulled her blade from Hotaru's and set her feet, dropping into a fighting stance once more, both blades held before her. "He killed my brother. I will have his head."

"You will not." Her voice remained calm. From the corner of her eye, she saw Kachiko kneeling beside the body of the Crab. She had looped a strip of fabric tight around Yakamo's bloody stump and was twisting it into a tourniquet. Hida Yakamo had already slipped into unconsciousness from blood loss; he might yet die anyway, but from her few interactions, the young Crab deserved better than to be stabbed to death in cold blood as he lay helpless on the ground.

The gathered courtiers had begun to whisper in earnest now that their evening's entertainment took another unexpected turn. From a simple moon viewing party to a duel between samurai who were successors to their clans, to a confrontation between the Crane clan daimyō and a deadly swordswoman. There was a distant part of Hotaru's mind that appreciated that this moment was likely to be the pearl of court gossip for the rest of the season. No doubt that before a week had passed, the number of people claiming to have been present would have grown to preposterous portions.

"I do not wish to kill you, Hotaru."

"Convenient, for I've no wish to die," Hotaru replied, earning a chuckle from the onlookers. "And even more, I've no wish to see a young and promising samurai forever tarnish their reputation through one ill-thought out act. Sheathe your sword, Hitomi. You have won your duel, but there will be no killing today."

She was distantly aware of commotion behind her as more people arrived, but she dared not take her eyes from the woman before her. She was confident in her own skill, but she and the

Dragon were both at a level where a direct confrontation between them would be less about the perfect execution of technique and more about who made the first mistake. She would do her people little good if she died here today.

Then a contingent of Dragon – most clad in hastily donned kimono – were sweeping between them. They flowed around her like a river, using their bodies to physically separate her from Hitomi. She risked a glance behind her to see that Yakamo was unmolested, still lying on the ground with Kachiko standing over him. For a brief moment, she wondered where his own clan members might be, but she was grateful for whatever kept them from this place. A battle between the Crab and Dragon in the palace gardens would do little for peace and stability in the realm.

"No!" Hitomi shouted. "No! I will have my vengeance!" Despite her shouts, a wall of her own people now separated Hitomi from all those gathered. The Dragon used the simple expedient of closing ranks and moving as one and Hitomi was left with the choice of turning her blades on her own people or accepting the inevitable and allowing herself to be led from the gardens. It was a close thing. Hotaru caught only glimpses of the Dragon's face as the flow of her clan members pushed her from the garden, and she wore an expression of absolute rage. There was none of the pretext of the perfect samurai mien; the woman was literally purple with anger and her blades, still held upright before her, shook with the fury of it. But even in her state, she could not turn those dreadful swords against the men and women who shuffled her from the garden, and in moments, the crowd had swallowed the Dragon, leaving Hotaru, Kachiko, and the prone form of Yakamo alone in a circle of gossiping courtiers.

Kachiko sighed, looking down at the unconscious form of the Crab and at her own bloodstained hands. "This is not going to do much for my reputation."

Before she could answer, the Crab arrived. There were no thanks offered, nor asked for. Hotaru and Kachiko simply stepped back from the son of Hida Kisada as the members of his own honor guard knelt and lifted him, almost reverently, from the ground. They turned without a word and carried the unconscious man from the gardens. Their entertainment over, the rest of the courtiers spread out through the garden once more, and the sounds of light conversation and tinkling laughter filled the evening sky.

Hotaru gazed at the woman beside her. For the first time, she noticed a rip in Kachiko's perfect kimono, a strip of fabric cut from the whole. With a shock, she realized it was the same strip that had been tied around Yakamo's stump, keeping the blood from pulsing completely out of his body.

"You saved his life." She didn't mean for the words to sound like an accusation, but from the slight wince across Kachiko's face, she knew she had failed. "Why?"

The Scorpion Clan was no stranger to death. Kachiko herself was no stranger to it. If the hotheaded son of the Crab Clan Champion got himself killed in an unsanctioned duel at the palace, what of it? It mattered little to the Scorpion. That reputation Kachiko had spoken of had been carefully cultivated, maintained with deception, lies, and pure ruthlessness. The Mother of Scorpions was many things, but no one ever mistook her for soft-hearted.

"Because it was the right thing to do?" Kachiko replied, before her lips twisted in a wry smirk. Not because of the sentiment, but that she, Kachiko, would believe it. "Honestly, I don't know," she said quietly. "Maybe because Hida Kisada would owe me a favor for saving his son's life, and the Scorpion have precious few allies these days. Maybe because I wanted to shock the other gossiping birds at this party and *really* confuse them. Or maybe you're rubbing off on me, Hotaru." She sounded almost sad as she said this, her gaze drifting to the spot Hotaru had stood moments before. Between Hida Yakamo and his would-be killer. "After all, you were risking your life to save the boy. If he had died, all that effort would have been wasted."

Hotaru felt warmth bloom to life within, but she kept the emotion from her face as she turned. "Come," she said, her voice low so prying ears couldn't hear. "Let us be gone from this place. There is nothing left to be gained here tonight."

Kachiko nodded, but her gaze drifted to something in the grass, and a brief look of pain shimmered through her eyes, so quickly it might've been Hotaru's imagination. She followed Kachiko's gaze and had to repress a shudder.

Yakamo's severed hand lay there, forgotten in the perfectly manicured grasses of the palace gardens. It would remain there until some servant chanced across it, or some animal came and carried it away, for none of the samurai caste would sully themselves by touching dead flesh.

"An amusing lesson there, don't you think?" Kachiko murmured. "What was once precious and vital, now reviled and outcast, all because of the single strike of a blade."

Hotaru swallowed. Kachiko was not speaking of Yakamo, but of her own clan and their current standing in the Empire. "Come," she said again, putting a hand on Kachiko's back, ignoring the slight tremble that coursed through it. "Let us go to the bathhouse and see you clean."

Kachiko's voice was almost too soft to hear. "Does the blood ever truly wash off?"

Hotaru knew the answer, but she kept silent as the pair moved together from the garden, leaving the blood and the severed hand of Hida Yakamo where it had fallen.

# 19

# Toturi

Toturi waited outside the Village of the Golden Blades. Daidoji Daisuke stood on his right and Utaku Kamoko – reluctantly – stood on his left. The Unicorn had been loath to leave her mount behind, but understood that, if the conversation they were about to have went badly, a single mounted person would be the target of every bowman arrayed against them. Toku stood just behind them, his fingers drumming nervously on the haft of his axe.

In the distance, some hundred yards away, stood a tight formation of soldiers. It was not an army, not by the standards Toturi would use. But he could see how the raiding party – fifty soldiers strong – would appear as such to untrained villagers. Toturi couldn't help the pang of loss somewhere deep in his chest as he gazed upon the Lion. Despite the armor that had been lacquered black and despite the lack of flags and mon, they were Lion. Even at this distance, the discipline and precision of their lines told him that as clearly as the missing banners would have.

These were his people, soldiers that had once been under his command. He had never given them orders to raid and pillage their neighbors, but he understood the tenets of warfare in the Empire. And he understood that the men and women standing across from him had no real choice in the matter. Samurai were not given the luxury of ignoring or disobeying orders from their rightful superiors.

That didn't excuse the raiding. It didn't justify the killing. But he understood it, nonetheless.

A trio of forms detached from the assembled soldiers and began crossing the field toward them. When Kamoko brought word of the enemy – and he had to think of them as the enemy now – Toturi's plans had solidified. He had chosen this field with purpose. It currently lay fallow, unplowed and unbroken, the earth packed firmly enough to make it easy for a body of soldiers to march across. Far easier than the narrow cart path that led into the village. On either side of the field were waving strands of wheat, almost ready for the harvest, the golden stalks standing nearly four feet tall. Those wheat fields were key to his strategy. By placing himself, in full armor and flanked by two more armored samurai, he had practically guaranteed that the Lion forces would take this approach.

The trio of Lion walked to within ten feet of Toturi and the others before coming to a stop. He didn't recognize them; his years as Emerald Champion had not allowed him to keep tabs on the rising young officers of his own clan as closely as he would have liked. The man in the center wore a helmet plumed in a luxurious mane that made the black lacquer of his armor moot. Even those without Toturi's eye would clearly mark him as a Lion with that helmet. He was younger than Toturi, perhaps twenty years of age, and Toturi could see the curiosity in his eyes. If he recognized his former Clan Champion and the former Emerald Champion, it did not show on his face.

Of the pair that flanked him, one was older and had a hard set to his features. A man who had seen more than one war, but, again, not a samurai that he recognized. The final soldier was more a boy than a man, probably on his first stint of duty to the clan and learning what it meant to be a samurai. It pained Toturi to think this campaign against unarmed Crane villages would be his first taste of what it meant to be Lion.

The central figure bowed formally, a bow which Toturi returned in kind. "I am Akodo Sachio," he said. "You stand between me and my objective, rōnin." He spoke the words in a calm, matter-of-fact tone, but with an underlying note of arrogance that almost made Toturi smile. He remembered that feeling, of being in command of an army, thinking that little could stop you. It was a feeling that shattered quickly when you finally did face something capable of answering back.

"I am Toturi," he replied. "A rōnin, as you've surmised. And my companions are Daisuke, also a rōnin, and Utaku Kamoko, Battle Maiden of the Unicorn." Each bowed in turn, though Toturi could see that both were tense. Despite choosing his path, Daisuke clearly had issues with being called a rōnin. But Kamoko's tension stemmed from something else; Matsu Agetoki was clearly not with this force, but they were still his soldiers. In Kamoko's mind, that made them just as valid a target for her vengeance as the man himself.

"Have you lost your horse, Battle Maiden?" the elder samurai snorted.

Kamoko's hand flashed to the hilt of her sword, a fraction of a second before Toturi's own hand moved. He caught her wrist before she was able to bare more than an inch or two of steel. She made no other outward move and her face remained expressionless, but Toturi could feel her straining against his hand. For his part, Akodo Sachio frowned at his lieutenant. It was a visible reprimand, if a small one, but the man offered no apology, nor did the Lion demand one. He did, however, have the courtesy not to mention the fact that Kamoko had tried to draw steel during what was obviously a parlay. Only a second passed before the Unicorn relaxed her grip and Toturi pulled back his arm, but he knew if he hadn't stopped her, more than one head might be lying in the dirt of the field.

Which would make his plan nearly impossible.

"You have not explained why you bar our path, Toturi the rōnin," Akodo Sachio said.

"The Village of the Golden Blades has engaged us to defend it," Toturi replied. He smiled at the young officer. "And that is precisely what we will do."

"You work for money?" the elder samurai scoffed. He looked as if he had swallowed something foul and wanted to spit, though even his discourtesy did not extend so far. "I know you are rōnin, but are you totally bereft of decency?"

"An interesting question," Daisuke said, the mocking lilt back in his voice, "from those who would slaughter helpless villagers."

Toturi sighed and raised his hand. "Enough," he said. "There is no need for us to insult one another. We came out here to give you a simple warning: attack the Village of the Golden Blades, and we will stand against you. You will not find an unarmed population fleeing their homes. Turn back."

Akodo Sachio stiffened. "And you think that two rōnin, a Unicorn, and a peasant boy with an axe can stand against two and a half score trained Lion warriors? I have heard the legends of the great Toturi, but never that he could slay samurai by the dozen."

"I heard of a Toturi, too," the older samurai added. "One who failed his clan, failed in his duty, and failed his Emperor."

He had been recognized, it seemed. So much the better. He ignored the jibes and replied simply, "No, Sachio. I cannot slay dozens of your warriors. If we were alone, you could certainly overwhelm us." He offered a small smile and another polite bow. "But I never said we were alone. If you wish to know the details of our forces, I'm afraid you'll have to join us in the village." He cast one hard glance at Kamoko as he turned on his heel and walked away.

If the Unicorn gave in to her desire for vengeance here and now... well, things would get interesting. He had accounted for that possibility, of course, just as he had accounted for the possibility – however unlikely – that the Lion commander would simply try to stab them in the back. Such behavior would violate all the tenets of warfare laid down in the Akodo Code, but one could never be certain. He had contingencies in place, but their greatest chance at victory hinged on his own people following the plan, and the Lion acting according to the dictates of the traditions that they held so dear.

The thought momentarily jarred him. The traditions that *they* held so dear? Did he no longer hold those same beliefs? And did he no longer consider himself a Lion?

He had no time to dwell on those thoughts as they strode back toward the town. As he did, he waved a hand three times over his head, a signal to the men and women who remained within the Village of the Golden Blades. At that signal, they filed forth. There weren't many, two scores and no more. They had no armor, and their weapons were repurposed farm implements. But they moved with purpose and confidence, stepping from the safety of their village to form a narrow line, spreading all the way across the fallow field.

Behind him, Toturi heard the barking laugh of the older soldier.

"That one is mine," Kamoko muttered through tight lips. "He needs to be taught some manners."

"You can't really blame him," Daisuke said, eyeing the line as they approached. "The whole situation is a trifle ridiculous." The villagers stood in a rough approximation of military attention, their mishmash of repurposed hoes, sharpened shovels, sickles, and machetes held loosely in their hands. None held bows or slings; there had been a few in the village, but Toturi had reserved them for another purpose. "Our great leader's forces don't exactly inspire confidence."

"That is the entire point," Toturi said softly. "We want them to be overconfident. We want them to see our pathetic forces and come rushing forward. The key to any good strategy is deception. We want the enemy to think us weak."

"Oh, yes," Daisuke agreed. "I understand the principle, of course, but I always thought that it went something like 'make them think you're weak when you're strong.' We've definitely accomplished the first part." Behind them, a drum began a steady beat. "It's the actually being strong that, I must admit, has me a little worried."

They passed through the line and Kamoko immediately quickened her pace, moving to where her horse, draped in its lamellar barding, awaited her. Toturi turned, letting his gaze fall upon the Lion for the first time since they began walking away. Sachio had likewise returned to his troops. Now, the block of fifty warriors moved forward at the march, a quick walk that allowed them to maintain formation. That formation, he noted, was ten soldiers wide by five deep. They took up only a quarter of the width of the fallow field, marching right down the throat of Toturi's forces.

It was a more careful approach than Toturi would have expected, given that Sachio had greater numbers, better trained troops, and the fact that Toturi had elected to fight in the open rather than among the buildings of the village. Sachio had enough warriors to spread out his front and engage Toturi all up and down the line of villagers. His armored soldiers should make short work of Toturi's forces if they engaged even at roughly even odds.

"Quite the tight formation," Daisuke observed in a dry voice, one hand resting lightly on his sword hilt. "Very disciplined for this backwater town in the middle of nowhere."

"He knows my reputation," Toturi acknowledged. "The boy is young, but not stupid. If he saw before him a formation of villagers, spread out to protect their village with their crude weapons, he would likely charge right in. But I am here, so he approaches with more caution and sets his own formation so that at each position, he will outnumber us unless we collapse our own line."

"Is that why we went to meet him?" Toku asked, the tremor in his voice giving away his fear. He stood beside Toturi, clutching his axe as he gazed on the approaching samurai. Any peasant facing down an approaching army of well-armed warriors would have been terrified, but Toku stood firmly, his jaw clenched in determination. "Because you wanted him to know you're here?"

"Yes, Toku," Toturi said, his eyes locked on the position of the Lion troops. They were not quite halfway across the field but showed no sign of slowing or increasing their pace. It appeared as if Sachio was committed to the advance but would hold the call for charge until the last moment, in case Toturi had a trick up his sleeve.

Which Toturi did.

"Ah, Lion pride," Daisuke commented in response to Toku's question. "It's so blissfully predictable, isn't it?"

"I don't understand, my lord."

This was not the time to be explaining war tactics and strategies, not with the enemy a few heartbeats from charging down their throats, but Toturi spared the boy a split-second glance and nodded back to the approaching Lion.

"Firstly, Toku, those samurai and ashigaru almost certainly have yumi tucked away in their gear," he muttered, referring to the bows and arrows many warriors carried into battle. "The biggest danger to the village is Sachio deciding to simply kill as many of us as he can with arrows. If they did that, half the village would be dead before we could close the distance. But knowing that I'm here, he will see that as a shameful, perhaps even cowardly, tactic. Matsu Agetoki has a reputation for pragmatism; he might accept that stain for a quick victory. But a young Lion samurai with his first taste of command?" He shook his head.

The enemy had continued to march closer. The distance now was down to a hundred feet or so. If it were Toturi's command, he would give the order to charge when that number dropped to fifty feet, letting his warriors gain the momentum of rushing forward into the enemy's thin ranks, but keeping the distance short enough to maintain his formation. He suspected Sachio would give the same command and that his soldiers would be as aware of the counter charge. Which meant there would be a moment where the Lion forces would be anticipating it, mentally preparing themselves for the rush into mortal danger.

It was at that moment, when their anticipation and fear would be at the highest, that they would be the most vulnerable.

"And the second reason?" Daisuke asked, helping him along.

"We need to dictate their movements to spring our trap. Which we should do just… about… now."

With the last word he raised his hand and dropped it sharply. A horn sounded at his signal, sending a clear, piercing note rising into the sky. From the tall wheat stalks on either side of the fallow field, Toturi's own soldiers rose. Their ranks had swelled to nearly forty strong on the march to the Village of the Golden Blades. They were not much better equipped than the villagers, but every bow the village had possessed had been passed into their hands. It was still not enough to arm them all, but two dozen strings thrummed as one as arrows came raining in from either side. Lions screamed and fell as their eyes flashed toward their young leader for direction.

It was a pivotal moment, for as the arrows fell among his samurai and ashigaru, their commander, Akodo Sachio, had to make a decision. He could break off his attack and try to outdistance the bow fire; he could order his forces to charge one of the three forces set against him; or he could split his army and try to engage the flankers peppering him with arrow fire. Toturi knew the correct answer and was not surprised when Sachio arrived at it.

"Charge!"

At the shout, the Lion surged forward, and despite the situation, Toturi felt a rush of pride in his clan… and a little surge of sadness at what was about to happen. It was no easy thing to ignore the enemy fire coming from the flanks and charge into the teeth of another force, but it was the correct tactical decision. The doctrine that Sachio operated under had been developed in part and thoroughly tested by Toturi. He knew the proper response to the close-in ambush, just as he knew the proper counter. It was not unlike a duel, the thrust and counter thrust of warfare an echo of individual blades flashing between two samurai, with the victory going to he who controlled the tempo and cadence of the fight. Toturi was about to seize that control, and as a result, loyal members of his clan would be sent to their next turn upon the Wheel. The knowledge came with a wave of guilt, but he could not allow the feeling to cloud his judgement or stop him from doing what he must.

Toturi raised his arm once more, circling his hand above his head. The horn sounded again, firing off three quick notes in rapid succession.

It was the signal for his own forces to charge.

The villagers around him surged forward, letting out a ragged battle cry. As they did, the bowmen at the edges of the field fired off one last volley before they, too, charged into the enemy's flanks. There was a thunder of hooves as Kamoko, atop her white battle steed, shot past him, her sable hair and the horse's snowlike mane both streaming with the speed of their passage.

Toturi didn't bother drawing his blade. As surely as if he was reading one of the countless battle scrolls at the Akodo Commander school, he could see how this fight would now unfold. He said a silent prayer to his ancestors, begging their forgiveness as the "army" of peasants and rōnin crashed into the Lion. The Lion, for their part, fought with bravery and tenacity. The lead forces smashed into his own charging villagers, and in those few seconds of fierce battle, the blood of the Village of the Golden Blades fell freely, watering the fallow field.

But then Kamoko was there. She and her steed worked as one, both fierce warriors in their own right, but far more deadly when working together. Her sword cleaved through a lamellar helm even as her mount's iron-shod hooves caved in the chest of an ashigaru rushing in from behind. The fury of her charge jarred the Lion lines, if only for an instant, but it was long enough for the villagers of the Village of the Golden Blades to find their rhythm and present a solid wall. It was time enough for the peasants who had followed him from that nameless village to reach the rear and flanks of the Lion, bringing their own makeshift spears, hatchets, and blades to bear.

It was time enough for the battle to be decided.

To his credit, Akodo Sachio knew it as well. Between the volleys of arrows and the first thunderous crash of his lines into Toturi's, nearly half of Sachio's soldiers had fallen. They had struck back, bloodied the Village of the Golden Blades, but when the encircling forces joined the battle, they knew it was over. Toturi had been in the young officer's boots; he knew the temptation to fight until the last breath, to die in a blaze of glory so that no rumor of cowardice or failure could attach itself to your name.

Fortunately, it seemed that today, Toturi's ancestors heard his prayers. As the Lion line, which had compacted to a tight square facing enemies on all sides, continued to shrink, he watched as the proud Lion took off his plumed helm and cast it to the ground. He called out to his men, and as one, they stepped back, throwing their own weapons down and raising their hands in surrender.

Toturi had seen this possibility and warned his own troops against it. As the Lion forces surrendered, the peasants, villagers, and rōnin took a step back, though they kept their weapons raised. There would be no massacre here today. On either side.

Toturi glanced at the sun, which had barely moved a finger's width. From the moment he had spoken with the young Lion to the moment of Sachio's surrender, less than a quarter hour had passed. He looked upon the field with equal parts pride and sadness. Pride at the villagers and members of his own band who had stood to battle and carried the day; sadness at the bodies that now lay upon the field. Those bodies belonged either to the men and women who had followed him this day or to those who called him kinsman, no matter how distant the relation. Despite the victory, it was hard to feel any real joy.

"Come, Toku," he said to the boy who had remained at his side when the others charged, trying to keep the weariness from his voice. "Let us go take the surrender of Akodo Sachio."

# 20
# Yakamo

F ever dreams plagued him.
He slumped over on his horse, only vaguely aware of the braided cord that kept him tied to the saddle. The stump of his arm felt as if a thousand stinging insects crawled and bit at it. His hand – his missing hand – hurt, as if it was not gone, but still attached and being twisted and wrenched in unimaginable ways. The heat of it, the near-unbearable heat, tore at his body, wracking him with alternating chills and sweats as he clung both to consciousness and to life.

And all the while, waking or asleep, he dreamed.

He dreamed of the Wall, and he dreamed of the dead. Bunzō, broken and twisted, crawled through his dreams, accusatory eyes glaring from the rotting, undead flesh of his face. His hands, twisted and claw-like, reached for Yakamo, raking at his flesh and tearing at something much deeper. Momoe, half the flesh missing from her body from the oni's terrible jaws, laughed then wept then laughed again, pointing a bloody, skeletal hand straight at his heart. His father, a gigantic figure several times larger than Yakamo knew the man to be, towered over him, and he, too, had joined the halls of the dead. He frowned in disapproval as behind him, the Wall crumbled and an unliving army shambled into the Empire.

Guilt. Blame. Disappointment. Destruction and despair. They haunted Yakamo's dreams and, try though he might, he could not pull himself from them.

"He will not live to reach the Wall."

He didn't know who spoke the words; he barely understood that they were words at all, for to his mind's eye they seemed to be coming from the rotting mouth of Bunzō.

"If he dies, his father will blame us. We'll be sent into the Shadowlands to act as permanent scouts," Momoe's corpse replied. Why would Momoe fear the Shadowlands? She was the best scout the Crab possessed.

"He's strong," another voice insisted. Sukune? When had his brother arrived? And why was he covered in blood? "Force the broth down and keep him lashed to the saddle. We'll travel day and night. Better to kill the horses than the son of the Great Bear. We will get him to the Wall, alive or dead. If there's still a Wall to get back to." He heard a sound like someone spitting. Sukune, bookish, courteous Sukune, who would have been much better suited to this mission, would never spit.

His head was pushed back, and lukewarm liquid filled his mouth. It tasted of brine and fish, and he gagged as he choked on it. Someone stroked his throat, forcing him to swallow. He felt the rush of the lukewarm liquid through his body, and for a moment, it seemed to cool the heat of the fever. Then it passed, and the pain set in once more.

"Change the poultice," Sukune was saying. "And clean the… stump."

"How do we know the Scorpion woman isn't trying to kill him with this foul-smelling glop?"

A very good question, Yakamo thought, as the bandages on his arm were bathed in cool water. Also, when had the Scorpion woman given them anything? Yakamo couldn't remember. He wanted to scream as they began to unwind the cloth, but he didn't have the energy. The best he could muster was a tremor.

"If Bayushi Kachiko had wanted Yakamo dead, all she had to do was nothing. I don't like it any more than you, but she saved his life. Why kill him now?"

"Because she's a Scorpion?" Bunzō's corpse grunted as it leered down at him, hands reaching for his throat. No. Not his throat. They were smearing something thick and viscous along his wound. It burned and tingled, but then seemed to numb the pain, or at least, deaden it some. Why did his missing hand still hurt?

"Well, it has yet to kill him, so we keep going. Bandage him and let us be gone. It's still a long way to the Wall."

For Yakamo, those days passed in a blur of pain and in the company of ghosts. Not just those with whom he had served on the Wall, but a countless multitude of souls, stretching back to when the first stones were laid. It was a long, gray line of duty and sacrifice, but it was also a long, gray line of death. And above them all, hovering like twin suns, were the eyes of his father, staring down at him, burning with judgement.

He welcomed the moments when the ghosts forced him to drink the fishy broth or when they slathered his wound with salve. He welcomed those moments because, if only for an instant, the stabbing pain pulled his consciousness closer to the surface and banished the eyes of the dead. Bunzō, Momoe, his father. He wasn't quite ready to join their ranks just yet.

Yakamo opened his eyes. And, for the first time in what felt like years, he knew where he was. His throat felt like a desert waste, bereft of even the memory of moisture. "Water," he croaked, and he did not recognize the weak and reedy sound as his own voice.

A cup was pressed to his lips and the cool liquid flowed down his throat. He drank greedily, gulping the water until he thought he would slosh when he moved. He forced his eyes fully open, blinking against the grainy crust that lined his lids. At first, he saw nothing, just a vague sense of light against the darkness. Then the light resolved into a blurry haze, and from there into the painted face of Kuni Yori.

It was not a welcome sight.

The spindly shindōshi peered down at him, his face painted in stark whites and reds and his eyes black and empty voids. Yakamo felt a strange sense of déjà vu as he remembered waking to that same face after his first desperate rush back to the Wall, a lifetime ago, it seemed.

"You have survived," Kuni Yori said in his dry, papery voice. "Good. The spirits have deemed that now is not your time. Your father has been sent for." His eyes moved down Yakamo's body, settling on his left arm. The abrupt end of his left arm.

Yakamo's eyes followed as if of their own volition. He didn't want to look, didn't want to see what Mirumoto Hitomi had done to him. But he couldn't stop them. His arm, even before the nest of bandages, looked shriveled and wasted, almost skeletal. He frowned; that arm should have been thick with ropy muscle, stronger than any Crab save his father. Instead, it was spindly, weak. Disgusting. And it ended. It just… ended. In a mess of sticky and stained bandages, that were nothing but blotches of red and brown against the grayish linen backdrop. He felt his stomach churn at the sight.

"It need not be this way," Yori said. His voice was soft, seductive. His eyes were not on the ravaged, wasted limb, but on Yakamo's face. "Your arm can be restored. If you are willing to do what is needed."

Yakamo didn't have time to consider the words, for the door to his chambers opened. Yori slipped back, disappearing into the shadows at the edge of Yakamo's vision. His pale visage was replaced with the broad and hearty face of Yakamo's father, towering over the bed.

"You're awake!" Hida Kisada boomed, and his voice seemed to fill the room. "Good. Now to get you healthy once more so you can join us on the Wall." He spoke with a boisterous cheer, but one that landed poorly to Yakamo's ears. It sounded forced, the forced cheerfulness that he himself had put on when comforting the wounded who would soon be returned to the Wheel. Was his situation truly so desperate?

He pushed the question aside and forced the words from his throat that he knew he had to say, no matter how bitter their taste. "I have failed you, father."

"No," Kisada said. "No, Yakamo, you have not. I have heard of your duel with the Dragon girl. She was armed with her favored weapon; you were not. She was wearing armor; you were not. Despite the girl having every advantage, you did not back down from her challenge. And from the message I've received from the Crane daimyō, you tried to turn the duel into an opportunity for aid for the Wall."

Yakamo blinked at that; he hadn't realized that Doji Hotaru had sent a message for his father. Of course, he hadn't been in a position to realize much of anything. "You lost a fight, son," Kisada said, and while there was regret in his voice, Yakamo thought he heard something else. Pride? "Anyone can lose a fight. But you did not fail us."

For a moment, he felt as if a weight had lifted, a weight he hadn't realized had been there, compressing his chest and making it difficult to breathe. For a moment, Yakamo felt light. Then he looked down at what remained of his left arm, and the weight settled on him once more, crushing and eternal.

"None of the clans are coming, father," he said. "I couldn't get anyone to agree to send us aid. And I came home maimed." The fingers of his remaining hand clenched into a fist. "What use will I be when the Shadowlands hordes come?" he rasped. "What use is a Crab who cannot hold a weapon? I failed you, and I failed everyone."

Kisada's face darkened with anger, but, Yakamo realized, not anger directed at him. "You did not fail the Crab, Yakamo," he insisted. "The Empire failed us. Every one of those soft, complacent northerners who has no idea of the horrors we protect them from has failed us. No, son. You did not fail. We were betrayed." He spoke the word with a deadly intent and Yakamo felt a shiver course down his spine. "And it is a betrayal that the Empire and the regent *will* answer for."

His father's words hit Yakamo with the force of a tetsubō. Had the Empire betrayed them? Had it gone so far? Yakamo wasn't sure; but what he did know was that in his father's words he heard a measure of salvation. Some of the shame he felt eased at his father's reassurance.

Kisada was interrupted as a thunderous boom reverberated through the great fortress, shaking the walls and causing motes of dust to stir in the air. Yakamo felt his heart skip, but neither his father nor Kuni Yori reacted. He knew what that meant; they were already aware of the problem.

The Shadowlands army had arrived.

Yakamo glanced at his missing limb and felt an anger and frustration boiling within him. How could he fight, as he was now? How could he help defend his family and his clan? And beneath that boiling anger, there was fear clawing at his belly. How could the Crab, without reinforcements from the rest of the Empire, stand against the army he had seen in the Shadowlands?

His father must have seen the understanding in his eyes, for Hida Kisada nodded. "Yes, the army has arrived. They have been staging on the plains outside the Wall for nearly two weeks, preparing their camps and building siege engines." His father offered a rare, wry smile. "It seems some of those engines have been completed and they are now ranging on the bastion." He turned to Kuni Yori. "See to his health, Yori," Kisada said. "I need him on the Wall, where he belongs."

"As you wish, Lord Kisada," the shindōshi replied, bowing low.

"I must go to the battlements, Yakamo. Rest and recover. We will push back this Shadowlands army as we have done with all those that came before it. Then we will see about the Empire's betrayal." With that, he turned and strode from the room, leaving Yakamo alone with Kuni Yori.

Yakamo was silent for a long moment, aware of the spindly shindōshi watching him with his dark eyes. All the Kuni family set Yakamo's teeth on edge; the men and women of the Purifier school were an undeniable weapon against the Shadowlands, but he had always thought them a sword with no hilt. Useful, yes, but as dangerous to the one who would wield it as it was to the enemy.

But now, the Shadowlands had come to his door. It had before, of course, but Yakamo knew that this time was different. This would be a battle such as the Crab Clan had not faced in generations. And while more of his people – more of his friends –

died, he would be here, sick, injured, and unable to do a damn thing about it.

Unless he was somehow restored.

Yakamo was no fool. His arm was gone. There was no bringing it back. Not even the most powerful healing invocations could restore a limb once it had been lost. But there were other powers in the Empire, darker powers. They were the reason the Kuni, who danced that edge between pragmatism and corruption, were both valued and feared. But if it could make him whole and strong once more… Was he willing to make that choice? Was he willing to pay that price? Because there was always a price. Whether it be blood, righteousness, or his very soul that Yakamo would trade for his arm, there was always a price to be paid. What was he willing to sacrifice for the lives of his clan? For his duty? For the Empire?

He closed his eyes, and in that darkness, he saw Bunzō, Momoe, and the others.

"You said you could restore my arm." Yakamo opened his eyes and looked to the Kuni. "What must I do?"

Kuni Yori smiled.

"It is a small enough thing, Yakamo. I only need your name."

# 21
## Hotaru

"The Lion delegation is leaving the capital, Lady Hotaru."

Hotaru ignored the interruption as she continued to work her way through the forms. The naginata sang in her hands as it flashed through a flurry of feints and strikes. She danced across the manicured lawns, body in constant balance, the spear a blur of controlled destruction. She moved faster and faster, striking to the beat of the song of battle that only she could hear until she felt the sweat pouring from her skin. Then, with the suddenness of a caesura, she stopped, panting and drenched in sweat as she set the butt of her polearm to the ground.

Only then did she turn her attention to the servant who had entered the garden. Hotaru had chosen the site of her practice with intention, and she moved through the forms a scant few yards from where Mirumoto Hitomi had defeated Hida Yakamo scant weeks ago. And where she had intervened on the Crab's behalf, preventing the Dragon from slaying her helpless opponent.

She didn't like playing at politics – at least, not to the degree that many of her kinfolk did – but she could not pass up the symbolism. Here, the Crane had stood against aggression and showed their willingness to fight to defend those who could not defend themselves. The message was clear: when it came to the aggression of the Lion, her clan would do no less than she did herself.

The servant – one of her own, not one of the liveried palace attendants – had waited patiently for his daimyō to finish her training. As she turned to him, he offered a deep bow, bending nearly double. "My apologies for interrupting, Lady Hotaru, but Doji Shingo thought you would want to be informed immediately of the Lion's departure."

Hotaru nodded. Matsu Tsuko had never formally accepted nor rejected her proposal. The shared stewardship of Toshi Ranbo should have been seen as a clear political victory for the Lion leader and a meaningful loss of face for the Crane, but apparently, it had not been enough. Every messenger she had sent to solicit a response or set up further negotiations had been politely rebuffed. If the Lion had departed the capital, it could mean only one thing.

"Then it is to be war," she said. The words sent a chill down her spine, but at the same time, they came with a small measure of relief. The time for politics was done. She no longer had to pretend that the border incursions from the Lion weren't happening; she no longer had to turn a blind eye to the atrocities and death taking place. She had advocated for peace, fought for it, even in the face of opposition from her own clan. She had wanted to find a way forward without bloodshed.

But if the Fates and Fortunes deemed it otherwise, then so be it. Matsu Tsuko would learn, just as Akodo Arasou had learned, that the Crane would not lie down and die.

"Summon all of my ambassadors and councilors," she said to

the servant. "Tell them to meet me in my chambers and to bring with them every scribe and courier they can gather." She thought for a moment before adding, "Ensure that no word of this reaches Kakita Toshimoko, nor the ears of the regent. What comes next must be the action of the Crane and the Crane alone. I do not want any Imperial involvement. The clans must see the Crane act as an independent and strong clan, not as a ward of the Empire. Understood?"

The servant bowed again. "Yes, my lady."

"Good." She considered her own sweaty, disheveled state. "Tell them to meet in one hour's time. Now, go."

The servant left, leaving Hotaru alone in the garden. She had much to do in the hour before her council would gather. She needed to visit the bathhouse. She needed to don appropriate apparel to set the tone for the meeting ahead. She needed to consider carefully what her orders would be and how to gather and marshal her forces for war. She needed to do many things, and she needed to do them all right now.

But her eyes were drawn instead to the place where Yakamo had lost his hand. The Imperial gardeners had removed the amputated limb and their careful ministrations had erased most of the signs that a duel had taken place on the spot less than two weeks ago. She thought she could see a few darker stains in the grass, where the shears of the workers had been unable to remove all of the blood-stained turf. But that faint scarring was all that remained, visible only to those who cared to look for them.

The Crab's warnings had likewise vanished, gone with Yakamo and his honor guard, presumably to the Wall to face the hordes of the Shadowlands alone. A flicker of regret coursed through her. She – all the clans, really – should send support to the Wall. But how could she when her people faced annihilation from the Lion? Would a company or two of Iron Warriors change anything for Yakamo and the Crab? Likely not, but they could mean the difference between life and death for some of her own people.

Still, as she pondered the fate of her clan and the upcoming war, Hotaru could not help but think about that patch of blood-stained grass and wonder at its chance of survival.

She spent the rest of the morning and the afternoon closeted with her advisors. A stream of couriers and messengers flowed from her quarters, out into the Imperial City and into the Empire at large. With the sudden departure of the Lion and the flurry of activity among the Crane, only the most politically obtuse could fail to see what was happening. Hotaru felt the rising tension in her courtiers and ambassadors, and in the suddenly increased traffic at her door. Functionaries from the other clans arriving with invitations to seemingly meaningless and trivial endeavors: tea with the Phoenix, a game of Go with the Dragon, a stroll through the gardens with the Crab's sole remaining representative at court, an invitation to a riding demonstration being held by the Unicorn. Those invitations had nothing to do with the activities presented and everything to do with gauging just how close the Empire was to being dragged into another war.

Only two of the Great Clans sent no representatives at all: the Lion, for which the reasons were obvious, and the Scorpion. In fact, Kachiko had been strangely absent since the affair with Yakamo in the gardens. The two had managed to steal only a moment here and there as each went about their duties, Hotaru trying to find a peaceful solution with the Crane and Kachiko… Well, Hotaru admitted to herself, she had no idea what Kachiko was doing. She wondered if the Scorpion was still trying to figure out who Chukan Hanako was, and why the Phoenix seemed to have such influence with the Lion. It no longer mattered to Hotaru; if Hanako had been stoking the flames of war for whatever reason, then her mission was successful.

By the end of the day, when the last of her courtiers and ambassadors had bowed and shuffled from her chambers, Hotaru was exhausted. But plans had been made and orders sent. Her forces had already been on alert, for while Hotaru had come to the capital hopeful that peace with the Lion could be reached, she knew the realities of the situation. Now those armies would march, moving from their rallying points deep within Crane lands to the borders where the Lion had been raiding and harassing her people.

She knew that the Lion had contingencies in place as well, and that their own forces would be on the march. It would be a race, then, to see who would reach the vital strongholds first. The most obvious target was Toshi Ranbo. It was there that Akodo Arasou had fallen, and where the tempo of the Crane-Lion war had changed. It was the most obvious root of the territorial disputes between her people and the Lion. And it would be the largest single symbol of victory or defeat. So long as the Crane held Toshi Ranbo, the Lion would never be seen as victors in any war between them.

But it was also the most fortified. Her experienced generals were already there, along with the most veteran warriors of the Crane. If Hotaru went there, her presence would stiffen the resolve of the populace, but it would make almost no difference militarily. On the other hand, there were several other palaces and castles of the Crane that *would* benefit from a skilled leader. Her presence at any one of them could mean the difference between victory or defeat, while simultaneously providing her a more centralized location to command the Crane's widespread forces.

But which one?

She was pondering that question when she heard footsteps upon the tatami mats outside her door. It was not the soft steps of her servant, but the heavier tread of booted feet. She looked up from her desk, instinctively grabbing the katana resting on its stand, in time to see the door to her office fly open and a servant come rushing in.

"Forgive me, Lady Hotaru," the girl said, dropping prostrate to the floor. "I know you gave orders around further visitors, but…" She trailed off, but Hotaru needed no further explanation. Behind the kneeling servant, a woman clad in the shining white armor of the Imperial Legions strode into her office.

"Lady Doji," the legionnaire said with a precise bow, the plates of her armor creaking as she did. "The Dowager Empress requests the pleasure of your company."

The chambers of the Dowager Empress were the definition of refinement and understated elegance. Even Hotaru, who had grown up in the Esteemed Palaces of the Crane and had seen the finest works the Kakita artists could produce, was moved by the beauty of it all. The quarters had been Hochiahime's when her husband had lived, and Hotaru had little doubt that they would remain in the possession of the Dowager Empress for the rest of her natural life. It would take a cruel hand to turn Hochiahime out; Yoshi would not dare, and Hotaru doubted that even the princes, when and if they could be found, would consider such a thing.

She was escorted into a reception chamber, decorated with intricate woven rugs imported from Unicorn lands and covered in cushions of the finest silk. The walls were hung with scrolls, most depictions of simple calligraphy, but executed with such precision that Hotaru could clearly see the Kakita and Asahina influences. A low table was already set with a tea service and the Dowager Empress herself sat before it. There were no servants present and even as Hotaru realized that, the Seppun palace guard bowed and, without another word, exited the room. Hotaru could not help feeling a nearly overwhelming rush of emotion; she had visited with the Dowager Empress once already, but it had been a much more formal affair. This was something different. To be left alone with the empress so soon after the murder of her husband was a sign of trust that, for an instant, almost brought her to tears.

"Please, Hotaru. Sit and take tea with me." The words were simple, but the empress spoke with a grace and refinement few in the Imperial Palace could match. The woman herself was close to fifty years, but not a single wrinkle or line marred her flawless skin. Songs had been written of her beauty, and while the blush of youth may have faded, her quiet presence was still undeniable. There was more to it than simply beauty; the Emperor was surrounded by beautiful women. It took something more to catch the eye of the ruler of Rokugan. In Hochiahime, that something more had been an almost preternatural calmness that radiated from her like sunlight, tempering emotions and gracing all those in her presence with a sense of peace. Hotaru knew well the pressures of rulership, and she could only imagine how dearly Hantei 38th had cherished that peace.

Hotaru bowed to the Dowager Empress, deeper than was required. "You honor me, Lady Hochiahime," she said. She knelt on the cushions, pulling her daishō from her belt and setting both blades to her left side, in such a way that it would be awkward and difficult to quickly retrieve them.

The empress said nothing as she began the careful and ritualistic process of pouring the tea. Each move was as precise as Hotaru's sword or spear work, executed with the same precision and grace.

The movements themselves were captivating, but for Hotaru, there was something more. The empress did not idly serve tea, not even to the heads of clans. Nor did she often meet alone with… well, anybody. And Hotaru could only imagine that the palace guards, in the wake of their failure to protect her husband, had taken the empress' security even more seriously. To be alone in her presence, and to be served by her hand, stirred a sense of wonder in Hotaru that she hadn't felt since her first days in the Imperial City.

They went through the tea ceremony in silence. The empress radiated the calm for which she was known, but beneath it there was… something. Hotaru couldn't quite place it, but it was like a deep place in a river: the surface may seem still, but somehow one could sense the power and turmoil churning somewhere far beneath. Fortunes knew the empress had plenty to be concerned about: her husband murdered, her children missing, and her empire on the brink of war. But Hotaru sensed something else, something more than the pain of a grieving widow or a worried mother.

Hope?

The ceremony concluded and left Hochiahime and Hotaru sitting across from one another, formalities dispensed. The empress took one more small sip and then moved her porcelain cup back to the tray in front of her. Hotaru saw the barest tremble, not of the cup itself, but in the tea that remained within, as Hochiahime set the cup down. She drew a small breath, almost as if she were gathering herself, before speaking.

"I have received a ransom note for Sotorii."

Hotaru felt a tremor pass through her own hands and quickly set her teacup down. Her mind raced as she failed to come up with a suitable answer. Why had Hochiahime come to her with this news? And was it good news or bad? Good, certainly, that at least one of the princes had been found, but to learn that he was in the hands of an enemy? Which enemy, and what concessions could be wrung from the woman if her child's life was on the line?

The empress smiled, and it was a small, sad thing that spoke far more of pain than humor. "I can read the questions on your face, Hotaru," she said. The use of her name brought an answering smile to Hotaru's lips. It was a reminder that while Hantei Hochiahime may have been the empress for many years, she was once Doji Hochiahime and had been very much a part of Hotaru's early life. By reminding her of that, the empress was framing the conversation not as the empress to a Clan Champion, but rather one between family members.

"Then I suppose I might as well ask them, my lady," she said. "Why are you telling me this? It brings me joy to think that Sotorii has been found, even if he is being held captive. But is this not a matter for the regent or the Emerald Champion? I would think the Imperial Legions would already be on the march."

The smile faded from Hochiahime's face, and for the first time, Hotaru could clearly see the pain and worry there. She did not know Sotorii well; what few rumors reached her ears about the prince suggested that he was perhaps a little too arrogant and spoiled for his own good. But how could the heir of the Empire *not* seem so to those around him? She was sure that to his mother, the boy was none of those things. He was simply her son, and with his father dead and brother missing, Hotaru could only imagine the torment and loneliness she must be experiencing.

"Yoshi is a good man," Hochiahime began. "But his concerns are split between advancing the Crane and his own power. I am not certain that finding my son fits into his plans for the Empire." For anyone else to speak those words aloud might have been considered treason, but Hotaru could not fault them. She had wondered the same herself. "And while I suspect Toshimoko would drop everything to find the prince if I were to ask it of him, the situation is... delicate."

"How so?"

"The informant who brought this to my notice is one many would question."

Hotaru blinked. Given the current climate, she couldn't imagine *any* source of information coming to the Dowager Empress and bypassing the regency not being viewed with skepticism, but there was one source that would be viewed with more than most. "The Scorpion?" she asked.

Hochiahime nodded, and Hotaru drew in a slow breath. She wondered if it was Kachiko who had delivered the message; it would explain the Scorpion's reticence over the past few days. It also explained why Hochiahime didn't wish to involve Toshimoko; her uncle had had little love for the Scorpion before Shoju's betrayal. Since the Emperor's murder, if a Scorpion told him Lady Sun would rise in the east, he would set his own eyes firmly to the west to watch for her approach.

"I still do not understand why you've told me this," Hotaru said. "I can understand your reluctance to bring this matter to the regent or to Toshimoko, but why me? I sympathize with your plight, for we are family as well, but I'm certain the Imperial Guard would aid you, with or without the regent's approval."

"And in so doing, drive another wedge into the already fracturing Empire," the empress said. "No, Hotaru. The Empire needs the Hantei's sons to return to make it whole, but you cannot hope to make something whole by splintering it further." She fell quiet, and once again Hotaru glimpsed the uncertainty and fear that boiled just beneath the surface. After a long moment, the empress shook her head once, decisively. "No. It must be you. My son is being held in Ryokō Owari Toshi."

Ryokō Owari Toshi. Or, more commonly, the City of Lies. It

was, at least nominally, a trading hub in Scorpion lands. A city, not unlike the City of the Rich Frog or Toshi Ranbo, that had switched hands more than once in its lifetime. In practice, it was a den of inequity run more by criminal gangs, bandits, and disaffected rōnin than it was by the Scorpion. Unless you believed the rumors that it was actually the Scorpion themselves in charge of those criminals. Hotaru had never been there. There was little of her own knowledge or expertise that could be useful in such a city.

But she did know someone who could.

*I see, now.* "It isn't me you need at all," Hotaru noted. "What you need is someone who can convince Bayushi Kachiko to help you."

But Hochiahime shook her head.

"The Mother of Scorpions has already offered her aid," she said, causing a ripple of shock to flutter through Hotaru. "I believe she makes ready to undertake this journey as we speak. Bayushi Kachiko has sworn that she will see my son freed and returned to me by any means necessary. I do not need you to convince her of anything." Again, that long, hesitant pause, and this time, in the weight of Hochiahime's gaze, Hotaru saw doubt. Not fear for Sotorii. Not worry over sending the wife of her husband's killer to rescue her son. But doubt in Hotaru herself.

That doubt stabbed at her as deeply as the trust the empress had demonstrated moved her.

"In this matter, I must put my faith in Bayushi Kachiko," Hochiahime went on. "As much as I love my sons, my first duty is to the Empire, and I will not allow them to be used as the levers that break it apart. But do not think for a single moment that I trust her." For the first time, the tumultuous emotions surging beneath the calm demeanor entered into Hochiahime's voice, and Hotaru could hear the anger and even the edges of hatred burning through the words. "I could never trust that woman, or any of her clan. How you can..." She cut herself off and drew a calming breath and gave another firm shake of the head. Hotaru kept her expression neutral. She was unsurprised that the Dowager Empress was aware of her relationship with Kachiko. They worked to keep the details clandestine, but in the Imperial Palace, there were few better informed than the empress.

"What matters is that I can trust *you*," Hochiahime finished. "I must use Bayushi Kachiko. I need her expertise. I need her access to Scorpion lands. I might even need the fact that she was married to the man who was the daimyō of that forsaken clan. But I also need someone at her side who will not betray me. Someone who has influence over her. And someone that I know will put the good of the Empire above her own needs."

The Dowager Empress looked directly in her eyes, and Hotaru felt the heat of that gaze. The woman known far and wide for her almost preternatural calm was a raging torrent within. There was a depth and power there that Hotaru had never before seen, not in the days of her childhood when Hochiahime had been like a favored aunt to her and not in the times Hotaru had visited the empress after she married into the line of Hantei. "You are that person, Doji Hotaru," Hochiahime said. "Am I wrong?"

Hotaru thought of the afternoon she had just spent preparing her clan for war. What would happen if she left the Crane to defend against the Lion without her? The landscape of war changed quickly, and strong leadership was required. Someone would have to make decisions; someone would have to lead the clan. In her absence, who would that be? How many of her people would die because she was not there to lead them?

And yet... the Empire needed a clear and stable succession far more than it needed her, or even her people. If the prince returned and claimed the throne, the regency would end. The conflict between the Lion and the Crane could be resolved by Imperial decree, a decree that she could not seek from Kakita Yoshi. Lives would be lost in the meantime, but how many more lives – not just from her clan, but from all the clans – would be lost if a scion of the Hantei line was not restored to the throne?

*Ancestors, guide me,* she thought in silent prayer. Do I abandon my people for the good of the Empire? Or do I abandon the Empire for the good of my people?

It was an impossible choice. And, no matter how hard she tried to push it down, worry for Kachiko rose up inside her. The roads of the Empire were no longer safe. Ryokō Owari and the surrounding area was a nest of Scorpion treachery and ill intent. Kachiko would be traveling alone, without bodyguards, without the authority or fear her name would bring. How could she allow Kachiko to face those dangers alone?

Her people. Her empire. Her love.

"No, Hochiahime." Her words, soft as they were, seemed to echo through the chamber. "You are not wrong."

# 22
# Toturi

The Village of the Golden Blades was no longer recognizable. Toturi surveyed the wall – palisade, really – that had risen around the village, intersected at four points by the cart paths that allowed the farmers and merchants a way in and out of town. Those "gates," though they were little more than gaps in the defenses now, were flanked by the skeletal scaffolding that would become watchtowers. Day by day, the Village of the Golden Blades was transforming from a modest farming town, indistinguishable from thousands like it across the Empire, to a fortified enclave that would never have to worry about raiding parties and bandits again.

The modest defenses wouldn't mean much if it came to true war, Toturi knew, but there was only so much he could do. When his forces left the Village of the Golden Blades, it would be as safe as they could make it. If the Lion, or anyone else, wanted to destroy it, they would have to invest some serious effort into the attack. If he were in command of the Lion, he wouldn't bother. The strategic gain wouldn't be worth the cost in lives.

But then, if he were in charge, the Lion would not be at war.

He felt the familiar surge of shame at the thought, but somehow, the sting of that shame was less than it had been. His failure had resulted in the death of the Emperor. His failure had put Matsu Tsuko in charge of the Lion and had installed Kakita Yoshi as regent. His failure had been the spark that ignited the fires of instability that threatened the very foundations of the Empire. He could not hide from that, not from himself and not from the rest of the world. The responsibility had been his, and he had failed.

But what could he have done differently?

He could not be by the Emperor's side every moment of every day. Could he have foreseen Bayushi Shoju's betrayal? The Scorpion had been one of the Emperor's closest advisors and, by all accounts, a trusted friend. All proverbs about the nature of the Scorpion aside, there was no reason to suspect Shoju had any plans to attempt a murderous coup.

But seeing to the safety of the Emperor and Imperial family had been his most important duty. And he had failed.

"Your forces grow by the day."

He turned to see Utaku Kamoko. She still wore her armor – he had yet to see the woman clad in anything else – and the new dents in the steel bore silent witness to her role in the battle. Her eyes were directed beyond the rough palisade to the encampment that had sprung up around the Village of the Golden Blades.

"Did your scouting bear fruit?" he asked.

She shook her head. "We found no sign of Agetoki's forces. If he intends to attack this village again, his scouts are keeping a low profile." She shrugged. "Trying to train up horsemen while scouting for the enemy is… challenging."

In the weeks since the attack on the village, the trickle of people coming to his banner had turned into a flood. Now, what they had ironically dubbed Toturi's Army was beginning to resemble the actual thing. He had delegated the organization of the peasants, rōnin, and even a few wandering samurai to Daisuke and Toku while he oversaw the village fortifications. Kamoko had volunteered to lead the scouting parties and help train up what small force of cavalry they could muster. Daisuke and Toku had done better than he could have expected; the encampment surrounding the village would have done any Lion regiment proud. Still, most of those who had come were not soldiers; they were men and women either displaced from their homes by the conflicts sweeping the Empire, or those who had grown tired of watching all that they built over the course of their lives torn down. They were people seeking a better way, but unsure of how to find it.

"I think many of them will stay here," Toturi said at last. "The village will need help for the harvest, and now with the walls going up, it will be a place of safety."

"I'm afraid you are wrong, my lord."

He turned his gaze from the camp to look at the Unicorn, trying to hide his surprise. They had not known each other long, but he could not think of a time when Kamoko had so directly contradicted him. "How so?"

"These people are not here for safety," the Unicorn said. "They did not come to be farmers. They are here because they can see that something is broken in the Empire. How many of the rōnin in those ranks do you think were rōnin a year ago, or even a month ago? Many are like Daidoji Daisuke, looking to change things but unable to do so through the normal politics of the Empire." She shook her head, her dark locks bouncing like a horse's mane. "No, Lord Toturi. What you have is a force unlike any in the history of the Empire, perhaps stretching all the way back to the Founding. These are not people who want to fight for their clans or their personal glory. These are people who want to fight for a better world, for all of us. You have given them a path to do so. The promise of full bellies and a roof over their heads will not easily sway them from that path."

Toturi considered her words, her passion, as he gazed over the rows of tents laid out in precise lines next to the fields. "Perhaps you are correct, Kamoko," he said. As he did, he felt the familiar weight of responsibility that never seemed to ease. "But if that is the case, then what are we to do with them?"

Defending this village from slaughter seemed a simple enough action, but Toturi knew it would not be long before full scale war broke out across the Empire. And when that happened, things would no longer be so clear. "It is a simple task to say you wish to protect the innocent," he said, "but what do you do when the innocent and guilty are intermingled on all sides? Are the Lion peasants who die on Crane steel any less innocent than the Crane that fall to the Lion? What of the raids that your own Battle Maidens conduct across your borders? How do I use this new model army in a land where warfare and death are as much a part of our traditions as venerating our ancestors and taking tea? If Matsu Agetoki himself was defending a village from a ravening horde of Iron Warriors, would you stand by his side, so firm in your cause?"

Kamoko was quiet for a long moment, and Toturi wondered if he had gone too far. The Unicorn had never confided her desire for vengeance on Agetoki to him; he only knew of it through Daisuke's tale. But if she was going to counsel him on how to use the forces that had come to his banner, then he needed to know where she stood.

"I would stand by him," she said at last, each word sounding as if it had to be pulled bodily from her. "Spirits of my people, of my mother, forgive me, but I would. Until the innocent were safe, I would fight at his side. Even his." She turned and met his eye, and in her gaze, he saw both an unshakable resolve and the deep fury that burned within. "But when that fight was done, my lord, I would cut him down. I would cut him down without mercy and without remorse."

"And vengeance would be yours." Toturi nodded. "And Agetoki's wife? His sons? His daughters?"

"What of them?"

Toturi smiled, a smile tinged with sadness. "I mean no insult, Kamoko. By every tradition of the Empire, you have the right to your vengeance. And by those same traditions, Matsu Agetoki's loved ones, once you take your vengeance, will have the right to theirs." He looked from the bustling war camp to the industrious village and in them saw the dichotomy of the Empire he loved. "I only wonder, Kamoko… when does it end? Matsu Agetoki slays your mother; you slay Matsu Agetoki; Matsu Agetoki's family comes looking for you. And so on."

"My mother died defending Unicorn villages from unprovoked attacks. Matsu Agetoki will die for carrying out those attacks on the defenseless. Can you stand there and tell me that those things have equal weight, that they are both equally worthy of vengeance?" The hint of anger had been honed to a cutting edge, and Toturi knew that he had to tread carefully. He did not think that Kamoko, even angered, would attack him. But he did not want to drive her away either. She was a skilled warrior and a valuable presence on the battlefield, but even more so, he felt something in the Unicorn's presence. Nothing romantic, though Kamoko was vibrant and beautiful by any standard, but a shared understanding of the world, perhaps. He sensed in her a kindred spirit, a person that could become a true friend. That was a rare and precious thing in the Empire, and he had no wish to squander it.

But it was also why he felt the need to press her on her quest for vengeance in the first place.

"No, Kamoko. *I* do not think they have the same moral weight. But is any parent's death just when seen through the eyes of their child? Is any child's death just when seen through the eyes of a parent? I do not deny you your right to seek justice for those you lost; I only wonder if the Empire can ever truly know peace if we settle every matter at the tip of a blade."

"Perhaps not, Lord Toturi," the Unicorn said. "But I will not simply ignore my mother's death. What path is there for justice? What is the point of the Empire if we cannot protect the innocent and punish the guilty? Peace is all well and good. But peace without justice is little more than slavery."

"And justice without peace is the tyranny of the strong," Toturi countered. "Make no mistake, Kamoko – when it comes to war, justice is the sole province of the victor. My people know that better than most. And we both know that justice is a word known only to the samurai. Ask Toku about justice. Or, better yet, ask some of those villagers you passed on your way to my camp if they would prefer justice or peace."

Kamoko narrowed her eyes at that, and Toturi felt a flash of regret at the words. They both knew that those peasants were almost certainly dead. "Forgive me, Kamoko," Toturi offered into the silence. "I go too far at times. A holdover from my days in the Dragon monastery, where such contemplations were encouraged."

"Remind me never to visit the Dragon monasteries," Kamoko said flatly. "But there is truth to what you say, my lord, though it does not change the fact that my mother was killed needlessly. Nor does it change the fact that those Crane peasants you mentioned have neither justice nor peace." She looked, first to the industrious village and then to the equally industrious war camp, seeing, Toturi thought, the same dichotomy of the Empire that he saw there. "I cannot simply abandon my search for justice. My course is set. If I do not try to find my own justice, then it will not be found."

"As you say," Toturi agreed. "And perhaps *that* is the true problem that we face. Perhaps we all need someone to turn to, to help us find justice when it seems there is none to be found."

They fell into silence then, each lost in their own contemplations, as around them villagers and soldiers alike went about their tasks. Toturi strove to remember the lessons learned among the Dragon, to take these respites for what they were; a calm in the ever-raging storm of life. But he could not fully quell the turmoil in his mind. The peasants and rōnin that had flocked to him saw their numbers grow daily, and Toturi could no longer deny what they were swiftly becoming. It seemed the Fortunes truly did want him at the head of an army, but to what end? How could he use that force to unify the Empire? How could he use it to give justice not just to the samurai, but to the peasantry who were seen as acceptable collateral damage in the struggles of their betters?

Stopping the attack on the Village of the Golden Blades had seemed the right thing to do, but he had no desire to arbitrarily throw his support in with the Crane. The Crane were no less guilty than the Lion when it came to the border wars and political strife. Nor could he simply travel the lands at the head of an army, stopping attacks on the peasantry whenever he chanced across them. That sounded noble enough, but it would have no impact whatsoever on the broader situation. He could defeat a hundred Akodo Sachios, and there would be a hundred more, waiting to carry out the orders of their daimyō.

Toturi sighed as the solution rose up before him once more. The princes needed to be found. To have any chance of meaningful change, the Empire needed to evolve, and it could not do that without an emperor on the throne. But Toturi could not search for the princes at the head of an army, even if he wanted to.

One last time, he considered abandoning those who had come

to him, slipping away and resuming the search for the heirs to the throne. It was a fleeting fancy, and one he soon discarded. Restoring the line of Hantei was important, but it was no longer his path; he would leave it for others to walk.

But if he could not restore Prince Sotorii to his rightful place, and if he could not parade across the Empire hoping to be where he was needed when the time was right, what options were left to him? And how long could he move at the head of an army before the clans saw him as a bigger threat than their fellows and moved against him?

"There is no clear path forward," he muttered, breaking the silence.

"No," Kamoko agreed. "But if we cannot see the way, then we can trust in our ancestors and the Fortunes. I do not think they have forsaken us, my lord." She rested one hand lightly on his shoulder and gave a not-so-gentle squeeze. "The way forward may not be clear now, but it will become so. For both of us."

Toturi grunted, pushing away the worries. "Then let us make the most of the time between now and then. If you are to find your justice, and if we are to build an empire that gives peace and justice to all its people, then there is much to do." He surveyed the village one last time before turning to the command tent, rising in the center of the war camp. "Let's be about it."

# 23

# Yakamo

Yakamo felt the darkness around him like a physical force. He knelt in the very center of the top of Kuni Yori's tower, the thin fabric of his hakama no barrier to the harsh winds that ripped across the parapets. The stones were cold beneath his knees, digging into his flesh and numbing his legs, but he scarcely noticed them. His torso was stripped naked, bare to the stabbing wind. His right hand rested against his right thigh. His left arm – what remained of it – dangled loosely from his shoulder.

His left hand *still* hurt. He could not explain it, for there was nothing there to cause him pain. But he felt it, nonetheless, burning and twisting as if the nothingness of the missing limb were itself a fire. The severed stump of his forearm glistened red in the darkness, the bandages stripped away. Candles, as thick as his remaining wrist and some standing two feet high, encircled him. Orange flames danced and flickered madly, but despite the constant howl of the wind, they did not die.

Yakamo shivered. He could feel the gathering of the spirits, their presence swirling around him like a storm. He had felt them before, when he had been healed after battle, or when the shindōshi called on them to rain fire and earth upon the creatures of the Shadowlands. But these spirits felt different, infused with a malevolence that chilled him more than the biting wind. In the grip of that otherworldly ire, Yakamo felt the cold hand of fear clutching at his chest.

Kuni Yori, clad in his formal robes and his face bearing the bone-white paint of his order, stepped into the circle of light. The dancing shadows pooled in the contours of his body, sharply contrasting his angular features and emaciated limbs. He thrust his arms into the air, and as he did, a peal of thunder rolled across the sky, loud enough to shake the tower. The wind shrieked in response, until Yakamo had to kneel forward, hunching his shoulders so that it would not bowl him over with its force.

Still the candles did not go out.

Kuni Yori stood like a bared blade, the wind parting around him, touching him less than it did the flames. He thrust his hands higher into the air and started to chant. The words that poured from the shindōshi's mouth were not of the Empire nor any foreign land whose speech Yakamo had ever heard. From the tortured expression that danced on Kuni Yori's face, they were not made for the human tongue. Each phrase seemed ripped from him, as much a scream of pain as an imploring of the spirits. The words stabbed into Yakamo like knives, clear and sharp despite the winds, which continued to swell with each of Kuni Yori's shrieks.

Yakamo forced his head up, looking beyond Kuni Yori to the sky. Lord Moon and the innumerable stars had vanished, swallowed by the racing clouds called forth by the storm. Lightning flashed, a crimson streak that slashed the clouds like a bloody whip.

"Hida Yakamo," Kuni Yori shouted, his voice raw and frayed. "They have come! I have called upon the spirits, and they have answered."

Yakamo felt the presence of the spirits surge, and with them came a sudden flood of familiar darkness. The tainted, almost tangible darkness of the Shadowlands. His skin crawled, recoiling from the oily touch, and Yakamo clenched his teeth. These were not the elemental spirits that Yakamo knew; these were not the benign servants of the ancestors and gods. This was something else.

You knew what Yori was offering, Yakamo. Do not pretend you did not. Doubt flooded him. This was wrong. This was a betrayal of what it meant to stand on the Wall, to fight against the darkness. Should he turn back? Could he?

His eyes fell upon his withered arm and the sense of his own failure washed over him like a wave. He had failed in the Shadowlands, and Bunzō, Momoe, and the others had died as a result. He had failed to defeat Hitomi, and it had cost him his competence as a warrior. He had failed to convince the regent's court to come to the aid of the Wall, and that failure might well cost him his people, the Empire they protected, and their very existence. Worst of all, he had failed his father. No matter the words spoken, he could not escape the look of pity and disappointment that haunted his dreams. The litany of failures seemed a physical force, one that crawled into his open mouth and stole his breath, silencing any objections.

Another ear-shattering peal of thunder split the night. Raising his head, Yakamo blinked rapidly against the wind, not believing what his blurred vision was showing him. He could *see* the spirits. They were lithe, twisting things, made of ethereal fog. Each was no bigger than a weasel, and they moved through the night sky with the same predatory grace. They had heads and torsos reminiscent of people, but their bodies tapered off into drifting smoke. Their eyes burned with the same sullen glow as the flashes of lightning above. As they swarmed across the tower top, they reached with grasping fingers, their clawed hands ripping at the fabric of reality itself. They seemed to gather at an invisible seam, stacked atop one another on either side, talons digging into the nothingness. Then they pulled, and reality faltered.

Like a tear opening in silk, the edges of the night were peeled back, frayed threads dancing in the wind, and Yakamo found himself staring into chaos. He had no other word for it, for the landscape beyond that rift was like nothing he had ever envisioned. It was a formless, shapeless tangle of darkness and color, a scintillating, oscillating riot of movement. He couldn't name a single feature, yet looking upon it brought a sharp, stabbing pain to his head. It held his gaze and try though he might, he could not look away. Then the sound hit him, drowning out the wind and Kuni Yori's cries of ecstasy and pain. It was an almost physical thing, a wall of noise so intense that, at first, it had no meaning. But then it resolved into something Yakamo recognized quite clearly.

Screaming.

The noise was the wailing of countless voices, all crying out in pain and terror. It sent a spike of fear into Yakamo's heart, but even that paled to what came next. There was a shape resolving in the turmoil. The turmoil, he realized, of the Realm of Torment itself.

What had Kuni Yori done? What had Yakamo agreed to?

"He comes!" Kuni Yori shouted, his piercing shriek cutting through both the howling of the wind and the howling of the damned. "Make ready. He comes!"

Yakamo had no idea what Kuni Yori expected of him, but even if he had, he doubted he could have done anything about it. All he could do was stare at the portal to the depths of the Realm of Torment and watch as an oni emerged. No, not an oni, he realized. An oni *lord*, one of the rulers of the Realm of Torment, second only to Fu Leng himself. Fear filled him, an unnatural fear that had little to do with his own feelings. But beneath that fear was an undeniable sense of power. That power called to him.

At first, the demon seemed as formless and shapeless as the chaos in which it resided, but as it moved closer to the rift between the realms, it began to coalesce. For a moment, Yakamo thought he saw something insect-like and alien, but then the shape shivered and melted, resolving into a form much closer to a man. Though no less terrifying.

The oni stood taller than Yakamo, towering over eight feet. It was by no means the largest oni he had seen in his years on the Wall, but it exuded menace in a way that turned his blood to ice. With every inch of movement, it seemed to take on more substance, as if the act of pulling itself into the mortal realm freed it from the formless chaos of the Realm of Torment. The oni's skin took on an ominous shade, a pale red that spoke of rust and decay. Chitinous plates, almost like the steel plates of the ō-yoroi Yakamo wore during the heaviest fighting on the Wall, covered it, lending the oni a breadth that made it seem stocky despite its towering height. Horns protruded from the creature's forehead, sweeping to either side before cutting back at sharp angles. Its eyes burned with fiery intensity, glowing with an orange light above a mouth that was obscured by a half-dozen mandibles that looked as sharp as knives.

But worst of all were the oni's arms, which did not end in hands; as if in a mockery of all Yakamo's ancestors, they bulged into a pair of chitinous crab-like claws. Those claws reached out, the joints twisting at unnatural angles, grasping at the edges of the rend in reality as the demon pulled itself from the nothing and onto the tower top. As it emerged, it threw back its head and howled, the roar drowning out the storm and shaking the foundations of the world. The sound threatened to shatter his eardrums, and it brought with it a charnel stench of things long dead. It should have terrified him, but Yakamo found that he was past the point of fear. He looked at the demon filled with an emptiness to rival the nothing from which it emerged.

"Your name, Yakamo!" Kuni Yori shrieked. "It demands your name! Speak it, and you will be restored."

Yakamo realized in that moment that there was still a choice to be made. The chain of events that had led him here might have cascaded out of his control, but he did not have to go through with this final step. He could clamp his teeth together and refuse to give the oni his name, and with it, the power to influence the Mortal Realm. It might well cost him his life, for who knew what the oni, deprived of the reason it had been summoned, would do? But death seemed an easy thing. If he did not die, it would mean giving up his life as a warrior, for how could he fight as he was now? In either case, it would mean leaving the fate of the Wall in the hands of others. And it would mean knowing that he would never again see even the pride in his father's eyes.

Yakamo made his choice.

"My name is Hida Yakamo, son of Hida Kisada, part of an unbroken line that stretches back to the Fortune Hida," he shouted. "I name you, demon. By my ancestors and the Fortunes, I name you. Yakamo no Oni, my name is yours!"

As he shouted the words into the storm, the wind howled to hurricane strength. But unlike before, when it pushed against him, trying to bowl him from the tower, this wind seemed to tear right through Yakamo. It swept through him, passing flesh and clawing at the very core of his being, and he felt something go with it. Some part of what made him *him* was caught in that torrent and broken from his soul.

But it did not leave him empty.

In its wake he felt a new strength surging within him, a torrent of energy that dwarfed the storm around him. For one brief instant, he understood what it was to be a god.

Then his left arm exploded in agony. He threw his head back and screamed, his cry and that of Yakamo no Oni blending into one unending roar. What remained of his left arm swelled and writhed and he felt bones snapping as his flesh twisted and grew. Tendrils of ropy muscle erupted from the stump of his forearm in a shower of pus and gore, twisting around one another and taking new shape.

He clawed at the stones of the tower with his right hand, and he felt them crack beneath the force of grasping fingers. He stared in horror as his left arm continued to change, the flesh knotting together in new patterns. It seemed to go on forever, an unending litany of pain as he and Yakamo no Oni howled in concert.

When it was finally done, it was not his severed hand that had returned to him. What he held up before his face was the serrated and chitin-covered claw of a giant crab. It dwarfed his human hand, opening and closing seemingly of its own volition with a *click-clack-click-clack*. The chitin – the same blue-gray as the colors of his clan – grew almost to his elbow, where it faded into his regular skin. The muscles of his left arm, which had withered in the weeks of convalescence, now bulged once more, straining against his own skin. The pain had fled, and it had taken rational thought with it, for he could only stare at what had become of his body.

He forced his eyes away, aware that Kuni Yori's piercing incantations had started once more. He looked up in time to see Yakamo no Oni standing a few paces away, a twisted nightmare against reality. The oni's own left claw was gone, leaving a ragged stump where its claw – the one now grafted to Yakamo's flesh – had been. His eyes met the oni's and for the briefest moment, he saw his own face, mirrored over the demonic features. But the oni was already losing substance, growing translucent, fading in the raging winds. The candles that somehow still burned in the fury of the storm flared, rising several feet into the air, as Kuni Yori's voice reached a crescendo. The mouth of the demon irised open in a final, soundless roar, and with another gust of wind, Yakamo no Oni was gone.

The storm died as suddenly as it had begun. Kuni Yori's incantation stopped and silence fell, broken only by Yakamo's ragged breathing. He was still on his knees, one hand feeling the rough press of the stone against his palm. The other...

His stomach churned as he gazed at the monstrous claw that was now part of him. The sight of it sickened him, made him feel less than human. But there was something else as well. He could feel the undeniable power of it, the strength that infused not only the claw, but coursed through the rest of his body, flowing from the chitinous appendage and into the rest of him. Though he still knelt against the stones, the lingering weakness from his injury was gone. Vanished, as if it had never been. With it had gone the pain of the transformation and a dozen other aches and pains he had scarcely been aware of. His eyes fell upon the stones beneath him, stones that had cracked under the grip of his right, human, hand.

Despite the churning in his stomach, a smile pulled at his lips. He was strong now, stronger than he had ever been before. With this strength, this power, he could stand as a champion against the Shadowlands. He could lead his people like a living banner, striking down whatever horrors Fu Leng might throw at them. With this power, he could prove, beyond the shadow of a doubt, that he was the rightful successor to the Crab Clan and a worthy heir of the Great Bear.

"Rise, Hida Yakamo," Kuni Yori said. The shindōshi's voice was hoarse and brittle. Yakamo rose to his feet, seeing that the ritual had taken a toll upon the man. Beneath the bone-white makeup, Kuni Yori's face looked sallow, his eyes rheumy. Despite his appearance, Yakamo sensed an echo of the same dark energy that was coursing through his own veins. "The spirits have answered my call; you are made whole."

Yakamo glanced at the claw once more, and this time, neither mind nor stomach rebelled at the sight. Kuni Yori was right; he was made whole. Perhaps the provenance of his healing had required the powers of the Shadowlands, but was there any sweeter justice than turning those self-same powers against that darkness?

Yakamo smiled, straightening to his full height. For the first time, he willed the claw to open and close, watching as the serrated pinchers clenched shut with a grip that could snap steel. His smile widened, showing teeth, and he felt a feral need somewhere deep within. He needed to test this newfound strength. He needed to feel the bone-crushing power as his claw closed over something's head and popped it like a melon.

He needed to kill something.

"Come," Kuni Yori said, as if reading his mind. "The battle yet rages, and your presence will be a boon to our forces. Don your armor, warrior of the Crab. Take up your weapons. And lead your people to victory."

A final peal of thunder split the sky at those words and a wordless, eager growl escaped Yakamo's lips. This time, the Shadowlands would be the ones to know fear, despair, and death. He turned toward the trapdoor leading down into Kuni Yori's tower and, ultimately, to the field of battle.

He was aware of the eyes upon him as he strode down the battlements. He wore his great armor, the massive steel plates dented and scarred from the blows of countless battles, but never broken. That protection came at a price; the armor weighed enough that even the biggest of men were encumbered by its mass. But not Yakamo, not anymore. He barely felt the armor, just as he barely felt the weight of the iron tetsubō, carried in his right hand. That massive club should have required two hands to wield, but Yakamo spun it as easily as a wakizashi.

But it was not the ease with which he moved in his armor, or the casual way in which he carried the length of iron, that drew all eyes to him. Nor was it Yakamo's presence, though word of his return from the capital and his injury at the hands of Mirumoto Hitomi had spread up and down the Wall like wildfire. Every eye was drawn to the claw. As he approached, the low conversations of the soldiers on the parapets trailed off as they stared openly at Kuni Yori's work. Yakamo did not begrudge them those stares, nor did he acknowledge them. Familiar faces gaped at him in shock; he ignored them and continued down the Wall, to the bastion where his father and his father's generals planned. He heard the whispers that trailed in his wake, but he ignored those as well.

*Let them talk.* Let them speculate on the how and why of his emergence. It didn't matter to Yakamo. He had been in the Imperial City when the massed army of the Shadowlands had arrived at the Wall. He had been tied to the saddle of his horse, missing a limb and dancing on the border of life and death when the first assaults had begun. And he had been preparing for Kuni Yori's ritual when the most recent wave from the creatures of Fu Leng had broken against the ramparts. He could see the exhaustion in every face, feel the despair of every wounded samurai standing at their post. The Shadowlands army, uncountable in its numbers, was still out there, darkening the plains like a carpet of ants. It was only a matter of hours before they staged their next assault.

*Let them come.* Yakamo would show them the depths of his newfound power. He would break their assault and throw them from the Wall. He would show his people that they need not fear that this was the end.

And he would show his father that he was worthy of being his son and heir.

He found Hida Kisada in the central bastion, bent over the sand table that showed the length of the Wall. His brother, Sukune, stood slightly apart, looking uncomfortable in his armor. His sister, O-Ushi, was gesturing at the table. "They are pressing up and down the Wall. There have already been several minor breaches at the smaller outposts. But nowhere so much as where we stand."

"Because they know if they break us here, the rest of the Wall will crumble," Yakamo said as he strode into the room.

All eyes turned to him. He saw the anticipated shock in the stares of the generals. He saw the flash of revulsion across Sukune's face as his mask of indifference shattered. A slight gasp escaped his lips, a sure sign of the cowardice and unfitness of Yakamo's brother. O-Ushi watched him with a carefully blank expression, but he did not miss the widening of her eyes nor the slight step she took backward. Both of his siblings could not keep their eyes from his restored – and much improved – arm. Their shock at seeing him was like a balm, and it brought a smile to his face. He could practically smell their fear.

It smelled delicious.

It was his father, however, who surprised him.

Hida Kisada smiled.

The Great Bear rarely smiled and Yakamo could remember no more than a double handful of times when that smile had been directed at him. He felt his chest swell with pride and he stood taller. "You are looking well, son."

"I feel well, father," Yakamo replied. He raised his left arm, opening and closing the claw with a sharp click that echoed in the bastion like a hammer strike. "Kuni Yori's gift will be put to good use. The foul creatures of Fu Leng cannot stand against the might of the Crab, especially now." He saw his brother flinch back at the snapping of the claw. "You disagree, brother?"

Yakamo could see the sweat beading at the brim of Sukune's

helm. His brother's face was pale, but he offered a minimal bow. "I am glad you are well, brother. I am perhaps unsettled by the rumors of darkness and fire atop Kuni Yori's tower the other night, and the appearance of a claw that belongs on the arm of an oni–"

"Yakamo, stop!"

Yakamo turned his head to stare at his father, wondering why he had shouted at him. Only then did he realize he had crossed the intervening space between the door and Sukune. His brother's hands were locked around the base of Yakamo's claw, straining against him. The claw itself, Yakamo realized, was clamped around his brother's neck. Sukune's feet dangled in the air.

Yakamo barely felt the weight of him.

He looked at his brother's eyes, which were wide and starting to bug out of his head as he fought for breath. He was vaguely aware of O-Ushi grabbing her iron-shod tetsubō and his father restraining her with one outstretched hand. It would be so easy. All he had to do was squeeze just a little harder than he was now and Sukune's neck would snap. The raw strength of his new limb awed him.

Sukune made a small, strangled noise, and Yakamo blinked.

By the Fortunes and ancestors, what was he doing? He opened his claw and Sukune collapsed to the ground coughing and sputtering, face slowly turning from ugly reddish-purple back to its normal tanned flesh as he fought for oxygen. Yakamo could see the bruise already forming at his neck, along with a few points where the rough chitin had broken the skin and drawn blood.

"Forgive me, brother," he said. Even to his own ears, the words sounded hollow, and he did not kneel to help Sukune to his feet. The man had insulted him, after all. Hadn't he? Yakamo couldn't really recall, but it didn't matter. What mattered was the power he had displayed. That power would be the new mainstay of the clan. It would be how they threw back the Shadowlands. "I forgot myself for a moment."

He looked over to his father and sister, both of whom were staring at him with blank faces. O-Ushi still had her tetsubō at the ready, and Yakamo could see the tremble in her hand. He had to stifle a sneer. Who were they to judge him? They didn't know what he had been through in recent months. They didn't know the power he now wielded.

"Yakamo," Kisada began, but he was cut short as the sonorous alarm bells that dotted the Wall began to sound. O-Uchi turned to the nearest window, gazing out at the Shadowlands horde.

"They come," she said. "Another major push."

Yakamo met his father's eye and held it for a long moment. In his father's gaze, he saw a faint hint of uncertainty, but there was something else there. Something stronger. Expectation? Hope? He could not place it, exactly.

"Go to the second bastion," Kisada told him. "The fighting has been greatest there. The command is yours." He paused to give Yakamo, and his arm, an appraising look. "Show us the power you claim, Yakamo. Show us that the spirits have chosen you as their champion."

I will.

Yakamo slammed the claw to his chest in salute and turned toward the exit, his brother's crumpled form forgotten behind him.

# 24

# Hotaru

H otaru watched the people pass through the gate, moving in and out of the Imperial City, and felt a strange sense of symmetry. Toshimoko had waited for her at this very spot when she first entered the city, so long ago it seemed. She wished he were here now. His blade would be a welcome addition for what was to come. But as far as the Emerald Champion was concerned, Hotaru was in her chambers, dealing with the thousand tasks needed to marshal the Crane against the advances of the Lion.

She felt a wave of guilt wash over her. Guilt at deceiving her uncles; Toshimoko was dear to her, and Yoshi had some right to know what she was about to undertake, especially since those already concerned with rising Crane influence might look askance at the Crane Clan Champion rushing off to the rescue of the prince. But she felt even more guilt for abandoning her people on the eve of war. Her officers had their orders; they knew what they must do. But she could tell them nothing more than she had an Imperial duty that would take her from the heat of battle. It was a risk; if her soldiers came to believe that their Clan Champion had abandoned them, it would have a measurable effect on their fighting spirit. But if she could save the prince, and put an end to the senseless war, how many of those same soldiers might be saved? And how could she deny Hochiahime's request? How could she let Kachiko face the dangers ahead by herself?

She couldn't. Which was why she found herself here, waiting for the Scorpion. She had tracked Kachiko down – never an easy task – and the pair had made hasty plans. They could not be seen leaving the palace together; such a thing would attract the eyes of every servant and courtier and set their tongues to wagging. When it was discovered that both she and Kachiko had left, better that nothing indicated that they had done so together. They would meet here, at the gates, and begin the long journey to the City of Lies. It would take the better part of a fortnight to reach the city, and then their task would truly begin.

Hotaru scanned the crowd, watching for the familiar form of Kachiko, but also watching the faces of the people that passed by. The samurai all wore the same emotionless mask, schooling their faces to impassive stillness no matter the situation. Some of the peasants and merchants, those of higher classes, tried to do the same, though their expressions were far easier to read. The lower status peasants didn't even try to hide their emotions; she could see the joy and pain, the laughter and loss, in every smile or frown that passed by. But there was one emotion she saw on every face, one common thread that tied everyone in this city together, and it reaffirmed her decision to leave the fate of the Crane in the hands of her generals.

Fear.

In every face that passed her, laughing or serious, shadowed or joyful, Hotaru saw fear. She saw it in the furtive glances that the citizens darted at one another, in the quickened pace that people took when they passed each other on the street. She felt it in the music of the city, always frenetic, but now beating with an almost manic rhythm. The citizens of Otosan Uchi were afraid; and why wouldn't they be?

The Emperor was dead, his heirs vanished into the night. Two of the most powerful clans in the Empire were moving toward open war. The heir to the Crab had come down from the Wall, warning of the dangers to come, and had left the city maimed and tied to his horse. The whispers of war that had drifted on the air since the Emperor's murder had become open shouts, telling of the chaos and mayhem to come.

Which was, she reminded herself, exactly why it was so important to retrieve Sotorii from his captors and put him back on the throne. A strong ruler, with a firm guiding hand, could put this madness to rest.

"Are you ready to depart, Hotaru?"

She jumped – literally jumped – at the words, her knuckles tightening on the haft of her naginata. Hotaru wore simple traveling clothes, her kimono and hakama woven of plain cotton with a hempen overcoat. They bore no decoration and were dyed in muted browns and grays. Her hair was tied back in a warrior's tail rather than in the elaborate styles her servants normally prepared for her, and tucked under a conical straw hat. A pack rested at her feet. She still wore her daishō – and carried her naginata, of course – but she had done her best to assume the role of rōnin. She had garnered a few strange looks as she left the palace grounds, but once she had passed through those gates and into the city proper, no one had looked at her twice.

Hearing her name, spoken so close and with such familiarity, had been a shock. But it was nothing compared to the shock she received when she turned toward the speaker.

Bayushi Kachiko stood there, having walked to within an arm's length of Hotaru without her even realizing it. That wasn't surprising; Kachiko might draw the eye of everyone in the room as soon as she stepped in, but she could also blend into any landscape as silently as a ghost. She had opted for clothing much in line with what Hotaru was wearing, though instead of browns and muted grays, the Scorpion was clad in shades of black and… darker black. That, too, was unsurprising. She carried no weapons, or at least, no weapons that Hotaru could see. Which was also what Hotaru had expected; Kachiko might be deadly with her blades, but she was not one to give away the advantage of surprise.

None of that startled the Crane as she regarded the Scorpion. It was something much simpler, much more fundamental, that captured Hotaru's attention.

Bayushi Kachiko was not wearing a mask.

In all their years together, Hotaru had never seen the Scorpion without some form of face covering. Those masks had ranged from painted porcelain to translucent veils, though every one was elegant, graceful, and designed to draw attention to the face that wore it. In recent years, she had only seen Kachiko wearing the lacy butterfly mask that Hotaru herself had gifted her. That mask was diaphanous and clung to every contour of Kachiko's face. It did not hide her face, not really. The Scorpion looked no different without it.

And yet…

Seeing her without it, with truly nothing between them now, tugged at Hotaru's heart. Kachiko seemed smaller somehow, more fragile. She was no less beautiful; her unmasked features made Hotaru's heart race no less than seeing the Scorpion in her finest, most elaborate palace garb. But there had always been an edge to Kachiko's beauty, a sense that it was as much a weapon as the hidden blades that could appear in her hands without warning.

Now that edge was gone, and the softness of Kachiko's face, her true face, gazed up at Hotaru.

Her hand rose of its own volition, the backs of her fingers brushing against Kachiko's cheek. For a brief moment, Kachiko leaned into the caress, but only for a moment. Then they were both pulling away, suddenly aware of the crowds that continued to swirl around the gates of the Imperial City.

"Your mask…" Hotaru trailed off. Kachiko knew she wasn't wearing a mask; telling her as much seemed a pointless endeavor.

"What better way to go unseen as a Scorpion?" A small, almost vulnerable smile rippled across Kachiko's face before it vanished. "It's just another mask, Hotaru," she said with a dismissive wave. "One I have worn before. I do not wear it at court, but it serves me well in other settings."

Just another mask. Hotaru shook her head. She loved Kachiko, there was no sense in denying it, but sometimes the woman was… well, a Scorpion. They all wore masks, of course; every samurai knew it. The emotionless mien of the perfect warrior was exactly that, a mask donned as surely as one donned armor. But it wasn't the same as wearing a literal mask that hid your face from the world.

Or was it?

Had Kachiko ever had the chance to truly be herself, she wondered? Or, for that matter, had Hotaru? Perhaps in the late night moments with Kachiko when the world was still and no other eyes were upon them. Or in the times when she and Toshimoko sparred in the dojo, where the ebb and flow of swordplay drowned out everything else. But apart from those times, when was she truly, wholly Hotaru? Not at court, for there the games of politics precluded ever showing one's true nature. Not on the battlefield, where being known by your enemy was tantamount to defeat. Not even among the palaces of her people, where the mantle of leadership meant that she must always present a carefully constructed persona.

"Hotaru." Kachiko was smiling at her again, and Hotaru couldn't help but feel that the woman had read her mind. "The road to the City of Lies is long," she said, not chiding. "Better that we get started. We can speak of masks along the way, if you wish."

Hotaru nodded, reaching down to shoulder her traveling pack. Kachiko, too, had a satchel over one shoulder, though it seemed much lighter than Hotaru's. It gave Hotaru pause. Had Kachiko ever traveled rough, she wondered? There would surely be an inn along the way, but in the two weeks' journey before them, they would certainly find themselves sleeping under the stars at times. It would be easier if they could ride, but only the wealthy could afford horses, and mounts would draw unnecessary attention. Better to keep a lower profile. But how would Kachiko handle the rigors of the trip?

She gave herself a mental shake. Kachiko was the one who had offered to make this journey, she reminded herself. She was the one who told the empress she would find her son. If Hotaru knew anything about the Scorpion, it was that she would be prepared for whatever they might find.

"Let us go, then," she said. Kachiko fell in beside her, and together, the two walked through the long tunnel that passed beneath the walls of the capital.

The wonders of the capital quickly gave way to the countryside as Hotaru and Kachiko made their way out of the city and into the Imperial lands that surrounded it. The road was a mix of crushed stone and hardpacked dirt that formed a surface almost as hard as the paved roads of the city. If they stayed upon it, Hotaru knew that it would carry them from the Imperial lands to Kakita Palace, through the northern lands of the Crane and all the way to Last Breath Castle, the stronghold of the Matsu family of the Lion, not far from Beiden Pass. Through that pass, they would find the lands of the Scorpion, crossing through Yogo and Shosuro provinces until they reached Ryokō Owari.

They did not use the main road. The Lion were marching to war, and Kakita Palace was as likely a target as any in the Empire. Instead, they would skirt around the village of Tsuma – another place to be avoided – and travel the network of cart paths and dirt roads that crisscrossed the main thoroughfares of the Empire. Once they were deep in the heart of Crane lands, they would be safe from the encroaching Lion forces, though Hotaru knew that did not mean they would be truly safe. Bandits upon the roads were always a risk, and to the casual observer, the pair of them were an easy target.

She smiled at the thought; any bandit who decided to impede the two of them would be in for a surprise.

"These lands are more peaceful than I thought they would be."

Hotaru glanced at Kachiko, still feeling a rush of heat when she gazed at her unmasked face. A layer of road dust had settled in her hair, and a faint sheen of sweat glistened on her brow, but strangely enough, Hotaru found that even more beautiful than the stunning vision that prowled the halls of the Imperial Palace. Bent with the weight of her pack and swathed in traveling clothes, she looked far less the courtly seductress and more just another traveler upon the road.

"We are still very close to the capital," Hotaru replied. "Too close for bandit gangs to be comfortable with. Even Matsu Tsuko, no matter what she thinks of the regent, would not bring war to these lands. An army this close to the walls of the Imperial City would bring the wrath of all the other clans down upon it."

"And do you think there will be trouble once we cross into the lands of the Crane?"

There was no accusation in those words, but Hotaru felt a sting, nonetheless. The Crane lands were hers, after all. She felt the twinge of conflicting duties once more; how could she protect her own lands when she was busy protecting the Empire as a whole?

"Probably," she said at last, sighing with the word. She glanced down at her daishō, which marked her as samurai, regardless of the manner of her dress. That alone should guarantee them food and shelter at any of the villages or farms they passed, but… "Even if we do not encounter bandits," she went on, "there will be little welcome for us, even at the villages. The Lion have already raided numerous settlements along the border, burning crops and razing them to the ground. Those people have to go somewhere. I suspect we will find many towns bursting at the seams. If we find them intact at all."

"Which is why we must retrieve Prince Sotorii. Whatever the cost."

Hotaru frowned at the note of fear in Kachiko's voice. For a heartbeat, she was almost certain she had imagined it. Kachiko was not one to fear anything. She had not backed down from the Imperial Court even after her husband had murdered the Emperor and her clan had withdrawn in shambles. She had not backed down when a giant of a Crab youth had towered over her, telling her to leave. She had not backed down when a slew of masked assassins flowed through Hotaru's door and tried to overwhelm them. Kachiko's words, spoken in the quiet spaces between the two of them, came back to her.

"If it is not the world that I wish it to be, then I will bend it to my will until it is at least a world where those I love need not live in fear."

"Do you fear the fate of the Scorpion if Sotorii takes the throne,

Kachiko?" she asked quietly. "Is that why you told the empress you would find him?"

Kachiko did not answer for a long, long moment. They walked in silence, moving briskly down the highway, passing merchants pulling slow-moving carts and getting passed by the infrequent messenger or other horseman. The silence stretched so long that Hotaru thought Kachiko simply wasn't going to answer, or that she had offended the woman by bringing up her husband's betrayal. But at last, the Scorpion sighed.

"I fear for us all," she replied in a near whisper, "if Sotorii ascends the throne."

That was unexpected. Hotaru frowned as several questions leaped to mind, though she only spoke one. "Why?"

"I can't explain it." Kachiko's lips thinned, and she gazed over the line of trees in the distance, her brows drawn together. "The boy is… different, Hotaru. I watched him in the palace. He is arrogant, yes, as all boys raised in the lap of power can be. But there is something else. Something no one can explain, though I know that many among the Emperor's councilors felt it, as well. There was some effort to convince Hantei that Daisetsu would make the better heir." She shook her head, loose locks of raven hair dancing across her shoulders. "But I do not know what I fear more: Sotorii upon the throne, or no one at all. I pray to my ancestors and the Fortunes that watch over us that the prince, if placed upon the throne, can be guided."

Hotaru felt a wave of unease at Kachiko's words. She had heard nothing of Sotorii's fitness to rule; no rumors about the boy had reached her ears. She was seldom at the Imperial Court, but for such a thing to not leave the halls of the palace was almost unfathomable. For the concern to have been kept so close, meant that it was a deep concern indeed.

But that was not all. Kachiko's desire to "guide" the emperor sent a chill through Hotaru. She could not deny her feelings for the Scorpion, but she *was* a Scorpion. Was there a difference between someone like Kachiko being the power behind the throne and someone like Shoju claiming it through force?

Had the Lion asked the same question when Yoshi assumed the regency?

The irony of it almost made her laugh out loud. It seemed no matter who sat upon the throne, there would always be those who took issue with it. If that was the case, could the Empire ever truly know peace? Or was her dream of a Rokugan that did not turn to war as the solution to every problem just that – a dream?

"If we do find Sotorii," she said, her voice soft, "I'll make sure he remembers the Scorpion were the ones who helped him return to his throne."

Kachiko said nothing. But she slipped her hand into Hotaru's, squeezing gently as they walked down the road.

They saw their first burned-out village five days after departing Otosan Uchi. By Hotaru's estimation, they were still two days' journey from Lion lands, which meant Matsu Tsuko's soldiers were pressing deep into Crane territory. The simple wooden houses of the villagers had burned almost to the ground. There was no lingering scent of their destruction on the winds, no residual heat as they picked their way through the village.

"This is old," she mused aloud. "Weeks old, at least."

"Before Matsu Tsuko and her delegation left the capital," Kachiko agreed.

The village had been small, no more than a dozen buildings built around a central structure that had either been the headman's house or perhaps a teahouse or inn. Most of the homes were little more than blackened logs and broken timbers. The central building had been set alight as well, but it had been roofed with clay instead of thatch, and its framing had been done with thicker lumber. The walls were gone, and the interior destroyed, but some of the structure still looked sound. Hotaru wondered if the people would return, when the war with the Lion ended and peace came once more to Rokugan. Would they rebuild, starting over in the literal ashes of their old lives? Or would the Daidoji family who ruled this land simply assign new tenants to the village? The Crane could not afford to have valuable farmland sit idle, after all.

"It saddens me, Kachiko," she admitted, as they made their way through the ravaged town. A town that, not long ago, had been bustling, full of life. "I understand why Matsu Tsuko wants to make the regent look weak. And I understand why her anger fell upon the Crane. But it is always the innocents who pay the price for our games of politics and power."

"We did not make the world, Hotaru." Kachiko's voice, while sympathetic, was practical. "We must live in it as best we can. But this village is a reminder." She glanced at the sky, at the position of the sun, and frowned. "The closer we get to Beiden Pass, the more dangerous the roads will become. We should be careful."

Kachiko was right, of course. And there was little she could do about it now. The best thing for the peasants, for all the Empire, was to complete her mission. If the Hantei line was restored to the throne, the petty squabbles between the clans would be set aside.

They moved on in silence, walking through the ashes of the burned village, following the dusty cart path that served as a road. With the village at their back, the journey once more seemed almost idyllic, though Hotaru knew that was an illusion. The pair had left the main roads behind two days ago, and while farmhouses and villages still dotted the landscape, they were seeing fewer and fewer people. Many had likely fled, abandoning the area and their livelihoods in the hopes of holding on to their actual lives. Hotaru knew that they would not be seeing any Crane soldiers. From a purely military perspective, there was nothing here worth defending, not this close to the Last Breath Castle of the Lion. The thought saddened her, but that was the reality of war.

They had moved into the foothills of the Spine of the World mountains, climbing steadily toward Beiden Pass, when the danger Kachiko spoke of finally found them. They were, technically, still in Crane lands, the province held by the Daidoji family. But this close to the three-way border with the Lion and the Scorpion, such things meant little.

A quintet of people, three men and two women, stood across the road, blocking their path. Even at a distance, they showed signs of rough living, their clothing stained and tattered. The men had scraggly facial hair, as if they couldn't be bothered or didn't have the means with which to shave. They all bore weapons, stout clubs and knives.

"Perhaps they're lost and looking for help," Kachiko said, a hard edge creeping into her voice. She knew as well as Hotaru what this was.

Hotaru reached up and loosened the ties that held the wooden sheath on her naginata's blade. She had been using the polearm as a walking stick, its weight as comforting and familiar to her as her haori. "Stay behind me if you can. Wielding this takes considerable space."

Kachiko didn't reply. Neither had slowed their pace, walking purposely toward the people that barred their path. Now, the Scorpion slipped back half a step, her hands disappearing into the broad sleeves of her own overcoat.

"What have we here?" the apparent leader of the highwaymen sneered as they moved to within easy earshot. Up close, the five were even more disheveled than they had seemed from afar. Hotaru noted the thinness of their limbs, the hollowness of their eyes, and felt a flicker of sympathy. She could understand their plight, but it did not excuse what they were doing.

"Step aside," she said in return. "Please. Find a village and honest work. I do not want to kill you."

"Don't worry, *Lady* Crane," he said with a sneer. "We won't hurt you or your little friend cowering behind you. *If* you do exactly as we say." He pointed at her with a dirty finger. "We want your money, and your coats, and whatever weapons you might have. You can keep your lives and your virtue. If you have any." The words were calculated insults and would have had many a samurai clearing steel and cutting the bandit down before he had finished speaking them. But Hotaru felt only pity for the man.

"I can give you some zeni," she allowed. "It is all I have with me that I can spare. I'm afraid our coats and our weapons are not up for negotiation."

"Neither is our virtue," Kachiko added behind her. "Though in looking at the lot of you, I think I would rather give up my life."

The man stared at her incredulously, the shock on his face plain. His face reddened such that Hotaru feared he might be having a fit, but then he broke out into harsh, mocking laughter. The other four soon joined him, and the sound of their dismissive mirth grated against her nerves. Hotaru was sympathetic to their plight, but she was still a samurai. There were limits. She snapped her arm out to the side, flicking the naginata so that the sheath went flying from it, revealing eighteen inches of razor-sharp steel.

The laughter died.

"Or, if you prefer, we can cut you down where you stand," she offered.

The five exchanged furtive looks at that and Hotaru could feel their confidence slipping. She offered a prayer to her ancestors that they guide her clear of these desperate fools. But it seemed her ancestors were not inclined to listen.

As if at some unspoken command, all five highwaymen surged forward. There was no attempt at respectable combat, no acknowledgment of any of the virtues of the Akodo Code. Instead, they simply tried to overwhelm Hotaru, eliminating what they saw to be the bigger threat so that they could deal with Kachiko at their leisure.

It cost the first to move their life.

Kachiko's kunai flashed, sinking into the eye socket of the man who had demanded their money and burying itself to the hilt. He went down in a twitching heap, but the other four leaped over his corpse, snarling in anger and fear as they brought their crude clubs to bear. Hotaru stood her ground, rooting her feet into Earth, and swept her naginata not at the enemy, but rather their weapon. The blade of her polearm cleaved through the first club to get within range, smashing through the hardened wood to cut deep into the woman who swung it.

She, too, went down.

The bandits were on her then, pressing close, trying to get within the reach of the polearm and deny her the ability to bring the weapon to bear effectively. Hotaru smiled as she whirled among the bandits. She blocked another club with the spinning haft of the naginata as she danced in the midst of the three remaining attackers. Her lead hand grasped just below the blade of her weapon as she dropped low, almost into a split, and a club passed harmlessly overhead. She thrust the naginata forward as she sprang back to her feet, driving the steel toward the recoiling enemy.

The blade parted flesh and another attacker fell away. She had lost track of Kachiko in the fight, and the woman seemed to materialize behind one of the two remaining bandits, her tantō flashing across his throat. She was gone again almost as fast, disengaging from the melee with astonishing ease as her victim crumpled to the ground.

The remaining bandit staggered back, her eyes wide in shock. The battle, if it could be called that, had taken no more than a few seconds, but she now found herself alone. She looked back and forth between Hotaru and Kachiko, her eyes wide in terror. Then she threw down her club, turned on her heel, and sprinted away from them.

"Running away, are we?" Kachiko said, watching the woman flee. The Scorpion held another kunai, blade grasped in her fingers, but her eyes tracked the would-be bandit as mercilessly as the predator for which her clan was named.

"Kachiko, don't," Hotaru sighed. "I doubt she'll be much of a threat to anyone now."

Kachiko's lips twisted in the barest of smirks, and the knife vanished from her fingers.

Hotaru glanced down at the bodies, one of which still had Kachiko's kunai jutting from its eye. With a frown of distaste, she quickly pulled it free, stabbing the blade into the packed earth of the road a few times to clean it before handing it back to Kachiko.

"Do you think they were Crane, Scorpion, or Lion?" she asked the other woman as she looked at the bodies. She didn't touch them, but she did scan their features and clothing for anything that might indicate who they might have been, before whatever hardships in their lives had forced them here. She didn't find anything, but then, she really didn't expect to.

The Scorpion shrugged in response to Hotaru's question, slipping her kunai back beneath her coat. "I don't know. And I don't think it matters. They gave us no choice, regardless of their clan. I do think we should hurry, though; I've no desire to meet more bandits on the side of the road. The sooner we can shelter behind the walls of Ryokō Owari, the better."

Hotaru took a moment to clean the blade of her naginata and recover the sheath that had been cast off to the side. Then, the two set off down the road, neither looking back at the bodies that they had left decorating the path. Hotaru could feel their presence, though, another reminder of what the Empire had become since the fall of Hantei.

They had to recover the prince and set things to right. And the violence here today would be a candle against Lady Sun compared to what they would likely have to do there.

Could violence truly be the precursor to peace? Could it be any other way?

Hotaru did not know. But she knew her path, and she knew her duty. She would find both in Ryokō Owari.

# 25
# Toturi

"**M**atsu Tsuko's forces are on the march."

Toturi looked up from the low desk – really just a pair of planks balanced on two of the large clay pots that used to carry water – to see Daisuke, Kamoko, and Toku enter his tent. He had moved his own residence from the village proper to the encampment that now surrounded most of the Village of the Golden Blades. It had been Kamoko who had spoken, but when he raised an eyebrow and gestured for the trio to sit on the cushions scattered before his desk, it was Daisuke who stepped forward.

"I received word from some of my contacts," the Crane rōnin said, a hint of urgency beneath his normally refined voice. Toturi knew those "contacts" were likely courtiers and ambassadors in the courts of the Crane. "The Lion have abandoned the capital and declared Kakita Yoshi a false regent," Daisuke went on. "They claim that he seeks to subvert the will of Heaven and take the throne for himself. That, or decree the Crane an Imperial family and name Doji Hotaru the rightful heir. They are no longer content with raiding the borders of Crane lands. Their armies are on the march, though from what I've been told, none move toward the Imperial City. Instead, they are moving into Crane lands in force. My sources have sent word that Matsu Agetoki has been given command of the expeditionary forces and prepares to make war upon the Crane."

Toturi tilted his head back and closed his eyes for a moment. When he had been an initiate at the Dragon monastery, the senior monks had spoken of meditation as a sacred communion, a way to connect the mind and spirit with the divine. They had insisted that, if you could simply sit and listen to the universe, you could feel the pull of the will of Heaven. Toturi had never achieved such enlightenment himself, but there were many among the Dragon who claimed to have done so. Now, however, in that moment of silence, he could feel the pull of a thousand twisting threads.

If it was the will of the divine, it felt surprisingly similar to a noose closing around his throat.

"Doji Hotaru would never take the throne," he said, ignoring the tug of destiny, if only for the moment. He opened his eyes and leaned forward, placing both hands on the desk before him, the reports forgotten. "I may not like the woman" – she had killed his brother, after all, and inadvertently thrust the responsibilities of the Lion upon him – "but she would not betray the Empire. And while Kakita Yoshi might use his power to advance the interests of the Crane, that old fox would never dream of pushing out the rightful heirs."

It had been a week since he had spoken with Kamoko, convinced that there would be no "right" side in a war between the Crane and Lion. The history between the two was long and staggeringly complex, with plenty of blame and countless atrocities on both sides. But if the Lion were reigniting hostilities under a clearly false premise, could he be so certain that there wasn't a "right" side anymore? And if they were on the "wrong" side, could he truly stand against them, his own kinsmen? The rank-and-file soldiers no doubt believed that they were fighting a righteous war for the future of the Empire.

But how could he stand by and do nothing?

Toturi sighed. "Does Agetoki march on Toshi Ranbo?"

It was the most obvious choice. Violence Behind Courtliness City – and if there was a place in all the Empire which had better earned its name, he did not know of it – was one of the deepest roots in the conflict between the Lion and the Crane. The Crane's current administration of the city, won not through conquest but rather political maneuvering, was a thorn in the Lion's side. His brother had died trying to reclaim the city in the last Crane-Lion war. If Matsu Tsuko truly wished to make a statement against the overreach of Imperial power in regard to the Crane, there was no better place to send Agetoki and his soldiers.

The Crane knew that as well. Doji Hotaru was not a fool, and Toturi knew that the Crane Champion would have ordered the city heavily reinforced. A battle in Toshi Ranbo would be a bloodbath on both sides, but at least it would be a fight between two armies who had known such a conflict was inevitable.

"No, Lord Toturi." It was Toku who replied. The boy continued to grow, and not just under Toturi's direct instruction. Kamoko and Daisuke had both taken to the boy, and had been teaching him in areas where Toturi had his own weaknesses, like horsemanship and the finer niceties of the courts. It was a shame that the strict caste system of the Empire would never let the boy rise much higher than a subcommander of ashigaru. How far might he go if his potential were not limited by his station?

"Lord Agetoki has bypassed Toshi Ranbo," Toku continued. "His forces march on Kyotei Castle."

Kyotei Castle sat between Otosan Uchi and Toshi Ranbo. It

was another stronghold with a long and bloody history between the Lion and the Crane. And like its larger neighbor, it, too, had changed hands many times over the centuries. In and of itself, the castle was of little import; its defenses were solid, but far easier to overwhelm than those of Toshi Ranbo. It held a position of moderate strategic value in the grand scheme of things.

But it did sit directly on the route from the capital to Violence Behind Courtliness City.

"It's a direct challenge to the regent," Toturi said, mind turning on the problem. "If the Lion take a Crane stronghold so close to the capital, they can position their armies to march on the Imperial City itself." The idea that even Matsu Tsuko might possibly entertain such a notion was not only foreign to him but brought an actual wave of churning sickness to his gut. Such an action would make Matsu Tsuko no better than Bayushi Shoju; worse, since she would be dragging the entire clan into her treason. "If the regent responds, it will appear as if he is coming to the aid of the Crane, and all of the clans will see Matsu Tsuko's fears as being realized."

"And if he doesn't," Kamoko added, "the only nearby forces the Crane have to reinforce Kyotei Castle will be from Toshi Ranbo itself." It was tactically brilliant. If the Lion took Kyotei Castle, any Imperial forces would be locked into the capital, since they would not want to be perceived as aiding the Crane. At the same time, Crane armies from the southern Crane lands would have to deal with the problem at Kyotei Castle before they could hope to reinforce the armies at Toshi Ranbo. With one stroke, Matsu Tsuko and Matsu Agetoki would pin down the Imperials, isolate Toshi Ranbo, and reinforce their political position that the entire war was justified by the favoritism of the mostly-Crane Imperial Court.

Toturi nodded at the Unicorn's assessment. "And it would be

foolish in the extreme for the Crane to send any help from their forces at Toshi Ranbo. Doing so would only weaken them further."

"But surely the Crane will do something," Toku said.

"Doji Hotaru has little choice in the matter," Daisuke broke in. "The Crane do not keep as large a standing army as the Lion. What forces we do have are scattered all up and down the borders, trying to guard against raids, like the one the Lion attempted on this very village." He jerked his head, indicating the town outside the tent and sending his topknot bouncing. "That, or they are reinforcing Toshi Ranbo itself." He offered a slight, wry smile. "Matsu Tsuko has been planning this a long time, it seems. One could almost admire her, if it weren't for the fact that one's clan was about to be butchered. To make matters worse, the Crab sent a delegation to the Imperial Palace, requesting help at the Wall. A great Shadowlands army gathers. But with the threat of war between the clans, my little birds suspect that no help will be forthcoming for anyone."

Toturi felt the tightening of the noose even further. No one had suggested to him that they intervene. How could they? It was *his* clan, his people, and Kyotei Castle, though it housed hundreds of innocents, was not the Village of the Golden Blades. By every rule of warfare, it was a valid military target.

A valid military target made vulnerable by the widescale attacks on villagers and farmers. A target that, if the cards turned a certain way, could plunge not just the Lion and the Crane into open warfare, but could pull all the clans into war with them. Toturi knew Kakita Yoshi; he did not think the man would rush to the aid of Kyotei Castle. If nothing else, the wily Crane was a realist, and would understand the fallout of such an action. He should allow the castle to fall.

Unless he had already been driven to the point where he did not care. If Matsu Tsuko's campaign was successful, if she convinced the Empire that Kakita Yoshi's regency was nothing more than a puppet regime for the Crane, the only choices left to him would be a high likelihood of facing the headman's axe as a usurper or ordering the Imperials into the fray on the side of his clan.

With that thought came a vision of Bayushi Shoju, standing before the body of the Emperor, bloody blade in hand. The rage Toturi had felt when he discovered the Scorpion had clouded his vision, but in that flash of memory, Toturi could clearly see the sadness on Bayushi's face. Had it really been there? Or was his own mind playing tricks on him?

Toturi shook the image from his head. Perhaps he needed to meditate on it, to try to truly understand what took place on that night, but now was not the time. Now, he had a decision to make, and whatever he did, the shape of the Empire might be changed forever.

Why couldn't the Fortunes just leave him in peace?

He crushed the fleeting thought beneath the iron fist of discipline and turned to look into the eyes of each of his companions. They had not been together long, but he had grown to trust and care for each of the trio before him now. In Kamoko's eyes, he saw her hunger for vengeance against the man who killed her mother. But he saw temperance there, too, a willingness to follow his command. If he decided this was not a battle for the army that had formed around him, she would not leave. She would not abandon her vengeance, but neither would she abandon his cause, whatever it might be. In Daisuke's eyes he saw the worry for his clan and people, a worry that Toturi shared for his own clan. But there, too, he saw a willingness to follow where Toturi led. In Toku's eyes, he saw something else. An admiration and hope that added to the crushing weight of responsibility that Toturi already bore. In those eyes, he saw the idealized version of the samurai reflected back at him, the protectors and champions of the people. How the boy managed to hold on to that image when he had seen firsthand the reality of war was beyond Toturi, but he could not deny the duty that it put upon him.

"Spread the word," he said. "We march with the dawn."

# 26
# Yakamo

Yakamo roared, and the Shadowlands filth cowered before him. As he charged, the goblins retreated, until they were pushed up against the parapets of the Wall. That was good. It made them easier to kill. He swung his tetsubō with a speed and power that, when it connected with the skull of one of the monsters, he didn't even feel it. Instead, he felt only the ring of iron against stone as the club smashed through the goblin's head like a rotting melon and struck the Wall with enough force to send chips of stone flying.

Any damage to the Wall should have shocked Yakamo, but he barely noticed. Instead, even as his tetsubō was rebounding from the stone, he was reaching out with the claw at the end of his left arm. Two snips and another pair of goblins died, their ribcages crushed beneath the force of his grip. A fourth swung a jagged sword at him, and he simply swept it aside, letting the blade strike the armored chitin. In response, he struck the creature with such force that he lifted it from the Wall and sent it sailing over the parapets.

Yakamo howled, an almost animal sound of anger and triumph as he watched his enemies flee before him. He was vaguely aware of the other Crab within the bastion. They were engaged in their own desperate fight, and the weaklings were barely managing to hold their own. He knew he should care about that, but the fury of battle had fully claimed him. All that mattered was that his enemies die.

A roar answered his own, and he spun, hair and mustache whipping wildly as his eyes settled on the ogre that had just torn a samurai in half. It snarled at Yakamo and hurled the upper half of the dead warrior at him, throwing it with the speed and force of a battering ram. Yakamo swatted the corpse aside as easily as he had the goblin.

"You dare challenge me, filth?" he roared. "Come. Come and die like your fellows!"

The ogre charged, heedless of the goblins and samurai it swept aside in its passing. The thunder of its footfalls shook the bastion and Yakamo knew that, not so long ago, he would have felt the tremors of fear in those reverberations. Now, he threw back his head and laughed. The ogre clutched a massive bearded axe in one fist and swept it down, cutting diagonally as if to split the Crab from his left shoulder to right hip. No person alive could have parried that strike, not with the full weight of the ogre's massive body behind it.

Yakamo didn't parry the ogre's wild swing. He swept his tetsubō up to meet it. The two weapons clashed with a sound like thunder, and for the first time since the crab claw had formed, Yakamo felt pain. The tetsubō was torn from his hand and went bouncing across the bastion floor, a noticeable dent in the solid piece of iron from where the ogre's axe had struck it. He let out a cry, this time of pain, as ligaments and joints were stretched to the snapping point.

But the ogre had fared even worse. The heavy axe head, wrought in the dark forges of the Shadowlands and imbued with the taint that permeated those lands, shattered. It exploded into hundreds of metal shards that peppered the ogre's flesh and sank deep. The creature stumbled, its brutish face slack in shock as it stared at what remained of its weapon.

Yakamo reacted with an instinct not his own. As the ogre stumbled forward, he swung his crab claw like a mace, bashing the already staggered opponent on the top of its exposed head. That dropped the ogre to its knees, and the claw was already reaching out. The serrated pincers closed around the creature's throat… and snapped shut. Even through the desensitizing chiton, Yakamo felt thick muscle and bone break right before the monster's head tumbled off its shoulders.

Yakamo smiled. Then he spun, snatched up his tetsubō, and charged back into the fray.

It went on like that for some time, until even the seemingly limitless fury that filled him had been exhausted and Yakamo was roaring not in anger, but in pain with each swing of club or claw, forcing his muscles to respond. It was enough, if only barely. After what seemed an eternity, but Yakamo knew was little more than an hour, the assault broke and the waves of Shadowlands creatures retreated, falling back to their own lines outside of the range of arrows, siege engines, or the incantations of the shindōshi.

As the chaos of battle drained from him, it took what little energy remained with it. Yakamo slumped to the cold stones of the battlement, not even bothering to find a crenellation to lean against. With his exhaustion came a strange realization; he had no real memory of the battle that he just fought. He remembered fighting; he remembered reveling in the death of his foes. But outside of that, it was a blur. He distinctly did *not* remember commanding the samurai and ashigaru that manned the bastion, and when he looked around him, he saw the reality of that failure.

There were so many dead.

The bastion was littered with corpses. Many belonged to goblins and ogres, lesser oni and other creatures of Fu Leng. But the others were the shattered bodies of the Crab. They lay everywhere, cast aside like broken dolls, and Yakamo could see that fewer than two dozen of the men and women defending the bastion still stirred. When he first arrived, there had been more than a hundred. Which meant that more than three-quarters of the forces under his command had perished.

How many had died because he had lost control and instead reveled in the death and destruction of his enemies? How many of his kinsmen would still be alive if, instead of giving in to his newfound power, he had focused on commanding those whose lives had been placed in his trust?

Weak, all of them. If they had been strong, they would have survived.

The thought came from nowhere, shocking him with its callousness. None of the samurai and ashigaru who defended Rokugan from the Shadowlands could be called weak. They gave their lives in defense of the innocent; they fought so others might live in peace. Only the strong could make such a sacrifice.

Then they should have lived. The alien thoughts continued through his head, unheeded. They are supposed to be warriors. They shouldn't need constant direction and supervision to do something as simple as crushing their enemies. If they died, it is because they were weak.

An image of Hiruma Bunzō, his legs shattered, covered in his own blood, demanding that Yakamo leave him, flashed through his mind. With it came a spike of pain that shot through his left arm and made him clench his jaw to prevent a scream. But the image, and the pain, at least cleared his head.

There was still work to do.

The survivors were stirring, rousing themselves from the stones as they turned to the task of finding the wounded among the dead. They were all veterans of the Wall. They knew the drill, and went about their duties without Yakamo having to order it. But why were they casting such furtive and even fearful glances in his direction?

He ignored their looks and set about tossing the dead Shadowlands creatures over the battlements. The monotonous nature of the task – grab a body in his claw, drag it to the edge, hurl it into the darkness beyond – left his mind free to focus on what, by the ancestors and Fortunes, had happened during the battle. He had arrived with the bastion under attack. He had joined the fray. And that was it. What had happened afterward was nothing but a blur, though now that he could think clearly again, one thing was glaringly obvious.

It was obvious from the casualties the Crab had suffered that the bastion had been very nearly overrun. But no reinforcements had come. He was sure of it, not only because his faulty memory couldn't recall it, but because the dead and wounded Crab were all those who were stationed here. How close had the attack come to succeeding, if whatever reinforcements were left had been deployed to situations even more dire than his own?

How many more such attacks could they withstand?

He knew the answer. Not many. The minutes since the enemy had been driven from this bastion continued to tick by, and still no aid came. No fresh soldiers to stand the watch in their place. No shindōshi with their soothing incantations to the Water spirits. Even the youths that served as messengers and carried food and water to the soldiers between assaults were absent.

Had his father decided that Kuni Yori's blessing was not a blessing after all? Had he ordered the reinforcements to stand down?

A new bubble of rage rose within him at the thought. How dare he? How *dare* he? He had taken on this burden for his father, for his people. If that old and broken man thought that he could simply shove Yakamo and the embarrassment of his bargain aside, then Hida Kisada would learn differently. He would learn the true power of the pact that Yakamo had made. And if he did not learn well, then perhaps it was time for the Crab to have a new daimyō.

"Water, Lord Yakamo?"

The small, trembling voice cut through his thoughts. He realized that his breath was coming in short, panting gasps, not from battle fatigue, but from a building rage that he had scarcely been aware of. A girl, no more than ten, stood by his side. She carried a bucket and a long ladle, which she held up to him. Her eyes were wide with fear, and they were very carefully *not* looking at the claw that had replaced his left arm. The ladle trembled in her grip, causing droplets of water to splash over the side.

He felt another irrational surge of anger. His soldiers needed that water. But he stepped down on it hard. What was happening to him? Was this what it meant to give his name to an oni? Would he be forever filled with this ill-timed anger?

"Thank you," he said, stifling a growl as he took the ladle from the girl. The water slid down his throat, dampening the rage a little. Yakamo took a deep breath, drank another mouthful, and finally felt the cloud of darkness that had settled over him begin to lift. He dropped the ladle into the bucket with a clunk and the girl scurried away, taking the water to the next soldier in line.

He tried not to be hurt by the relief on her face.

Around him, the Wall was coming alive with the support that he expected after a battle. The water girl was not alone. Several children moved among the survivors, offering food and drink. A lone shindōshi, aided by a pair not quite old enough to fight, moved through the ranks of the wounded. Yakamo noted that most were being treated with poultices and bandages rather than mystical healing. No shindōshi could call upon that power indefinitely, and it seemed it was being reserved for only the most extreme injuries.

There were reinforcements at last. Yakamo saw a few fresh faces among the injured. Of the hundred plus soldiers that had weathered the first attack, it looked like two score had regained their feet. Better than his initial estimations, but still far too few. After a quick calculation, he saw he had two dozen reinforcements, though some already bore wounds, indicating that they had been shifted from other areas of the Wall. That put him at less than three-quarters of the strength the bastion should have held.

Yakamo walked to the parapet and gazed out at the Shadowlands. He could see them there, in their thousands. Mounds of the dead littered the field, with the piles of corpses rising a dozen feet at the base of the Wall. But even now, even with the newfound power that the oni arm had given him, Yakamo knew it wouldn't be enough.

He expected that to reignite the rage that now seemed to live just beneath the surface of his skin. But it didn't. Instead, it filled him with a tiredness that went straight to his soul. This was what he had tried to warn the fools in the Imperial City about. This was where the Empire's focus needed to be. Instead, they turned their blades against each other.

By the Fortunes, they were so bloody stupid.

And unless his father had a trick up his sleeve, their stupidity was going to kill them all.

One of the new arrivals approached, and like the child before him, the man locked his gaze on Yakamo's eyes, refusing to acknowledge the claw. "Lord Hida," he said with a bow. "What are your orders?"

His orders. A few moments ago, he had been wondering if his lack of orders had led to the demise of more of his soldiers. But what orders could he give? There were no clever gambits, no twists of tactical genius. There was only the army of the Shadowlands, his depleted forces, and the Wall. In that moment, he missed Hiruma Bunzō like never before. What he wouldn't give to have the Laughing Crab beside him, with a quip to bolster the morale of the warriors who knew that, on this day, they were going to die. They were all going to die.

There was only one order to give.

"We hold."

# 27
## Hotaru

R yokō Owari Toshi. Journey's End City. The City of Green Walls.

The City of Lies.

Hotaru had heard tales of the city, but she had never visited it. There was little that would draw a samurai of her repute to a place with such a nefarious reputation, and that was before one considered how deep it was into Scorpion territory. Now, as she and Kachiko moved across the hills at the base of the Spine of the World mountains, traveling along the River of Gold, the city revealed itself in the distance.

It was beautiful from afar. The river flowed through fields of poppies, and while the flowers that were the entire reason for the city's existence were not clothed in the deep crimsons of their bloom, their vibrant stalks still covered the hills in a lush carpet of emerald. That green was reflected in the walls of the city proper, the limestone quarried from the Spine of the World, where a quirk of water and earth tinted the stone so that it was almost indistinguishable from jade. Those shining green walls were nearly as breathtaking as the enchanted walls of Otosan Uchi itself.

It had come as a shock to see the city within.

Beyond those brilliant walls, a rambling warren of wooden buildings and alleyways sprawled out like a maze, a mix of living quarters, shops, and warehouses so densely packed that even at a distance, they seemed to be straining against the limits of the walls. Where the river widened into the Bay of Drowned Virtue, a stone quay ran along the shore, with wooden piers reaching into the water like greedy fingers. While most of the buildings looked simple, even shabby, several palaces and temples towered above them, tiled roofs stained the brilliant red of the poppies.

"Welcome to Journey's End," Kachiko said, as they joined the steady flow of movement toward the city's gates.

"Will we have any trouble getting inside the city?"

The Scorpion offered a small smile. Hotaru was just getting used to seeing her full face, and that smile sent little jitters through her heart, though there was an undercurrent to it that seemed almost smug. "No," was all Kachiko said.

Hotaru left it at that, and they marched toward the gates. It was a mixed lot making their way into the city; Hotaru saw merchants with laden wagons being pulled by oxen, peasant farmers with hand carts loaded with early spring vegetables, even a group of monks wearing the robes of the Fortune of Wealth, making a pilgrimage to the great temple. Only half the people on the road wore masks; amidst the others she could pick out citizens from most of the Great Clans and a dozen minor clans.

"I wasn't expecting to find so many of the other clans here."

"They follow the coins," Kachiko replied. "A desire for wealth is universal, regardless of clan colors. It's one of the many things you can find in Ryokō Owari."

"And the other things?"

Kachiko's smile took on a mischievous bent. "Intrigue. Murder. Debauchery. The usual things for any city. And opium, of course. The processing centers produce literal tons of opium, but not all of it gets processed for official uses. There's always a portion that disappears."

Hotaru felt a surge of disgust at the thought. She knew that the opium trade – officially only sanctioned for use as medicine – had a more illicit side, but she hadn't expected Kachiko to speak of it so casually. "How can the Scorpion allow that?"

"Allow it?" Kachiko shrugged. "In truth, Hotaru, we cannot prevent it. There is too much money involved, and too much demand. If we tried to clamp down, the situation would only slip faster through our fingers."

"But surely you could do something," Hotaru insisted. The flow of people had slowed, forming into a queue as travelers reached the gates of the city.

The Scorpion arched an eyebrow at her. "Really, Hotaru. I know that the Crane and Scorpion have very different views of the world, but surely you are aware of the reality?" She shook her head in an almost affectionate manner. "It costs us far more in terms of resources and life to try to stop the problem. We know who the players are. We keep our eyes on them and make sure that they do not get out of hand. The idea that the opium gangs have free rein in the city is just one of the many lies told here. They know the limits." Her voice took on a more serious, almost sinister tone. "And they know what will happen if they break those limits." As quickly as it came, the darker note left her voice, and Kachiko returned to being almost flippant. "Really, it's for the best. The theft and violence are kept to a minimum, and if someone oversteps, the gangs take care of the problem quickly and on their own because they don't want the Shosuro getting involved. The Empire gets its opium, the… recreational… demand has an outlet, and the criminals police themselves." She shrugged one dainty shoulder. "An elegant solution to an ugly problem. And one no one will be changing anytime soon."

Hotaru set her jaw, knowing the Scorpion was right. For all that they had in common, and for all that she cared for, even loved, Kachiko, they did come from very different backgrounds. And right now, this was Kachiko's world. The City of Lies had existed much longer than either of them, and would continue to exist long after Hotaru had gone to her ancestors. She wasn't here to change the city, and she had no illusions about changing the Scorpion.

She was here to rescue the prince.

She turned her attention back to the walls as they made their way toward the gate. The traffic here flowed much more quickly than it had when approaching Otosan Uchi, or the Esteemed Palaces of the Crane for that matter. The reason why became evident a few moments later.

The guards at the gates – a pair of Scorpion ashigaru wearing masks of plain linen – were barely looking at the entrants. Instead, each group seeking to pass through the gates handed the guards a small cloth satchel and were immediately waved through the gates of the city. Hotaru blinked in surprise and glanced at Kachiko.

"Do you not inspect those that would enter Ryokō Owari?"

Kachiko had bent down slightly, letting her hair fall in front of her face. When she straightened, Hotaru felt a sense of loss. The Scorpion had donned a mask again. This one was not the butterfly mask that Hotaru had gifted her, but a much simpler affair of painted porcelain. It covered more than half her face in a curving teardrop that swept from her right eye, across her left and curled down toward her chin. The blood-red enamel was edged in black with delicate swirls of ebony. It obscured her features and with her hair pulled back, Hotaru almost did not recognize her.

"There is no need," Kachiko said simply. "All are welcome in the City of Green Walls. Provided they can pay the entry fee."

"Entry fee?" The idea of having to pay money to enter the city was just one more mind-boggling aspect of the Scorpion's culture. "What of the farmers? Surely, they don't pay to sell their wares in the city?" There were numerous farmers around them, and Hotaru could see that they were, indeed, passing over small pouches, presumably full of coins.

"Everyone pays," Kachiko replied. "The farmers raise their prices enough so that the cost of entry is covered. The merchants do the same. Everyone who steps through that gate knows what the City of Green Walls is about, and what to expect when they enter. There is a reason why the shindōshi built a temple to the Fortune of Wealth here, Hotaru."

Hotaru shook her head but let the matter drop. They had almost reached the gates of the city. She wondered for a moment if she should try to cover her hair. But she was not the only Crane standing in line. What had brought *them* to the City of Lies, she mused. She saw more than one samurai among them; were they rōnin? Emissaries? Not the latter, for like every other clan in the wake of Hantei 38th's assassination, she had ordered all formal ties with the Scorpion severed.

Informal ties, of course, were another matter.

They were at the gates, and without a word, Kachiko passed over a small pouch that Hotaru hadn't even seen the woman produce from somewhere beneath her coat. Between the knives, masks, and now this, Hotaru wondered how there was any room for the woman herself, but it was only a passing thought. As they stepped through the gates, she was consumed by the music of the city.

It bustled with the same frantic energy as the Imperial City, but here, the song of the city was different. The Imperial City was a complex melody woven with different harmonies that came together in a song that was rich and complex but, ultimately, whole. The City of Lies was different. It was as if a dozen competing songs were being played at once, in a constant point and counterpoint with syncopated interruptions that rose from nowhere. There was no unifying theme to it; the songs clanged against and battled each other for dominance. The only constant was the music of the coins, dancing underneath it all, the foundation on which all was built.

Kachiko allowed her a moment to drink it in, but only a moment. "Come, Hotaru. There is someone we must meet," she said matter-of-factly. "Follow me, and keep your sword close. Now the true danger begins."

The interior of the sake house smelled of alcohol and something else, something that reminded her of burning tree sap with a slight floral overtone. She didn't recognize the smell, but she knew it, nonetheless. In this place, in this city, it could only be one thing; somewhere within the establishment there was a room where the opium smokers dwelt.

Hotaru had been to war; she had fought and bled, and she had taken life. She had shown mercy to her enemies and passed judgment on her own people. She had kept company with raucous soldiers and done her share of carousing. But as she surveyed the interior of the sake house, she realized that, in some ways, she had still led a sheltered life. She had frequented many sake houses, inns, and geisha houses in her time, and she would not have said that any of them were particularly upscale. She realized now that she would have been wrong.

The sake house was dark and filled with smoke. The smoke of the opium drifting from somewhere deeper in the house mingled with the thick tobacco smoke spilling from the pipes of the men and women at the tables. Both were overshadowed by the woodsmoke from smoldering fires in the braziers around the room. The entire place lacked adequate ventilation, and Hotaru felt a lightheadedness settle over her.

The clientele barely paid them any attention as they settled in to a table pressed up against one wall. Or perhaps it was better to say that the other patrons actively avoided looking at them. No one wore clan colors and apart from the dyed white hair of two women seated on the other side of the establishment, the only other obvious markers of clan were the masks of the few Scorpion in the room, including Kachiko.

"What are we doing here, Kachiko?" Hotaru asked. She had followed the woman through the bustling streets, and each turn that Kachiko took led them deeper into the rambling warrens, through a labyrinthine network of narrow, twisting alleys and crooked streets, where ramshackle buildings loomed over them and blocked out the sky. If there were parts of the city where the light of Lady Sun never touched, Hotaru would not have been surprised.

The people that moved through those tangled paths with them largely ignored the two women. They garnered a stare or two, but Hotaru's daishō – to say nothing of the naginata she carried – and Kachiko's mask kept any from approaching. To Hotaru's eye, the people who lived in these squalid streets were little different than those anywhere else in the Empire, but she sensed a harder edge beneath the surface. The people in the sake house had the same air.

"Meeting our contact," Kachiko replied easily. She wrinkled her nose at her teacup, not bothering to drink the murky liquid that looked more like muddied water than proper tea. "She will be here shortly."

Hotaru had not seen Kachiko contact anyone on their journey to this place. No one at the city gates had paid them any heed, and Hotaru would have bet a sizable portion of the next harvest that they had moved through the city with near-perfect anonymity. How Kachiko's cohort would know when to find them, or where to find them, was beyond her, but she had long since given up on trying to understand the vagaries of the Scorpion. Instead, she sipped at her sake and waited, trusting that Kachiko knew what she was doing.

It was not a long wait.

No more than ten minutes had passed when another woman slipped onto the bench beside them. Like Kachiko, she wore a simple mask, this one made of painted wood. She wore muted colors, all grays, browns, and blacks that Hotaru knew would blend into the city equally well in day or night. The woman, perhaps only seventeen years old, moved as silently as the smoke curling through the room. One moment, they were alone; the next, the girl was settling onto the cushions with liquid grace.

"Ayame," Kachiko said by way of greeting, unperturbed by her unannounced appearance.

"Lady Kachiko," the girl replied. She executed a seated bow with the same effortless grace with which she had joined them.

"Report, please."

"The prince is being held by one of the firefighter gangs," Ayame replied without preamble. "Those that call themselves the Fire Eaters."

Hotaru knew of firefighters. Or at least she had heard stories of them. The cities of Rokugan were mostly made of wood, and having groups of peasants ready to come to the aid of the populace should a fire break out seemed like a just cause. And the firefighters *did* fight fires when one occurred. But they also reveled in extortion, charging businesses and citizens a "fee" for their protection. Even that, if reasonable, wouldn't have raised any eyebrows; the firefighters had to be ready to risk their lives to keep large swaths of the city from burning should a spark be ignited, and that entitled them to some compensation.

What earned them their criminal status was that when someone didn't pay their fee, their home or business inevitably went up in flames. And the firefighters were always there to watch the "unprotected" buildings burn. If that weren't enough, the various gangs also fought one another for territory, sometimes leading to pitched battles in the streets that left dozens dead. Hotaru had no doubt that in a city like Ryokō Owari, they were also involved in the opium trade and other criminal enterprises.

Including, apparently, the kidnap and ransom of princes.

"How did the prince come to be here in the first place?" Hotaru demanded. "After his father's murder, both Sotorii and Daisetsu vanished. How did he end up here, in the City of… Green Walls?" she finished, not sure if she should use the more informal moniker in front of Kachiko's agent.

"I do not know, Lady Crane," Ayame replied, and Hotaru could hear the undercurrent of irritation in her voice. Not at Hotaru, she realized, but at the fact that there was a secret out there that the Scorpion had been unable to ferret out. "The prince's likeness is well known, and even if it wasn't, the regent sent sketches of Sotorii and Daisetsu to every major city in the Empire. He should have been seen. Here of all places, someone should have seen the prince enter the city. But I cannot find any who will acknowledge such."

"Nor will you," Kachiko said. "Do not worry, Ayame. I see only two possibilities: someone was paid very well for the prince being smuggled through the gates and then forgotten, or all those who were aware of his passage into the city were killed." She paused. "Or both, I suppose." None of the possibilities seemed to bother Kachiko.

"Whatever the reason," Ayame was saying, "the Fire Eaters operate out of the Fishermen's Quarter of the city. We have found several locations where the prince might be being held." She pulled a small scroll from beneath her kimono and unrolled it on the table. It was a map, presumably of the Fishermen's Quarter. A half-dozen buildings were circled. Ayame pointed out three of them, all located close to the river itself. "These three are warehouses. Mostly used to store smuggled goods. This one" – her finger stabbed at a smaller building set deeper into the quarter – "is a gambling hall. It gets a lot of traffic. Not a good place for a prince to be held."

Her finger moved on to the next building. This one, too, was on the river, but positioned at the far edge of the district. "This used to be a pottery, but it's been in disrepair for years. We know the Fire Eaters own the building, but no one has kept a close eye on it since it's been abandoned." She tapped the paper thoughtfully. "That changed when your message reached us. We have noted some signs of activity there, but it is still relatively quiet." Her finger moved to the last circle, this one sitting in the center of a residential area. It was a large house, almost a manor by the standards of the poor district. "The home of Oh Moriyasu. The current leader of the Fire Eaters, though their organization is loose enough that it's difficult to say for certain."

Hotaru wondered who "we" was. She knew that Kachiko had a network of informants within Otosan Uchi that rivaled – exceeded, really – any of the Great Clans. Kachiko had also long been rumored to be the spymaster for the Scorpion Clan. Hotaru had never asked her directly; such activities were considered… impolite.

As Clan Champion, she understood the necessity of maintaining such networks. Empires lived and died on three things: armies, food, and information. Each Great Clan was a nation unto itself, and she had her own networks of scouts and informants. But no clan could rival the Scorpion when it came to knowing what was going on within the Empire. Hotaru realized that she was getting something that those outside the Scorpion Clan rarely witnessed: a glimpse into the inner workings of their intelligence network.

Kachiko was studying the map and though the mask she wore hid most of her features, Hotaru could see the calculations flashing through her eyes. "Six choices," she mused. "Six targets, each one a possibility for finding the prince." Her gaze shifted to Hotaru, a note of challenge in her voice. "Where would you put him, Hotaru?"

Hotaru had never contemplated activities of a criminal nature, but she had sat among the best tacticians in the Empire. This was not so different from the battlefield. In the prince, the Fire Eaters had a valuable resource that they would want to protect, but also a tremendous weakness that they needed to keep from prying eyes.

"Not the gambling hall," she said. "Like Ayame said, too many people. Too much of a chance of the prince being seen. The 'manor house'" – the moniker was generous, but Hotaru didn't know what else to call it – "would provide the prince some level of comfort. Since they know who they have, they wouldn't risk treating him too poorly. But, again, it sits in the middle of a busy area." She mentally crossed it off her list of possibilities, aware that both Kachiko and Ayame were watching her with dark, appraising eyes.

"The warehouses, then," she said at last, "or the abandoned pottery. They provide some measure of privacy, and all four are large enough that suitable quarters for an 'honored guest' could be arranged."

"That is our assessment as well," Ayame said, and the faintest of smiles flickered across her face. Surprise? Respect? Or amusement that the noble Crane could skulk in the shadows with the Scorpion? "We await your word, my lady."

"How many have you gathered?" Kachiko asked.

"Two dozen."

"Good." Her eyes, behind her mask, went cold and dark as onyx.

"There are rules in Ryokō Owari Toshi, and this cannot be ignored. We strike at sunset. Send ten to the gambling hall. Deal with the Fire Eaters. Try to avoid hurting the citizens, if possible, but I do not want any Fire Eater to escape. Five should be sufficient for the house, if done appropriately. Oh Moriyasu will not see Lady Sun again."

She spoke calmly, not raising her voice. The only indication of the anger boiling within her was in the cold glittering of her eyes. It sent a chill down Hotaru's spine. This was a Kachiko she had heard rumors of, but never seen. A Kachiko that could order the death of dozens of people without batting an eye. It shouldn't have bothered her; after all, every time Hotaru went into battle, her words sent far more people to their next turn on the Wheel. But it did make Hotaru think of masks once more… was the ruthless Kachiko a mask that the Scorpion donned when it was needed? Or was the warm and loving woman that shared her bed the mask?

Kachiko continued to study the map. "Teams of three for each of these," she said, indicating the warehouses. "Observe first. If there are too many, our forces will regroup here." She tapped her finger at an alleyway located roughly equidistant between the warehouses. "If you find the prince, do not strike until Hotaru and I are present. If you do not find the prince, eliminate the Fire Eaters. We will deal with them, root and branch, this night."

"What of the pottery, my lady?"

Kachiko smiled across at Hotaru. "I think Hotaru and I will see to that personally."

# 28
# Toturi

Toturi rode into the Lion camp under a flag of truce.

He felt a pang of loss as he moved between the tents. He was surrounded by an army of his clan, and he was not in command of it. In fact, by his own decision, he couldn't really call them his clan anymore. He was rōnin. Without clan, without master.

He had chosen his exile; it had not been imposed upon him. But he could not simply return to them… not with the weight of his failure pressing down upon him. Even if he did return, what then? Would he challenge Matsu Tsuko for leadership of the Lion and risk fracturing the clan? Or would he retire to the countryside and watch the peasants farm the land? Perhaps a return to the monasteries of the Dragon and a life of quiet contemplation? He shook his head. No. There was no easy path back, not until the stain of his failure had been washed clean.

Still, he saw the hope of his return in the eyes of more than one Lion soldier as he made his way to Matsu Agetoki's command tent. He understood that hope; the glory of war was oft spoken of at court, but that glory could only be enjoyed by those who lived. In Toturi's return, they saw a new possibility; perhaps there would be no dying today. Those eyes brought a heavy burden of guilt to Toturi's soul, for while he wished as strongly as they that no blood be spilled, he knew it would not be.

He saw something else, too. Not all the soldiers who watched his passage through the camp looked at him with hope. There were those among the warriors of the clan who eyed him with the contempt reserved for traitors. He could not blame them; he had arrived at Kyotei Castle at the head of an army, and he walked through their camp flanked by a Unicorn and a Crane.

Daidoji Daisuke still wore his nondescript rōnin garb, but his silvery hair marked him as Crane for every eye to see. Toturi had no idea how the Crane managed to keep his hair dyed the silvery white through the rigors of their journey, but he suspected the Crane would sooner die than let one strand of his silky locks show its true color.

Toturi, too, wore the colors of a rōnin, but he had traded his simple kimono for black-lacquered armor. He had been hesitant to bring the Crane and the Unicorn to this meeting. Daisuke's presence was sure to inflame the Lion – which it was already doing with some of them – and though he trusted Kamoko's restraint, he still could not be sure what she would do when she came face to face with Matsu Agetoki. In the end, the fact that the Unicorn was *not* a rōnin, but rather a decorated Battle Maiden, won him over. Her presence would lend weight to their party, perhaps enough to make a difference.

Besides, he wasn't certain that Kamoko would have listened if he had ordered her to stay at the camp, and the first lesson he had been taught was to never give an order unless you were certain it would be followed.

They had arrived to find Kyotei Castle already under siege.

Matsu Agetoki's forces had encircled the stronghold and were laying siege to it. According to Daisuke, the castle garrison was small, a pittance by the standards of places like Toshi Ranbo. The castle had little chance of standing against the forces arrayed against it. From what Toturi could see, if nothing changed, Agetoki could take the castle in a matter of days.

Toturi, on the other hand, now rode at the head of a column that numbered hundreds of troops. They were green; more than half had never swung a blade in anger or fired an arrow at anything larger than a rabbit. But there was a core to them of the finest steel in the Empire; waves of "rōnin" had come to his banner. Most were from the Lion and the Crane, but there were representatives from every major clan. A small contingent of Battle Maidens – nearly thirty of the warrior women on their amazing mounts – had arrived only the morning before and placed themselves immediately under the command of Utaku Kamoko. He had watched those rōnin carefully and had come to a realization: they were among the best their clans had to offer.

Toturi had spent half his life looking deeply within himself and the other half training and commanding armies. He had learned how to recognize gifted warriors, and the rōnin who had come to support him were just that. He hadn't been able to watch them all drill, though on the long march from the Village of the Golden Blades, he had certainly tried. And in that observation, he saw a universal truth. The men and women who had walked away from their current lives to join him on his march were all talented warriors. They came in all ages and sizes, and they bore a mix of armor and weaponry that would make it difficult to integrate them into any standard formation, but their skill was undeniable. Such a force could easily take on five times their own numbers.

The same could not be said of the peasants that had come to

him. They had only the training his core of rōnin could give them, and while they had made great strides, it would still take two or three of them to face down even one samurai in battle. By his best estimation, his force, with their elite core and the growing skills of their novices, could handle an army half again their own size and come out bloodied, but victorious.

But Matsu Agetoki's army wasn't half again their size… it was nearly four times as large as his own.

"The commander's tent, Lord Toturi." The Lion subcommander who had been escorting them stopped before a large pavilion. A pair of Matsu berserkers were stationed outside, the women staring at the trio with visible menace. But they said nothing, simply pulling back the tent flaps and allowing Toturi and his companions to enter.

For Toturi, stepping into that tent felt like coming home. Everything within it was laid out precisely as dictated by the Akodo Commander School doctrines, right down to the position of the cushions used for when the commander received guests or discussed strategy with his officers.

Matsu Agetoki knelt behind a small table that had already been set with tea. He wore a simple kimono in Lion yellow and brown, though Toturi had little doubt his armor was close at hand. As they entered, he rose and offered a deep bow. "Welcome to my camp, Lord Akodo," he said, his rich baritone reverberating through the room. "And you as well, Daidoji Daisuke" – another bow – "and Utaku Kamoko. You are all welcome here."

Toturi felt the Unicorn stiffen at his side as she came face to face with the man who had killed her mother. She said nothing, but he could feel the tension in her, like a tightly coiled spring ready to snap into motion at the slightest touch. Toturi stepped slightly ahead of his companions and gave Matsu Agetoki a bow of his own. The man had shown respect so far, and courtesy dictated that it be returned, whatever personal matters might lie between them. "Thank you for receiving us, Lord Agetoki."

"Please, sit," Agetoki said as he did so himself and began carefully pouring tea into the cups set on the table. "Just because we are in the field, there is no need to dispense with the small comforts."

Toturi pulled his daishō from his obi and set them to the side as he knelt upon the cushions. Daisuke followed suit. For a moment, the silence stretched as Kamoko's hand hovered near the blade of her katana. Toturi braced himself. If the Unicorn lost the internal battle with her desire for revenge and struck here, the Akodo Code would dictate that he and Daisuke stand by and watch while the soldiers cut her down.

The Code would be sorely disappointed. If it came to it, he would fight by her side, but he offered a silent prayer to his ancestors that it not be so. Kamoko's hand clenched around the hilt of her katana almost spasmodically, but she did not bare steel. Instead, she slid her hand down and pulled both scabbards from her obi, taking her place at the table.

They all took a moment to sip their tea and at the first taste of it, Toturi felt another surge of homecoming. The leaves were a mountain blend from the Akodo lands and one he had not tasted since renouncing his position as Emerald Champion. He indulged in a second sip before setting the cup firmly back on the table. Daisuke had followed the dictates of courtesy – no surprise from the Crane courtier – but Kamoko had not even touched her cup. An insult, but a small one, and one that Agetoki seemed content to ignore.

"While I am glad to see that you appear to be doing well, my lord," Agetoki said after setting his own cup down, "I am somewhat saddened to learn that you have arrived at my camp at the head of a rōnin army. A rōnin army that, or so I have been informed, is composed largely of Crane." He took another sip. "And, of course, I have heard of your other exploits in opposition to your clan." He nodded, and a cloth divider that led deeper into the tent moved. Toturi recognized the young Lion officer that stepped forth. His armor was a little more dented and there were tufts of hair missing from the mane of the helmet he carried beneath one arm, but it was the same subcommander that had assaulted the Village of the Golden Blades.

"Akodo Sachio," he acknowledged.

The youth, scarcely older than Toku now that Toturi could get a look at him outside of the battlefield, bowed in response, but said nothing.

"Imagine my surprise when I learned that one of our raiding parties was thwarted by the former Clan Champion," Agetoki said. He smiled, and to Toturi's eye, that smile seemed a genuine mix of irony and bemusement. "The Fortunes do enjoy their twists and turns, don't they?"

"Raiding party?" Kamoko's voice was calm, with the edge of steel beneath. "You mean band of murderers. What possible value can be gained by burning the villages of unarmed peasants?"

Agetoki nodded, the smile never leaving his face. He leaned forward slightly. "A fascinating topic, and since the strategy has run its course, I don't mind discussing it with you. There have been border raids as long as there has been a Rokugan. But you know that. The Battle Maidens engage in them readily enough." He offered Kamoko a stiff nod, which she ignored.

"But what Matsu Tsuko and" – he put one hand lightly on his own chest – "with some modesty, I, devised is a variation on that long-standing tactic. The goal, you see, is to force the enemy to disperse their units, pulling soldiers from their far-flung fortifications in order to reinforce their villages. If they don't do this, they'll be seen as cruel and unjust rulers by their own populace, possibly sparking rebellion. If they *do* send soldiers, which of course Lady Hotaru did, at least to the degree that she was able, then they weaken those same fortifications to a degree that makes them easier to claim on the field of battle. Of course, there are certain fortresses the enemy simply can't afford to weaken. Toshi Ranbo, Kakita Palace, and the Esteemed Palaces of the Crane. Which means that reinforcements for the villages must be pulled unevenly, further weakening their entire defensive network." He took a sip from his tea and the smile he offered was almost shy. "It's been a rousing success and, at the risk of sounding overly brash, one that I've been quite proud of."

The earnestness of the man as he sat, calmly drinking his tea and discussing a strategy that had put an untold number of civilians to death, chilled Toturi. He had planned campaigns with death tolls that haunted his dreams, but he had never been immune to the real price of war. For Matsu Agetoki, the deaths seemed irrelevant. Pieces on the board devoid of thought or feeling. He glanced at Daisuke. The young rōnin's face was absolutely still, his eyes calm. But his hand had shifted, moving an inch closer to the hilt of his katana.

Utaku Kamoko, however, was not so calm.

"It's no better than butchery," Kamoko snapped. "But then, you know all about butchery, don't you, Matsu Agetoki?"

Agetoki blinked, his smile slipping just a hair. "Have I offended you in some way, Lady Unicorn?" he asked cordially. Kamoko's jaw tightened.

"Do I look familiar to you, Lion?"

The Lion general studied her for a moment and, just as with his description of his campaign against the Crane civilians, Toturi saw open and honest appraisal there. Matsu Agetoki was not angry. He was not reveling in his victories. He wasn't touched by the deaths of his soldiers or of those he deemed his enemies. He was proud, as all Lion were proud of their military accomplishments. But for the rest of it, he showed as much emotional investment as Toturi would playing with pieces on a Go board.

It sent chills down Toturi's spine.

"I'm afraid not, Kamoko," Agetoki said at last. "I have had skirmishes with the Unicorn before, but they were many years ago."

"Utaku Kumiko. Do you remember her, Lion?" she practically spit the words. Toturi heard the shifting from outside the tent as the Matsu berserkers reacted to the raised voices. Daisuke's hand crept closer to his blade. Toturi closed his eyes for a moment, drawing a breath. This was not the plan. They were not here to assassinate Matsu Agetoki. It would do nothing but get them killed. He had little doubt that the next Lion in the chain of command would step into Agetoki's place and Matsu Tsuko's plan for the Empire would march on. His army, on the other hand, would vanish like a whisper on the wind.

He opened his mouth to speak, to try to de-escalate the situation, but Matsu Agetoki was already speaking. "Ah, yes. Forgive me, Kamoko; I didn't make the connection. The Battle Maiden commander who died during the Lion-Crane war when our raiding spilled over into Unicorn villages. She was a fierce warrior; she fought bravely and died well." His words were matter of fact without mocking or malice.

"She was my mother. You led her and her forces into a trap, and you killed them all."

"I have killed many people, Kamoko. As have you. Such is the nature of war." He offered a slight, seated bow and turned to Toturi, dismissing the Unicorn in the next breath. "Now, on to other business. Toturi, I suppose since you fought against young Sachio that you have not brought an army to reinforce the Lion?"

Kamoko's face was flushed with anger and her whole body

trembled. Toturi could see that it was taking every ounce of control for her not to draw her sword and drive it through Agetoki's heart. Daisuke had yet to speak, but his hand still hovered near his blade. Both of his companions were ready to strike, and Realm of Torment take the consequences. But Toturi kept his voice even, hoping that his own calm would spill over to his comrades.

There would be bloodshed soon enough. But he did not want this meeting to end in it.

"I have come to try and convince you to abandon your siege, Agetoki," Toturi said.

"And why would I do that?"

He was prepared for the question. He doubted it would matter, but the words rolled immediately from his tongue.

"Because you are a true son of the Empire. Because you are a skilled enough strategist and versed enough in politics to understand the long-term ramifications of what you're doing." Toturi leaned forward, locking his eyes onto Agetoki's. "If you do not abandon this course, your actions could pull the entire Empire into a war it cannot survive. It will make the last Lion-Crane war look like a border skirmish. The men and women that swell my army's ranks see this; it is why just as many Lion have come to my banner as Crane. The Shadowlands are restless, Agetoki. If the Empire falls to its own internal struggles, they will rise up and swallow us all. We must remain united. Surely you can see that?"

Again, the careful consideration as Agetoki weighed his words. "What you say is not impossible," he allowed. Toturi felt a surge of hope, but it was short lived. "But it is just as likely that by proving the regent's weakness, the Lion will *save* the Empire. How can we be whole if the Emerald Throne is not strong? How can we stand against the Shadowlands without proper leadership? The weakness at the Imperial Court is like gangrenous flesh. It cannot be left to fester. We must remove it, or it will spread, and the Empire will die." He offered a small, apologetic bow to Daisuke as he said, "And should we deliver a fatal blow to the Crane at the same time, then perhaps it is finally time they lose their status as a Great Clan and fade away into obscurity."

To his credit, Daisuke didn't respond with anything but a cold smile. Toturi, however, felt the anger creeping into his own voice. "You would risk the Empire, and the lives of everyone in it, to destroy the Crane?"

"For the glory of the Lion and the duty I owe to our clan, I would risk everything."

Toturi nodded. He stood and beckoned for Kamoko and Daisuke to rise as well. "Then we have said all there is to say. Thank you for the tea, Matsu Agetoki. You can look forward to the pleasure of our company again in the morning."

"It will sadden me to put an end to one of the Lion's greatest generals, Akodo Toturi. May your ancestors guide you to a better life on the next turning of the Wheel."

Toturi gave a curt nod that could – generously – be considered a bow, turned on his heel, and left the tent. Their escort was waiting for them but kept a respectful distance as the trio made their way out of camp.

"You know, Kamoko," Daisuke said, speaking for the first time, "if you should find yourself in a position where you just can't bring yourself to kill that man, let me know. I would be more than happy to be next in line."

In the predawn moments, just before Lady Sun crested the horizon in the east, Toturi stood in front of his assembled army. It was *his* army, Toturi's Army, in a way that no army he had ever led had been. These were not his clan members come out of a sense of duty. These were not men and women who wanted to use the conflict to cover themselves in glory. No daimyō, champion, or Emperor had appointed him to this position or ordered him or anyone else to muster here.

Every person who stood before him had come here of their own free will, ready to fight and risk their lives to protect the Empire they loved. They had done so for two reasons. The first was because they saw the rot at the Empire's core, the same rot that had allowed their Emperor, the Light of Heaven, to be murdered. They saw the rot in the famine and disease that inevitably followed in the wake of war. They saw it in the bandits and criminals – some starving and desperate, others mere selfish opportunists – that had flooded the roads and turned traveling between villages into a life-risking affair. And they saw it in the samurai raiding parties that now slaughtered villagers and farmers wholesale, people with no real chance to defend themselves.

They saw the rot, and they could no longer sit idly by and watch the Empire that had sheltered them fall into the darkness. They saw the rot, and they said, "Enough."

But that was only half the reason they had gathered here. Toturi knew that he, himself, was the other half. In him they saw not a disgraced Lion general, nor the Emerald Champion who had failed to protect his Emperor, but rather, an almost legendary figure. They saw the man the Emperor had handpicked to lead his armies, the man who had slain the Emperor's murderer in personal combat, and the man who had walked away from power and prestige to wander the Empire, in search of a better way for peasant and samurai alike.

Toturi wasn't sure that he *was* the man they saw, but that no longer mattered. Even if he was not that man, he had to *become* him, for the sake of those that had flocked to his banner. As he looked out at the camp, lit by hundreds of flickering torches as they waited for the first gray brush of dawn, he felt a swell of pride, not in himself, but in the men and women who stood before him. Their faces were lost in the shadows of torches and twilight. They wore no uniforms, no clan colors. He could not tell man from woman, young from old, veteran from recruit as he looked out over them. They were one army, one people, united in a way that the Empire had not been since the Day of Thunder.

"Today," he said, voice ringing out, "we do not fight for pride. We do not fight for glory. We do not fight to advance the goals of this clan or that. Today we risk our lives not as Lion or Crane. Not as Unicorn or Scorpion. Not as Dragon or Phoenix or Crab. We risk our lives to restore the Empire that we all knew, an empire of peace and prosperity, to its rightful place. We stand against those who would shatter peace to advance their own power. We stand against those who would slaughter innocents and pretend it is justice. We stand against those who would bring the twin demons of plague and famine to our people. No matter what banners they carry, it is not the Lion we fight this day. It is the corruption that has taken root in the Empire and spread not just to my former clan, but to *all* clans. We will fight against that corruption and whether we go to victory or defeat, we go knowing that our ancestors and the Fortunes smile down upon us."

He surveyed his army one last time as he felt the first rays of Lady Sun break over the horizon, shrouding him in a halo of light. He hadn't planned that, but as the light fell over the faces of the army arrayed before him, he saw the effect it had on them, the hope and wonder that it filled them with. It was as if the Sun Goddess herself had anointed him in their eyes.

He put the weight of that particular burden from his mind as he spun on his heel. His katana flashed from his scabbard and he raised it high. Then, with one sharp motion, his arm fell, pointing the tip of the blade toward the castle in the east.

Or, more pointedly, toward the Lion army that stood between him and Kyotei Castle, a piece of iron caught between the anvil of the castle and the hammer of his forces.

"Forward!"

# 29
# Yakamo

They held.

Three times the assaults came, and three times Yakamo's forces pushed them back. In each attack, Yakamo felt the rage burning within him, weakening the foundations of his sanity. He fought two battles each time the Shadowlands filth poured over the parapets. The first was fought against the goblins and ogres and demons, and it was a fight of muscle and iron, of sinew and blood. His pact with Kuni Yori and Yakamo-no-oni served him well in that battle. Without the supernatural strength of the ritual, without the unnatural vigor and power of the claw, he would have fallen a dozen times over.

And without him, the bastion would have fallen.

He saw the reluctant acknowledgment of that truth in the faces of the soldiers that stood next to him. They had gone from horror at the sight of him crushing his enemies in the grip of the crab claw to numbness to acceptance. Now, he could see in more than one face something akin to gratitude. His fellow soldiers knew that they would not be alive if it were not for Hida Yakamo.

That did not help him fight the second battle, the one against himself. Or perhaps it was against the demon blood of Yakamo-no-oni coursing through his veins. Each time the Shadowlands creatures made the Wall, he felt it surging, demanding control. His vision dimmed, and he saw everything as if through a red-tinged fog. Except for the blood, which splashed vibrantly with every swing of his tetsubō, every crushing grasp of his claw. It would have been so easy to give in to that rage. It called to him. It tempted him with even more power.

But the ever-growing number of his own dead held him back.

They had no time to remove the Crab fallen from the Wall. Instead, they were stacked against the rear parapets like cordwood, a bulwark of flesh and a constant reminder of the fate that awaited them all. None of the soldiers left even glanced at the corpses anymore; the uncleanliness of the dead no longer bothered them. How could it, when they had spent so many hours side by side with their fallen comrades?

"How long can we hold?" The words rang oddly in his ears, low and slurred.

Yakamo turned to the speaker. The woman before him lacked the size and strength of his own sister, but she still stood on her own two feet. That was more than a lot of them could boast. He remembered her name: Hida Mihoko. An ugly bruise marred her face and her left cheek had swollen to the point where Yakamo doubted she could see from that side. Something in her face was clearly broken; the pain had to be intense, but Mihoko didn't acknowledge it.

Like Yakamo, she knew she was already dead. What was pain to the dead?

"Another attack," he answered. "Perhaps two."

They had received a trickle of reinforcements over the long day, but not enough to come close to replenishing their losses.

He now had fewer than thirty fighters whose injuries – and they were all injured – were minor enough to not impact their abilities. He had as many more walking wounded who could still swing a sword, but they wouldn't last long against a serious push. From the runners, he knew that they were doing better than any of the other bastions.

There would be no more reinforcements.

Mihoko nodded. "I wish the Fortunes had picked a nicer day for it."

Yakamo grunted at that. No day on the Wall was ever particularly nice. Lady Sun seldom broke through the clouds that were a perpetual shroud over the Shadowlands. Those clouds were unusually thick today, stretching as far as the eye could follow on either side of the Wall. Were they remnants of the storm that had formed when Kuni Yori sealed his bargain with Yakamo-no-oni? Or was it just another day?

As he gazed up at the gathering storm, he felt an energy there, a building torrent. As if the skies themselves were ready to get on with it. Yakamo couldn't blame them; he had tried everything, given everything, and still it had not been enough.

He was still going to fail.

He threw back his head and laughed. He couldn't help it. What had it all been for? How much blood had they spilled, just in the past few days, to protect an empire that couldn't be bothered to help them in their hour of need? An empire that was too concerned with their own infighting to see the monster on their doorstep.

"Yakamo?" Mihoko asked, voice hesitant. He must have looked like a madman, but he didn't care. In that moment, he understood Bunzō like he never had before. Laugh, so you don't cry. Laugh so the crushing weight of duty on the Wall didn't drive you mad. Laugh so the sacrifices – life, limb, mind, and soul – could be forgotten, if only for a moment.

"Laugh, Mihoko," he said, tears spilling from his eyes. "Laugh. Let the bastards hear our joy." She stared at him for a long moment until something in her face softened. A chuckle broke through her impassive mask. It grew into a titter and from there into a guffaw, until the woman clutched at her sides and howled with mirth. It spread from there, up and down the Wall, as the battered defenders found some solace in the absurd. Yakamo laughed until the pain in his sides was deeper than the pain of the many wounds he had sustained in combat. He laughed until his voice was hoarse and ragged and he had no more tears to cry.

He laughed and laughed and ignored the spasming pain in his left arm, as if the demon's limb was rebelling against the very idea of joy.

They came again with the dawn, and Yakamo knew that it was over.

They could not stand against the numbers arrayed against them. He saw the truth as the horde surged toward the Wall. The siege engines sounded, but slowly, their tempo slackened by the fact that there were not enough bodies to man them. Sporadic blasts of fire and lightning opened holes in the enemy ranks, but they closed almost at once. Within seconds, the Shadowlands creatures were scurrying spider-like up the stones.

His remaining soldiers took up their positions. Those that still had ammunition rained arrows down into the upturned faces of goblins and ogres. Others hurled discarded weapons and chunks of armor, anything to dislodge the climbers. But it didn't matter. The enemy would reach the Wall in their thousands, and when they did, there was nothing Yakamo and his fellows could do.

Nothing but meet their deaths with courage.

And take as many of the creatures with them as they could.

A peal of thunder sounded, loud enough that the Wall itself seemed to shake, and bolts of white-hot lightning traced patterns across the sky. Lady Sun was rising to the east, but the clouds were so thick that she did not bring light, only a lessening of the darkness. Yakamo felt the energy building in those roiling skies, as he had the day before. It seemed to echo in his own head and made his claw *click-clack* open and closed, as if in response to the energy of the storm.

The first goblin head appeared over the crenelation. He barely noticed the snarling face of the creature. His claw snapped out, and another body joined the pile of bones at the base of the Wall. But another replaced that. And another. An endless amount, scrambling over the edge.

Yakamo smashed his tetsubō down on yet another goblin skull and swept two more from the Wall with his claw. But he heard shouts of pain and panic, and felt the pressure on his right side increase. He knew what that meant. The enemy had gained a foothold and were pushing their way onto the battlements. He risked a glance in that direction and cursed.

An ogre had gained the top of the Wall.

The monster roared as it heaved itself over the Wall. Even as Yakamo turned, he saw the ogre's weapon, more a rusty club of iron than anything that could be considered a sword, crash through the guard of one of his soldiers, dropping them to the ground.

"Ancestors curse you," he growled.

"Go, Yakamo." Mihoko, who had been battling at his side, didn't turn her gaze from the Wall. "I will hold here."

He didn't second guess the woman. He doubted the line could hold much longer, with or without him. He simply stepped back from the front and ran toward the ogre at a dead sprint.

He reached the beast just as it closed its fist around the throat of another warrior. With a wordless howl, Yakamo brought his tetsubō smashing down on the monster's elbow. The sound of the joint separating was like another peal of thunder and the Crab fell from the ogre's nerveless fingers. Without hesitation, the warrior took advantage of the ogre's bellow of pain to drive his wakizashi deep into its guts, spilling them across the parapet.

There was no time to see if the man was okay. No time to accept his thanks. Yakamo whirled to the parapets, to lunge back into the defense of the Wall.

It was already too late.

He turned just in time to see Mihoko go down beneath a swarm of goblins, overwhelmed by the sheer number of the monsters. All along the length of the bastion, he saw the same scene repeated. A dozen samurai fell, and the rest backed away, forming into a tight knot as more and more Shadowlands filth gained the battlements. Yakamo reached down and pulled the man he had just saved to his feet, propelling him toward the group of defenders. Two goblins interposed themselves, and he crushed them as easily as he would a pair of beetles.

They joined the rest and, for a brief moment, the battle stalled. He found himself back to back with members of his clan, standing at the center of an ever-growing circle of goblins, ogres, and lesser oni.

At least it wasn't the undead. Yakamo would die here, but at least it would not be at the hands of some former Crab whose body had been brought back to life through dark incantations. He would die on his feet, surrounded by his fellow warriors, and he would take as many of them with him as he could. He could think of worse ends.

"What are you waiting for?" he bellowed in defiance to the hordes that surrounded him. "Come on! Let's end this!"

As if in answer to his shout, another peal of thunder sounded, and Yakamo felt a wave of darkness wash over the Wall.

For a moment, he thought that some new, Fu Leng-cursed entity had joined the fight. Perhaps a true oni had come, a lord of the Realm of Torment, one that wore Yakamo's face. But then that same wave of darkness flowed into his veins, filling him with newfound vigor. He felt the thousand aches and pains that he had been carrying through the battle fall away, even as a dark strength swelled his limbs and pushed back the exhaustion.

And then, the dead that had been stacked against the back parapet of the battlements moved.

First one, then ten, then in a constant undulating ripple, the butchered Crab samurai rose. Like enormous pale worms, they slid off the wriggling piles of their own dead and climbed to their feet, still holding the weapons they had died with. Despite the surging wave of power that filled him, Yakamo felt the undercurrent of fear. He had faced off against the corpses of his friends. But never like this; never had the bodies risen on the very field of battle where they fell. The dead had always been his weakness, and now they were about to pull him down.

Was that why the Shadowlands creatures had waited, because they knew that the dark sorcerers of Fu Leng were weaving their profane incantations?

If so, why did they look so surprised?

The surprise spread up and down the Wall as the fallen samurai lurched forward. Every man and woman remaining in his command braced themselves, backing together in an even tighter knot, until their shoulders were pressed tightly against their fellows.

But the dead did not come for them. The grasping claws and upraised swords fell not upon Yakamo and his survivors. Instead, they lurched past the Crab, tearing into the creatures of the Shadowlands. He heard the yelps of surprise, even fear, from the goblins as the melee, which had a moment before paused in a fragile and seemingly timeless moment, exploded anew.

All up and down the Wall, the dead joined the fray. But they did not fight on the side of the Shadowlands. The fallen Crab had resumed their duties and tore at the invaders with tooth and nail and forgotten weapons, driving them back until it was the Shadowlands monsters and not the Crab who had been pushed up against a bulwark of their own dead.

For a long moment, Yakamo could only stare as the battle passed him by. He was frozen, both by the shock of what he was seeing, and his own fear of the undead. Power surged in him once more, filling his veins and his mind. It demanded to be used. It wanted to break and smash and kill.

And it had a target for its malice.

"Drive them from the Wall!" he shouted.

Yakamo charged forward, shouldering his way between the dead that had, only a moment ago, petrified him with fear. He swung tetsubō and claw alike with wild abandon, crushing the life from the goblins and ogres that dared stand in his path. His soldiers – his living soldiers – hesitated for a moment longer. He felt their shock as the son of their daimyō dove headlong into the midst of the dead, fighting beside the unliving to push the Shadowlands back.

Shock gave way to action, and the dozen or so warriors that could still fight threw themselves into battle. All up and down the Wall, the surviving Crab stood shoulder to shoulder with the walking dead. Together, they drove the enemy back. In the chaos of battle, Yakamo could hear the unspoken questions of his clansmen. How had the dead risen? Why were they fighting against the Shadowlands when every time before, the undead had been their enemy?

But even as they pushed the Shadowlands back, Yakamo knew the truth. He felt it in the surging power that flowed through him, starting in the oni claw and flowing outward from there. He recognized the energies that swirled around them and infused the undead. He had felt them before. In the Shadowlands when the oni had killed Momoe and Bunzō. When Kuni Yori called an oni lord from the Realm of Torment and into the Mortal Realm.

When he had given the demon his own name, Yakamo-no-oni, and had been forever changed.

This was the power of the Shadowlands, the power of the dark spirits that the shindōshi of the Empire refused to call upon. It was the power of the Realm of Torment, and some part of Yakamo, deep within the center of his soul, recoiled against it.

But that part was weak, and he crushed it as easily as he crushed the skull of a goblin that dared stand before him. There was no room in him for weakness. Not anymore.

When it was done, Yakamo stood at the parapet, staring out at the Shadowlands army retreating before him. The Wall had held; the enemy had been defeated. The risen dead had dealt them an unexpected blow, and despite their numbers, he knew that this time, they would not regroup. They would fall back, disappear into the barren hills of the Shadowlands itself. They might come again, but not until their masters understood what had happened.

The siege was over. This battle, at least, was won.

He stood shoulder to shoulder with the corpses of the men and women who had died defending the Empire, and he felt nothing but hate. Not for the undead; he scarcely thought of them at all, except to chide himself for ever fearing their presence. They were another tool, a weapon, to be used to make the Crab stronger.

No. He felt hate for the lazy, closed-minded, fawning servants of the regent. All the death and mayhem around him could have been prevented. It was *their* fault that so many Crab had fallen. It was *their* fault that they had to resort to methods the rest of the Empire would consider disgraceful. Yakamo snorted. Such a ridiculous idea; not a single one of them had ever had to test the strength of their convictions against the strength of an oni's blade. Their concepts of righteousness and virtue wouldn't stop that oni from tearing off their heads.

They needed a reminder that it was the Crab that kept them safe. And they needed a regent – no, an emperor – that understood that.

And given what had happened this day, Yakamo had an idea just who that emperor might be.

Hida Yakamo, son of the Great Bear, successor to the Crab Clan, threw back his head and laughed.

No one laughed with him.

How could they?

They were all dead.

# 30
# Hotaru

Despite being long abandoned, the pottery smelled of sludge and baked clay.

Hotaru had seen potters' workshops before; there were many skilled artists among the Kakita who produced pottery, ceramics, and porcelain of such beautiful and delicate nature that it could stand beside any painting or work of art. The pottery on the banks of the River of Gold was not that.

It was more factory than workshop, the type of place where clay pots were produced with little eye to artistry and then fired in massive kilns, all to feed the constant demands of the city. How or why it failed, Hotaru had no idea, but as they approached the building, it was evident that it had.

The entire stretch of the riverbank, nearly a mile in length, looked as if it had fallen on hard times. The long shadows of dusk underscored that decay, drawing the eye to the broken shutters and missing shingles. Most of the buildings appeared to be warehouses or workshops, with the latter being the type for artisans who needed access to large amounts of water in their crafts. The warehouses were run down, with gaps showing between boards, the shutters on many windows hanging at odd angles or missing entirely. The workshops were a little better, but not by much. They also passed at least two buildings that had burned to the ground, leaving nothing behind but piles of charred wood and blackened timbers.

The pottery itself could have easily been mistaken for a warehouse, were it not for the dozen clay chimneys jutting through the roof. It, too, showed signs of disrepair, but Hotaru could see faint rays of light trickling from around the closed shutters and through the gaps in some of the boards. She saw no guards in the doorway or lurking in the shadows. In fact, the streets here were largely empty.

At least that emptiness would make their approach easier. If the prince was inside – and given that Kachiko had chosen this place for the two of them to surveil, she had a strong suspicion he was – they would need to act decisively.

"Do we have a plan?" she asked Kachiko.

Kachiko arched a slender brow at her. After their meeting with Ayame, they had gone to a house that was some sort of haven for the Scorpion. There, Kachiko had traded in her kimono for loose-fitting garments in grays and blacks, and a cloth mask that fully covered her face, leaving only her eyes uncovered. For the first time in Hotaru's memory, the Scorpion openly bore weapons. A wakizashi rode her hip and a number of kunai were strapped to her belt.

For her part, Hotaru had swapped out her simple traveling clothes for a set of garments found at the Scorpion cache. Instead of the shadow-blending attire that Kachiko wore, she had opted for what appeared to be another set of traveling clothes, but the kimono and hakama both had thin bands of metal and bamboo woven into their fabrics. It wasn't as good as actual armor, but it was better than nothing, which was her other option. She still carried her naginata and had her daishō at her waist.

"I think you'll approve of my plan, Hotaru," Kachiko said. "We – or you, at least – are going to go for the direct approach."

Hotaru felt eyes upon her as she walked toward the door to the pottery. There were a pair of doors, one a broad sliding door on a track that was meant for wagons, and one that was normal sized. It was to the latter that she went, making no effort to hide her approach. Kachiko had reasoned that the Fire Eaters wanted a meeting. It might not be the appointed time or place, but they had sent a ransom note, after all. They were unlikely to shoot an obvious samurai approaching their hideout full of arrows as soon as they saw them.

Or so Kachiko had said.

She was out there, somewhere. The Scorpion had slipped into the darkness as soon as Hotaru began her approach. Hotaru had tried to track her, but as she had so often in the throngs at court, Kachiko simply vanished. She had no idea where the Scorpion was now, or what she was doing; her only instruction was to "provide a distraction" while the Scorpion located the prince.

There was only one way to provide the type of distraction that Kachiko would need. As Hotaru approached the door, she tilted her head, first one way, then the next, stretching the muscles. She flexed her fingers on the haft of the naginata and drew a deep breath. She felt the music of the city shifting around her, picking up pace, taking on a more driving rhythm.

There was a moment of doubt as things reached a crescendo. If Kachiko was wrong or if, for whatever reason, the Scorpion was deceiving her, Hotaru's actions could be viewed as criminal. Even worse, she could be about to launch a one-woman assault on a perfectly innocent group of people. Once she started, there would be no going back. It came down to trust: trust in Kachiko and the information her people had acquired. Trust in the Scorpion. In the City of Lies.

I trust you, Kachiko.

As she reached the door, Hotaru took two bounding steps and turned her shoulder, crashing the full weight of her body into the rotting wood. It burst open, and she was inside. She registered only two things before the instincts of battle fully claimed her. First, the area beyond the door was broad and open, the potters' wheels removed. It was lit by lanterns hung from the high beams and felt to Hotaru more like a dojo than a pottery. Second, it was full of rough men and women, all of whom were armed.

They wore heavy haori made out of a rough fabric that reminded Hotaru of sailcloth. In their hands they clutched an array of clubs, knives, and short axes, many of which she realized were repurposed boating implements. While they had clearly been aware of her approach, they had just as clearly not been expecting her to burst into their midst. It left them momentarily shocked.

Hotaru took full advantage of that moment.

The music of the city became the music of battle, and Hotaru danced into the midst of the Fire Eaters. Her naginata wove into her melody and where the notes carried her, death followed. As the blade slipped past the guard of the first Fire Eater and slashed across his throat, she was aware of others first recoiling in surprise and then surging forward, a frantic upswell of notes.

She spun the polearm, using blade, butt, and haft, turning aside their weapons as her feet carried her through the dance. Always centered, always in balance. She moved like water and struck like air, and two more Fire Eaters fell, their blood spilling onto the hard-packed dirt of the pottery.

She had moved through their ranks and now stood on the far side of the room, away from the door. Four of the Fire Eaters were on the ground, and she could tell at a glance that three of them would never rise again. The fourth, whom she had struck with the spinning haft of the naginata, might live provided her blow had not broken his skull. Eight remained and they all stared at her with the same wide-eyed mix of horror and surprise.

"Who are you?"

"I am Doji Hotaru, Clan Champion of the Crane," she replied formally. She offered the barest of bows. "And I have come for the prince."

At those words the faces of the Fire Eaters paled and their eyes darted around as if expecting to see a hundred ashigaru crashing down on them. When the soldiers did not appear the man who had spoken cleared his throat. "You are welcome to the prince," he said. He hesitated and added, "If you pay the ransom."

The insolence of the man shocked her. He was a peasant who dared to lay hands on the rightful heir to the Emerald Throne. He had just admitted as much. And to add to the insult, he thought to *sell* the prince back to them. Hotaru did not understand what could lead these Fire Eaters so far away from the path. They did not follow the Akodo Code, but how could they lack all sense of decency?

"There will be no payment," she said by way of response. "The only reward you receive is prison, and that only if you surrender. If you do not, your reward will be death."

"There are eight of us and one of you."

She could hear the fear in the man's voice. He was trying to gather the tattered remnants of his bravery, but he knew that he and his companions were caught. "There were twelve of you," she noted. "And while you might think it, I am not alone."

As if in answer, a man cried out and then fell, dropping from a mezzanine that Hotaru hadn't noticed in her initial scan of the area. He hit the ground like a sack of millet, and a small hunting bow fell from his limp grasp. One of Kachiko's kunai sprouted from the hollow of his throat.

Kachiko appeared a moment later. She was not alone. A young man strode after her, hands clasped behind his back. He stood straight, his chin lifted in the air. Despite the fact that his kimono was stained and rumpled, he somehow managed to convey a sense of regalness. He wasn't that much younger than Kachiko. A half-dozen years at most. But something about the way he looked down on them – literally and figuratively from his high perch – made him seem more the petulant child than the heir to a mighty empire.

Without taking her eyes off the Fire Eaters, Hotaru bowed. "Your Imperial Highness," she said.

"Your Imperial *Majesty*," he corrected, his voice high and clear. "Really, I thought the Crane of all people would be better about such things."

His voice, and the ingratitude in it, grated in Hotaru's ears. She felt a surge of irritation, even anger, rising within her. She was the Champion of the Crane, and such disrespect was an insult not only to her, but to her entire clan. He was not the Emperor, not yet. There were ceremonies and formalities before Sotorii could rightfully claim that title. By every dictate of courtesy, she had the right to chastise the prince in turn. She fought down her ire and resisted the urge; now was not the time or place.

Hotaru rose and turned her attention back to the Fire Eaters.

"It's over. Lay down your arms."

It hung there for a moment. The Fire Eaters still outnumbered them; they had to be considering trying to overwhelm Hotaru. Or perhaps, simply fleeing the scene. The path to the door was clear, though Kachiko had already demonstrated that she could take the life of anyone who tried to run. If they tried it, Hotaru knew some would escape. She wished them well of it if they did; she had little doubt that doing so was a death sentence. The Fire Eaters were done; their only choices left were prison or death.

She saw the moment when the leader realized the same. "We should never have gotten involved in this," he muttered. "I should have never listened to that girl." Hotaru blinked in surprise at the words, wondering if she had heard correctly, but the man was already dropping his weapon. The others followed suit, and in short order, Hotaru found herself standing over eight kneeling Fire Eaters, their heads bowed in defeat. They would need to be questioned, their motives uncovered. Moments later, Kachiko and the prince had joined her.

Kachiko had pulled down her veil and replaced it with the lacy butterfly mask that did more to accent her beauty than conceal it. As the prince and the Scorpion walked out onto the main floor of the pottery, Hotaru could see a strange look in the prince's eyes. It was not one she particularly liked. Men had looked at Kachiko before, of course. It was something Hotaru had grown accustomed to whenever she was in the Scorpion's presence. Jealousy was a ridiculous notion, especially when Kachiko herself encouraged those eyes on her, and for the most part, Hotaru could ignore it.

But something about the prince's covetous gaze set her teeth on edge.

Kachiko had one hand resting lightly on the prince's bicep, and it was unclear who was guiding whom as the two stopped at Hotaru's side. Hotaru bowed again, a proper bow this time, and one that Sotorii barely seemed to notice. His eyes were locked on the Fire Eaters and his expression had shifted to something eager. Something hungry.

Kachiko must have noticed the look as well. "Do not worry, Prince Sotorii," she said. "I will see to it that they are properly dealt with. The poppy fields always need workers." She took a step toward the door. "Come, let us get you to Shosuro Palace. We will leave these criminals to the magistrate."

"No."

The word was spoken flatly, but there was something beneath it that sent a shiver up Hotaru's spine.

"You have been through quite the ordeal, my prince." Kachiko tried again, her voice soothing, almost hypnotic. "You must be tired. A fine meal and a hot bath will do much in washing away the unpleasantness of this night." A smile fluttered across her face, as her fingers reached out and lightly stroked the prince's arm. Barely a touch, but one Hotaru knew he felt. "I will have the servants at the palace put out their finest for you."

She was flirting with him, or at least, she was walking the line between seductive and scandalous. Try as she might to ignore it, Hotaru felt the sharp pang of jealousy deep within. Was Kachiko truly trying to win the prince's affections, or was she simply tempting him to leave this place, and its people, unscathed? She didn't know, and she hated that she didn't know. Kachiko's games, and their intent, were always ambiguous.

The prince turned toward Kachiko and for a moment, Hotaru thought that the Scorpion's words would have their intended effect. But then something flashed behind the prince's eyes and a cruel smile came to his lips.

"Those things all sound wonderful, my dear," he said. Hotaru barely stopped herself from flinching at the diminutive. Kachiko was of the Bayushi line and one of the highest ranking samurai in her clan. No matter how flirtatious she might have been, it was not appropriate for the prince to call a high ranking noble and the Mother of Scorpions, "my dear". Even then, Kachiko was the widow of the man who murdered Sotorii's father.

His behavior was not normal, not by any standard of Rokugani society. Was that a remnant of his ordeal? Or was it something else? She didn't have long to ponder it because the prince turned to her.

"Kill them."

The men and women at her feet stiffened. They looked up at her, eyes suddenly pleading.

"Prince Sotorii," Kachiko said, voice ever-so-slightly chiding. "It is not appropriate. Lady Hotaru is the Clan Champion of the Crane, not a common executioner. If you wish these men dead, let the Scorpion attend to it."

"The Crane?" Sotorii scowled. "You mean the clan that has usurped my throne?"

Anger flared to life within Hotaru, even as Sotorii continued. "My captors told me many things, Kachiko. I am wise enough to separate the truth from the lies, but can you tell me that the regent is not a Crane? That a Crane wasn't appointed as the new Emerald Champion? *Appointed* by another Crane?" The prince looked as if he wished to spit, but then realized such an act would be beneath him.

"Prince Sotorii" – Hotaru tried to keep the anger from her voice – "it would be wise to question these men and women. As for Kakita Yoshi, he was named regent by your father's council. While Kakita Toshimoko's own appointment might be irregular, it was by no means a usurpation of your rightful place on the throne."

"Then prove it," Sotorii demanded. Again, Hotaru had to stop herself from flinching at the whining note of petulance in the would-be Emperor's voice. "I don't care what lies this filth might spew. I have given you an Imperial command. Kill these traitors!"

Hotaru opened her mouth, about to declare that she had *not* been given an imperial command because he was not yet the

Emperor. But Kachiko gestured, a low, quick hand flick of her hand down by her hip, subtle enough that Sotorii did not notice. Hotaru looked at Kachiko and she felt a new chill crawling down her spine.

Kachiko was afraid. No. She was *terrified*. None of it had shown in her own voice, but now that she was looking for it, Hotaru could see the slight tremble in her hand and the blankness of her expression. This wasn't her normal mask, but something very different.

"Please, Hotaru," Kachiko said. Her voice was clear, calm. Hotaru couldn't place it, but now that she was aware, she couldn't unhear it. "Do as the Emperor bids. Those who dared kidnap our lord deserve only death. As the ranking Scorpion in this city, I deem it so."

Emperor. Kachiko knew the boy was not the Emperor. But she knew, as did Hotaru, that he *would* be. And from the sneering petulance on his boyish face and the undercurrent of fear within Kachiko, Hotaru realized it would be foolish to disobey him now. He might not be Emperor – yet – but as the crown prince, he had a right to pronounce judgement on his kidnappers. And even if he didn't, here in the lands of the Scorpion, Kachiko's declaration had just sealed their fate.

It wasn't a matter of if they would be executed; the only question was whether or not Hotaru herself would carry out their fate. Hotaru had dispensed justice in her own lands and, when necessary, with her own hand. The penalty for these Fire Eaters' crimes warranted death, and no one could say differently. But she did not want to kill them.

If it had just been her and Sotorii standing here, she would have refused, crown prince or no. But she couldn't ignore the subtle pleading in Kachiko's eyes. Kachiko, who in all the years Hotaru had known her, had never pleaded for anything. The realization chilled her. Kachiko either knew something she did not, or she sensed, as Hotaru did, the inherent *wrongness* in the eyes of the prince. And she needed Hotaru to do this.

If Hotaru refused, the prince would be within his authority to have her killed. And not just her, but Kachiko as well. Perhaps not now, not as merely the heir presumptive to the throne. But he *was* the presumptive heir, and when they returned to Otosan Uchi, he would almost certainly be crowned Emperor. No matter what happened here today, a rational Emperor would not order two of the highest ranking nobles in Rokugan to be executed, especially when the realm was already hanging together by the thinnest of threads.

But as she looked into Sotorii's eyes and saw the quiet pleading in Kachiko's, Hotaru knew that Sotorii was not a rational man.

Hotaru stepped forward, and her naginata swept down, moving with the crisp precision of years of training. Before the first Fire Eater's head had hit the ground, the second was already dying. She moved down the line, quickly, efficiently. The prince's kidnappers, who had only moments ago surrendered to her because she had promised them their lives, died by her hand. In that moment, she hated the prince for making her do this, for making her forfeit her given word.

But she did it, nonetheless.

When she reached the end of the line, she found herself staring down into the face of a woman who was probably no older than Hotaru but looked twenty years her senior. A life of hardship had aged her, and as she gazed up at Hotaru and the blade that was about to fall, she spoke.

"You deserve him. Lady Sun have mercy on you, for your prince will not."

The woman's head joined the others to the accompanying music of Sotorii's delighted applause. "Excellent, Lady Hotaru," he stated. "Perhaps the Crane are loyal after all. Now, I believe there was mention of hot baths and warm food? I find myself in strong need of both. Let us call on the Shosuro, and we can speak of returning to the capital as quickly as we can. I have an empire to rebuild."

With that, he strode from the pottery, Kachiko beside him. But the Scorpion gave Hotaru a brief look just before she turned away, and the gratitude in those eyes warmed Hotaru's heart, even as the warning there chilled her insides.

Left alone, Hotaru took a moment to survey the bodies, laying where they had fallen. She felt dirty, tainted, and the words of the Fire Eater echoed in her ears.

Lady Sun have mercy on you, for your prince will not.

She prayed that those words would not turn out to be a prophecy.

# 31
## Toturi

An army stood across the open field. They were arrayed in neat blocks, their ranks dressed with a precision that spoke of long discipline. Toturi sat atop his horse, taking in the formations of the enemy. He almost didn't need to bother, for he and Agetoki were students of the same school of warfare. He knew the formations and doctrines of the army across the field as well as if they were his own.

At the front of Agetoki's lines stood blocks of archers, lightly armored and with arrows stuck into the ground before them. Toturi noted that the Lion commander had elected to leave most of his ranged combatants with the force that still encircled Kyotei Castle. He could not fault Agetoki for that decision; keeping the garrison inside the walls of the castle was vital to crush the relief force Toturi had brought to bear. Still, he was glad for it, nonetheless. There would be a butcher's bill to pay today, but if his count was right, he had at least as many bowmen as the Lion had arrayed against him. His lines would not disintegrate before they reached the enemy front.

Behind the bowmen came the yari-armed ashigaru. It was these soldiers that worried Toturi the most. Their long polearms bristled menacingly, with blocks of soldiers five ranks deep. Breaking through those lines would be costly, in terms of both time and blood, and it seemed Agetoki had realized as much. While most of his archers remained around the castle walls, every pikeman he possessed stood ready to repulse Toturi's army.

Next in the formation came the samurai and their personal retainers. These would be the most skilled of the Lion, at least on the individual level. They had the training to match any of Toturi's own men. Behind them stood the cavalry. There were not many; the Lion had never put much weight on horse-mounted warriors. They were of little use in a siege, and a good formation of pike could stop them cold. Or so the reasoning went. The Unicorn had shown time and again how effective they could be in open-field battles, but despite his own personal urgings, the Lion schools had never adopted the tactics or techniques. His own cavalry, small as it was, outnumbered Agetoki's, but that was the only formation where he had numerical superiority.

If he followed the Akodo doctrine, Agetoki would use his archers to pepper Toturi's army as they advanced, then open gaps in the polearms for the archers to retreat behind the lines. The pike would stop his infantry and, at the opportune moment, push forward and open their own ranks to allow the shock troopers of the samurai and their personal retinues through. Those warriors would smash into Toturi's lines in a close engagement, leaving the cavalry to sweep around the flanks, further disrupting Toturi's formations and cutting off any reserves. The only real unknown for Agetoki was Kyotei Castle itself, but with a blocking force of five times the castle's garrison, the Lion general had little enough to worry about on that front.

It was a brilliant execution of the Akodo doctrine with an attention to detail that Toturi could only admire. That same doctrine had a very precise answer to the tactical situation that Toturi found himself in: retreat. His training dictated that, when facing a much larger force, he split his own army into several harrying elements and spend the next month harassing Agetoki's supply lines, ambushing his patrols, and doing everything he could to win a war of attrition. Only when he had whittled down the Lion should he engage Agetoki on a more level playing field.

Except, in doing so, he would condemn Kyotei Castle. And if Kyotei Castle fell, the regent might commit Imperial forces against the Lion, turning Matsu Tsuko's accusations into prophecy. The doctrines of the Akodo Commander School would not serve him here.

So, he did what every good commander did when presented with an impossible situation: he broke the rules.

"Are you absolutely sure about this?" Daidoji Daisuke asked from his side. The Crane had donned armor, but unlike Toturi who wore his layered lamellar armor, the duelist had contented himself with the lighter ashigaru armor. "I was a great disappointment to my teachers when it came to matters of war, but isn't this all a bit… nontraditional?"

Toturi grunted. "Don't worry, Daisuke. The archers will have much on their minds. Besides, that is why I had everyone who could handle a saw building shields."

Shields had not seen regular use in the armies of Rokugan for centuries. The philosophy of war had shifted to favor pike and bow for ashigaru. And with the exception of the Mirumoto, samurai had always preferred fighting with a two-handed grip on the katana. The shield had given way to the sode, the heavy armored shoulder plate that could provide some protection from arrows while leaving both hands free for fighting.

But the concept had not vanished, even if it had fallen out of use. No one in Toturi's army possessed an actual shield, but they had plenty of skilled craftsmen among the peasants who had joined them. It had not taken long to put together enough planks of wood and bits of leather to equip each soldier in Toturi's vanguard with something akin to the shields of old. They were heavy and awkward, but thick enough to weather the arrow storm and meant to be discarded as soon as the no man's land between the lines was crossed.

"I'm sure that's a great comfort," Daisuke replied. "But I hadn't expected our samurai to be leading the charge." Toturi could sense Toku shifting on the horse beside his. The boy was not a natural rider, and with one hand occupied by the simple banner – a brown wolf on a field of gray – that had somehow been adopted as the symbol of this army, he sat on his mount uneasily. Toturi remembered the conversation with Toku, and the reason so many peasants had come to fight at his side.

They knew he would not throw their lives away.

"Our tactics must adapt to the situation," Toturi replied. "Our ashigaru" – he used the term, even though the peasant volunteers didn't really meet the definition – "do not yet have the discipline to cross an open field under fire by enemy archers and breach a wall of pike. The rōnin do, or at least, they have the training for it. And the shields will dilute any casualties we might take."

"As you say, Lord Toturi," Daisuke replied. "But I hope you won't think less of me if I'm glad that my place is by your side, acting as a bodyguard, and not in the vanguard."

Toturi frowned, not because he found fault in the Crane's words, but because they were so contrary to the drives of most samurai. Glory would be found in the vanguard, not sitting by Toturi's side, keeping him safe should Agetoki's assassins reach him. To most samurai, that glory was more important than life itself.

But Daidoji Daisuke was not the only rōnin that had come to him with a different view of the world. His army would not hesitate to fight; not one of the rōnin had so much as blinked when they learned they would lead the assault. But they placed duty higher than glory or pride, and they held life sacred. They would risk it, but only if the cause was just. The thought of it filled him with a deep sense of gratitude and responsibility. These men and women – peasant and rōnin alike – had put their lives in his hands. He owed it to them to spend those lives as frugally as possible.

Toturi glanced to the left and right, making sure one last time that his forces were arrayed properly. His vanguard spread out before him, but unlike the enemy, he did not have his green troops out front. There were three groups: the core of rōnin stood in the center, with two units of peasant fighters to either flank. Toturi had no intention of trying to exhaust Agetoki's arrow supply with the bodies of his least capable warriors; instead, he would send his rōnin – veteran fighters all – right down the throat of the enemy. The archers would support them, trying to disrupt Agetoki's bowmen. With the shields and their own archers for cover, they should reach the pikemen relatively unscathed. At that point, the quality of the rōnin that had come to his banner would be revealed.

He had one more surprise up his sleeve. Kamoko had left with the entirety of her Battle Maidens before Lady Sun had graced the field. Sending out the cavalry meant he had no real reserve to speak of, but Kamoko had her orders. When the moment was right, she would appear.

All was ready. He had done everything he could to give them a chance at success. All he could do now was trust in the people who called themselves Toturi's Army.

He looked at the banner that Toku held and offered up a silent prayer that his ancestors smile on them this day. Then he met Toku's eye.

"Signal the archers."

The boy grinned. There had been no time to teach him – or any of the other peasants come to his banner – the complex signals of the battle fan. Instead, they had elected a more venerable – though still effective – system. Toku raised a horn to his lips and blew. Three loud blasts sounded over the battlefield. At the prearranged signal, Toturi's archers marched forward. He felt the tension from the other side of the battlefield as the soldiers there shifted, and their own archers reached for their arrows.

Toturi closed his eyes and offered up a final prayer to his ancestors and the Fortunes. He prayed not for victory – though if either wanted to lend a helping hand on that front, he certainly wouldn't refuse – but for as many of the men and women who had come to his banner as possible to make it through this day alive. The thrum of bowstrings sounded across the battlefield and the whistling of hundreds of arrows flying through the sky came almost on its heels.

The first volley of arrows from the archers of either side targeted their counterparts. Toturi's archers were spaced in a long skirmish line with gaps between them to allow the rōnin to move freely through their lines. As he watched those first arrows fall, Toturi felt a little surge of relief. Agetoki's archers were in tight block formations, and only those in front could pick out individual targets. The rest fired in volleys, their arrows describing arcing waves through the sky. The spread formation of Toturi's bowmen thinned their casualties, at least some. Where the arrows hit, men screamed and died, but Toturi's archers answered in kind, and every bowman in their long, well-spaced skirmish line had a clear line of sight to the enemy. They might not be able to concentrate their fire as much, but their arrows began taking a toll on Agetoki's archers.

"Send the rōnin," Toturi said, keeping his voice calm and even. Toku blew another signal, and the block of rōnin began their march.

Toturi could only watch as his rōnin moved through those skirmish lines, entering the killing field. Agetoki's archers understood the risk, and their fire shifted at once to the infantry.

Arrows arched into the sky, and at their apex, he heard a wordless shout from his rōnin. The rough-hewn shields were raised, edges overlapping. A sound like hailstones on wooden rooftops echoed across the battlefield as the arrows struck home. Toturi could see that, despite the protection, some of his rōnin had fallen, but only a handful. The rest marched on, the discipline of the samurai allowing them to walk into that rain of razor-edged steel at a steady march.

They had to close more of the distance before he could order the charge, lest they arrive at the enemy lines too winded and tired to fight effectively. Toturi watched while his soldiers marched across the field, and with every volley, a few of his forces were left behind. He maintained an outward calm despite feeling every one of the losses as if the arrows were striking his own flesh. Nerves twisted his stomach and the order to charge forward, to close the distance at a speed to minimize casualties, danced on tip of his tongue. But he had to be patient. He had to wait.

Nearly four hundred yards had separated the two armies, a distance just out of the effective range of the bows. The rōnin had closed half that distance at the march, and it continued to drop. Agetoki's archers were beginning to lower their point of aim, firing on a flatter trajectory. It would make angling the makeshift shields more difficult. His own archers continued to punish the opposing archers, firing with impunity. The weight of the enemy fire had fallen off by at least a third.

One hundred and fifty yards. Soon.

The distance between the rōnin and the archers fell to a hundred yards.

"Now, Toku," he said, and the boy once more raised the horn to his lips. The signal, one long sonorous note, signaled three things, and they all happened at once.

As the note reached the rōnin they dropped their shields, pulling their weapons as they lowered their heads and sprinted forward. His archers, who had also been moving slowly forward as they engaged the enemy, shifted their aim. Instead of covering the rōnin, they now directed their fire to the pikemen. The result was evident a moment later when the long lines of pike began to react to the arrows that were falling among them. The disruption caused a moment of chaos and the cries of pain warred with the shouted orders.

The enemy archers managed one final volley, before they had to turn and sprint for their own lines, desperate to reach safety behind the forest of pikes. Their flight spurred the rōnin on as the disarray of the pike armed ashigaru bought them a brief window in which to act.

But the signal had not been for Toturi's rōnin and archers alone. As the last lingering note died away, Toturi took his eyes from the charge of the rōnin. On the flanks of the battlefield, his peasant forces had begun their march. The sound of their drums brought a feral grin to Toturi's face as the two separate divisions of soldiers surged forward. They were all green troops, but they had been trained as extensively as possible by the rōnin who, even now, were slamming into the wall of pike.

"Now," Toturi growled, his fist clenching on the reins as he saw the two lines meet. The shift of targets from the archers had sewn disarray into the enemy spearmen, made worse by the sudden need to open their formation and let their own archers through. That disruption bought his rōnin priceless moments to get in among the ranks of pike.

Many fell. No amount of disarray could completely break the formation of a wall of well-disciplined pikemen. But they cut deep into the ranks of ashigaru. He had ordered the rōnin to maintain a tight formation, and when they crashed into the enemy, they had not spread out across the entire frontage of their lines. They struck like a hammer into soft metal, folding it around them. There was a danger there, for the ashigaru on either side began to turn inward, seeking to bring their spears to the flanks of the rōnin.

"Archers. Signal three," Toturi barked. Toku, anticipating the command, responded at once, and a staccato series of notes rang out.

Toturi's archers shifted focus once more, moving with a precision and timing that made him proud. The officer corps of his new army consisted mostly of older peasant farmers, practical men and women who understood how to get the job done. There was no ego, no glory, just a sense of duty to Toturi and their fellows. At their command, arrows began falling among those ranks of pikemen who were trying to collapse on the rōnin's flanks, breaking their formations and buying time.

Time enough for the wave of his ashigaru to close the distance.

The Lion were skilled and disciplined, and Toturi's green troops weren't completely able to catch them in the flank. With the precision of years of drilling, the pikemen wheeled back, presenting a forest of steel to Toturi's second wave. He saw the twin groups of his ashigaru, most armed with much shorter spears, axes, or broad chopping blades reach the opposite ends of the Lion line. The pike might have avoided taking the charge in their flanks, but their rapid change of formation had been hasty, and the peasant soldiers were now among them.

Arrows sailed overhead, as the enemy archers made it to the rear and began trying once more to thin the ranks of his own bowmen. Toturi's archers responded in turn, but true to Toturi's plan, they continued their advance, moving forward under fire, pausing only long enough to send answering volleys at the enemy. Those volleys did not target the archers alone; every other soldier was under orders to fire instead at the ranks of Lion samurai, still waiting for the pike to open a path.

Toturi's army had bit deep enough into their ranks that the Lion pikemen couldn't easily do so, at least not in a way that would hold his own forces at bay. Tangled in their own weapons, they began discarding the long spears, drawing the smaller, machete-like blades they carried as backup weapons. Even at this distance, Toturi could see that the skill of his rōnin was winning the battle of attrition; they fell, but they did not go down easy.

They fought on a carpet of dead pikemen, and Toturi's soldiers were stuck in deep and would not be easily dislodged. He could see the Lion samurai preparing to join the fray. The fire from the enemy archers had ceased – their forces were too intermingled for the Lion to risk firing into their own people, but his own archers still harried the enemy.

Still, even from his perch several hundred yards away, Toturi could feel the momentum shifting. His forces had surprised the Lion, getting past the bowmen and largely neutralizing the long reach of the pikes. His troops had made it to the enemy lines, and if they weren't unscathed, they had taken far fewer casualties than Matsu Agetoki could have expected.

But they were still outnumbered, and the initial shock his army had inflicted upon the Lion soldiers was fading. The lines solidified, and he could read the increased pressure as the larger force continued to collapse around his own, pressing in from the flanks.

So far, his plan had worked, but the battle was balanced on a razor's edge. The next part was going to be vital. And there was nothing Toturi could do to influence the outcome but trust in the strength and will of those who had joined his cause.

He moved his horse forward and raised his voice.

"Push!" he roared over the din of battle, his voice echoing across the blood-stained plains. He heard the call echoed up and down the line as his entire army took up the cry.

Each unit had their part to play, and they knew their orders well. Despite his call, the rōnin did not push forward; Toturi knew that the last thing they wanted was to shove their way through the pike and into the teeth of Agetoki's samurai. Instead, those in the center of the line stopped their advance entirely, focusing instead on holding firm in the face of the increased pressure. The two lines of peasant ashigaru bowed outward, pushing left and right in a sudden and furious onslaught of steel.

Their goal was simple: link up with the other elements of Toturi's army and form a singular front.

The pikemen had discarded their polearms, leaving Toturi's rōnin with the advantage in reach and experience both. But the deep ranks of the enemy meant that they were always facing fresh opponents. He saw the line shiver and he knew that they were dangerously close to the breaking point. In that moment, he felt the fingers of doubt. His soldiers, the men and women who put their trust in him, were dying. If Agetoki's forces disrupted Toturi's plan, a massacre would follow.

He could order a withdrawal. They had a contingency for it, but if he did, Toturi knew that they would never strike this deep again. Matsu Agetoki was no fool; this battle had already cost him dearly. If Toturi withdrew now, Agetoki would break off his siege of Kyotei Castle and hound them until he brought them to bay. It might save Kyotei Castle and buy the garrison time to properly reinforce itself. It might prevent the Empire from being dragged into a full-scale civil war. It might mean those things, but it would definitely mean the end of Toturi's army.

Matsu Agetoki had underestimated them; he would not do so again. He would use his full force to hunt them down, and while there was no way he would capture or kill them all, they would be forced to scatter. As a fighting force, they would be done.

The battle would be won or lost here and now. The next few moments would be the key. "Hold!" he shouted, pushing his horse even closer to the battlefield. "For the love of your ancestors! For the grace of the Fortunes! Hold! For the Empire!"

"For the Empire!" Toku shouted at his side, waving the banner furiously in the air.

"For the Empire!" Daisuke's voice added to the call.

"For the Empire!" The call echoed up and down the lines, taking on the steadiness of a chant. He could see the confusion in the faces of the enemy. They had been called to war to fight against their traditional enemy in the Crane. Instead, they found themselves facing the former leader of their own clan, the former Emerald Champion, and a group of rōnin and peasants who seemed to think they were fighting for the survival of the Empire itself.

Toturi empathized with them; pitied them in a way. This was a fight that never should have been necessary. But it *was* necessary, and he would see it won.

In order to get this far, he had committed every soldier he had to the fray. The only reserve left to him was the three of them: Daisuke, Toku, and himself. His forces had linked up, and his archers continued to peel away at the fringes of the enemy line, but he could see that the pikemen were desperately maneuvering to open their ranks enough for Agetoki's samurai to join the battle. When that happened, his army would slowly be ground to dust.

"Now, Kamoko," he whispered. The Unicorn could not hear him, of course, nor was she close enough that he could have used the signal horn. His forces were fully engaged and had pulled as many of the defenders from the siege as they would. It was up to Kamoko to recognize the moment, to know the proper time to strike. Her detachment had moved around the battlefield, beyond the eyes of the watchers and scouts, circling the opposing armies. If she had been successful, then they would have a chance at victory. His last surprise, his final hope, rested on Kamoko, the Battle Maidens, and the Crane themselves.

The part of the Lion army that Agetoki had left to the siege surrounded Kyotei Castle, but to encircle the castle and prevent anyone from escaping, their lines were necessarily thin. A small, mounted force could be on them before they knew it, and while Kamoko had no chance at breaking the siege with the forces available to her, her contingent could cause enough chaos to open a window for the Crane to sally forth.

If the Crane garrison fell upon Agetoki's army from the rear, they had a very real chance of achieving a victory. Toturi had no way to communicate with the Crane commander. He had no idea as to the conditions within the castle. For the tactic to work, he had to trust that whoever oversaw the castle would recognize and seize upon the opportunity.

That was a risk, but as far as Toturi was concerned, it was the smaller of the two risks his plan faced.

The minutes ticked by and with each passing moment, the momentum of the battle continued to shift. There were no tactics left, no brilliant strategies by him or Agetoki. This was a war of attrition, and, if Kamoko failed or deviated from her duty, it was a war Toturi would lose. He could see Matsu Agetoki's personal banner, set back from the lines by a couple of hundred yards. Just like Toturi, he had chosen a spot on the edge of missile range, but close enough to effectively command. It was roughly halfway between the two fronts of Kyotei Castle's walls and the line where the battle against Toturi's army now raged.

If Kamoko could lead her forces on a strike to allow the garrison of Kyotei Castle to sally forth, she could just as easily order the charge against Matsu Agetoki. She had her orders, and she knew that the success of their mission depended upon the Unicorn opening a hole in the besieging force for the Crane to join the battle. But if she decided that her vengeance was worth more than the lives of the people who had come to Toturi's Army, then the day was lost.

He acknowledged the possibility, but Toturi had faith in Kamoko, just as he had faith in the rest of his army. She would succeed, he told himself. She would not put her own personal vengeance over everything else. He continued that mantra in his head, as more of his army fell and the Lion continued to edge forward, swallowing his lines.

Toturi could not see the gates of Kyotei Castle. The melee that separated him made it impossible to see anything beyond the chaotic swirl of bodies. But he didn't need to see the gates to know the moment when the battle shifted.

It began with chaos in the ranks of Matsu Agetoki's bodyguards. For one worried moment, Toturi thought that Kamoko may have taken the opportunity to strike directly at the Lion general after all. But then, he would have seen the charge of her cavalry as they fell upon the command group. Instead, what he was witnessing, barely visible over the swirl of the still-raging fight, was Agetoki's reaction to the unexpected.

A moment later, drums began to boom, echoing from the walls of Kyotei Castle. And a new sound, the roar of the Crane soldiers as they rushed their ancient enemy from behind, and pandemonium erupted over the battlefield.

"That is a welcome sound," Daisuke said, an audible note of relief in his voice.

Toturi nodded. "It seems like Kamoko has been successful and that the Crane have accepted our invitation."

"We're going to win!" Toku shouted. His horse caught the boy's excitement and spun, forcing the peasant to juggle reins, horn, and banner for a moment.

"It's not decided yet," Toturi warned as the boy got control of his mount. "Do not assume victory until you have their surrender. Or until they're dead at your feet."

"Yes, my lord." The boy grinned, fierce and triumphant. "But your plan worked! The Unicorn got through the siege, and the Crane have come. What can the Lion do to stop us now?"

"That, perhaps," Daisuke noted, pointing toward the battlefield. Agetoki's cavalry had finally entered the fray. They moved at a canter, not yet committed to the charge. But they weren't headed toward the battle, where Toturi's infantry held against the ashigaru of the Lion. Nor were they headed to the Crane who were now visible, charging toward the Lion's rear. Instead, they were sweeping around the lines.

Heading, Toturi saw, for *him*. Agetoki's banner waved at the front of that formation, his colors snapping wildly in the wind. Apparently, the Lion General, seeing the inevitability of his own defeat, was taking the only path left to him.

If his armies could not win, he would slay Toturi. In a standard Lion army, such things would be of little import; the chain of command would pass the responsibility on to the next commander, and so forth down the line. But Toturi's army truly was *Toturi's* Army. Without him at the head, it would dissolve. Agetoki might lose this battle, but he could still ensure that Toturi would not be a thorn in the side of another Lion commander.

For a moment, Toturi wondered if the Lion general had outmaneuvered him. The thought brought a brief, sardonic smile to his lips. His forces were fully committed. He had no reserve. The only guards he had were one Crane duelist and a boy. His cavalry, the only force that might respond quickly, was somewhere on the other side of the battlefield. They might reach him before Agetoki, but it would be a race, and only if they had the presence of mind to see what was happening. Had Matsu Agetoki fallen into his trap, or was it the other way around?

Daisuke brought him from his reverie. "Perhaps, Lord Toturi, now would be a good time to exercise a tactical repositioning."

The sardonic smile deepened. "You can say, 'run,' Daisuke."

"As you say, my lord. Now would be a *very* good time to run."

# 32
## Toturi

They rode for their lives and the thunder of approaching death followed them.

"This is hardly what I would have expected from the brave and noble Emerald Champion!" Daisuke shouted over the clatter of their own horses' hooves.

"Any commander should know when it is wiser to retreat," Toturi shouted back. "Remember that, Toku."

"Yes, my lord," the boy said. He still held on to Toturi's banner, though he had lost his horn. The way the boy was bouncing in his saddle made Toturi fear that he would be thrown from it at any moment.

Agetoki and his own cavalry had swept around the lines of the battle and set their sights on Toturi. The Lion's cavalry contingent was quite small, fewer than a hundred riders, but supplemented by a score of Agetoki's personal bodyguards. A hundred against three were not odds that even the bravest of samurai would stand against, and Toturi had opted for the better part of valor.

Their flight was not blind, though. He had held position long enough to watch for Kamoko and saw when her Battle Maidens had entered the fray. Thank the Fortunes and whichever of his ancestors had been watching over him, she had seen Matsu Agetoki and his cavalry ride forth, and was smart enough to guess where they were heading.

She had not tried to follow the Lion, as Agetoki swept around the eastern edge of the battle. Instead, she had instantly wheeled her forces and rode west, hoping to reach Toturi from the other side of the field before Agetoki did. Toturi saw no reason to sit idly by and wait to see if salvation or death would reach him first. He had shouted for Daisuke and Toku to follow and had spurred his horse to a gallop, heading directly for Kamoko's cavalry.

It would be a near thing. Toturi had a jump on Agetoki, and their steeds weren't weighed down with heavy barding. But they were mounted on horses that had been taken from farms, and neither Daisuke nor Toku had much experience in riding. Agetoki's cavalry was just that; soldiers bred to the saddle on mounts trained for war. The ground shook with their hoofbeats, and the rumble of death approaching from behind grew deafening.

"We're not going to make it!" Toku shouted, and Toturi clenched his jaw. The last thing he wanted was to be cut down from behind while fleeing the enemy. But he could see Kamoko's riders clearly now, the woman herself at the front. In that moment, she looked like a Kakita painting of the ideal Unicorn. The horsehair plume of her helmet streamed out behind her as she leaned forward in the saddle, lance canted and ready to be thrust forward at the moment of impact. Her white steed surged beneath her, muscles bunching and expanding with a beautiful rhythm. Behind Kamoko came a broad vee of the remaining Battle Maidens, all a near-perfect copy of the picture Kamoko presented. The rest of Toturi's cavalry followed in their wake.

"Ride!" Toturi shouted. "Straight at the Battle Maidens. Trust them to know the way."

They didn't have much choice in the matter. His horse was now at a dead gallop, a speed that it would not be able to keep up for long. It had the bit in its teeth, and even if he tried to guide it, Toturi doubted the horse would respond. He could feel the tension and panic in the beast between his knees. All he could do, all Daisuke and Toku could do, was hold on and hope that they didn't get trampled by their own reinforcements.

It hung that way for a frozen moment. Toturi could practically feel the breath of the Lion mounts on the back of his neck and his world had been reduced to the sound of hooves and the charge of the Unicorn. Then the Battle Maidens were whipping by him, passing so close that the edges of his haidate – the armored guards that covered his thighs – scraped against one of the Unicorn's.

The sound that followed was terrible, and he knew from experience that it was one that Toku and Daisuke would never forget. Despite the cost of human life, it was the screams of the horses and the crash of the impact that seemed to echo through the mind. Then Toturi, Daisuke, and Toku were through the lines, and he fought desperately with his horse. He managed to slow the beast, then turn it, using reins and knees to spin it back to the battle even as he tore his katana from its sheath.

And not a moment too soon. The opposing cavalry forces had crashed together, but unlike the infantry, the lines were not static. The two groups were intermingled, fighting a dynamic, moving battle, and some had punched completely through the lines, their pursuit of Toturi unhindered.

He barely got his blade up in time to intercept the sweeping pass from the rider, and then he was plunged into the thick of it. The Akodo Commander School taught personal combat, as did every school in Rokugan, but it focused on foot. His techniques were not meant to be executed on horseback.

But in life, you adapted, or you died.

A broad sweep of his blade tore one rider from his saddle, to be trampled beneath the hooves of his own compatriots. He recovered from the swing and, guiding his mount with his knees, dropped the reins and smashed his katana into an upraised tetsubō, tearing it from its wielder's hands and unhorsing the rider. He tore his wakizashi from its sheath with his off hand and hurled it, catching a Lion warrior who had battered Toku's guard aside in the back. It reminded him of the first day in that nameless Lion village so many months ago, when the boy had come to his aid.

Then they were clear, and a lull settled over the battle.

He understood why a moment later.

Kamoko and Matsu Agetoki sat on their horses in the middle of a ring of soldiers. The cavalry on both sides had fallen back, both instinctively understanding that a personal matter was to be settled here. A quick assessment showed Toturi that Kamoko's cavalry had done well in the brief clash, despite being outnumbered. They had taken losses, but not as many as the Lion, and the two forces were now at parity. The broader battle still raged, but there, too, Toturi could see that victory was in their grasp.

There was no need for this fight. The battle was done. He should call upon Agetoki to surrender. Too much life had been lost already. Besides, there was no guarantee that Kamoko could defeat the skilled and clever general. Why allow this pointless duel to continue?

But he did not move to stop it. If he did, he doubted Kamoko would ever forgive him, and the Unicorn Battle Maiden had earned more than just his trust. She had earned his admiration and comradeship. He may have believed her vengeance folly, but he had already made his position clear. The choice was hers, and it had been made. His duty now, as both her commander and her friend, was to support that choice.

He guided his mount to the edge of the circle that had formed around the pair. He caught Kamoko's eye for the briefest moment and raised his blade in salute. She gave him a fierce nod in return.

"Matsu Agetoki," she called. "You have murdered far too many innocents in your raids and butchery. My mother was among them. I claim the rights of vengeance. I challenge you on the field of honor!"

Agetoki removed his menpō and Toturi could see a look on his face that was an equal mix of bewilderment and determination. His eyes, briefly scanning the crowd, found Toturi. The Lion general offered him a mounted bow, low in the saddle, which Toturi returned. He may have gotten the better of the man, and Kamoko may well have been justified in her claims, but he was still a Lion and a samurai. The Akodo Code dictated courtesy, and when offered, it would be returned.

"What a strange turn of events," Agetoki said, almost conversationally. "It seems that I am beaten." A bitter smile twitched one corner of his mouth, before he turned to Kamoko. "I will accept your duel, Utaku Kamoko, though, if I am being honest, I do not understand the justification for it. We have made many orphans today, on both sides." He shrugged, as if to show his indifference to the cost of war. "But I do so on two conditions. Win or lose, my army is allowed to quit the field. You may call me a butcher, but I know when a battle is lost. There is no need for further death."

He directed the words not at Kamoko, but rather at Toturi, who nodded. "Send a rider to your soldiers," he said. "And I will do the same to mine."

It took only a moment to arrange. Kamoko clenched her jaw and stared at the Lion general with barely restrained impatience.

But Toturi was grateful to Agetoki for the reprieve. He did not wish to kill the rank-and-file Lion, who were fighting a war they truly believed was just. "Your second condition?" Kamoko demanded, when the din of battle had faded and both armies had pulled back.

"We fight on foot. I assume you want a fair duel, and I fear the Lion doctrine is not as focused on cavalry training as it could be." He bowed once more to Toturi. "An oversight, perhaps."

Kamoko had dismounted even before Agetoki had finished speaking, but Toturi wished she had taken a moment more to consider. She was under no obligation to accept the terms, especially with Agetoki admitting the defeat of his army. Toturi had no doubt that the Lion general would have accepted a mounted duel, even if it was not his strength. By agreeing to his terms, the Unicorn was giving up her biggest advantage. Toturi almost objected, but he saw the look on Kamoko's face and held his tongue.

She would have her vengeance, and she would have it in a way that cast no doubts over the righteousness of her cause or the validity of her victory.

One of her Battle Maidens came forward and took the reins of Kamoko's mount. Across the battlefield, Toturi could see that the Lion, the Crane, and his rōnin and peasant army had fully disengaged, separating into three blocks of troops. Good. Whatever happened here, the battle was over.

"I accept your terms, Lion," Kamoko said. Her voice was cold, but calm.

"Excellent," Agetoki replied, stepping from his own mount. One of the Lion came forward and took his horse away.

The ring of soldiers around the pair had tightened and Toturi was struck by the strangeness of it all. Moments ago, they had all been trying to kill each other. Now that the battle was done, and despite the exhaustion he saw on their faces, despite the wounded being ushered to the back of their respective lines for aid, he saw no anger, no hatred on either side. They had done their job, and now that the work was done, it was time to move on. It was the attitude of most professional soldiers; one couldn't afford to let emotion get in the way.

Kamoko, however, was the exception. Despite her best efforts, she was exuding a palpable aura of anger as she faced Agetoki.

"If she loses, do you think Agetoki will accept my challenge?" Daisuke asked. "No offense to you or the Lion, Lord Toturi, but I think the Crane would be better off if Matsu Agetoki was not a factor in the coming war." His hand gripped the hilt of his katana, as if he longed to take it from its sheath. Toturi had seen the Crane duelist in action; his speed was nearly preternatural. There was no way Agetoki could best him. In battle, yes. But in a duel? The Lion would have no chance.

But it wasn't going to be necessary.

"She isn't going to lose, Daisuke," he replied. Kamoko had dedicated her life to this moment, and now it was before her. Toturi had absolute faith in the Unicorn.

The two had squared off in the center of the ring of watching soldiers. Neither were iaijutsu duelists; both stood with their katana raised, points canted slightly toward their opponent. A silence fell over the battlefield, one that even the horses and birds seemed loath to break. Both samurai stood motionless, eyes locked upon one another, searching.

Searching for the fatal weakness, the fatal flaw. Every swordsman had one, the blind spot that would one day spell their doom. For some it was as simple as a wound that had healed badly, limiting the range of motion just enough for another to take advantage. For others, it was a question of mental quickness, recognizing the perfect moment a fraction of a second too late. For others still, it was about willpower, allowing the destructive tendrils of self-doubt to creep in and erode the foundation of confidence that was vital to any warrior.

If you could find that weakness in your enemy, you could exploit it. When that happened, duels rarely went past the first strike. But that pregnant moment, that long lingering pause before either samurai moved, where each spent everything they had trying to find their opponent's weakness, was grueling.

It was why, in a duel like the one that Toturi and the others were now witnessing, the person who moved first usually found their life's blood spilling onto the ground.

Toturi was holding his breath. He hadn't made the conscious decision to do so, but he was, nonetheless. So were those around them. They could sense the building energy. They could all feel it, electrifying the air like the moments before a lightning strike.

Matsu Agetoki flashed forward, moving faster than a striking serpent, his blade blurring into a silver bar as he struck.

Toturi had not seen his weakness. Though he had been watching, searching, as had every person gathered in the circle of witnesses, he hadn't identified it before the Lion struck.

Kamoko had.

The Unicorn didn't move as fast as the Lion; she didn't have to. She didn't bother trying to block Agetoki's blade. She moved, twisting her body by bare inches, taking her head off the line of Agetoki's strike. Toturi distinctly saw wisps of her hair, slid free from her helm in the fury of combat, sliced away as Agetoki's blade glided by.

Her own katana struck in the same moment.

She slipped Agetoki's blade in an eyeblink and turned back, thrusting upward with the chisel-point of her sword. They both wore armor, but it didn't matter; Kamoko's strike took the Lion general just beneath the chin, punching upward through his palate and into his brain. For a split second, they stood like that, silhouetted against the afternoon sky, as the world around them held its breath.

Kamoko pulled her sword free and stepped back.

Matsu Agetoki, General of the Lion, the mind behind the strategy that had set the Crane countryside aflame and the killer of Utaku Kumiko, Kamoko's mother, crumpled to the grass.

# Epilogue

The prince's laughter set Hotaru's ears on edge. There was no music in the boy; and that is what he was, a boy, no matter his years. The laugh was harsh, mocking, a discordant string breaking from being plucked too hard. It was the laugh of a spoiled child who reveled in pulling the wings off flies and getting the servants in trouble.

"Did you hear her, Hotaru?"

She glanced over to see Sotorii, red faced from laughter, with Kachiko leaning close. A tiny surge of jealousy flashed through her at the image. For the entirety of their journey, the Scorpion had been at the prince's side, always ready with a soft laugh or fleeting touch.

Hotaru didn't believe for a second that it was genuine. Kachiko was doing what she always did, manipulating and gathering power. Given Prince Sotorii's disposition, Hotaru couldn't blame her for it. The prince was not a man whose bad side she would want to be on.

But it still set her teeth on edge and made her glad that this nightmare was almost over. What had the firefighter said? *Lady Sun have mercy on you, for your prince will not.* She suppressed a shudder and offered a smile of her own to Sotorii.

"I'm afraid I did not, my prince."

"Your Majesty," he corrected, and his brows drew together in a scowl. "I've told you before, Crane. It's Your Majesty, not my prince."

"You know the Crane," Kachiko said, briefly catching Hotaru's eye as she did. The look in the Scorpion's own was almost apologetic. "They are sticklers for propriety."

"Yes, well. I suppose we can forgive the insolence until the enthronement."

"Which should be soon, my prince," Hotaru added. Thank the ancestors, for she did not think she could travel with the boy much longer. Not and keep her head after he assumed the role of Emperor.

"Look there, Prince Sotorii." Kachiko pointed toward the east. Lady Sun had passed her zenith and the eastern horizon was growing dark. But there, in the distance, was a glimmer, a reflection from the descending sun. "The Enchanted Walls. We will reach the city, and your throne, on the morrow."

The prince walked to stand beside Kachiko. "Good," he said as his gaze swept the glimmer in the distance. Deep in his eyes, an answering glimmer transformed his face into something hungry. "My empire needs me. I have much to do."

Hotaru tried to ignore both the chill that swept through her at those words and the arm that slipped around Kachiko's waist.

Yakamo stood at the head of an army.

There were Crab in that army, ashigaru and samurai. But it was not only the Crab that stood beneath his banner. Ranks of the undead, animated, he knew now, by the prayers and incantations of Kuni Yori, stood in blocks near their living brethren. The dead were not alone. Yakamo did not fully understand what had happened in the wake of the defeat of the Shadowlands army, but their ranks had been further reinforced.

He couldn't help the snarl that came to his face as he saw the goblins, ogres, and lesser oni that fleshed out the army before him.

"You understand the need of it?" Hida Kisada stood next to him, and while he, too, wore an expression of distaste, his voice was firm.

"Yes, father," Yakamo replied. And he *did* understand. He had questioned Kisada in the past, had wondered at his motives and strategies. But no more. The Empire had sealed their own fate when they had forced the Crab to stand alone. Otosan Uchi had forsaken the Crab, the Wall, and the sacred duty owed to every man, woman, and child in Rokugan. It had begun under the line of Hantei and continued with the regency of the Crane. Neither had earned the right to rule.

"Rokugan needs an emperor who will properly stand against the Shadowlands," Hida Kisada said. "If that means using our enemies to our gain, then that is what we must do."

"I understand," Yakamo said again. He felt the tingling power in the claw that dangled from his left arm. "The Empire must have a strong leader at the helm. And if they will not come to the Shadowlands, we will bring the Shadowlands to them. Let them know what it is to fight against real enemies. Let them come to understand the taint that those horrors bring. And when you ascend the Emerald Throne, let them feel the terror and relief of having a true warrior of the Empire upon the throne."

And, some small part of him added at the back of his mind, let them all know that one day, it will be Hida Yakamo who ascends the throne.

"I am proud of you, my son," Hida Kisada said, resting a hand on Yakamo's shoulder. "You are as worthy an heir as any could hope for. You will lead the Crab to greatness."

Yakamo expected to feel something at those words. He had longed to hear them, but now that they were spoken, he found he felt… nothing. It was a welcome change. He did not need affirmation; he had something far superior. He had power.

"Take this army," Hida Kisada went on. "March on the capital. Bring the Empire to its knees. And secure the throne for me. The Hantei line is done. It is time for the Hida to assume control."

Yakamo smiled. *That* he could do. Let the salvation of the Empire begin.

"As you command, father."

"What will you do now, my lord?"

Toturi sipped his tea. He was seated, along with Daisuke, Kamoko, and Toku, at a table in the study of Doji no Tsume Takashi, the young man in command of Kyotei Castle. Takashi had personally led the sortie that crashed into the rear ranks of Agetoki's army and set in motion Toturi's victory.

"You are, of course, welcome to stay here as long as you wish," the young man continued. "We owe you our lives, after all. But I do wonder what plans you might have before you."

Toturi took a moment to consider. Takashi had opened the gates of his castle to Toturi's army and treated even the lowest of his peasant soldiers with respect. Takashi's healers had seen to their wounded, and he had feasted them from the castle's stores. Despite that, Toturi couldn't help but feel the Crane's welcome was forced. Given the history of Kyotei Castle, and the fact that almost half of Toturi's forces were made up of disaffected Lion, he couldn't blame the man.

"We will not burden you long, I think," Toturi said at last. "I have explained the reasons we came to your aid, and I am sure you understand that, our force being what it is, we have no real desire to become embroiled in a broader war between the Lion and the Crane."

Takashi nodded. "Your help was welcome, nonetheless. The actions of the Lion in this war have been…" He trailed off, realizing that he was talking to the former Champion of the clan he was about to insult.

"They have been, indeed," Toturi said with a small smile. "But I think you will find what comes next to be a more conventional war. Matsu Tsuko's strategy was brilliant, but her attempt to pull the regent into open conflict with the clans has failed." He sighed and set his teacup back on the table. "This war is only beginning, Takashi. Matsu Tsuko will not abandon her plans over a singular setback. She will seek allies among the other clans, and she will find them. And Doji Hotaru will do the same. I fear that, despite our efforts, the conflict will not end. But it will be a war between the clans for their own supremacy, not a war to discredit the Emerald Throne and whosoever sits upon it. We have accomplished that much, at least." He offered his host a wry smile. "Despite that, I think the regent might be a little uneasy if I linger too long. Having the former Lion Clan Champion sitting at the head of an army, within striking distance of Otosan Uchi, might make Lord Yoshi a little uncomfortable."

Takashi bowed his head in acknowledgement. "What will you do?"

"We move west."

He spoke the words without really thinking about them. They had come unbidden into his mind, but as they fell from his lips, he could sense the rightness of them. Was it his ancestors or the

Fortunes guiding him? Or was it simply the process of elimination? East would take them to the sea. South to the walls of the Imperial City, and north right into the heart of the conflict between the Crane and Lion. But what would he find to the west?

It didn't matter. He would trust in fate and the Fortunes to guide his hand. The conversation turned to mundane matters as Takashi played the courteous host. Toturi let Daisuke take the reins of that conversation. He was tired; tired from battle and tired from the weight of the responsibility he carried. But it was not time to rest. Not yet. He smiled politely as the conversation droned on, and longed for the moment when he could lay his head down.

Many hours later, Toturi found himself atop the walls, surveying the field of battle. Despite his exhaustion, sleep had escaped him. He wore a heavy kimono, bound tight against the wind that howled across the parapets, as if trying to tear him from the walls. If he looked at the fields below, shrouded in the cloak of night, he could see they were full of bodies. Those bodies would be reclaimed and given funeral rites, but it would take days. In the meantime, the scavengers would feast.

There was a lesson there, but his tired brain could not fathom it.

"I did not expect to find you here, my lord."

He turned and offered a weary smile to Utaku Kamoko. The Unicorn, too, wore a simple kimono, bright with the colors of her clan. She still did not consider herself rōnin. He wondered what would happen when her clan chose a side in the coming war. Would she leave him and return to their ranks? Or would she don the black?

"I cannot sleep," he admitted. "I told Takashi that we move west, and so we will, but I cannot say why."

Kamoko came to stand by his side, shoulder to shoulder, looking over the battlefield. "Something has guided you thus far," she said after a quiet moment. "Trust that it continues to do so."

"I suppose," he said, wishing that he had the same confidence in himself that those around him seemed to hold. "And what of you?" he asked. "You have found your vengeance. Matsu Agetoki is slain. Where does your future lie?"

She sighed. "I do not know, Lord Toturi. It was the right thing to do. But you were right as well. I feel no different now that Agetoki is gone." She smiled. "In fact, I take more pride in the fact that we saved this castle than I do in the death of the man who killed my mother. What does that say about me?"

"That you value life more than death, Kamoko." Toturi scanned the battlefield. Lord Moon's light disguised the bodies from this distance, cloaking them in shadow, making them seem like nothing more than natural shifts in the land. "It is something that I have struggled with as well. We are taught that duty and glory are sacred, and death is a price to be willingly paid in the pursuit of either." He paused, considering his words. There were those who would deem his next words outright blasphemy of the Akodo Code. But he said them anyway.

"I think we have been lied to, Kamoko. Or, perhaps, we have twisted the Code beyond its original intent." Kamoko blinked at that, but she did not seem to take offense, for which Toturi was grateful. "In either case," he went on, "I think I have come to understand what this army is truly about. It is about *life*, Kamoko. It is about stopping the senseless violence and the endless war, and finding another way." His smile turned ironic, and he felt a heat behind his eyes as he blinked back the tears that wanted to gather there.

"I have spent the last decade fighting one war or another. I grow weary of it. I am not sure I understand how to take this army and use it to save lives, but I know that is its purpose. I see it in every downtrodden peasant that joins our cause, every rōnin that quietly walks away from their life of privilege to fight at our side. They sense it, too." He clenched a hand over the hilt of his sword, sensing the irony there. "There must be a way forward where our disputes aren't all settled at the tip of a blade."

"We will find it, Toturi." The Battle Maiden's hand on his shoulder held the same warmth as the tears that slid down his cheeks. "Together."

Deep beneath the Imperial Palace in Otosan Uchi, a beautiful young woman knelt alone on the flagstones.

The stone basin before her shimmered with black liquid, reflecting the orange light of the lanterns that burned from their hangers on the walls of the otherwise bare chamber. The woman smiled at her own reflection, admiring the unlined and beautiful features that stared back up at her.

"The way has been cleared. The prince returns. And you will follow after."

She reached into the bodice of her kimono and produced a single yuri petal. The delicate white lily fell into the liquid. It floated there for a moment, white upon black. Then, as the blood that filled the basin saturated the delicate veins of the flower, the petal slowly darkened to red. It sat lower and lower in the blood until, with a final abruptness, it slipped beneath the surface and disappeared.

As it was swallowed, a single ripple flowed across the basin. It disrupted the reflection, and for the barest instant, the face that stared back at her was torn, half that of a beautiful young woman, and half that of a demon.

Chukan Hanako smiled.

# Acknowledgments

This novel has been a passion project for us. We have spent countless hours adventuring through Rokugan and the works of those who have come before us have provided inspiration not just for this book, but for many of our other works outside the Emerald Empire. It has been a pleasure to be given the opportunity to become a part of something that has provided us with so much joy. As such, we must first thank the original creators of the setting: John Zinser, Dave Seay, Ryan Dancey, Dave Williams, DJ Trindle, Matt Wilson and John Wick. The world you created came to life at our table and provided memories that we'll cherish. We know we're not alone in that.

We would also like to thank the current stewards of L5R, the good people at Asmodee, for giving us the chance to put our stamp on the world of Rokugan. It is always challenging to build castles in someone else's sandbox, but the folks at Asmodee were committed to a collaborative process, which we appreciate to no end. Our thanks to Charlotte Llewelyn-Wells, Brian Mulcahy, and Katrina Ostrander for their editorial guidance and for keeping us grounded in the setting and the lore of the ever-changing saga that is the *Legend of the Five Rings*. And to the rest of the team at Aconyte Books for doing the thousand other tasks necessary to turn a manuscript into a real live book out there in the world.

Finally, we'd like to thank the fans of *Legend of the Five Rings*. Whether you're rolling dice, flipping cards, reading books, or playing a board or video game, none of this would be possible without you.

Julie & J.T.

# About the Authors

## Julie Kagawa

JULIE KAGAWA is the *New York Times* bestselling author of the Iron Fey, Shadow of the Fox, Talon, and many more series exploring worlds magical and mundane. She has written books for people of all ages, including children's chapter books, middle grade adventures, a wealth of young adult novels, and adult fantasy works. She was born in California but now resides in Kentucky horse country with her husband and a pair of stubborn Australian Shepherds.

## J.T. Nicholas

J.T. NICHOLAS writes science fiction and fantasy and has been a fan of both genres since picking up his first TSR novel more than 30 years ago. He is the author of the New Lyons Sequence, *Stolen Earth*, *Re-coil* and other novels. As a military brat, he has lived in more places than most and has moved dozens of times, an experience that taught him that no matter where you go, we all have more in common than we might think.

# Legend of the Five Rings

For more than thirty years, the epic fantasy saga of *Legend of the Five Rings* has been told through a beloved series of tabletop games, novels, short stories, and more.

The setting for *Legend of the Five Rings* is the land of Rokugan, a rich fantasy setting inspired by the samurai cinema of Akira Kurosawa and the history and folklore of Japan, China, and other Asian nations. In Rokugan, shapeshifters, dragons, and gods walk beside mortals, and warring samurai clans clash for power and prestige, duel for love and revenge, and defend against the demonic invasion of the Shadowlands.

To find out more about *Legend of the Five Rings* and to discover other ways to explore the land of Rokugan, visit: LegendoftheFiveRings.com

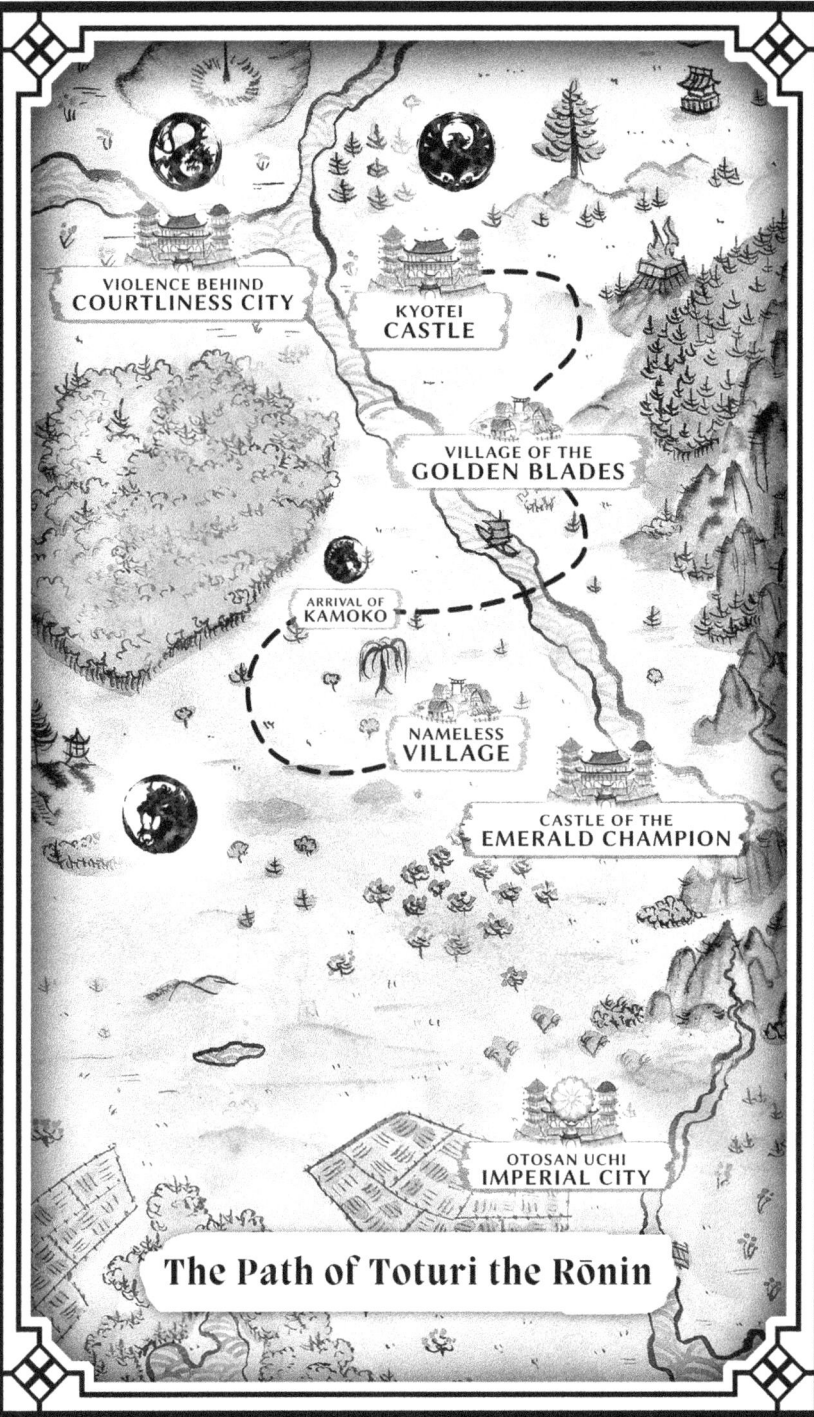

# Acknowledgments

This novel has been a passion project for us. We have spent countless hours adventuring through Rokugan and the works of those who have come before us have provided inspiration not just for this book, but for many of our other works outside the Emerald Empire. It has been a pleasure to be given the opportunity to become a part of something that has provided us with so much joy. As such, we must first thank the original creators of the setting: John Zinser, Dave Seay, Ryan Dancey, Dave Williams, DJ Trindle, Matt Wilson and John Wick. The world you created came to life at our table and provided memories that we'll cherish. We know we're not alone in that.

We would also like to thank the current stewards of L5R, the good people at Asmodee, for giving us the chance to put our stamp on the world of Rokugan. It is always challenging to build castles in someone else's sandbox, but the folks at Asmodee were committed to a collaborative process, which we appreciate to no end. Our thanks to Charlotte Llewelyn-Wells, Brian Mulcahy, and Katrina Ostrander for their editorial guidance and for keeping us grounded in the setting and the lore of the ever-changing saga that is the *Legend of the Five Rings*. And to the rest of the team at Aconyte Books for doing the thousand other tasks necessary to turn a manuscript into a real live book out there in the world.

Finally, we'd like to thank the fans of *Legend of the Five Rings*. Whether you're rolling dice, flipping cards, reading books, or playing a board or video game, none of this would be possible without you.

Julie & J.T.

# About the Authors

## Julie Kagawa

JULIE KAGAWA is the *New York Times* bestselling author of the Iron Fey, Shadow of the Fox, Talon, and many more series exploring worlds magical and mundane. She has written books for people of all ages, including children's chapter books, middle grade adventures, a wealth of young adult novels, and adult fantasy works. She was born in California but now resides in Kentucky horse country with her husband and a pair of stubborn Australian Shepherds.

## J.T. Nicholas

J.T. NICHOLAS writes science fiction and fantasy and has been a fan of both genres since picking up his first TSR novel more than 30 years ago. He is the author of the New Lyons Sequence, *Stolen Earth*, *Re-coil* and other novels. As a military brat, he has lived in more places than most and has moved dozens of times, an experience that taught him that no matter where you go, we all have more in common than we might think.

# Legend of the Five Rings

For more than thirty years, the epic fantasy saga of *Legend of the Five Rings* has been told through a beloved series of tabletop games, novels, short stories, and more.

The setting for *Legend of the Five Rings* is the land of Rokugan, a rich fantasy setting inspired by the samurai cinema of Akira Kurosawa and the history and folklore of Japan, China, and other Asian nations. In Rokugan, shapeshifters, dragons, and gods walk beside mortals, and warring samurai clans clash for power and prestige, duel for love and revenge, and defend against the demonic invasion of the Shadowlands.

To find out more about *Legend of the Five Rings* and to discover other ways to explore the land of Rokugan, visit: LegendoftheFiveRings.com

# Legend of the Five Rings
## THE CLAN WARS BEGIN

Continue your journey into the realm of Rokugan...

Warring samurai clans fight with swords and magic to protect their domains from demonic incursion in these exciting novels from Aconyte Books.

Journey across the land of Rokugan and glimpse the legendary Great Clans and Imperial families in this lavish full-color artbook.

Explore the different facets of the Emerald Empire and play through the story of the Clan Wars through board games.

Step into the role of a samurai and embark on epic quests in these roleplaying games from Edge Studio.

Undertake dangerous missions into the Shadowlands in the first ever video game set in the world of Rokugan. Find Shadowveil: Legend of the Five Rings on Steam today.

and more...

explore the latest at
## www.LegendoftheFiveRings.com

© Asmodee North America. Legend of the Five Rings and the L5R logo are TM of Asmodee North America

## Go deeper into the Emerald Empire in epic new novels!

Follow dilettante detective Daidoji Shin as he solves murders & mysteries amid the machinations of the clans.

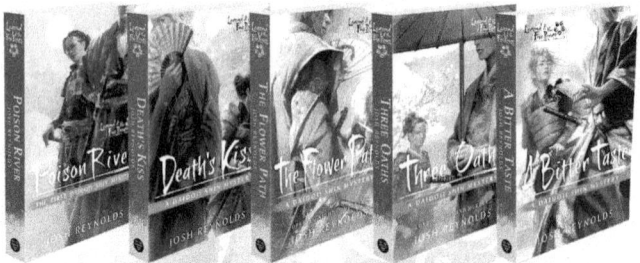

Enter the Spirit Realms in enthralling supernatural adventures.

A forgotten evil threatens the Emerald Empire.

Explore the heroes of Rokugan in exciting novels and novellas.

ACONYTEBOOKS.COM // LEGENDOFTHEFIVERINGS.COM

www.ingramcontent.com/pod-product-compliance
Ingram Content Group UK Ltd.
Pitfield, Milton Keynes, MK11 3LW, UK
UKHW010714050825
7235UKWH00027B/293